Spectacular Praise for
A Game of Fear
and the Inspector Ian Rutledge Mystery Series

"These World War I–era Scotland Yard mysteries are tangled and sophisticated and fun."

—R. L. Stine

"You're going to love Todd."

—Stephen King

"The melancholy tone that distinguishes the Rutledge series is a reminder that war never ends for the families and friends of lost loved ones. It just retreats into the shadows."

—*The New York Times Book Review*

"Excellent. . . . Todd has rarely been better at creating a creepy atmosphere to enhance [a] nuanced exploration of human darkness. Rutledge remains one of today's most fully rounded mystery leads."

—*Publishers Weekly* (starred review) on *A Game of Fear*

"*A Game of Fear* continues the high standards readers have come to expect from Todd. It is a testament to both authors' considerable talents, and a wonderful tribute to the late Caroline Todd."

—*South Florida Sun Sentinel* on *A Game of Fear*

"A superior example of crime fiction, a haunting exploration of war and its legacies and a sterling reaffirmation of its authors' humanity, *A Game of Fear* offers escapist pleasures—including a breathless climax—while simultaneously eliciting thought on intellectual and moral issues."

—*Free Lance–Star* (Fredericksburg) on *A Game of Fear*

A Game of Fear

A GAME OF FEAR

An Inspector Ian Rutledge Mystery

Charles Todd

WILLIAM MORROW
An Imprint of HarperCollins*Publishers*

P.S.™ is a trademark of HarperCollins Publishers.

A GAME OF FEAR. Copyright © 2022 by Charles Todd. All rights reserved. Printed in the United States of America. No part of this book may be used or reproduced in any manner whatsoever without written permission except in the case of brief quotations embodied in critical articles and reviews. For information, address HarperCollins Publishers, 195 Broadway, New York, NY 10007.

HarperCollins books may be purchased for educational, business, or sales promotional use. For information, please email the Special Markets Department at SPsales@harpercollins.com.

A hardcover edition of this book was published in 2022 by William Morrow, an imprint of HarperCollins Publishers.

FIRST WILLIAM MORROW PAPERBACK EDITION PUBLISHED 2023.

Library of Congress Cataloging-in-Publication Data has been applied for.

ISBN 978-0-06-290560-4

23 24 25 26 27 LBC 5 4 3 2 1

This book is especially for Sammy. His endless energy and capacity for love was a comfort for those who knew him. Sammy was the light of his home and all those that lived with him. Dogs, cats, and people will miss him desperately.

Hunter was a kind and gentle dog most of the time. His happy smile greeted everyone the same. Sammy's companion and cohort, they were inseparable. Hunter could sit for hours as long as he was touching someone. Sammy and Hunter shared a loving home where they received as much love as they gave. It is never easy to say goodbye to anyone or even a pet who has shared years with us. The loss of these two wonderful spirits is deeply felt and their fond memories will be with us forever.

I

London, Late Spring 1921

Too often, Rutledge thought as he shut the door of the flat, carried his valise to the motorcar, and set out for the coast of Essex, humor has a malicious twist to it.

Word had got around that Markham had assigned him the murder inquiry in Essex, and as he quickly cleared his desk and took the remaining files down to Sergeant Gibson, he was accompanied by a cacophony of noises that were supposed to represent ghostly sounds. He made the best of it, but he knew that in some cases the noises were intended to remind him of his haunted war years. Of shell shock. Sharper sounds, pencils rapidly tapping the edge of a desk, more like the rattle of machine-gun fire than Marley's chains—faces hiding their intent behind friendly grins, while their eyes, staring at him, were cold—and Markham in his doorway, watching without any expression at all . . . He'd had to clench his teeth to prevent swearing at them and instead pretend to be amused.

When he'd questioned Markham about the need to send the Yard to Essex in the first place, the Chief Superintendent had said shortly, "Well, *something* happened, that much we know. I don't put much stock in the rest of it. Sort it out. The Chief Constable feels obligated. He says he knows the family. Otherwise he'd have left it to the local man."

Spring was coming to Kent as Rutledge crossed the county line. The orchards were in bloom, great splashes of white or a soft pink everywhere he looked. The hop fields were a low, bright green, just breaking through the soil, not yet ready for the hordes of Londoners who came down to string up the vines.

The reason he'd chosen to drive this roundabout way, rather than through East London, was a light lunch with Melinda Crawford, at her house. He'd promised her more than once that he would come down, then had had to put off his visit. Not that he was deliberately avoiding her. Twice she'd stood by him in a time of great need. Once when word had come that his parents had been killed in a boating accident off the Isle of Skye. And again when he himself had not known where to turn or who to trust. What's more, she'd been a close friend of his parents and a part of his childhood. He'd always been fond of her.

The thing was, she saw him too clearly—knew him too well. And he'd had to struggle since war's end to keep Hamish from her. The voice in his head that had never left him, never given him peace, since the Battle of the Somme in '16. She knew a little of that part of his war—but not the worst of it.

She was Army, generations of Army. And he wasn't sure how she would feel about his guilt.

And so he tried to keep his distance when he could.

She was expecting him. When he came up the drive, the door opened as he braked to a halt by the steps.

"Hallo," she said, smiling. "You made good time."

Rutledge grinned in response. He'd let the big touring car out on the straight stretches. As she must have known he might.

He got down, walked up the steps, and kissed the cheek she presented.

"You're looking well," he told her, and meant it. She was wearing a woolen dress in a shade of dark red that she preferred, and with it a heavy gold locket on a gold chain. He knew what was inside it—her late husband's likeness, painted by a master, giving the sitter a warmth and life that had intrigued Rutledge as a boy. He could remember asking often "to see the Colonel, please, may I?" And she would open the tiny clasp and show him the handsome man in the uniform of another century.

"Come in. Lunch is in half an hour. And you can tell me about this latest inquiry of yours."

"I don't know that it will turn out to be much of an inquiry at all," he said, following her into the high-ceilinged hall, where Shanta was waiting to take his hat and coat.

He didn't add that it was one of the reasons he felt he could spare the time to come this roundabout way through Kent.

"Essex, you said on the telephone?"

"Yes, the village of Walmer, on the coast."

He followed her into the library, where she offered him a whisky, then poured a sherry for herself before sitting down across from him.

"The problem is, a murder was witnessed—but no body was found at the scene. Nor has one turned up. At least it hadn't, by the time I'd left the Yard."

"Surely sooner or later someone will be reported missing?"

"That's always what we hope will happen. The witness, meanwhile, has told the local man that she recognized the killer."

"Then why has the Chief Constable asked for the Yard to step in?"

"A very good question, one I asked Markham." He smiled wryly. "Except for the fact that the name she gave him is of someone who is already dead. The killer, apparently, is a ghost. And for all we know, the victim is one as well."

Melinda was clearly intrigued. But she said only, "Well. If anyone can get to the bottom of it, you will. Now, give me the news from London." She went on, asking about his sister, Frances, and a number of friends they had in common, until Shanta appeared in the doorway, announcing that lunch was served.

It wasn't laid out in the long dining room, which could seat twenty guests with ease. Instead, a small table had been set in Melinda's sitting room beside the fire that was always blazing at any time of the year. She'd spent her youth and the early years of her marriage in India, and claimed that she had never learned to tolerate the English chill.

It was a pleasant hour or so. Rutledge, looking up at the clock on the mantel, reluctantly rose to take his leave. "Duty calls," he said.

Melinda didn't protest. She understood Duty.

She hadn't mentioned the inquiry at all after that initial bit of conversation when he arrived. Now, at the door seeing him off, she said, "There's an airfield very close by Walmer, as I remember. Is it anywhere near this house where your only witness lives?"

"There are several wartime airfields along the Essex coast. How close one may be to Benton Hall I don't know. Why?"

Melinda frowned. "As I recall, there was an incident there during the war. A death that was never explained. You might keep that in mind."

Rutledge regarded her for a moment. "How did you come to know that? Nothing was said about any incident in the report I was given."

She looked up at the tall man standing on her doorstep, and said blandly, "A friend of mine was the commanding officer there when it happened. He took it quite hard."

Melinda Crawford was probably the most astute woman he'd ever met. In her lifetime she had experienced more than most, and her contacts among Army and Foreign Office people were legendary. He was never really certain what she'd had a hand in, for she never spoke of victories—or defeats.

He said, "Is there anything else you can tell me?"

"No. I only remember it because it upset a friend."

Rutledge let it go—he knew her well enough to understand that this was all she intended to say. Otherwise she wouldn't have waited until he was leaving. He kissed her again and went out to his motorcar. She waved farewell as he left, her dark red dress a splash of bright color against the facade of the house as he rounded a bend in the drive.

He made good time to Gravesend, where the ferry crossed the Thames to Essex.

I t was another two hours to Walmer, up the main north road and then a turning into a network of country lanes. It was flat terrain, crops and grazing, with fertile soil that often turned to mud after the winter rains. He was delayed twice, by a slow-moving muck cart, and again by half a dozen geese waddling across the road from a farm pond.

The village proper was set on a hill that sloped down to the water. Here the River Chelmer met the Blackwater Estuary, where long fingers of land protected it on either side all the way to the sea, like a deep inlet.

Rutledge drove through the streets, noting the odd tower on one of the churches, then found his way down to the harbor. The sea was invisible from here, but the estuary glinted in the sunlight. He found several pubs and the usual shops that catered to several fishing boats and one or two smaller craft. One of the pubs was called The Salt Cellar, with its large wrought iron cellar hanging above the door, and the other The Viking, with a sign of a suitably fierce and bearded figure brandishing an axe. Weather had faded the painted background to a dull gray, but someone had touched up the head of the axe, and the brightness caught the eye. The windows were grimy, the general appearance as faded as the sign above the door.

Beyond the harbor were the salt flats and the weathered wooden sheds where seawater from the flooded flats was pumped into basins, cleaned, boiled, then dried, before the flakes were raked up and shoveled into tubs. The business of supplying salt had once been king here, just as wool had before it, but it was no longer quite so profitable, and so Walmer had faded into a quiet backwater. Rutledge had a sudden memory of his grandmother keeping Walmer Salt in a special jar with a ceramic top.

Satisfied that he had a general plan of the village in his head, Rutledge turned back to the police station on one of the side streets just off the High. There he was informed that Inspector Hamilton was having a very late lunch in the back garden of an hotel just down the way.

He left his motorcar at the station and walked there. The High was fairly busy, women stepping in and out of shops as they did their marketing, while overhead gulls swooped and called. It was impossible to see the harbor from this part of the village, much less the sea. It could, he thought, be any inland village, except for the gulls. It was almost as if Walmer had turned its back on the water, now that it was no longer the main source of income.

The Swan Hotel was small, no more than four stories, gray stone with large windows. He stepped inside and was shown to a rear door leading out into the garden. Half a dozen tables had been set out there, for dining and drinking in fair weather, but the lone man seated at one of them was paying little attention to the sunny day. His head was buried in what appeared to be reports, spread out in the space where his empty dishes had been pushed aside, and he didn't look up as Rutledge crossed to his table.

"Just set it there," he said, motioning beyond the dishes. "Where it won't drip."

"Inspector Hamilton?"

He looked up then. A small man, slim but strongly built, with graying dark hair and a trim moustache, he was at first annoyed by the interruption. Then realizing that Rutledge was neither a waiter nor anyone else he recognized, he got to his feet and said, "You must be the man from London."

"Yes. Ian Rutledge."

Hamilton nodded, collected the papers he'd been studying into a stack and tucked them into a slim case by the table leg, before indicating the other chair. "I'm almost embarrassed to speak to you," he began with a sigh. "But the Chief Constable insisted that we call in the Yard. He's actually related to the woman who is the only witness. His daughter was married to her late son. The war."

Rutledge sat down. "Is she a reliable witness, do you think?"

Hamilton sighed. "Until this past weekend, I'd have said yes. She's nearing fifty, I expect, in good health, has a good head on her shoulders. At the start of the war, an airfield was laid out on part of her property. Requisitioned, not by her choice. But she made the best of it, looked after the men stationed there, most of them young lads a long way from home. Well, her own son was in France. She gave them the run of her tennis courts and the gardens, with the stipulation that nothing be destroyed, and even allowed them to drink at tables she set up just beyond the maze." He smiled. "Kept them out of mischief, she said. And gave them a place to unwind after a flight, without coming all the way into town. Not that it kept them from enjoying the fleshpots of Walmer, mind you, especially on a Saturday night. Quite popular those men were too. Or so I heard. I was glad I didn't have a daughter."

"Widow, this witness?"

"Yes. Her husband died in 1910, and she had only the one lad. He was a pilot himself, had sixteen kills to his credit before he was shot down. That nearly broke her, but she soldiered on, and the men at the airfield rallied round, taking turns looking after her. It was rather nice of them."

"Tell me about the ghost who is said to be our killer."

Hamilton watched the gulls for a moment, then said, "I wasn't here when it happened, of course. But about halfway through the war, one of the officers at the field got into his motorcar, heading for the lane that led out to the main road, but he was going at a great rate of speed. Then without warning he veered into the hedge that separated the house grounds from the airfield. He hit it full force. Never slowing, according to witnesses. When the lads got to him, he was dead, his chest crushed by the steering wheel. It was quite a shock."

"Accident or deliberate?" Rutledge asked. He could hear the echo of Melinda's words in his head.

Hamilton shrugged. "They couldn't find anything wrong with the motorcar. But apparently Captain Nelson had been having a rough patch. He'd had three close calls in the air, barely making it back to a field in one case, coming down in the water in another, and limping

home in a third. Forty verified kills to his credit, a fine pilot. Most of
the lads didn't last as long as he had. Half the town came to his funeral.
He'd told a friend he was out of luck, and that seemed to haunt him.
That came out at the inquest, but other than that, no one could understand what had happened."

"How old was he?"

"About your age. Not quite thirty, at a guess."

"You seem to know quite a bit about it. Even though you weren't
here."

Hamilton moved his chair slightly and stretched out his legs. "My
wife sent me cuttings from the local paper. It's only a weekly, but some
of the other newspapers carried the story as well. Must have made a
change from the war news, which wasn't very hopeful at the time."

"What did local gossip have to say?"

"Nobody wanted to call it suicide. They seemed to prefer to believe
his luck had run out. Just as he'd said. That it was a freak accident."

"That hardly makes him a ghost." Rutledge watched the gulls overhead, waiting for the Inspector to answer. "Did he haunt the field afterward?"

"No." Hamilton hesitated. "But the odd thing was, the story got
around that he was sometimes seen on the field as a pilot took off—
but only by a pilot who didn't come back. That he foretold bad luck.
Warned a man of his danger. However you might look at it."

"Has he been seen since then?"

"That's even odder. The Ministry was starting to dismantle the
field after the war, and before the work was finished, a half dozen
village lads decided to go there one night to find the ghost for themselves. And they saw him. They came home frightened out of their
wits. When a number of the village men went back to see what was
happening—more likely to hunt for a human prankster than a ghost—
the airfield was empty. They didn't even start a hare or a stoat. But the
boys couldn't be persuaded that there was no ghost. They were that
certain of what they'd witnessed." Clearing his throat, he added, "My
youngest son was one of them."

"He still claims it was a ghost, even today? Or has he forgot his fright?"

"Oh yes. He won't talk about it. But one look at his face when he came home convinced my wife he'd seen *something*. I tried to talk to him about it when I got home, but he refused to say anything. Whether it was a ghost or not, who can say?"

"And the woman who lives in the house? Does she believe in ghosts?"

"Lady Benton? The Hall had once been a small monastery, a sister house to one in France. Under Henry VIII the monks were turned out and the abbey was about to be dismantled when it was granted to a Benton ancestor for some prowess or other at a tournament. He'd unseated the King or some such, depending on which historical record you want to believe. The ancestor came posthaste to have a look at his new property, tore down parts of the abbey, and turned what was left into a manor house. Quite a handsome one, in fact. It would probably be poetic justice to say the ghosts of the dispossessed monks got their own back by haunting the house. What's more, the village has a long memory—you'll hear the house referred to as 'the Abbey' more often than it's called the Hall."

"Most manor houses claim to have ghosts," Rutledge commented.

"If there's one here, I've never heard tales about it. Although they do tell visitors at the Abbey that one kitchen maid a century or more later swore she heard bells in the night, calling the monks to their prayers."

Rutledge smiled. "Indeed. What about the victim in this case?"

Hamilton shrugged. "Apparently she didn't recognize *him*. Nor could she say whether he was real or imaginary." He toyed with the handle of the knife on his plate. "I can't tell you what has caused her to be so wholly convinced that she saw a ghost do murder. I even spoke to Dr. Wister, to see if there was any medical reason. And he knows of nothing that might cause her to have such hallucinations."

"How will she take to my poking about?"

"Truthfully? I think she'll welcome it. This business has unsettled her. Not surprisingly."

Hamilton began to rise, collecting his papers. "You could do worse than staying here at the hotel, by the way. There's a small inn not far from the Abbey, but it's mostly for drinking. Not much of a kitchen and only two very small rooms."

Small rooms. The thought made Rutledge shudder inwardly, his claustrophobia awakening with a vengeance. He'd been buried alive in the trenches and had barely survived, leaving him with a dread of confined spaces. It was one of the reasons he never took a train anywhere, the thought of sharing a cramped compartment putting him off.

"Thanks for the warning. I'll bespeak a room here."

As they crossed the garden to the rear door of the hotel, Rutledge asked, "Who was the victim of the airfield ghost?"

"That's just it. We've no idea. Nor does Lady Benton. Captain Nelson had no enemies. Unless you count the Hun pilots."

I t was going on seven o'clock, but Rutledge went to call on the doctor after settling into the hotel.

"You've come about Lady Benton," he said, after Rutledge had introduced himself.

"Inspector Hamilton told me that he'd spoken to you about her."

"Good man, Hamilton. He told me about his village while I was digging a bit of shrapnel out of his shoulder, just outside Ypres. I remembered that when I was finished with the Army. I wanted a quiet surgery where there were no broken bodies lined up on stretchers and no time to do a decent job on any of them. And Walmer suited me when I came here to take a look."

Dr. Wister was young, perhaps thirty-five or six, but he looked ten years older. Rutledge wondered if he drank—there was something about his eyes that suggested long nights and unpleasant dreams. As if sleep was hard to come by.

Physician, heal thyself. It didn't always work.

Wister gestured to the chair in front of his desk, as he walked around it and sat down. "She's perfectly sane. I'm not convinced her eyesight is what it ought to be. But this business with the ghost and a murder . . ." He shook his head. "I don't know what she actually saw— only what she believes she saw. It was late, dark—and Hamilton would be happy to learn that it was nothing more than a bit of undigested dinner. Like Scrooge. He's used to dealing with evidence. And apparently there isn't any."

"For a start, could she describe the victim? What sort of weapon was used? Was any blood found at the site? I understood from Hamilton that Lady Benton believes she recognized the killer. But was she as certain about any other details?"

"I don't think anyone actually asked that many questions. I expect Hamilton searched, but never found any evidence to support what she'd told him. Including blood. He's always thorough. Still . . ." He cleared his throat. "Women living alone sometimes start at shadows. Hear noises where there are none. They worry about their safety, and she lives in a very large house with no live-in staff."

"What did you do for her? Give her a sedative, to help her sleep?"

"Well, it was the next morning, when she came in to report what had happened. Hamilton brought her to me, because she appeared to be in some distress. I got the rest of the story out of her over some very hot, very sweet tea. Apparently she'd locked herself in her room until first light, then drove herself in. No breakfast, of course. But I'm a doctor, I listened closely, and I didn't judge. Because I could see that she believed every word of her story."

Changing the subject, Rutledge asked, "Who did the post mortem on Captain Nelson, when he was killed?"

"Dr. Gregson, my predecessor. He died in the influenza epidemic, but he was a fine record keeper." He gestured toward a cabinet against the wall by the windows. "I looked up the report, after speaking to Lady Benton. Just to satisfy myself that Nelson was dead. Internal injuries were severe. The wheel crushed his chest. That hedge is very old, with trunks as thick as trees, and at the rate of speed he was said to have been going, the motorcar suffered heavy damage as well. Otherwise, he was a healthy young man, nothing physically that might explain what happened, like a sudden heart event—and nothing that might have worried him to the point of ending his life. That's to say, no fatal illness developing. Emotionally—that's another matter. I dealt with men in France. Gregson didn't. There might have been something that he missed."

Rutledge looked away so that Wister couldn't read his eyes and see what was there. But the doctor had something else on his mind.

"A suggestion?"

"By all means."

"Be careful. Interviewing Lady Benton. You don't want to make matters worse by making her doubt herself. Not doubting her account, you understand—herself. There's a difference."

"I understand."

"Do you? It's important that you do. I'm the one who will have to pick up the pieces long after you go back to the city."

Rutledge stood up. "You will have to trust that I know what to do. How do I find the house?"

Wister reluctantly gave him her direction.

Then, at the door, Rutledge asked, "What became of the motorcar? Afterward?"

"According to Gregson, it was left there until after the inquest. In the event it was needed. And then there was the wait while the Captain's sister was reached in America. Finally the commanding officer saw that it was removed and disposed of—it was bad for morale. And Lady Benton insisted as well. She told him it was distressing to her staff to see it there. The Major cleared it with Gregson, of course. He made a note of that too. For the record. What became of it after that I can't tell you."

Rutledge thanked him, and left.

When he drove out to the Hall, several miles north and east of the village, he passed the ruins of the gatehouse that had once marked the entrance to abbey lands. The base was flint, but there wasn't enough left to judge more than its size. A mile farther along he came to gates of the house itself, set into the high wall that appeared to encircle the estate. They were closed.

He could see what must have become of the original gatehouse, for the wall was flint, the tall pillars on either side of the gates as well. The original builders hadn't wasted good materials.

He'd hoped to find them open, even at this hour, but perhaps after what had happened, he thought, Lady Benton wasn't eager to have either visitors or curiosity seekers.

It was as he was reversing to return to Walmer, that he noticed the gates themselves.

Tall, wrought iron, inset into the pillars and rising in a graceful arch. There was half of a brass scroll on each that came together in the center when the gates were shut as they were now.

He'd taken for granted that it simply gave the name of the property. But it wasn't the name, it was a single word.

Lachrymosa

Rutledge stared at it.

Latin. A place of weeping . . . Tearful.

He could feel Hamish stirring in the far corners of his mind, and as he drove back to the village, he knew he was in for a long night.

R utledge ordered his dinner standing at the desk in Reception, then went up to his room. The sky was still clear and sunlight lit the roofs he could see from his windows, but it didn't brighten his mood.

His meal was brought up, and he'd barely finished it when the darkness began to come down.

C orporal Hamish MacLeod was dead. His bones lay in the black mud that was once a battlefield and now a cemetery. Yet it was more difficult for Rutledge to think of him there than it was to deal with the voice in his head that seemed to come from outside it, just by his shoulder. Where Hamish had stood through so many night watches, waiting for the dawn and another attack across No Man's Land. They had shared a friendship, two very different men from very different backgrounds, brought together by war. The young Scot had been a natural soldier, with an eye for tactics and strategy, a good mind, and a strong sense of duty. His acute hearing had often saved them from night attacks and quickly pinpointed the source of a concealed sniper's shots.

Yet it was that strong sense of duty that had led to Corporal Hamish MacLeod's death. During the bloody and seemingly endless battle of the Somme, for interminable weeks of attack and counterattack, he had seen as his duty the welfare of the exhausted and dispirited men under him, keeping them alert, keeping morale high, making certain that they faced each day ready for whatever was thrown at them. And when orders came down to take out a German machine gun that would stop the next offensive, he had called the assault what it was—sheer murder—and after repeated, useless sorties that failed to stop the German gun, Hamish had finally refused to lead another suicidal attempt to break through to it. Rutledge as the commanding officer had tried to persuade him to change his mind, and Hamish had flatly refused. Neither man realized how close the other was to breaking—neither man could find a way out of their dilemma. And in the end, faced with Hamish's steadfast refusal, Rutledge had had no choice but to order his Corporal shot. It had been the only way to prevent what amounted to a mutiny and regain control of his men.

Rutledge had just delivered the coup de grâce to the dying Scot when a ranging shell from their own side fell short and buried them all, the living and the dead, in the same grave. Only Rutledge had survived, his face pressed against the body of his dead Corporal, finding a tiny air pocket until that too gave out and rescuers pulled him unconscious out of the black and stinking mud.

He had fought on, haunted by the memory of what he'd been forced to do, haunted too by the voice in his head that had become his only way of denying that Hamish was dead. And when the war ended and he was sent home, Rutledge brought the voice with him. Survivor's guilt, Dr. Fleming had told him at the clinic: the desperate need to blot out what he'd done, for his own sanity's sake. Like so many officers, dealing with the terrible burden of having sent hundreds of men to their deaths while he himself escaped with a few superficial wounds, Rutledge had found his own salvation. Or so he'd believed in the darkest corners of his mind.

Shell shock, the rest of the world called it, and Rutledge had done his best to keep that secret, struggling back through the harrowing nightmares and the punishing voice in his mind just enough in 1919 to return to the Yard. He struggled still, but at least he functioned now. For as Dr. Fleming had told him on his last day at the clinic, "It's important for you to realize, Ian, that you *must* win this battle for your mind. And Hamish won't help you there. I can't either. You must fight with all the strength in you to win. Or when the darkness comes down again, it won't lift."

Sometimes that was his greatest fear.

And there were also nights when he could almost wish that it wouldn't lift, that there would be peace, finally, in oblivion.

Then somehow he found the strength of will to fight through the nightmares. Unwilling to give in. Or give up.

He had learned that they were not the same . . .

2

Rutledge slept finally as the sun was rising. But the bustle in the street beneath his window woke him again shortly after seven. He got up, shaved with cold water, and dressed, then went out to walk the streets of the village for half an hour before he was able to consider his breakfast. And after he'd eaten, he waited again, but this time until he was sure the Hall would be open.

And so it was just after nine when he turned in through the open gates and followed the drive up to the main door.

It was, he thought, an unusual blend of architecture. In front of him was an imposing facade nearly two stories tall, soaring to a slender tower that was more ecclesiastical than defensive. Above the massive door was a lovely mullioned window, with coats of arms in stained glass. The remains of what the monks had built? A graceful Elizabethan center seemed to embrace another wing, very likely built from the very stone that had come from the rest of the abbey. Several oriel windows decorated the upper floors, their diamond panes catching the morning light. Smaller than other grander houses of the day, the Hall was in perfect proportions for its size.

Hamish, stirring in the back of his mind, said, "It's verra' isolated."

True enough. It was clear that the abbey had had quite large holdings, and their buildings as well as this house had been designed to last, the center of their own universe.

Looking up at the facade, Rutledge was reminded of what Wister had said about women living alone in large houses. How did that affect Lady Benton, or what she'd witnessed? He remembered that his sister, Frances, had been uncomfortable alone in their parents' London house when he'd left for the war. Even though she'd lived there all her life, she'd kept on the live-in housekeeper who had served their parents, and the cook as well. While in a way they had made her feel safer, they hadn't been able to fill the emptiness his departure had brought. Between the lines of her letters, he had sensed her loneliness, even though she had tried to hide it.

Had the departure of the men at the airfield played any part in Lady Benton's ghost? But then it had been several years now. Not a recent loss . . .

He got out and went up to the door, ringing the bell.

It was several minutes before it was opened by a middle-aged woman in a black dress that looked very like a uniform.

"May I help you, sir? The house is not open until ten o'clock."

"My name is Rutledge. I've been sent by Scotland Yard to inquire into the murder Lady Benton reported."

She looked him up and down. "Do you believe her?" she demanded, standing in the doorway like Horatius at the bridge, holding it against the entire Etruscan Army.

He didn't smile. "Until I have spoken to Lady Benton, I can't tell you whether I believe her or not."

That appeared to be a satisfactory response. The door was swung wider, and the woman said, "Wait here, and I'll see if she's receiving visitors."

He stepped into a large hall, almost two stories high and boasting a hearth that would easily roast an ox or two. But instead of the usual array of weapons and armor that were typical decor, this hall had a single ornament, standing where a high window let light fall across it: a large painted wooden statue of a woman, her head to one side and her face half hidden by her veil. The weeping Madonna.

He was struck by her features, what he could see of them. Delicate and yet strong, her sorrow expressed in the dark, haunted eyes, and the sad mouth. He was reminded of a marble statue he'd seen in Belgium, of a young Madonna with the child who would become Saint John. But he pushed that memory away almost as soon as it had formed. The statue here, he thought, must have come from a church Lady Chapel. Perhaps from the Abbey church? She appeared to be very old, fine lines in her robes indicating the drying of Time as the wood aged.

Looking around him again, he realized that the hall must once have been just such a chapel—the high ceiling with its bosses, which marked the points where the ribbing connected, the traceried windows no longer filled with stained glass. The hearth had been added, to make the hall habitable in cold weather. There was a distinct chill here, even on a sunny morning.

He was still admiring his surroundings when a voice behind him said, "She's all that was left of the monks' chapel. And that was because they had hidden her when the King's men broke down the doors. I've been told that the Abbey church was built of Epping Forest oak. But she's French."

Turning, he saw a tall, slim woman in a gray dress, a pale lavender scarf at the throat. He might have put her age at forty-two or three. Her hair was still a pale gold, and her eyes were blue.

"Good afternoon, Inspector. I'm Felicia Benton." Her voice was patrician, and cool.

"Ian Rutledge, Lady Benton. I've come to hear your side of the story."

She smiled at that.

"My sitting room is through there." She turned and he followed her through several large public rooms, beautifully decorated and kept, into a smaller room that had a comfortable, lived-in air. She gestured for him to sit down.

"We don't have visitors on Mondays and Tuesdays. Keeping the house pristine for viewing takes a great deal of time and energy. It's open the rest of the week."

"How large a staff do you have, Lady Benton?"

"Seventeen. They keep the house clean, and they sit in each of the public rooms when there are visitors. To answer questions and make certain nothing is touched. I also have a cook and a housekeeper, because I don't have time to run the house and take care of myself. The staff takes turns serving in the small café in the only remaining part of the house that belonged to the monks, the crypt."

She was calm and quite self-possessed, hardly the sort of woman he'd have expected to report a killing involving a ghost.

"The death duties have been dreadful," she went on. "My husband, and then my son. We struggle to keep the estate going, and it requires a great deal of money. It's the statue of the Virgin that most people come to see. According to the house archives, she was carved in France in the tenth century, and given to the monks here when they opened the house in the eleventh century—apparently because the abbot here was a relative of the abbot at the mother house. The rest of the Abbey is Elizabethan, with very few changes in some of the rooms. And the portraits of course are rather well known. We have a lovely Charles I by Van Dyck, a small portrait of Anne Boleyn as a child, a Queen Elizabeth in armor at Tilbury, speaking to the troops. Among others. We're bombarded by requests to sell them or donate them or lend them, but I want to keep them here as long as I can do."

"Quite a responsibility," he replied.

"Sometimes I wish I could simply let it all go. But I can't. It was my husband's and my son's duty to keep it in good order and pass it on. I can do no less."

She was simply explaining, not asking for his sympathy. "No one lives in but me," she added. "I'm the only witness to whatever it was that happened."

"How many rooms are there in the house?"

"Seventy-five, not including the garrets where the servants used to sleep. By today's standards they hardly count as rooms. Some fifty are closed. They aren't on display or aren't needed, like most of the bedrooms and the nursery, and so it's easier on the staff to keep them shut off. We do look in once a month to be sure all is well."

"And you don't mind living here alone?"

"Why should I? It's my home. There are memories here of my husband and my son that I treasure." She looked around, her eyes sad. "Eric loved the house. When he was little, he'd explore, then come and ask one of us to tell him about a clock in the Blue Bedroom, or the birds on the wallpaper in the small cabinet room. He led some of the tours after his father died, and the visitors adored him. And he could answer all their questions without referring to the book we keep in each room, identifying all the treasures on display."

He smiled. "Then it's comforting, not lonely."

"Yes, very much so." Then she gave him an amused glance. "I even hear the monks singing, when the wind is up. In a way that's comforting too."

Until now, she had seemed to be quite rational, capable, and as normal as the doctor.

Something in his face must have changed, because she laughed, adding dryly. "We have a multitude of Elizabethan chimneys, and God knows how many cracks in the brickwork. The wind finds a way in. I'd rather think of monks singing than more repairs needing my attention."

He had the grace to apologize, although he wasn't quite sure what the apology was for. "I shall remember that when my own chimneys whistle." Changing the subject, he went on. "I understand there's an airfield just beyond the boundaries of your property?"

"Yes. It was actually part of the estate, but as it was suitable for an airfield, the Ministry took it over. Well, we weren't using it, it was fallow at the time. I've petitioned to have the land returned to the estate, but there is some talk of preserving it for history. I don't quite see how, most of the buildings were dismantled in early 1919. There are foundations, the airstrip itself, and the ruins of a building or two. Hardly anything worth the trouble of preserving. Oddly enough we do hear of a visitor or two there. Mostly curiosity, although some of the men have returned, bringing their families to see where they served. Or their families come to see where they were posted, those who didn't come back. There were quite a few of those."

"Has the Captain's family ever come back?"

He'd caught her off guard with his question. But she didn't ask him which officer he was referring to. She knew.

"I—if they did, they haven't called at the house."

"What really happened to him?"

She sighed, shaking her head. "I don't know. Men went off in their aircraft, even though they knew that most seldom survived past two or three missions, and they fought with what skill they had and great courage. I talked to a good many of them, when they came up to the house. They laughed, there was horseplay—they were so *young*. Dear God. But you had only to look into their eyes, and see old men lurking there."

He understood what she meant. He'd seen recruits change after their first battle. The boy gone forever.

"Was he suicidal, do you think?"

"I don't know." She considered the question, but he knew she must have thought about it again and again since the man's death. "He hid his feelings well. I liked him, you know. A charming man, intelligent, well read. We would talk sometimes. I invited him to dine here several evenings, because he was curious about our library. And he stayed until midnight once, reading a book. It was part of a collection, or I'd have given it to him to take back with him. But he never talked about himself. Of course, he was older than most of the flyers. Perhaps that was it."

"Why do you think he came back from the grave to kill a man whose body we still haven't found?"

He wasn't sure what he'd expected, what her answer would be.

She surprised him. "I don't know. I only know what I saw," she said simply. "I had wondered, waiting for the police to come, if it was something that had happened some time ago, and somehow I was able to witness it years later."

Frowning, he asked, "Are you saying that you believe he might have killed someone in the past?"

"I'm not sure what I'm trying to say. I do know what I saw. I am at a loss to explain it. Even to myself." She shrugged slightly. "I know Inspector Hamilton believes I'm mad. And Dr. Wister wonders if I am ill, and he hasn't been able to diagnose that illness yet. Perhaps both men are right. All I can tell you is that madness doesn't run in my family. At least there's no record of it occurring."

Every time Rutledge thought he had formed an opinion of Lady Benton, she showed him a different face.

"Who was the victim?"

"I have no idea."

"How was he killed?"

"I'm not even certain it was a man, you know. He was there, and then he fell, and the—his killer—rushed forward to stand over him. And then he looked—he looked up at my window, as if he knew I was there, watching. I stepped back. When I dared look again, there was nothing there. Neither the victim nor the killer. Just the night." She shivered.

"Perhaps you dreamed it?"

"I was awake, Inspector. Fully awake. I'd gone to the window as I often do to watch the moon rise. My husband and I would stand there and watch it together, some nights. And so it has become a habit for me. After a busy day, it's in the quiet of the night that I miss him. And—as you say. It's comforting."

He asked her then if he could see the window.

"Yes, of course. This way." She led him through another series of rooms to a second staircase. "This is the newer part of the house—that is, not the fabric, but the interior. My husband's father won a great deal of money on the Derby, and brought the living quarters into the nineteenth century. I have been very grateful."

He had kept his bearings, and thought that the room they entered was in the east wing, overlooking the distant estuary. It was large, and actually quite pleasant, with a high ceiling, the wallpaper dark blue with a pattern of silver fleur de lis, the colors picked up again in the draperies and the carpet as a soft gray and blue. After the formal state rooms he'd passed through, this one was bright, with three windows across the outside wall.

"My father-in-law slept in the old Master Bedroom suite until he redid these rooms, and then moved the family across to this wing, with real mattresses and conveniences." She had crossed the room as she spoke and reached up to pull the curtains wide. "We always slept with these open—heresy to my husband's old housekeeper, who believed that one must shut out the miasmas of the night."

As Rutledge joined her, he could look down on a narrow terrace with steps leading down to the lawn. Wide borders enclosed this, set in patterns of colors. It was a private garden, he thought, with a small fountain in the center and wrought iron chairs, painted white, at the far end.

"Where were the figures?"

"They came up from the left—the direction of the airfield. There's an arch in the hedge just by the terrace. One was ahead of the other, and when the second figure appeared just below us, by the terrace steps, the other man stopped and turned. He was just there, near the little fountain. It's a cupid, a pretty little thing. Then he backed away as the second man started forward. See where the colors change from red to pink? There, more or less, is where he stopped again. And the second figure kept moving toward him . . ." Her voice trailed off.

"And what happened next?"

She took a deep breath. "The man with his back to me—the victim—was moving when his knees suddenly seemed to buckle—and he went down, falling slowly forward onto his face." Her voice changed. "I—he didn't move, you see. Not after that. And—and his companion—his companion looked up at this front of the house, as if he could see me here in the window. But he couldn't—I'm sure of it—I wasn't close to the glass."

Rutledge thought she was trying to convince herself. And so he waited.

She drew another deep breath, trying to steady herself. And failed. "I stood there, frozen. Then—then he walked forward. He passed the man on the ground without a glance. Still looking up. Moving straight toward the terrace, and the doors there, as if he intended to come into the house. That's when I recognized his stride, you see. And even in the moonlight, as he drew nearer, I recognized his *face*. It seemed to glow from within, somehow. I was in a panic. I knew who he was—and I knew he was *dead*." Her fear was real, even now, her hands trembling although she at once clasped them together to stop it. "I turned and rushed to lock my door and even pushed that chest across in front of it." She turned slightly to point at a tall chest just by the door. "By the time I could cross back to the window, he was nowhere to be seen—but the other man—the one who had fallen down—was gone as well."

She kept her eyes on the sunny window, refusing to look at Rutledge. Striving to bring herself under control and failing.

He said gently, "Are you certain the other man was dead?"

"Yes—I—he—it was the way he lay, you see. *Crumpled*. Not struggling or moving."

"He couldn't have used the other man's movements to get to his feet and flee?"

"Where could he have gone? The only way out of the garden is by the arch in the hedge. His killer was between him and any escape."

"Did you hear a shot?"

"Oh, no, there was no report, no flash."

"Did anyone try to break into the house?"

"No. I didn't sleep. As you can imagine. When it was full light, and I could hear people stirring downstairs, doors opening and shutting, as the staff arrived, I moved the chest again, unlocked the door, and went down to the terrace doors myself. But they were all right." She smiled, more anxiety than humor. "I expect ghosts don't *need* to break in, do they?" When she looked up at him, there were tears in her eyes.

Before Rutledge could speak, she said quietly, "I'm not mad. At least I don't think so. I did *see* what happened. I wasn't dreaming or walking in my sleep. I unlocked the terrace doors and went out onto the grass. It was still wet with dew, and I realized that I'd forgot to put on my slippers. I knew just where the men had stood. Where one had fallen. But there was no blood. The grass wasn't even bruised . . ."

"How could you be sure of the right place? In the night, the colors of the flowers would have been white or gray. You couldn't judge their colors."

Lady Benton shook her head. "I've lived here for so many years. Do you think I couldn't find my way around this house *or* the grounds, in the middle of the night?"

"Did the police—Inspector Hamilton—come up to your room to see the scene as you'd shown it to me?"

"No. Once there was nothing in the garden to support my account, he was more embarrassed than he was interested. Well, to be fair, in his place I wouldn't have believed me, either."

"And you are sure the man you saw was the Captain? That's a good distance, it was dark."

"I've told you. I recognized his walk. And—and his face glowed. I could see it clearly."

"You mentioned that before. How do you mean, glowed?"

"Yes, all right, think me silly or mad or whatever you please. But it was—I could see his features clearly. Even as frightened as I was."

He found himself thinking that fear sometimes heightened the senses, rather than dulling them.

She turned away from the window, crossing to the door. He had seen what he needed to see, at least until he knew more to look for.

And so he followed her, and they started back through the house to the sitting room. Their footsteps echoed in the passages and on the stairs, and as Lady Benton started to open the door that linked the newer rooms with the other part of the house, they could hear voices on the other side.

"Tours," she said, despair in her voice, her hand still on the knob. "I'd forgot. We book small private tours on the days we're closed to the public. There's one this morning." She turned to Rutledge. "We'll have to wait. They will be staring if I come through. Word has got around, I expect."

"We can wait," he said, and walked to the windows in the small lobby where the stairs debouched. There was an outer door here as well, the upper half glazed rather than paneled. It appeared to open into a walk sheltered by a line of high hedge. "Where does this lead?"

"Around to the stables, which is where I keep a motorcar and my staff leaves their bicycles. There are no horses. I miss riding. Just behind the stables are the tennis courts. No one uses them now." For a moment she stared out the glass. Then she said, "Am I breaking down? Are my nerves going? The doctor wanted to give me sedatives, to help me sleep. I tossed them into the dustbin. You're a policeman. *Was* there a murder?"

"I don't know," Rutledge answered her gently. "I won't, not until I've looked into your account." It wasn't the answer she was hoping to hear. And so he added, "I shouldn't worry about it too much, if I were you. You believe in what you saw. There must have been something there."

"I could have kept it to myself—I needn't have called the Inspector." Her fingers were twisting together again. "I did what I believed to be my duty. Now when I go into the village, people stare. I've taken to doing my marketing elsewhere." She touched his arm lightly. "Will you promise me something?"

"If I can."

"If—if you should discover that what I saw was only a figment of my imagination—or, well, a dream—will you tell me first? Before you speak to Inspector Hamilton or to London?" She lifted her chin, making the best of it. "I should like to be prepared, you see."

3

Rutledge looked down at her drawn face. "I can't promise. But I will do my best."

"Yes. I understand. Thank you." She turned. "I believe the tour has moved on. If you will excuse me, I must see that all is well in the café and elsewhere. Can you find your way out? Or if you wish, you have the run of the house. If there are questions, ask anyone. There is nothing to hide."

Rutledge thanked her, and then, rather than go through the house again, he let himself out the unlatched door and walked down to the stable block. It was not large, for there was a separate carriage house with its apartment above for the coachman. They were locked, and from what he could tell they hadn't been tampered with. That meant the barns for the farm stock were somewhere else. He found Lady Benton's motorcar in a small shed that had been erected expressly for it between stable and carriage house. There was fencing, with a gate, that separated the buildings from the farm lane that gave access to them. It was closed at present. Across the lane there was another fence, but as far as he could tell, the pasture was empty. That brought up another question—who ran the farms that supported the estate?

He glimpsed the tennis courts—two of them—noting that there were no nets, and weeds were beginning to push their way up through the grass.

The kitchen was in this wing of the house, facing the stables. There was a kitchen garden with a cutting garden just beyond.

He circled the house, counting six other doors, not including the one through which he'd entered the house or the one that he'd used just now to leave it. One of the six was the pair of long doors opening into the terrace below Lady Benton's bedroom. Nine in all, counting the kitchen. Not unusual in large old estates when dozens of servants came and went from the kitchen and the gardens, while the owners and their families and guests were free to use any door they chose. But this house, with only one person in residence, was vulnerable. The locks, as far as he could see, were a generation old. Anyone could find a way inside, and hide in rarely used rooms or closets and attics.

When the visitors left, he would have to come back and explore more thoroughly.

He'd deliberately ended his search at the terrace and the private garden where the events of Friday night, whatever they might have been, had occurred. He'd come through the hedge and the black iron gate that kept out trespassers, then stopped to consider the expanse of grassy lawn, the two flower borders running down each side, and the cupid fountain in the center. It seemed a little larger than it had from Lady Benton's windows. After a moment or two he walked out onto the lawn, moving toward the fountain and the bed of pink hyacinths. And there he turned to look up at the windows of the east front.

Remembering something Lady Benton had told him—that she and her husband often slept at night with the curtains open—he realized that on that particular floor, not open to the public, in all the windows, the drapes were drawn across. Save for hers.

A man who had just killed might look at the house to see if he'd been watched. And his gaze would be drawn at once to the window where the drapes were open. Where, in a dark room, someone might be standing, invisible to him on the ground.

Yet there was no sign of any altercation here on the neatly trimmed grass. Still, he quartered the garden, examined the beds on either side for footprints in the soft earth, and even looked into the wide basin of the fountain. Above his head, the cupid stood balanced on one foot, a bow in one hand and a quiver of arrows slung across his shoulders. He was looking down at Rutledge from a tall pillar of carved roses, forming a platform for the toes of his right foot, a stone smile on his chubby face.

Where the hedge enclosed the far end of the garden, there was a pair of wrought iron chairs, where one might sit and admire the range of color in the borders against the backdrop of the house and the tall chimneys rising from the rooftops.

Hamish, who had been silent since Rutledge had arrived, spoke suddenly, startling him. The voice was derisive.

"Did ye expect to find anything?"

Without thinking, Rutledge retorted, "What should I have found? What do you see?"

And cursed himself for answering Hamish aloud.

"An empty garden. Ye must ask yoursel', why yon Captain? Why did he kill the ither man, and no' the reverse?"

Rutledge stopped. "The Captain is already dead . . ."

"Aye. Ye canna' kill a dead man."

But you could. When he only lived in your own mind, you could put a revolver to your own head, and pull the trigger.

The thought ran through his mind before he could prevent it.

And heard Hamish's deep chuckle.

Forcing himself to concentrate instead on the task at hand, after a moment he looked up again at the windows of Lady Benton's bedroom, then purposely walked forward, almost to the foot of the terrace steps, keeping his gaze fixed on them, as he'd been told the killer had done.

But he couldn't have said whether she was there watching him or if the room was empty. The glass reflected only the cloudless bowl of the sky above his head. It must have done much the same in the night.

Then he turned to his right, where according to Lady Benton a path ran through another opening in the hedge and down to the airfield.

But he'd already explored that facade of the house, where lawns spread out under the windows and ornamental trees offered shade. Where was this path? He hadn't seen it.

Rutledge went back through the gate in the arch, and walked toward the distant airfield beyond the manicured grounds.

There was hedging beyond the lawns, forming a tall, dense boundary that enclosed them, and it ran right around from where he was standing to the stable block and tennis courts to his far left. He could just see the weather vane on the stable rooftop rising above the deep green of the hedge where it ended at the lane. The hedge itself was old, threaded with wild clematis and other vines, trees that had taken root and flourished, not well trimmed like that around the private garden. And it appeared to be unbroken . . .

Turning slightly to his right, Rutledge caught sight of a rough opening. Not a formal arch, more a break where many people must have come and gone over the war years. This then must have been how the men from the airfield came up to the house.

He crossed the lawns toward it.

The abbey had been set on a long, lofty ridge, rather like that in Walmer, where the harbor was on flatter land and closer to the water. Here, there was no water—just a vast meadow running toward distant wind-twisted trees. At one time it must have been marshy ground, possibly reclaimed over the centuries for a sheep run. Solid enough now, from the looks of it. And if he was any judge, Rutledge thought, the meadow was north and a little east of Walmer, which would put it closer to the sea.

The monks had chosen well. Raiders might come up the estuary to look for plunder and stumble across a village where Walmer stands now. There was not even a river here to lead them to the Abbey.

He turned his attention to the path, now overgrown and showing no signs of recent use. As far as he could tell, not even a Constable had tried to make his way down to the airfield.

This was a good vantage point to examine it, although there was hardly anything left to see. Rutledge stopped and scanned it.

There were only broken foundations now where a building had once stood, just as Lady Benton had told him.

The offices, quarters, and mess, along with other miscellaneous structures had been taken down, save for one or two smaller huts scattered out by what must have been the runway, farther to his left. Paths still snaked among the ruins, worn to bare earth by the feet of men posted here for the duration of the war.

The runway had been flattened and smoothed, the wiry meadow grasses and brambles kept short. He thought he could see where the aircraft had been parked, dark patches of oil and fuel spills still marking the line, backed up by the maintenance shops as well as the short observation tower where officers could stand to watch aircraft taking off or landing. Other foundations he could only guess at, but the long shapes of the barracks were clear enough, and the square that had been the mess.

Hamish said, just at his shoulder, "Here are the ghosts. The buildings that are gone."

And in a way it was true. Men had lived and died as they served here.

This was not the time to explore, but he walked a little way down the path in the hope of seeing where the damaged hedge might be, indicating where Captain Nelson had wrecked his motorcar. But from this angle it was not visible. Nor was there any indication of a lane in and out of the field. He rather thought the entrance was the lane that passed by the stables. But that could wait.

Over his head the sky was a bowl of blue with only a few clouds, and he remembered meeting an officer of an Essex regiment who talked about the breadth of the sky in this part of the county. And it did seem larger than the same sky in London or even in Kent.

Reluctantly turning away, he walked back to the house, looking for the crypt. He quickly learned that there was no outside access to it. Which made sense. For the great hall had been part of the original church choir and Lady Chapel, and the crypt would have been beneath it.

In a corner of the great hall, he found the arch and a flight of twisting, dimly lit, shallow stone steps worn by centuries of feet, and as he made the final turn, he could hear voices and the clink of cutlery and china. The smell of food wafted up to him.

The ceiling was low and the space partially taken up by heavy stone pillars supporting the church above, with a long counter to one side marking off the service area. Round tables filled the bays between the pillars, and there were some ten or twelve visitors sitting at them. The counter was piled high with trays of little cakes and thick sandwiches, there were dishes and cups, silverware at the end where a woman sat to take money, and a large kettle of what must be hot water for the tea in the caddy beside it.

The woman behind the counter smiled at him, asking what he'd have, and he ordered a cup of tea and one of the lemon cakes. She was younger than Lady Benton, with a sweet face. She set his selections on a tray, and after he'd paid for them, he carried the tray to a table in a corner.

Voices echoed here, and he caught snatches of conversations as visitors talked among themselves.

"I liked the blue room, best—"

"How long do you think it takes to dust everything—?"

"Mind you, the bedrooms are quite nice, but aren't the beds rather small—?"

"If there are horses in the stables, can I ride—"

He'd just finished his food when the woman who had opened the door to him that morning came down the stairs, looked around, and spotted him. Threading her way through the tables, she said quietly as she reached him, "May I join you?"

He noticed that she had avoided his title.

"Please do."

"I'm the housekeeper. I've been here at the Abbey since 1908." She sat down. "I have asked Lady Benton if she would like to have me stay in the house for a while. Until this—situation—has been resolved. She won't hear of it. I would like to ask you to advise her to bring someone in. Only temporarily, of course. She might listen to you."

"Truthfully? I don't think I could persuade her. It might frighten her, if I tried," he replied.

She regarded him impatiently. "I don't believe she's safe."

"Why?"

She glanced over her shoulder, making certain that she couldn't be overheard. "I believe her when she tells me that someone was on the grounds, that Friday evening. I don't know who they were or what they were about. But she's not *safe*."

"Why?" he asked again. "Is there anyone who might wish to harm her?"

The woman bit her lip. "No—I can't imagine why anyone should. But then why put on such a display when they must have been sure she was watching?"

That, Rutledge thought, was the first practical view of what had happened on Friday night.

"Who would do such a thing? To what purpose?"

"You're the policeman, I expect you to tell me the answer to that."

"There's the question of who is to gain if something happened to Lady Benton. Who inherits the Abbey, if she were to die?"

"It's left to the National Trust. There's an elderly cousin some-where, Wiltshire, I think. But he wants no part of the house. Never did, as far as I know. I don't believe he's ever set foot in it. At least not in my time here."

"Perhaps," Rutledge said, "he's changed his mind." Or someone in his family had finally realized what he had so cavalierly dismissed.

But she shook her head. "It's not likely. According to Lady Benton." She glanced over her shoulder again. Then added, "There are valu-ables in the house. Paintings, silver, books. And she owns some nice bits of jewelry. If someone frightened her into moving into the village even for a few days, the house would be vulnerable. He could take his time going through the rooms."

"Have you ever had a visitor who aroused suspicion—asked too many questions about certain objects or appeared to be—different from the usual run of person who comes through?" Rutledge asked.

She sighed. "A few times. One of the gardeners is rather burly. We had him ask one man to leave. There was no trouble. Still, it was worrying."

"What about insurance? For the more valuable pieces?"

"I don't know. She doesn't tell me such things. And I expect it's quite expensive. There's that alcove in the Green Drawing Room. Meissen figures, shepherds and shepherdesses, harlequins. And there's that silver salt boat in the grand dining room. A galleon in full sail, that piece. Of course, it would be more difficult to sell, it's too well known. Still, that's why there's always someone sitting in the rooms when we're open. Too easy to scoop up a small treasure, pocket it, and walk out."

"You're suggesting that the events in the terrace garden were a cover for robbery. Has anything actually gone missing?"

She shook her head. "Not that I know of. Not that we've discovered so far." Leaning forward on her crossed arms, she said earnestly. "A ghost. And a dead body that didn't exist. It doesn't make sense, does it? It's as if they *were* putting on a show—whoever they are. And there must be a reason for it."

"Was Lady Benton close to the officer who died when his motorcar crashed into the hedge?"

Surprised that he knew about the Captain, she answered, "He reminded her of Eric, I think. Her son. She missed him so. And she took the Captain's death hard. I mean, she knew the risks. He flew, after all. And he was good at it. I expect that was how he expected to die. Not like that. Surely."

Or it was possible that the waiting had become its own burden.

"*Was* it suicide? Or accident? No one seems to have an opinion about that."

Frowning, she shook her head. "I don't know. I don't think that anyone does—"

Someone called, "Mrs. Hailey, so sorry to interrupt—"

The woman glanced over her shoulder, toward the speaker at the foot of the stairs, an older woman dressed in dark blue. Turning back to Rutledge, Mrs. Hailey said, "I'm needed. But you will think about speaking to Lady Benton?"

"Yes." It wasn't a promise, he told himself.

He watched her walk away, her head bent to listen to whatever problem the younger woman had brought to her to solve.

Hamish said unexpectedly, "Do ye think it was housebreakers playing at ghosts?"

The deep Scots voice seemed to echo through the undercroft, and Rutledge dropped his teaspoon, bending to retrieve it as he covered his surprise.

A great deal of trouble to go through, he replied silently, when the Abbey could be entered in the middle of the night, without fanfare. It could be the middle of the morning or later before anyone noticed a broken lock on a little-used entrance.

"Aye, then why yon charade? Even the Chief Constable wonders if Lady Benton is no' well in the heid. The question is, will there be ither ways to frighten her—and leave doubt in the minds of those around her?"

"That's possible," he agreed. Rutledge rose, collecting his dishes and setting them on the little tray before taking it up to a small table, where a smiling young woman whisked them out of sight. "But what are they after? Robbery? Having her committed? Or are they simply tormenting her, for the sake of making her life a misery? If she cared about the Captain, seeing him murder someone is quite a clever way of hurting her."

He'd made his way out of the undercroft and was passing the statue in the great hall, when a thought occurred to him. "It wasn't her family who dispossessed the monks. I don't see any gain in punishing her for what her husband's ancestors did."

"But she didna' see a monk."

Leaving by the main door, he went out to his motorcar and turned the crank.

Behind him, the house was quiet, the flurry of visitors dwindling as the afternoon wore on. Save for those still in the undercroft.

Looking up at the handsome facade, he thought about Lady Benton's day. She prepared for visitors in the early morning, and then kept an eye on everything that was happening in the house, until it was time to close. Even then she must have to walk through the public rooms, turning out lamps, making certain no one had been left behind—looking to see if anything needed to be dusted or polished or even put back exactly in its place. When her staff left, what did she do then? Take a tray of food to her rooms, and shut off the rest of the house? He wondered if she could put Friday out of her mind. Not just the responsibility but the knowledge that she was alone. It wouldn't be surprising if that led to an overly active imagination . . .

Rutledge was about to step into his motorcar when the main door opened. He was surprised to see Lady Benton herself come through and call to him.

"Are you leaving?" she asked, the slightest trace of anxiety in her voice. "Did you find any answers?"

He walked around the motorcar to meet her, realizing he shouldn't have gone away without at least speaking to her.

Smiling, he said, "No answers. Not yet, Lady Benton. But I need to explore a number of avenues before I can reassure you that all is well. I would like to know, for instance, if lads from the village might have put on a show—"

He'd intended to relieve her worry, but instead, she had flushed a little and cut him off, saying, "Don't. Don't treat me like a child. I know what I saw, Inspector. I know it was real. At least, that it wasn't a pair of boys trying to play at frightening me. Those were men I saw."

"I'm sorry," he said at once. "I was not suggesting that you were wrong. But I must eliminate any possibility of someone playing a prank or trying in some way or for some reason to frighten you." When she didn't seem to respond, he added, "There are certain things a policeman must do. For instance, look at every possible fact. Until he does that, he can't begin to narrow his suspicions."

She raised a hand to her throat, clearly embarrassed. "Oh—yes—all right. I'm sorry. I thought perhaps—but that was rather silly of me, expecting you to clear away this mystery, your first day. Carry on, Inspector. If you have more questions, you know where to find me." And with a smile that tried to be understanding and patient, she stepped back inside the hall, and closed the door behind her.

He set out up the drive, intending to return to Walmer, but when he reached the gates, he changed his mind and instead turned in the opposite direction.

Nearly a mile up the road, he came to the inn that Hamilton had mentioned.

It really was little more than a pub. Small and not particularly well kept, the windows dusty and the sign above the door hanging on rusty hinges. Looking up at it, he saw that the name of the pub was The Monk's Choice. And the painting was of a jolly man in a monk's habit lifting a tankard, a broad smile on his face and a barmaid on his knee. Bawdy and disrespectful.

Intrigued, Rutledge pulled up in the small yard, and got out.

The first thing he noticed was the slant of the roof above the first floor. He could imagine how the ceilings inside sloped as well, taking up half the space. For a tall man, such a room would be worse than merely cramped.

As Rutledge was standing there, he had a feeling he was being watched, but there was no one about, and no one that he could see working in the fields across the road from the pub. He was dressed like a Londoner, and his motorcar was distinctive. And it was quiet enough that he could hear birds singing in the trees to his left. Curiosity, then, he told himself, and crossed the yard to the door.

It was heavy, creaking open into a fairly large single room, with a bar in the middle and tables on either side.

No one was behind the counter, and he stood there looking around. The theme of monks wasn't carried on the inside. Instead, the interior was rather plain, the tables old and scarred and the chairs looking as if they'd been used by the monks themselves in the eleventh century.

But it was surprisingly neat, unlike the exterior.

There was a door behind the bar that must lead to a kitchen, he thought, and a flight of stairs that went up to the two small rooms Inspector Hamilton had mentioned.

Someone started down the steps, and an unshaven man in shirtsleeves and apron appeared. He stopped halfway, stared at Rutledge, and said, "Not open until four o'clock." There was not a welcome nor warmth in his voice.

"You don't serve lunch?" Rutledge asked, curious. He noticed that the hand gripping the stair railing was grimy, and the other hand held a pail, half hidden by the legs of the man's trousers.

"No."

"Do you take rooms for the night?"

"No." The word was even more curt.

"Sorry to have disturbed you," Rutledge said, and turned to leave.

But the man asked, "Not from around here, are you?"

Rutledge replied, "I came up from Kent." When there was no further response, he added, "Actually I came to visit the Abbey. A man raises a thirst going through so many rooms."

"I wouldn't know. Never been there."

He had reached the door and was about to open it when the man asked, "In the war, were you? At the airfield?"

Rutledge turned back to face him, there on the staircase.

"A friend served here," he said. "The Captain who was killed crashing into the hedge."

"Bloody fool."

"Did you know him?"

"No. Heard about him. Always a daredevil, so they said. Some of the lads came here to drink."

"What did they think? Accident or suicide?"

The man's expression had been sullen. Now it was blank. "They never said."

But Rutledge thought they had.

"The news was a shock to everyone who knew him. He didn't seem the sort to kill himself. And he was too damned good a pilot to die in a hedge," he said.

The man didn't reply, staring at Rutledge without any expression. Then he turned and walked back up the stairs, disappearing from sight. Rutledge could hear his footsteps crossing the loose boards on the floor above.

Rutledge stood there for a moment longer, then went out the door and turned the crank.

Feeling eyes on his back, he straightened and looked up at the two windows that must mark the first-floor rooms.

In the one on the left, the curtain twitched very slightly and then went still.

Rutledge stopped briefly at the police station. Inspector Hamilton was at his desk, and he looked up as Rutledge was shown in.

"On your way back to London?"

Rutledge smiled. "Hardly. No, I came to ask what you know about The Monk's Choice."

"Thinking of taking a room there after all?"

"I think not. I stopped in before coming back to Walmer. What's the history of the pub?"

"It's been there for some forty years, at a guess. The owner's father, one Jack Newbold, was a tenant farmer at the Abbey until he was turned off for drunkenness. He moved into a derelict house on the road and turned it into a pub. God knows where he found the money. Still, it seems he was a better publican than he was a farmer, and The Monk's Choice did surprisingly well. Fred, the son, hasn't prospered, since he took over. Didn't have his father's head for business."

"Any trouble with the police?"

"Not really. Rowdiness, mostly. The pub was popular with some of the men at the airfield, and for a time was respectable enough to escape attracting the attention of their officers. Custom dropped off after the war, I expect." He concentrated on the pen he'd been rolling in his fingers. "Walmer lost quite a few men. As did the Abbey. Lady Benton had to mechanize the Home Farm, to make up for their loss.

Most of the women who work with her at the house are widows. Were you aware of that?"

"No, I wasn't."

"Three of my own men didn't make it back." He set the pen aside, and looked across the desk at Rutledge. "The thing was, Fred New-bold, Jack's son, was rejected by the Army. All his mates marched off to war, and he was left behind. It—affected him. He hasn't been himself since then."

"Why was he rejected?" What he'd seen of the man on the stairs, he was healthy enough to have served.

"Something to do with the heart. Doctor Wister can explain it, if need be."

Rutledge thanked him and left.

As he drove on to the hotel's yard, Hamish said, "In the old days, a public house like yon would belong to smugglers." The deep Scots voice coming from the rear seat was as real as it had been in life.

Without thinking, Rutledge answered aloud. "What else is it hid-ing?"

He was about to turn into the yard when he heard laughter coming from the open windows of the lounge.

Given that warning, he left his motorcar in the yard, and walked around to the rear where the garden tables were set out. The door there led by the kitchens, and he stopped in, asking a harried young woman if he could have a tray in the room.

"When this lot has gone, sir—would that be soon enough?"

"Yes. That's fine."

"There's a menu in Reception. Just tell them what you'd like."

He went on down the passage, which came out by the stairs and Re-ception, and he found himself in the overflow of guests, standing about chatting. Making his way through them, he found the menu on a stand outside the dining room, made his choice, and gave it to the grinning woman at Reception.

She made a note of it, and then said, "It does make the heart light to see a happy young couple." When he didn't immediately agree with her, she went on. "There wasn't much time for engagement parties during the war. People got married when and where they could, didn't they?"

The memory of his own engagement party came flooding back, and he made some answer, then turned and went up the stairs to his room. The sound of voices seemed to follow him, even when he shut the door.

Jean Gordon's parents had held the affair in their own home, and he remembered doing his duty, asking all the women who had no partners to dance, and Melinda was there, although he knew she wasn't particularly pleased that he'd proposed to Jean. He'd not been particularly pleased himself that she hadn't been as glad for him as he'd hoped. But he'd been in love, blind to the truth.

He'd danced with Kate that night, Jean's cousin, and saw reflected in her eyes a sadness for him, and tried to ignore it. Jean was bright, beautiful, spirited—and utterly selfish. And Kate knew that. He wished now with all his heart that he'd been a wiser man and had chosen Kate instead. But it was too late.

Too late . . .

His room looked out on the back garden he'd just come through. Several people had taken tables there, the murmur of conversation drifting up to him, but not the words. They were dressed for the party and had gone out for a breath of fresher air. He crossed the room and looked down at them. Then knew he had to get away.

Leaving the motorcar where it was, he began to walk. And soon found himself in front of St. George's churchyard, two streets over. Above his head the westering sun struck the tower, touching it with light.

Hamish said, out of the blue, "Where did they bury the Captain?"

There was an iron gate set in the stone wall surrounding the church-yard, and he opened it, stepping onto the path that led to the church door. But he turned aside and began reading the names on the grave-stones. He walked by many too old to be deciphered and searched in-stead for newer ones.

Hamish was saying, "There mayna' be a stone."

It didn't matter, he couldn't go back to the hotel until the guests had left. And so he kept on, ignoring the voice, moving about the uneven ground as he searched.

He finally discovered what he was looking for well behind the apse, as if those who had provided a place of burial had been of two minds about how the man had died.

Clearly there hadn't been any family to claim the body . . .

It was a plain stone with only the man's name—*Roger Anthony Nelson*—his rank of Captain, and his dates. Rutledge realized that he would have been twenty-nine on his next birthday, had he lived.

There was no information about his parentage or how he'd died. And there was no one else by that name close by, no one who might remotely be related.

Why hadn't the body been sent back to wherever his family lived?

He was still standing there, considering the stone, when someone spoke just behind him.

"Did you serve with him?"

4

Rutledge turned sharply to find a young woman a few feet from him. Her approach across the thick grass had been almost silent. Even Hamish hadn't heard her.

"Sadly, no."

"He would come into the pub sometimes—the Salt Cellar, down by the harbor. If he was still there at closing, he'd walk me home." She had brown hair and brown eyes, and was pretty in a very soft way. "I liked him. Quiet, nice manners. I'd have gone out with him, if he'd asked. But he never did."

"What did you talk about, as he walked with you?"

"Books. Music. He had a volume of poetry he lent me, and sometimes we talked about that. *Wings of Fire.* Do you know it?"

He did. He could quote from it by heart. He'd carried it in his pocket most of the war.

But he said, "I think I've heard of it."

"It was about the war. He liked it because he thought the poet had been there and knew what was true about it."

The poet had been a woman in Cornwall who had never seen France. But the man she loved had . . . She had seen it through his eyes.

"Where was he from? The Captain?"

"Somerset, I think. He lived near the Quantock Hills, and spent much of his childhood exploring them. He liked nature, and walking. He knew so much about birds." She smiled. "He'd hear one sing, and recognize it straightaway. I could hardly name the ones I actually saw."

"He was a pilot, I think?"

"Oh, yes, he loved to fly. He was posted to the airfield not far from here."

He began to walk back the way he'd come, and she fell into step beside him.

"I stop by here sometimes," she went on. "I expect he must be lonely with no family to come and visit."

"Were they dead? His parents?"

"I believe so. He always talked about them in the past. But he had a sister. You'd think she might want to come at least once, and leave flowers."

"Did he have friends in the squadron? Anyone in particular?"

"He was older than most of them. They called him the old man. I couldn't tell whether that was a term of respect or not."

"It can be. He was a survivor. They would respect his record."

"They would come into the pub from time to time, but they preferred the hotel bar. It was livelier. I think that's why he chose ours. Just local people there most of the time."

"I was told there was a pilot out at the airfield who liked to show off. Was that Captain Nelson?"

She shook her head. "I've heard people say that. My guess is, he had to look the part of the air ace. The white scarf and leather jacket, laced boots. He showed me a photograph once, and we laughed about the man in the picture. He called it his other self. He was dressed for riding in it, and I liked it."

"Was he sad, do you think?" They had left the churchyard behind, and he could see the houses nearer the harbor just ahead of them.

"I never saw it, if he was. Just—quiet. I was never much good at flirting with the patrons. Georgie, now, she could make every man who came in feel that he was special. But it was me *he* wanted to talk to."

Rutledge, reading between the lines, could see that she had fallen in love with the quiet flyer. She had told him as much when she'd admitted she would have gone out with him.

It also explained why she had talked so freely with a stranger. There was probably no one she could tell how she'd felt, not at the pub, nor in her personal life.

"How did he die?"

"His motorcar crashed."

"Here? Or in France?"

"Here. At the airfield," she told him reluctantly.

"Accident?"

She was silent for a time, then she said, "I wish I knew. I've wondered. It's worried me, because I'd have helped him, if I could. But you can't help what you don't know about, can you? He never said anything to me."

"Did he have any enemies?"

"He never said, if he did."

Rutledge could see the pub ahead of them, down the street another thirty feet. From this vantage point the wrought iron salt cellar above the door identified it clearly.

They were almost there when she added, "I wondered . . ."

"Wondered?" he pressed when she didn't go on.

"Well, there was Lady Benton. But she was old enough to be his mother, wasn't she?" The woman stopped short. "Here. I never should have said any of that. I don't know why I did. You're just like him! The Captain. Well, a stone would speak to him, wouldn't it? He had that same way of listening, and before you knew it, you'd done most of the talking, hadn't you? Are you a flyer too?"

He smiled. "Infantry. I was in the trenches."

But she wasn't reassured. "How did you come to know him, then? Why were you at the graveside? Why were you asking me questions?"

Rutledge said, "I wanted to know him better." It was clear she knew nothing about the alleged ghost, or what it was said to have done. "Is that so wrong?"

She stared at him, confused.

"You spoke to me, remember?" he added gently.

"So I did," she said finally. She rubbed her forehead. "I don't know. It's been bottled up. All this time. Georgie, and even Ivy, who serves in the dining room, would tease me about my posh beau. But it wasn't that. I mean, not to him. And so I kept it in, how I felt. And nobody knew how I cried when I heard. It liked to'av broke my heart."

"What is your name?"

"Liz." It was reluctant.

"Liz," he repeated. "I'm sorry. It must have been difficult for you."

Tears filled her eyes. "I know what I am. I work at the pub down here by the docks, and I'm not likely to meet someone like the Captain in the ordinary way. At least not someone who didn't want more than I was prepared to give. It was the best thing that ever happened to me, and I wanted it to go on forever, even though I knew it wouldn't. He'd be shot down—transferred—the war would be over and the field would be closed—or he'd just stop coming to The Salt Cellar." She wiped the tears away angrily. "I just wanted something I could never hope to have."

She turned away, walked off briskly, hurrying down the street to the pub, head down.

Rutledge didn't follow her, although he waited until she was safely inside.

Hamish said, "Puir lass."

"Why does everyone simply call him *the Captain*? Why did he come to The Salt Cellar? Was it really to get away from his rowdy mates?"

"He's deid," Hamish retorted. "Ye canna' ask him."

"Is he?" Rutledge turned and started back the way he'd come. "His ghost is accused of a murder."

Inspector Hamilton was just leaving the police station. Rutledge could read his hesitation—whether to pretend he hadn't seen the tall Londoner coming toward him but still some distance away or to wait for the man. In the end, he hesitated a bit too long and then couldn't escape.

"Just going home to my supper," he said gruffly, when Rutledge was close enough.

"I won't keep you. Does the town know the truth—that Lady Benton thought she had seen a ghost in her garden?"

Hamilton's mouth twisted. "Well, not the ghost part, precisely. We let it be known that a murder might have been done on the grounds of the house and we'd have to investigate. Still, we had to question people who'd been at the house the previous day, and talk naturally reached the village before tea. No way to prevent it."

That didn't explain Liz's lack of knowledge about the supposed ghost. But it did confirm Lady Benton's fear that people stared.

"Since the air station was shut down, have you had any scavengers about, looking for souvenirs or something worth selling?"

"Most people seemed to want to forget the war, once it was finished. We have a handful of visitors now, mostly the families of men who served here and didn't come back. Cheaper than going to France, I expect."

"Do they ever stop in here, to speak to you?"

"No. Well, not so far. They come and look, for what it's worth, and they leave. Not surprising, nothing much to see there today. Sometimes they visit the Abbey."

"Thanks. I'll leave you to your supper."

As if realizing he'd been less than helpful, Hamilton asked, "Comfortable, are you? At the hotel?"

Rutledge took the question as it was meant, replying, "Yes, thank you for asking."

"I don't know what else I can do to help you. I expect London will be pressing for answers. Sooner or later." He paused, torn between moving on and satisfying his curiosity. "What's your opinion of Lady Benton?"

"I think she believes what she tells us she's seen. But she has no way of explaining it, any more than we do. The lads who went to find the ghost as the airfield was being taken down—are there others like them who might decide to play charades with an audience of one?"

Hamilton was half-angry at the suggestion. "No. We're not that kind of town."

Rutledge didn't pursue it. "It was a possibility. I had to ask."

Slightly mollified, Hamilton said, "The truth? I don't see a way out of this, except to say that Lady Benton imagined it. That will be hard for her."

"We'll see," Rutledge replied, and with a nod turned back to the hotel.

He was just stepping into the lobby when someone behind him called, "Sir?"

Turning, he found a boy standing in the street, looking up at him.

"Hallo," he said, smiling. The boy must be eight or nine, he thought.

"Are you the man who came up from London?"

"I am. Scotland Yard," he answered.

"My mother would like to speak to you, sir. But you mustn't tell anyone."

"Now?"

"Yes, please."

"What is your name?"

"It's Edward, sir. My friends call me Eddie."

He followed the boy down the street, toward a long line of houses where the shops ended. They were much alike, wooden, two-story, sometimes three, well-enough kept up. As Rutledge and his guide reached one midway down the street, the boy pointed, and they went up the two steps. He opened the door and waited for Rutledge to enter before shutting it again.

"Mama?" the boy called.

She came out of the kitchen, walking down the passage toward him. A slim woman with gray in her brown hair and a tired face. "You're the policeman from London?" she asked.

"Inspector Rutledge. Mrs.—?"

"Dunn. Mary Dunn." She nodded to the boy, and he opened the

door just to Rutledge's right, standing aside so that he could enter. Mrs. Dunn followed, sitting on one of the upright chairs in the small parlor, leaving the single upholstered seat to her guest. He could see the effort she was making to keep her anxiety from showing.

"How can I help you?" he asked as he took the seat she pointed to.

"There was a murder at the House. The Abbey. Last week. But I've heard of no body being found. How can there be a murder without a body?"

"We don't yet know who the victim was."

"Did the Flying Corps hide it? The body? Is that why you can't tell who it is?"

Surprised, he asked, "Why should they do such a thing?"

"They didn't care much for deserters."

"Who is the deserter?" he pressed.

"Well, he wasn't one, was he? But they came here and told me to my face that he'd deserted. Why would they lie?"

"I'm afraid I've not heard about a deserter, Mrs. Dunn. Perhaps it would be for the best if you started at the beginning."

"I asked Inspector Hamilton. But he won't tell me anything."

He glanced at the silent boy standing by the front window, his face hard to read with his back to what was left of the light. Then Rutledge turned again to the woman sitting as upright as the chair itself.

"Nor can I answer your questions, until I know what they're about. Are we talking about someone in your family? A husband—son—?"

"My older son," she said reluctantly. "Gerald. He was mad about those airplanes. Not flying them, mind you, what made them run. If he heard of one close by, he'd go and look at the motor. And he could tell you all the parts, how they fit together, why they worked. How to fix them. When the war came, he volunteered. He'd just turned eighteen, and he wasn't interested in fighting, he wanted to work with the aircraft, and for a mercy—or so I thought at the time—he was posted *here*. Not in France."

She took a deep breath, as if to give her the strength to carry on. "All I cared about was having my boy close by. He'd come home when he could, and all he talked about were the aircraft, and the men who flew them. But that was all right, he was safe, wasn't he, and nobody shooting at him. Then one day in June of 1917, he didn't come home for his lunch, even though he'd promised he might, and after a bit, I sent Billy, my neighbor's boy, out to the field on his bicycle, to see what was keeping Gerry, I'd heard the flights go out just after dawn, and they'd come back just at tea. And the officers told me they hadn't found him, they'd looked everywhere, even London, but they hadn't found him. And then they said that when they did find him, he'd be *shot*."

5

Mrs. Dunn's voice broke on the last word. Then she cleared her throat and added, "Eddie and I didn't sleep for a week, listening for him at the door. Praying he'd come home. What I couldn't understand was why he'd give up what he loved doing, and leave without a word to anybody. Not even to me. When the war ended, and they began to tear down the airfield, all the buildings, I thought, he'll come home now, wherever he's been hiding. But he never has. And even when I asked his commanding officer why Gerry would even think of deserting, he just shook his head." Her gaze was fearful as she said, "Did he try to come home after all, and they found out and came and shot him anyway?"

Hamish was alive in the back of Rutledge's mind, as he tried to find an answer for the woman sitting ramrod straight in her chair, braced for the worst.

"That isn't how it's done," he said finally, putting as much kindness into his voice as he could. "Not in circumstances like these. He would have been court-martialed—tried in a military court. And whatever sentence was passed, it would be carried out at a different date and place."

"Are you sure?" she asked. "I've never asked. Until now, I didn't want to *know*."

Dear God, *was he sure?* But he managed to say, "There are exceptions. But not in Gerald's case." *He hadn't been on a battlefield, it wasn't in the midst of a push, with the men under him waiting, watching to see whether Hamish was going to obey the orders given him—*

"You are lying to me, I can see it in your face."

"No. I give you my word as an officer of the law." *But not an officer in the trenches, faced with mutiny—*

Rutledge forced the images from his mind. Forced himself to concentrate on the desperate woman across from him.

"Who else could it be, a dead man on the grounds of that house? Just there by the airfield?" She was pleading now.

"We don't know, Mrs. Dunn, if anyone has been shot."

"He'd wait there, maybe, and try to find someone to bring me word. I know Gerry—"

"Mrs. Dunn. Do you have a photograph of your son? In the event I find any evidence that Gerald has reappeared?" It was all he could think of to give her a little peace.

She rose, went to a table by the window, opened the single drawer, and took out a frame. Bringing it to him, she said, "This was his photograph in uniform."

Rutledge took it. Gerald looked very much like his younger brother. The same snub nose and round chin, given a few more years of maturity. His hair appeared to be brown, like his mother's.

"Thank you." He made to rise, handing the photograph back to Mrs. Dunn.

"I'm grateful," she said, clasping the frame to her chest. "Inspector Hamilton isn't a very sympathetic man. He was in the war himself, you see. He sees Gerry as a traitor, a deserter, and he couldn't care if he ever comes home. I'm Gerry's mother, and I know my son. He would never turn his back on his mates. He didn't desert. Something *happened,* and if I can't ever have Gerald home again, I want at least to know where he's buried."

———

He walked back to the hotel along streets that were nearly empty now. Since the war had ended and the airfield on its doorstep had been dismantled, Walmer seemed to have drifted back into its prewar tranquility.

Rutledge tried to keep his mind on what he'd just heard. He had no idea what had become of Mrs. Dunn's son. In France it would have been different. Deserter—missing in action—blown up as a shell came in—taken prisoner. A man might easily disappear. Here in England? A great deal more difficult.

But the incident—whatever it was—at the Abbey had brought back her loss, and even Gerald's body was better than the uncertainty she had lived with since 1917.

Rutledge came to the hotel and went inside.

For a mercy it was quiet now. The guests and the engaged couple and their families had left. He drew a breath in sheer relief.

A woman came out of the kitchen and said, "Was it you ordered dinner in your room, sir?" she asked in the voice of someone hopeful that he would say yes and she could finally go home.

"I left my order with Reception earlier." He gave her the room number.

"Thank you, sir. There was no one in when we went up just now. I'll see that a tray is brought up straightaway."

He turned and went up to his room. It had been a long day, and he had much to add to his notebook. But he stood at the window, looking down at the dark circles of the tables, empty now as a sunset chill set in. Postponing the inevitable, the voice waiting for him to turn out his lamp.

Hamish had been present more often of late.

Rutledge knew why.

He'd come back to London after a difficult inquiry in Shropshire, tired and more than a little unsettled, not satisfied as he sometimes was that justice had been done.

And the first person he'd met as he walked out of Scotland Yard after writing a report that had met official requirements but left out much of the distress that lay between the lines of words on a page, was Kate.

She had been to a service in Westminster Abbey and was walking toward Trafalgar Square when he'd encountered her on the corner by Big Ben.

"Hallo," he said in surprise as he recognized her.

"Ian," she'd exclaimed. And as she looked up at him, he could see a telltale redness around her eyes.

"Are you going somewhere?" he asked. "My motorcar is just there, I'll be glad to take you."

She bit her lip. "I quarreled with my parents, and told them I'd rather walk home. Rather silly of me, considering how far it is. But I don't think I'm quite ready to go directly there."

"It's too late for tea, and too early to dine," he said lightly. "But we could walk down to the bridge and watch the tide come up the river."

She smiled in spite of herself. "That sounds wretchedly boring. And somehow comforting."

"This way, then." Westminster Bridge was just below them, and together they turned. The streets were crowded at this time of day, but she didn't seem to mind, keeping pace with him as they walked in a companionable silence. When they reached the middle of the bridge, they stood by the parapet and looked down at the busy river, little boats moving up and down. It did seem comforting to her, monotonous as it was, and he waited, giving her time. He'd rather have comforted her himself, but that was out of the question.

Finally she said, "I do love my parents, I really and truly do. But sometimes they are so dense."

"I expect most children come to feel that way at some time or another."

"Did you?" she asked, looking up at him.

"When I told my parents that I'd rather be a policeman with the Met than follow my father into his firm, there was stunned silence. It took me several weeks to convince them that I wasn't trying to break family tradition, I just preferred police work to reading law and then spending my days in a courtroom. Even then, I think they expected me to see the light, finally, and give up this madness."

He hadn't talked about that before. It had been a difficult time, and he had regretted after their deaths that he had given them so much pain.

"Yet, here you are, an Inspector at the Yard. They would have been proud of that, wouldn't they?"

"I expect so," he said, not adding that he would never know just how they might have felt.

She sighed. "I spoke to my parents about working with refugees. They were horrified. They would much rather have me close by, settled and happy, grandchildren at their knee on Sunday afternoons."

Hiding his alarm, he'd said, "Are you still thinking about such work?"

"The truth is, I don't know that I'm up to it. I've talked to several people, and the stories they tell about simply surviving, all the while trying to do their work, dealing with government officials who want them just to go away—the language barrier—one can only do so much good. The rest is simply coping."

He said nothing. He agreed with her, but it was not politic to say that.

"But I think—I think too that I'm looking for an escape. To be perfectly truthful. And that's not what makes a successful worker."

There was an echo of Meredith Channing's voice in Kate's words. He heard it and felt a wave of sadness. Meredith had become a nurse to look for the officer she had married on his last leave—and realized too late that it had not been love, it had been compassion. Searching for him out of loyalty when he went missing. Driven by a guilt she couldn't accept.

"I must admit, there's some truth there," he agreed carefully. "It must require a great sense of dedication."

"Yes, I see that clearly. Sadly. I'm too stubborn to admit that to my parents, not just now." She turned to stare out at the river. "It truly was escaping, Ian. I wanted to live my own life, not live the life they believed is best for me. I thought in Romania or Armenia, I'd be out of reach."

He was relieved to hear that she was not leaving England. He was afraid it might be there in his voice, when he said, "I expect you made the right choice. They'll come around in time."

She shook her head. "I don't think they will."

He could hear an undercurrent in her words, but she didn't say anything more. Instead she squared her shoulders, smiled, and said, "You seem to come to my rescue when I'm unhappy. Could I persuade you to take me out to dine as well?"

"It would be my pleasure," he said. "Where would you like to go?"

"Somewhere my parents won't think to look," she replied.

And so he'd taken her to a small restaurant he'd found and liked for its excellent food and its quiet atmosphere.

It was both painful and at the same time a pleasure to sit across the table from her, listening to her conversation and watching the play of emotions across her face, the light in her eyes as she talked about things she enjoyed or felt strongly about.

Afterward he'd taken her home. She'd said, "Don't come to the door. Do you mind? I don't want my father to know I'd found safe harbor with a friend. I want him to worry about where I'd been all this time."

He'd said, "Are you sure that's best?"

She took a deep breath. "It is. For now. Thank you, Ian. I'm so grateful."

He didn't want her gratitude. He didn't want to be a safe harbor. He wanted to be more. But he said nothing, holding the door as she got down, and watched her cross the road, go up the steps to the Gordon house, and let herself in the door.

That's all there can be, he'd told himself. And drove home, to drink a stiff whisky and try not to think at all.

As he watched, someone came out the hotel's garden door and began to put candles out in little dishes. They flickered and danced in the shadows cast by the upper stories, but the flames were invisible where the last of the sun touched those closest to the back gate. He counted the tables. Nine of them.

The odor of cooking wafted up to him, coming from the kitchen below. Beyond the rooftops of Walmer, the sun was almost summer bright but casting long shadows.

There was a knock at the door, and when he opened it, a young man stood there with a tray and various dishes covered by a napkin.

When Rutledge had thanked him and set the tray on the small table, he discovered that someone had added a tart to his order.

Then he pulled the napkin across the food again and reached for his notebook, only to set it aside, and pour himself a cup of tea.

Anything to keep at bay what was to come . . .

His supper was cold when he finally forced himself to eat it, and set the tray outside his door for collection.

When at last it was fully dark, and the candles at all nine of the tables were clearly visible, he undressed, pulled the coverlet and top sheet down, and reached for the lamp, intending to turn it off. And stopped short. Turning back to the bed, he stared at the sheet he was about to lie on. He'd thought he'd seen shadows, the way the coverlet had fallen back.

Lifting the lamp, he brought it closer to the bed.

The sheet was smeared with dry blood. He knew too well what that looked like.

Ghosts didn't bleed . . . And the victim in the Abbey gardens hadn't bled at all.

He simply left it there, tossing the coverlet over the bed again, sitting in the only chair in the room, and waited for the darkness.

When he came down in the morning, Rutledge went to find the manager, who was speechless at first, shocked and disturbed by the request.

"Are—" He stopped and cleared his throat. "Are you sure, Inspector?"

"Come with me, and tell me what you see."

"I—um—I'll have the sheets—the entire bed—would you prefer another room?"

"No. Just see that it's gone before I've finished my breakfast."

"Yes—yes, of course, Inspector. I am so sorry—"

"Had anyone asked for me, last evening?" The boy, Eddie Dunn, had waited outside . . .

"Asking—no—that's to say there were a good many people here early on—a party for the young couple—we were quite busy . . ." His voice trailed off.

Rutledge didn't pursue the matter. His motorcar had been in the yard. It would have been easy enough to slip up the back stairs, unnoticed by the busy staff, open doors until the right room was found, and foul the sheets. The question was, had someone decided to play a little joke on the man hunting a ghostly killer? Or was it an attempt to persuade him that the ghost was another prank, and no harm was meant by either of them? That Scotland Yard was wasting its time in Walmer?

The manager was still apologizing as Rutledge left the office.

He chose a table in the corner of the dining room where he hoped he wouldn't be disturbed.

He had finally slept around four, drained and exhausted by the battering he'd endured as Hamish filled the darkness with one memory after another. Wave after wave of attacks across No Man's Land that had gone wrong because their intelligence had been wrong, he and the other survivors dragging the bodies of his men back across the wire, the wounded and the dead—the faces and the names went on and on. For he remembered them, all of them—he'd written the letters of condolences for every officer and man. Lies to families that let them believe that their loved ones had died swiftly and bravely, fighting for King and Country, their last thoughts about those at home. Keeping to himself the agony of their dying and their screams, the torn bodies and the blood.

The price of living, Dr. Fleming had called it. "You don't owe them your own death," he'd told Rutledge. "It was mere fate that you survived and they didn't. You can't carry that guilt with you, or you'll go mad. What you can do is honor them by not wasting the future you've been given."

Easier said than done . . .

It was one of the reasons he'd gone back to the Yard sooner than even Fleming had advised. Because he didn't know how much future he would have.

When he went back to his room after he'd finished his breakfast, he found the bed pristine, so perfectly made that it would have satisfied any barracks Sergeant.

That done, he went out to his motorcar, half-expecting that someone had tampered with it as well. But he could find nothing wrong.

Turning the crank, he got in and started out of Walmer.

He was still annoyed by the blood in the sheets.

Who had done that? Who had fouled his bed with blood? Was it a prank, or was it someone who wanted Scotland Yard to go away?

If that was the point, he told himself, they'd damned well gone the wrong way about it.

He followed the main road back to the Abbey, then continued past it, searching for access to the airfield without going through the estate. And as he'd thought while exploring the day before, it turned out to be the same lane that served the stables. When he came out past the long thick hedge, this end of it stopping just short of the lane, he left his motorcar in its shadow, and walked on.

And even though he quartered the entire installation, he found nothing to explain the disappearance of Gerald Dunn or what Lady Benton had claimed she'd seen.

Nothing, as well, to explain what Hamilton's son and his friends had seen here that frightened them when they had taken the dare to explore the airfield one night.

He looked in the handful of remaining buildings, but they were empty, no indication that a body had been left there until it could safely be reclaimed.

The long close-cropped grass strip where the aircraft had taken off was already losing its definition, returning to its natural state.

When he could, during the war, he himself had gone up a few times in the observer's seat. It had given him a different perspective of the battle. Once his craft had come within range of rifles in the trenches, and he'd heard the fabric tear when fire found them.

Now there was only the sound of the wind blowing.

It would be impossible to bury a body in a place where even a hare hopping across the flat meadow would be noticed. For one thing, there would have been a night watch on the airfield, and for another, given the number of men posted here, there must have been eyes everywhere, even in the dark. Had Gerald Dunn deserted after all, and was even now living in Manchester or perhaps London, afraid still to come home?

Turning back toward the hedges and the house beyond, he saw a figure standing on the terrace overlooking the lawns, waving.

He couldn't tell from this distance whether it was Lady Benton or one of her staff. That brought home to him how the household had heard and even seen the aircraft taking off or coming in. Without wishing to, this proximity had drawn Lady Benton and anyone in the Abbey into the life of the airfield.

It explained too why Lady Benton had allowed the men to use part of her grounds. If she had counted the aircraft that went out and the numbers that returned, she must have known the losses, and if there had been a crash landing, she would have heard it or even witnessed the flames.

He wondered if anyone from the house had seen the Captain's motorcar crash. With that thought in mind, he turned his gaze toward the long line of the hedge, searching for the exact spot where the vehicle had struck it. From anywhere on the airfield, it would have been easy to see where the hedge stopped and the farm lane led up to the main road. The Captain couldn't have misjudged that, even if he'd come from far out onto the airfield, where the aircraft were parked. And so whatever had gone wrong—driver error or mechanical failure—he must have struck the hedge just about—*there*. Close by the tennis courts? Trying for the lane, and failing to reach it because his steering had failed or he himself had lost control.

And yet he hadn't. There was nothing to indicate a crash.

Instead, the place where broken branches had healed over time, where the density of the hedge still showed healing scars, was closer to the long terrace he could see above the hedge. In fact, almost where the long terrace ended and the corner of the house marked the beginnings of the kitchen gardens.

And that must indicate that something had gone wrong with the steering . . . That he had swung to his left instead of his right because it had suddenly veered or locked or gone out.

Rutledge walked toward the hedge, and when he was close enough, he could see that he'd been right, it was here that Captain Nelson had died. Looking up toward the house, he could see the windows of the upper stories from where he was standing.

And someone looking out from that vantage point would have had a very different view of events. Would have seen the man in the motorcar struggling to regain control, and unable to stop himself from plowing into the hedge as the speed increased. Because the brakes too failed?

It could have looked, to those watching from the airfield, as if the motorcar was deliberately veering into the hedge. They could only see the rear of the vehicle turning wildly in that direction as its speed increased.

No wonder there had been a suspicion of suicide.

And if someone had witnessed that struggle from the windows, it might have looked like murder.

Then why hadn't he or she spoken up at the time? Was it because he or she hadn't understood what they were witnessing? And no one from the investigation into the Captain's death had thought to question anyone from the house. After all, his death would have been seen as a military matter, and only the officers and men on the airfield at the time would have been asked about it.

Rutledge turned away, and walked back to where he'd left his motorcar.

A death and a disappearance . . .

Were they connected? If so, how?

He was just turning from the farm lane onto the main road when he remembered that someone had waved to him as he was exploring the airfield.

Turning in at the Abbey gates, he drove up to the front door and knocked.

Mrs. Hailey opened the door to him, as she had done on his first visit.

"I thought I saw Lady Benton on the back terrace, waving to me while I was down at the airfield."

"Come in. I'll find her and ask." And she left him there in the great hall.

It was a good ten minutes before Lady Benton herself came into the hall, and said, "Inspector. Yes, it was I, there on the terrace. I have found some photographs of the airfield, if you'd like to view them. When the buildings were still there."

"Yes, that would be very helpful."

Two women and a man came into the hall from the rooms on display, and Lady Benton turned to smile at them. "The café is just there."

They thanked her and walked off toward the stairs down to the crypt.

She sighed. "We're short a member of the staff today. Margaret—Mrs. Hailey—is seeing to the door and watching in the first room. If you'll come this way?"

She led him back to the comfortable sitting room and went to a cupboard where she collected something, then turned and brought him a tin with a bouquet of roses on the lid. "My parents gave me this tin filled with chocolates when I was sixteen. I remembered it when I looked for something to put the photographs in. I'll leave you to look through them on your own, shall I? I must get back to the visitors. We don't have many today. But I'll be glad when they're gone."

As she hurried away, he took the tin to the desk by the window and sat down. Opening the lid, he found a collection of photographs inside. Some were of a small boy playing with his dog, a few with Lady Benton and a rather attractive man, smiling beside a Christmas tree in this very room. Others were of people he didn't recognize, and then he found the photographs of the airfield.

They were like others he'd seen here and in France, but they proved he'd been right when he'd guessed at some of the foundations. In one of the photographs a tall man with a military mustache appeared to be the officer in command, for he was standing with several other men, hands shielding their eyes, scanning the skies for returning aircraft. For someone had caught them unawares, their gaze worried, their posture stiff with the strain of waiting. And there were others of young men standing beside their aircraft or lounging in the mess, mugs of tea in their hands, cheeky grins on their faces. A few more showed men playing croquet on the lawns of the house or sitting in chairs under the shade of the ornamental trees.

He rather thought someone other than Lady Benton had taken most of these. Going through them carefully, he searched for the Captain, but he didn't seem to appear to be in any of them. Perhaps he'd borrowed her camera? For surely if she had taken the photographs, there would have been several of the same man . . .

He was just putting them back in the tin when Lady Benton returned, apologizing.

"Were they helpful?" she added, coming to help him gather up the photographs.

"Do you have any of Captain Nelson? I'd like to see them."

She bit her lip. "It was too painful to look at them, afterward. And so I took them out. I'll look them up another time, shall I?"

"Yes, please." He paused. "Did you witness his motorcar crashing into the hedge?"

"No—there was always so much to do—"

He couldn't tell whether she was lying or if she simply found it difficult to talk about.

He rephrased his question. "Did anyone else on your staff see what happened?"

"I-I never asked. I was so terribly upset. It never occurred to me—and no one said anything to me."

Possibly out of kindness? Knowing how distressed Lady Benton was. Such details would have only added to her grief.

"Did you go down, while he was still in the motorcar?"

"God, no. Of course I wouldn't have done."

"Surely," he pressed quietly, "someone came up to the house to inform you that he was dead?"

"Afterward—afterward one of his friends came up. And broke the news. He was terribly upset—he'd helped to lift Roger—Captain Nelson—from the motorcar. But he assured me that the Captain hadn't suffered. That he'd died swiftly, without any pain."

He thought that must have been a kind lie. Nelson hadn't died at once.

What was it that Melinda had told him? That she'd known the man in charge? And he'd taken the death hard.

Had he survived the war?

But Rutledge said nothing of that to Lady Benton. Instead he asked, "Was there an ambulance at the field?"

"Yes. For any man returning with wounds. There weren't many. Most of the deaths occurred over France, as you'd expect. Although some aircraft limped home and the pilot was hurt."

He thanked her then, and she saw him to the door.

There he asked, "You mentioned that one of your staff wasn't in today. Is she ill?"

"No. It was the anniversary of her husband's death. Patricia takes flowers to his grave on that day. Well, he's not actually buried—there's a memorial stone for him."

"Was your son brought home?"

"No. He's buried in France. There's a brass in the church. I leave my flowers there."

"Did you know a Gerald Dunn? A mechanic, I think. He is said to have deserted."

The name meant nothing to her. "Some of the men didn't choose to come to the lawns. Should I have had a reason to know him? In particular?"

"No, not at all. I happened to learn that he was actually from Walmer."

"Then perhaps he spent his free time with his family."

"It's possible," he agreed, and said goodbye.

Rutledge stopped in at the police station, found Hamilton in his office, and said, "Know anything about one Gerald Dunn, a mechanic at the airfield?"

"I've told you—I wasn't here during the war."

But Rutledge thought that Hamilton had known exactly who Gerald was, and his mother as well. He stepped into the cluttered room and sat down. "What became of him?"

"Look, I don't hold with deserters. The rest of us stood and fought—and died as well. He *ran*."

"He was posted to an airfield in England, where no one was shooting at him. Where he could walk home if he liked, whenever he was given leave. It makes no sense that he should desert. Did you look into Mrs. Dunn's repeated requests to investigate, when you came home?"

Hamilton shook his head in exasperation. "Two years later? When it had already been looked into officially? Everyone at the airfield had left by then, the buildings were coming down. It would have been an exercise in futility even to try."

"And no body, no unexplained bones, perhaps, came to light, as the work was being done?"

"No. *That* would have come to my attention."

Rutledge stood up. "Was Dunn's desertion before—or after—Captain Nelson's death?"

Hamilton looked down at his blotter. "That was in late May. 1917." He looked at Rutledge again. "Are you trying to tell me you think the two events are connected?"

"As you say. Everyone at the airfield has left. There's no way of knowing. But your replacement here during the war should have wondered about the possibility. Instead everyone labeled Gerald Dunn a deserter, and so nothing else was even considered, as far as I can tell. Gerald understood how aircraft worked. He could just as easily have known something about motorcars."

And Rutledge turned toward the door, leaving Hamilton sitting at his desk, consternation on his face.

Hamish said as Rutledge reached the street again, "Do ye believe what you told yon Inspector?"

Truthfully? he answered silently. I don't know. But I don't believe in coincidence when it comes to murder.

6

It doesna' explain what Lady Benton saw fra' her window. No' when the Captain is long dead, and for a' we know, yon lad Dunn as well," Hamish said as Rutledge walked back to the hotel, where he'd left his motorcar.

"Then why let her believe that one of the men was Captain Nelson?"

"To frighten her for anither reason. To punish her, even."

Which could very well be true. But that meant that someone who knew just how close she was to Roger Nelson must be behind the little scene in the garden. Otherwise, why not pretend to be her dead son instead?

But there he could answer his own question. No one could be sure just how she would react to seeing Eric in her dark garden. She might have rushed down to open the terrace doors, rather than watch what was happening from her window.

Melinda Crawford had told him that she knew a little about Walmer from a friend, who had been distressed by what had happened to Captain Nelson. What if there was more to learn?

Reaching his motorcar, he got in, pulled out of the yard, and started out of the village, heading north to Colchester. He needed to speak to Melinda, and he preferred to do it far away from anyone who might be interested in how he viewed the inquiry so far.

It was only twenty-five miles or so to this old Roman camp that had become a town. He'd passed through it a number of times in the past, sometimes stopping to dine in the Rose and Crown, one of the oldest inns in the country, a fascinating jumble of nooks and stairs and smoke-blackened timbers, a medieval gem.

The city was mostly Victorian now, and he found a telephone where he could speak privately.

Melinda was at home, and came directly to take his call.

"Ian," she said, and he could hear a certain wariness in her voice. "And how is your inquiry progressing?"

"Well enough. But I'd like to speak to the friend you mentioned as I was leaving. I need more information about the airfield and Captain Nelson."

"Ah," she answered him, the reluctance in her voice coming down the line to him. "That was Major Dinsmore. I'm afraid he took his own life shortly after the Armistice was declared and he was relieved of his command."

"Do you know why?" he asked, making certain his voice was steady. "Was it related to events at the airfield?"

"It was ill health, I was told. I hadn't seen Andrew for some time, the war kept him close to the airfield, but in August of 1917, I was passing through Chelmsford, and he tore himself away from his duties long enough to dine with me there. I was shocked by the change in him. He'd aged—thinner and grayer. Of course war had taken a toll everywhere, and at first I put it down to that. But before very long I began to wonder if it was something more—more personal, perhaps. Not just his responsibilities. I heard later that he was unwell in September 1918, that he'd had a very serious bout with the influenza. But he recovered and soldiered on, hoping the war would end by Christmas. As it did. Knowing Andrew, he returned to his duties far too soon. Several letters from him spoke of the fatigue and the cough that troubled him even in November."

"Personal—in the sense of his family, worrying about them?"

"I don't believe it was that at all. I spoke to several of his fellow officers at the funeral service, and they were remarkably reticent."

Melinda had a way of looking beyond the facade people put up. He himself had been all too aware of it, and had had to put up defenses against it when he was with her.

"Do you think he might have confided in someone else?"

He could hear her sigh. "I don't know. Sometimes it's easier to tell a priest or a stranger what's worrying you, than it is to tell those close to you."

"Was he married?"

"You're thinking he might have confided in his wife. I doubt it. She lived in Cornwall during the war—as far away from Zeppelins and soldiers marching off to fight or at home on sick leave as she could manage. A rather timid woman to be married to a soldier. He was quite fond of her, but she and I had little in common."

He could believe that. Melinda's life and the Army were closely intertwined, and she would have little to say to a woman who couldn't support her husband in time of war.

There was a silence down the line, and then Melinda said, "I was of two minds about telling you anything at all—I wasn't certain that the little I knew could be useful. That this inquiry was more about the present than the past."

"I'm not very sure what it's about," he told her frankly. "Just now, any thread could lead me to an answer."

"I'm sorry to hear it. Take care, Ian. Someone is being very clever. And that can be dangerous."

He didn't tell her about the blood on his sheets. Instead, he thanked her and put up the receiver.

Hamish said, "There's Lady Benton. She will ken the man—"

And Hamish was right, Rutledge thought as he went back to where he'd left the motorcar. Surely she could tell him more—she must have dealt often enough with Major Dinsmore.

Yet there was also something in Melinda's voice that worried him. Did it have to do with her friendship with the dead man?

Or was his own imagination running away with him, because he'd expected too much from that telephone conversation and had been disappointed?

He'd commanded soldiers on the Western Front. Not quite the same, perhaps, as commanding an airfield. But men were the same, the duties and responsibilities were the same, and the burden on a good officer to keep up morale and fighting spirit were the same. On the drive back to Walmer, he reviewed some of his own experiences in the trenches. But he could find nothing that could have accounted for one dead officer, under suspicious circumstances, and the sudden desertion or disappearance, of a capable mechanic at the airfield in 1917. That brought him full circle to the Abbey, and the lives of the people there.

If events on the airfield were just what they'd appeared to be, an accident and a desertion, then what was there about the *Abbey* that prompted the odd display in Lady Benton's private garden?

The last visitor for the day had left the Abbey and Lady Benton was making the final rounds when Mrs. Hailey let Rutledge in the main door.

"Is she expecting you?" the housekeeper asked skeptically.

"No. But I don't believe she'll mind answering a few more questions."

She swung the heavy door shut with a loud *thump* and shoved the great bar across, her way of letting him know what she thought about his questions. "That's all anyone has done—ask questions. With no answers forthcoming from the police. Or Scotland Yard, for that matter."

"What do you think we ought to be doing?" he asked as she led him from the great hall to the first of the state rooms.

"You come during the morning or the afternoon, but you are never here at night. There's no telephone in the house. If she needs help, there's no one to send. From her wing of the house, sounds from the other wing can't be heard. She'd never know someone was in the Abbey until it was too late."

"Are you suggesting she ought to stay in Walmer until we've discovered what's behind what she saw?" he asked as she opened the door into the next room.

"And leave the Abbey empty altogether?" There was disdain in her voice. "Didn't I tell you before that it made sense for someone to stay here with her?"

"You yourself, perhaps?"

"And what good would I be, in an emergency? Do you have a revolver with you?"

He had one. It was in the trunk beneath his bed, with his medals and uniforms and the rest of his war. But he wasn't allowed to carry one on duty.

"*She* does. I've seen it in the bottom drawer of her dressing table. It was her husband's."

"Can she use it?" he asked, suddenly alert.

"I expect she can. He'd have taught her."

Hamish said, "That will lead to trouble. Mark my words."

Ignoring the voice, Rutledge was about to ask if it was loaded, when they entered the third room, an elegant study with Empire furnishings and gilt-framed paintings. One, he recognized, was a likeness of the Duke of Wellington mounted on Copenhagen, his favorite horse.

Lady Benton turned from examining a spot on the carpet, saying, "Margaret, I think we ought to—" She broke off when she saw Rutledge.

"News already?" she went on.

"More questions. He says," Mrs. Hailey retorted. "Do you wish me to see to the rest of the rooms, my lady?"

"Yes, could you, please? And Mr. Rutledge and I will lock all the doors."

He followed her through to the private sitting room, and from there to each of the house doors. She didn't speak until they were out of Mrs. Hailey's hearing, then she asked, "What is it you wish to know?"

They had locked the door to the stable walk and were moving on to the garden room.

"Who was the officer in charge at the airfield?"

That surprised her. "Colonel Haverford. But he was seldom here, there were other small airfields under his command. And so Major Dinsmore carried out most of the day-to-day duties. There were two squadrons here, and perhaps a hundred or so men. They were supposed to guard the Channel crossings, but they were often assigned to cover the French coast as well."

"Did you come to know Major Dinsmore as well as you did Captain Nelson?"

She stopped in the passage they were walking down. It was dimly lit and he couldn't read her expression, but he thought she was angry.

"Why does everyone assume that I spent most of my time with Roger Nelson? I didn't. But I liked him well enough, and he reminded me, a little, of Eric and his father. After Eric was killed, I found that comforting. Roger's voice had the same timbre, and sometimes there was a gesture, a way he approached a subject—I could almost close my eyes and believe—but I knew, even as I did, that he wasn't my son. I wasn't in love with him, nor he with me. Is it so impossible to believe that we could have been friends?"

Rutledge remembered a time when he and Meredith Channing had been friends. And he found himself thinking that perhaps that was all he would ever have with Kate—a friendship. He understood loneliness, and he could hear that aching loneliness in Lady Benton's voice.

"I'm sorry if you took my question wrong," he said gently. "I would like to know more about the Major, and as he's dead—"

"Oh—I didn't know," she said, sadness in her voice. "I could see, those last weeks here, before the Armistice, that he wasn't well. But I took that—I believed that was the stress of command, and the war, and losing good men. I'd hoped that after the fighting stopped, he could find his own peace."

"That was clumsy of me," he told her. "Someone who knew him gave me the news."

"How sad for his wife. She was afraid of everything, he said, even dying or the Germans landing and herding everyone into concentration camps or some such. What we'd done to the Boers. She'd read about that, and she was sure the Germans would treat us the same way."

She moved on down the passage and came to the kitchen quarters, checking the locks on the door there. "His was a mathematical mind—navigation was his favorite subject, and he enjoyed looking at a collection of maps in our library. But he had very little time to relax, his duties mostly kept him down there, on the airfield."

"How did he take the Captain's death?"

Lady Benton turned to confront him. "How do you think? Everyone was devastated, it happened right in front of most of the men. They ran to the motorcar, tried to save him, but it was too late. It was the Major who held his body as they freed him from the motorcar. Can you even imagine how horrible that must have been?"

He could. Very easily.

As they moved on to the French doors, taking the servants' stairs to the ground floor, he said, "It must have haunted him."

"I expect that's the right word. *Haunting*. His death most certainly haunted me for months afterward. The Major too was never the same after that. Closed in on himself, somehow. He didn't confide in me, if that's what you're asking. Over the years I saw him frequently, but always in his capacity as commanding officer. We never talked in the personal sense. I only discovered his interest in navigation by accident. And I asked about his wife only because she never came to visit him. I'd wondered if she were an invalid perhaps." She paused. "I did wonder, at the end of the war, if he dreaded going home. He said something in passing, that war had been his life for so long that he was afraid of civilian life. It was an attempt to be amusing, but I could tell that there was more truth than jest in his remark."

Unwilling to go home to a woman afraid of her shadow and afraid of the world . . . Or was there more to the Major's death?

When they had finished all the doors and were back in her sitting room, she asked, "You always come back to the Captain's death. As if that was the beginning of everything. Even what I saw in my garden."

"I don't know yet where the beginning may be. And so I must look at all the possibilities. I continually ask myself why one of the men in the garden reminded you of Roger Nelson. Was it to frighten you into leaving the house? If so, it failed to accomplish that. If I were one of the two living men there, I'd begin to think of a better way to frighten you. Or dispose of you altogether."

It was rather harsh, but he believed she needed to be aware of her own danger.

Her eyes were suddenly large in a pale face.

"You sound like Margaret, trying to frighten me into allowing her to stay in. But I can't. I know this house, every sound, every smell, every *difference*. Having someone else to look after, to be sure she was safe, is more dangerous for me than being alone."

Rutledge could understand that.

"All right, for the sake of argument—what is the most valuable item in this house?"

Without hesitation, she said, "The weeping Madonna."

"If someone took it, he couldn't sell it. Or display it. Or in any way that I can see, benefit from it."

"Well, then, I've told you. The paintings. The silver. The heir-looms."

"But what if there is something else that people might be after? Was it ever rumored that the monks had buried their most precious posses-sions here—the Mass silver—their horde of gold—hoping to return one day and retrieve them?"

Lady Benton laughed at that. "Surely we'd have found them, when my husband's ancestors tore down the Abbey and built the house around the great hall. In the first place, there were never any rumors of that kind. The monks had a fairly good idea of what was going to hap-pen here. They'd have moved everything far away—smuggled it back to the mother house in France—sold it, for all anyone knows."

"Besides the Madonna, was there anything else here—a special crucifix, or candlestick—that was as famous? Bones that were said to have special powers of healing, drawing pilgrims?"

"You have quite a vivid imagination, Inspector." She smiled at him. "I believe there was an inventory taken at the time of Dissolution. And if there was anything in particular that my husband's ancestor wished to keep, he'd have seen it listed and taken steps to claim it. The only reason the Madonna is still here is that she's too large to remove without arousing suspicion. The first thing anyone coming into the church would have looked for, was her. The Abbey was dedicated to Our Lady of Sorrows. But the monks couldn't take her with them. Or feared to damage her by even trying."

He'd run out of possibilities.

"Still, someone must have waited—watched—until your light went out in the bedroom, and the drawn curtains were opened, knowing that you'd be looking down into the garden. A performance for one."

She clasped her hands together, a sure sign that she was distressed. "You really are trying to frighten me."

"No, drawing conclusions from what happened. We can guess that much. The *why* is the problem." He paused, remembering what Hamilton had told him. "There was another incident. When the buildings were about to be torn down—or just as the work had started—several village boys had come out to the airfield at night, on a dare. And something frightened them so badly they still refuse to talk about what happened."

"Oh. Yes. I'd forgot about that." She smiled a little. "I do recall the fuss when their fathers went to the field to see what had frightened them. And of course they found nothing. I put it down to the boys already being overly excited about slipping out of the house and venturing so far. A hare could have jumped out of nowhere, and they would have seen it as a monstrous thing. And later, when they'd calmed down, they were too ashamed to tell anyone the truth."

"Hamilton is convinced they saw something."

"He wasn't here at the time," she protested.

"He wasn't. That's true. But his son still refuses to tell him anything. And what if that event is somehow related to what you saw? What if this isn't the first time the Captain's 'ghost' has walked? What if it is a pattern?" He meant it in the figurative sense, not the literal. That there might have been another, similar, incident. But Lady Benton paled in shock.

She rose. "I think you'd better go now, Inspector. I shan't sleep a wink if you keep at me like this."

"I'm not being unkind. You need to know what I know, to keep your guard up. That's important."

"Thank you. You've done that very thoroughly."

He had no choice but to leave.

"Do you mind if I let you out the door toward the stables? I'd rather not try to close the main door on my own."

He'd seen the housekeeper manage it, but he said nothing, following her into the small foyer where she unlocked the door for him.

"Thank you," he said. "For giving me your time. As I learn more, I'll keep you informed."

"I appreciate that. Good evening, Inspector."

She closed the door behind him, and he waited, smiling for her sake, until he'd heard the bolts drive home. Then with a wave, he went off down the walk to the stables, cutting around to the front drive.

He noticed as he went that the weather was changing. The few fair days were over, there were rain clouds gathering and he could feel the coolness in the air.

Mrs. Dunn was waiting for him outside the hotel. He felt a wave of pity as he noticed how tired and wretched she looked, cursing himself for not going sooner himself to speak to her.

"I just need to know," she said diffidently, "if there's been any word about my boy."

"I'm sorry," he said, and meant it. "We haven't found a body. I have walked the length and breadth of the airfield, and I can tell you that there is nothing to indicate that anyone was buried out there. I have learned that the commanding officer during the war is dead, has been for some years. I can't ask him what he must have done at the time to search for Gerald, whether he came to the conclusion that your son was indeed a deserter or that something could have happened to him that accounted for his disappearance. I have been inside the Hall, and there is no indication that anyone working there was responsible. I haven't questioned everyone yet, but I shall, in due course. But so far, I can't find any reason that would connect the Hall to his disappearance." He added gently, "I have not forgot you."

Grateful tears filled her eyes. "Thank you, sir. You're the only person who would listen. Thank you." She turned and walked away, unwilling to let him see her relief.

He walked on into the hotel, having left his motorcar on a side street not far from the church, where no one would notice if he used it later.

After his dinner, he walked the streets of Walmer, passing the time until it was dark. The days were not yet as long as they would be, but the increasing clouds helped speed the light away.

Finally it was dark enough to provide the cover he needed. His Wellingtons were in the boot as well as an umbrella, in case of rain, and so was his torch. He left the hotel without having to carry anything with him, wearing dark clothing under a dark jumper beneath his overcoat, for the temperature had dipped with the cloud cover.

Walking without haste, he went to his motorcar and drove it out of the village, heading for the main road. There, out of sight, he changed direction and drove on toward the Abbey, passing it without stopping. Beyond it, he found the rough farm lane that ran between the stables and a fenced pasture, and cutting his headlamps, he turned down it. As he'd noted earlier, it continued for some distance beyond the house, past the boundary hedge on one side, and farm fields on the other, and ending finally at the airfield. Reversing over the rough ground, he put the motorcar out of sight in the protection of the tall hedge, and got down. Overhead the clouds appeared to have thickened, and there were no shadows. Changing his boots for his Wellingtons, he picked up his torch, thought twice about the umbrella, and began to walk, following the hedge past where the Captain had died, all the way to the path that led up to the lawns.

He didn't go closer, his movements could be too easily seen from the house windows. And there was no way of knowing just where Lady Benton might be, attending to a fraying carpet or a tilted painting, not afraid to move about the rooms as she pleased.

Leaning into the hedges, he waited. To his left the airfield sprawled in darkness, and sometimes he could hear soft scurrying in the hedges, as small animals ignored his presence.

This was the way the two men had come up, then walked toward the private garden.

He had no reason to believe anything would happen tonight—but the events of last Friday hadn't removed Lady Benton from the Abbey, and he was beginning to think that that was the intent.

And only someone who knew that she and Captain Nelson had been close could have created such a charade. Someone local, someone who had been here during the war—or someone familiar with Lady Benton herself . . .

Someone who knew or had even seen the treasures in that house?

Someone in need—or greedy—or for some reason intent on hurting her.

Hamish said, startling him, "If yon treasures are stolen, will the National Trust still want the house?"

An interesting point. But what could be done with house or property, here on a quiet bit of Essex coast?

"Ye need no' do anythin' with it."

Which brought Rutledge around to the owner of The Monk's Choice. Who held a grudge.

Who else held a grudge against this family?

It was an interesting possibility to consider.

Standing watch in the trenches, he'd watched the stars make their way across the night sky, but tonight there were only clouds scudding across, still thickening as he watched.

And no one came.

It wasn't until close on midnight that the rain finally began to fall. He felt the first heavy drops, and began to withdraw, leaving no mark of his own presence as he went. The house on the rise above him was dark. And there was no one on the airfield—he would have seen them before they could possibly pick him out against the darkness of the hedge.

His shoulders were wet, his dark hair as well, by the time he got back to his motorcar. Still, he looked it over carefully before turning the crank.

Just on general principles, he told himself, he turned to drive past where The Monk's Choice stood along the road. But it was dark as well, and quiet. Not even a dog to bark at the motorcar that passed by once, then reversed and perforce had to pass by it again.

It was raining hard when he pulled into the yard at the hotel, and then ran for the rear door. It was unlocked, for which he was profoundly grateful.

Peeling off his wet jumper and the shirt beneath it, he hung one over the chair back and hung the other in the wardrobe, leaving the door open.

His sheets were damp, but not bloody, as he turned out the lamp before going to bed.

Rutledge was grateful for that too, and Hamish's silence.

By dawn the rain was no more than a dreary drizzle, leading to a gray and dreary day.

As he came down for breakfast Rutledge was informed by the young man behind the desk at Reception that there was someone waiting for him in the dining room.

He was certain that it was Mrs. Dunn, but the man at the table by

the window who looked around as Rutledge came into the small dining room, then half rose as if expecting him, was a stranger.

Middle-aged, heavy-set, and shorter than Rutledge by a head, he
looked tired.

Rutledge said, "Scotland Yard. You wished to see me?"

"Yes, if you please. Could I join you for breakfast?"

"Of course." He took the other chair as the newcomer subsided into
the one he'd already taken.

Rutledge asked the woman serving them for tea and a menu, then
turned to his visitor. "Your name?"

"It's Wilbur, sir, Tobias Wilbur. I own a tea shop just down from
the greengrocers. Among other properties, in Chelmsford and Colchester. A man of business, you might say."

"How may I assist you, Mr. Wilbur?"

"I have an interest in the airfield that is close by the Abbey. I'd like
to buy it from Lady Benton. I understand she has petitioned to have
the property returned to her now that the War Office has no need of it.
I'm prepared to wait until it is fully in her possession, but perhaps she
would agree to signing some letter of intent?"

"Why do you want the property?" Their tea arrived, and Rutledge busied himself with that, not looking at Wilbur as he asked the
question.

"For many years, the Abbey, and particularly the Madonna, have
attracted a good many visitors. But that day has passed. It's my belief
that the airfield, restored, would be an attraction. An—er—memorial
as well." He amended quickly as he saw Rutledge's expression change.
"We will reconstruct many of the necessary structures, outfit them like
a museum, persuade young flyers to come here and offer rides. I understand that's quite popular. Perhaps a tea room, and something for the
little ones. I have seen a small but nice carousel for sale. It will require
a fresh coat of paint—"

Rutledge had heard enough. "Why do you think Lady Benton
would wish to sell the meadow? Or in fact wish to have an attraction
set up within view of her windows?"

"In light of what happened—two ladies were discussing events at the Abbey this past Monday. Ghostly villains, murder being done. On summer evenings, if she's agreeable, we could reenact what had occurred. I haven't been able to see her, I thought perhaps you could tell her what you've heard, and she would change her mind about seeing me."

Word was spreading. And the scavengers were beginning to arrive.

"I don't have Lady Benton's ear," Rutledge said, keeping his voice level, shutting down the anger rising in him. "Still, I don't believe she has any intention of selling."

"She would do well to work with me, you know. If there are secrets she wants to keep, private matters that are best forgot, they'll be safe with me. Not everyone will make that promise."

"That's enough," Rutledge said, making certain that his voice didn't carry beyond the man across the table from him. "I'd advise you to go before I lose my patience. You won't like what happens when I do."

Wilbur opened his mouth to argue, thought better of it, and rose, his tea untouched. But as he moved away from the table, he said viciously, "May I remind you, women are famous for changing their minds."

Rutledge began to rise from his chair.

Wilbur turned and scuttled for the door.

Rutledge waited until the man was out of his sight before sitting down again.

Hamish said, "Ye'd best not turn your back on that one."

Rutledge retorted silently, I'd like him to try.

A woman's voice said at his shoulder, "Your guest is leaving without ordering?"

"I believe he is." He turned to smile at her, but it didn't reach his eyes. He gave her his order. He didn't think she had overheard what was said between Wilbur and himself. "Do you know that man?"

The woman shook her head. "But I'm told he owns one of the tea shops. You wouldn't know it, judging from the people who work there. Terribly nice. I like stopping in."

Rutledge drove back to the Abbey, and when Mrs. Hailey opened the door, he asked, "Have you been annoyed by a man named Wilbur, hoping to buy the airfield, once it belongs to Lady Benton again?"

She stood aside to allow him to enter. "Oh, yes, indeed we have. I don't know what he should want with what's little more than a meadow. It's not good for much more than grazing. Even the monks knew that. The last time he came I sent him away with a flea in his ear, for disturbing Lady Benton with his nonsense." She glanced over her shoulder, to be sure no one was within earshot, and added, "What does she want with anything to remind her of the war? I ask you!"

"He called on me at the hotel, asking me to speak to Lady Benton on his behalf."

"The cheek of the man," she said in disgust. "Have you seen the circles under her eyes? I don't think she's sleeping at all. I'd like five minutes alone with whoever is behind this business, and tell him what I thought of him."

Someone came up the stairs from the crypt, calling to her, and the housekeeper said to Rutledge, "She's in her sitting room. You know the way."

It was a day for visitors, but apparently there wasn't a morning booking, for he found Lady Benton with gloves on, polishing a silver tray from one of the rooms. She looked up as he came in, smiled and said, "I mustn't keep asking you for news."

Rutledge shook his head. "Sorry. There is none. I keep waiting for whoever this is to show himself again."

That alarmed her. "Do you believe there will be more—apparitions, or whatever it was?"

"No, of course not," he told her quickly. "No, I meant, there's a reason behind what happened, even if it's no more than a prank someone thought up. And it will become apparent in time."

"Well, we have enough troubles without that. We're still shorthanded. One of the staff hasn't come in. I'm wondering if she's ill. But then she'd have sent word, wouldn't she? It's so difficult when you need every pair of hands. Will you be all right, wandering around on your own?"

"I'll find my way. Do I need keys?"

She took a ring of keys off her belt. "These should be what you need. Come back at noon, and I'll have Mrs. Hailey bring us a tray."

He began with the unused bedrooms. The house, he thought, could sleep twenty or more guests, and in great comfort. Many of the rooms were of late Georgian style and hadn't been redecorated. Those that were in current use in the last generations were early- and mid-Victorian.

More to the point, none of them appeared to have been used in quite some time, for a light layer of dust lay over the furnishings, showing no signs that anyone had been in the rooms in several weeks. Still, he could judge that they were all kept up—a tremendous effort for such a small staff.

He didn't open the door to her room, but found her son's, untouched, he thought, since Eric had gone off to war, except that it had been given more frequent care. As if Lady Benton saw to it herself.

He was just finishing the rooms for the butler and housekeeper, mattresses rolled up and nothing personal to be seen, when he heard Lady Benton calling, and realized that it was just after noon.

Rutledge joined her in the sitting room, where she had set out the food on a small tea table. There was soup, sandwiches, fruit, and a pudding, and as they ate, he told her his impression so far.

When the meal was over, he told her that he would like to finish his exploration, and she nodded. "I have an errand to run, I shan't be long. If you need anything, let Mrs. Hailey know."

He climbed the two sets of staircases back to the servants' rooms, taking up where he'd left off. He had just finished that floor and was about to go up to the Elizabethan attics, tiny cell-like rooms where the servants of the day had lived, when he heard Lady Benton calling him again.

Turning, he went back to the main staircase. She was at the foot, looking up, waiting for him to answer.

"Oh—there you are! Could you help me, Inspector. I have a small problem . . ." She hesitated, a little embarrassed to ask.

"I'm coming down." He joined her on the first floor, and then they went down the next flight as she explained.

"I went to Patricia's. Well, neither of us is on the telephone, and I had Mrs. Hailey make up a basket to take to her in case she was under the weather. But there's no answer when I knock. And I did wait, hoping she would call down to me, if she didn't feel like unlocking the door. But there was nothing—"

She realized she was running on, and stopped.

"I'm worried, as you can see," she went on sheepishly. "And I'm not really good at climbing in windows or knocking down doors."

It was a house of women, widows all, so he'd been told . . .

"I don't know that I'm good at knocking down doors," he said lightly, to cover his own concern. "But we'll raise her, or if not, I'll go for the doctor. We'll use my motorcar."

"Yes, thank you!"

They went out the front door, collecting the food basket on the way, and he helped her into her seat before turning the crank. The drizzle had become a misting rain for the moment.

"Where do I go?" he asked, joining her.

"She's just down the road, about three miles or so. Past that awful pub, and into the next village."

He followed her directions, and at the outskirts of the village, she pointed to a drive going into a tall, Victorian house set well back from the road.

"It's the Old Rectory, and her father retired here, when the new Rector came to take his place. She and her husband moved in after her father's death."

It was an attractive brick house, an avenue of flowering trees leading to the door. A turret with a pointed roof, very much in the Victorian style, rose to one side, and Lady Benton pointed to it. "There's a music room on the ground floor, and her father's study just above it. The third floor was part of the nursery."

He got down and came around to open her door. "Where does Patricia sleep?"

"Her room faces the drive. At the far end of the first-floor passage. She couldn't bear to sleep in the master bedroom, after her husband left for France. And he never came back. Artillery."

"What's her surname?"

"Oh. It's Lowell. Patricia Lowell."

Rutledge walked around to the side of the house, cupping his hands to call several times, but no one came to the window. Beginning to feel uneasy, he said, "Perhaps she's out—gone in to see Dr. Wister."

"She would have told Margaret or me, if she had done. And that wouldn't explain staying away two days."

"If she's ill, she's not able to respond. We'll have to find a way inside."

She had clearly been facetious about climbing in a window or knocking down a door. For now, Lady Benton said, "I'm really not sure—"

He turned to her. "I am sorry, but it's best to make certain she's all right."

The front door was rather massive, and he was hesitant to break a window. But the kitchen door had several panes of glass in the upper portion of the door, and he used a trowel he found in a trug beside the door to break one. Reaching in, he fumbled for the latch, and managed to open the door.

"Stay here," he said.

"No, she doesn't know you, you'll frighten her."

"I'm serious, Lady Benton. Wait here or in the motorcar."

She was already worried, but that frightened her. Licking dry lips, she said, "What's wrong? What do you think is wrong?"

"I won't know until I've looked." And he stepped into the kitchen passage, closing the door behind him.

7

Rutledge quietly made his way through the ground-floor rooms. There was nothing in any of them—parlor, dining room, music room, sitting room—to cause any alarm. Just an emptiness, a silence, that worried him.

He went back to the main staircase, climbing just as quietly to the first floor. He could feel Hamish just behind him. How many ruins had they searched together, expecting trouble, weapons at the ready. He shook himself to dispel the memory.

The house was handsomely furnished, but heavily Victorian, and he found the bedrooms to be much the same. He looked into each one, careful to leave what he suspected to be Mrs. Lowell's until last. Listening first for any sounds of movement inside, he raised his hand and knocked lightly.

There was no answer, and he called her name instead.

Silence.

Hamish said, "Ye must go inside."

Rutledge expected the door to be locked, but when he tried it, it opened.

The bedroom was very feminine, soft colors and lacy curtains at the windows, a silk coverlet on the bed, and a stand beside it with silk flowers in a tall, silver vase.

Hamish grunted as Rutledge crossed the threshold.

The room was empty. The bed neatly made, no clothes on the chairs, nothing out of place. Just the way Patricia Lowell must have left it before leaving for the Abbey.

Tidy. Like the rest of the house.

No sign of a struggle, nothing to indicate when or why she wasn't here.

He'd already looked in the other rooms. He was about to start on the attics, when Lady Benton called from the staircase.

"I can't wait any longer. Is she all right? Do we need the doctor?"

Rutledge went to the head of the stairs. "She isn't in her room. Or in any of the others I've looked into."

"She's not—?" she asked blankly. "But where is she?"

"I was just about to look in the attics—no, stay down there. I won't be long."

But he couldn't find any sign of Patricia Lowell.

Coming back down to the main floor, he shook his head. "Nothing. How does she usually get about? Come to work?"

"She has a bicycle. They all do. If the weather is very bad, they don't come to the Hall, or I come and fetch them in the motorcar."

They searched the outbuildings, but there was only a man's bicycle in the shed.

"Her husband's," Lady Benton said quietly. "It isn't hers."

They went back to the motorcar, standing beside it in the misting rain. He got his umbrella out of the boot, and opened it for her. Her face was pale but resolute as she said, "We must do something. This isn't like Patricia."

"Where would she go, if she felt ill and couldn't manage the distance to the Abbey? To a friend's house?"

"No, not when she was supposed to be coming to me. Or if there was some reason to go there, she would have let me know. Somehow."

"She left your house two nights ago, on her way home?"

"Yes. And she'd told me she was taking flowers to the churchyard the next morning. I knew it was the anniversary of her husband's death—I didn't expect to see her until later in the day."

He opened her door, and folded the umbrella as she got in.

Joining her, he said, "The churchyard? In this village or in Walmer?"

"His memorial is in Walmer. She wanted it there."

Reversing, he turned back down the drive.

"What about the broken window?" she asked, looking over her shoulder toward the house.

"We'll find a glazier. Right now, it's best to find Mrs. Lowell."

They drove in silence toward Walmer, passing the pub and then the Hall, finally coming into the village.

"Which church?" he asked.

"Where Roger is buried. Just there."

He found a place to leave the motorcar, gave her the umbrella, and led the way into the churchyard. Lieutenant Lowell's memorial stone was not far off the main path.

"She liked it here, in this churchyard. Even though it was farther away—just there." Pointing ahead of them, she indicated the stone.

It was newer than those near it, clearly recent, with no lichen or moss on it.

"She intends to be buried there, her name added to the stone," Lady Benton was saying as they crossed the grass to it. "Inspector— look. There aren't any flowers here."

They stood by the memorial stone, staring down at the empty grassy space before it.

Lady Benton, facing Rutledge, said, "I am at a loss."

But he was not listening. Hamish, loud in the back of his mind, was saying, "She's deid."

Rutledge wasn't ready to believe it. But he knew Hamish had to be right. It was the only explanation.

"Let me take you back to the Hall. You're needed there, and I will begin the search for Mrs. Lowell. For all we know," he went on, watching her expression as she went over the possibilities he himself was facing, "she might have been called away."

"Don't lie to me, Inspector," she said quietly. "Patricia would never do such a thing. Something is wrong. Dreadfully wrong. For one thing, her bicycle isn't in the stables where she keeps it while at the Abbey, I would have seen it when I went to my motorcar. And it isn't at the Old Rectory. We looked in the little shed where she keeps it. She left my house riding it, she never reached the churchyard here the next morning, because there are no flowers by the memorial stone. She isn't ill in her bed . . ." She stopped. "Who would harm Patricia?"

"Let's get out of the rain," he said. "I'll take you to the hotel for a cup of tea—or would you prefer to go home?"

"Not to the Hall. People will ask questions. And I know I can't school my face well enough to convince Margaret that all is well. I'd rather not frighten them."

"The hotel, then." He led her back to the motorcar, and they drove back up the High to the hotel.

He asked for a private parlor for her, and they were led to a small but pleasant little room overlooking the back garden.

They were divesting themselves of their wet coats when the tea came.

The woman bringing it in said with a smile, "The kettle had just come to a boil, but you'd best leave it a minute or two. I've added some cakes."

She set the tray on a small table, and left them then.

Lady Benton sat down by the little table, without thinking, accustomed to being the hostess.

She hadn't said anything on the short drive to the hotel. And now she sighed, looking down at the teapot in front of her. "I've known Patricia for a very long time. I can't imagine her being involved in anything that would harm me or the Abbey. She's a kind person, a conscientious person. If I ask her to take care of something, I know it will be done well."

"I don't believe I've met her."

"Did you go into the croft at all? She's in charge there. People like her."

He tried to recall the woman behind the counter. He had a vague memory of a pleasant young woman, smiling and helpful. Dark hair. Blue eyes?

"Not the sort of person to find herself in trouble. Or to leave me without a word. Something has happened to her, Inspector. What I don't understand is *why*."

"Any hint of problems in regard to her husband?"

"Good heavens, no. George was a lovely man, I liked him from the start, and I thought it was a fine match. He was one of Eric's friends, actually. That's how they met, you know. He came to a birthday party, Patricia was there, and if you believe in love at first sight, it happened that evening. Afterward, George found a dozen excuses to visit us, it was quite comic in a way, and then he'd borrow a horse or a bicycle, and we wouldn't see him for an hour or two. He'd come back to the Abbey, grinning, pretending he'd got lost on one of the country lanes or that he found a quiet place for a walk. Eric and I said nothing, we knew what drew him back to us. And we were as happy as George's 's parents when they were engaged. Eric was best man at the wedding."

She seemed to remember the tea, and poured two cups, passing him one of them.

"Well, you needn't hear their entire history. But I assure you, George had no enemies, and neither did Patricia." She handed him the plate of little cakes.

"Did she ever have problems traveling back and forth to the house?"

"Of course not. I do know she didn't care to pass that pub. Not that any of the patrons ever troubled her. It's just that the owner is rather odd, and he'd stand in the door sometimes, watching her ride past. I told her several times that if she had any misgivings about traveling that road, I'd send someone for her and take her home again. She assured me that she didn't need to be given special treatment."

"Still, she was younger than most of your staff. Is that true?"

"It is."

"I'll leave you here, if I may, and speak to Inspector Hamilton. He may have something that will help us."

Lady Benton frowned. "Patricia of all people would hate to be the object of curiosity."

"It's necessary, under the circumstances."

"I do understand. But her father was of the old school, that a lady never saw her name in the newspapers except for three times in her life. Her birth, her betrothal, and her death."

He left her then, walking from the hotel to the police station.

Hamilton was in his office. "You have heard of umbrellas, haven't you?" he asked, looking at the tiny droplets of rain on Rutledge's shoulders.

Ignoring the witticism, Rutledge got to the point. "Patricia Lowell. Do you know her?"

"One of the widows working for Lady Benton, I think," he said, all attention now. "Next village over but still my jurisdiction. What about her?"

"She's missing. Two nights ago, she left for her house apparently as usual, and she hasn't been seen since. I've been to the Old Rectory, and she isn't there. No sign of a struggle. What's more, there are no flowers on her husband's grave, even though yesterday was the anniversary of his death. According to Lady Benton, this was important to Mrs. Lowell, fair weather or foul, and yet it wasn't done."

Hamilton swore. "I'll start a search straightway. The Old Rectory has some land behind it, a small orchard, pasture for horses. Did you look into the outbuildings?"

"I did, and her bicycle is missing as well. At a guess, whatever happened took place between the Abbey and her house."

"The Monk's Choice is on that stretch of road. I'll have a Constable out there."

"What flower shop would she have used?"

"The Flower Pot—just off the High—is popular with the ladies. Start there."

"Don't waste your time at the Abbey. I was going room to room when Lady Benton asked if I'd go back with her to the Lowell house."

"Find anything useful?"

"No."

Hamilton grunted. "I shall have to apologize to her, before this is over. I'd not taken Friday night as seriously as it now appears to warrant."

Rutledge let that go. "There's a man named Wilbur who has been harassing Lady Benton. He's after the airfield, or the land it sits on. Do you know him?"

"Nasty piece of work," Hamilton said, rising. "War profiteer. Shoddy blankets, boot laces that rotted in the wet of the trenches. Nothing proved, he blamed his factory managers for the shortcuts. You aren't saying he's behind this business?"

"I doubt it. But I'm keeping an open mind."

The drizzle had stopped, and in its place, fog was coming in from the rivers, settling over rooftops.

In spite of it, Rutledge found The Flower Pot easily enough. He could understand why it was popular with the ladies, as Hamilton had described it.

The front window held everything the avid gardener might desire, from a selection of handsome pots to a variety of pretty gloves, and even a black-and-white cat stretched out asleep by the glass panes.

He opened the door, and walked inside. There were flowers everywhere, from live ones in buckets of water to silk ones in attractive vases. A middle-aged woman came forward to greet him.

The last thing he wanted was to start a rumor about Mrs. Lowell's disappearance. And so he said, "Mrs. Lowell has a standing order, I think, for flowers for her husband's grave?"

"Indeed, and on the date of their wedding as well." She frowned. "Although she didn't come in for them this time. Are you here to fetch them for her? I do hope she isn't ill?"

"When did she usually come for them? Morning? Afternoon?"

"Punctually at ten o'clock, sir. Even if it was raining. I always keep a little cellophane on hand to cover the blooms so they aren't ruined by the weather before she reached the churchyard." She gestured toward the array of flowers. "Shall I wrap her order for you, sir?"

"Yes, please." He waited while she did, and then paid for them.

"It's kind of you to help Mrs. Lowell. She's a lovely lady, and I know how much these meant to her. Do tell her I hope she feels better very soon."

He thanked her and left. Instead of going to the hotel, he walked on to the churchyard and carefully laid the flowers by Lieutenant Lowell's memorial stone. The pansies, violets, and daffodils added a splash of color to the grass, just now reviving after the winter.

That done, he started to leave the churchyard, but on impulse, he turned toward Captain Nelson's grave. And stopped short when he saw that the young woman from The Salt Cellar, the pub down by the harbor, was on her knees there. Liz was her name . . .

She looked like a wraith, for the fog was rolling in from the estuary. Still there was something in her posture, the slump of her shoulders, that led him to think she was crying. While it was his first instinct to be certain she was all right, this was very likely her only refuge, and he turned away instead. The tragedy was, her refuge was a dead man.

He left the churchyard, walking back to the hotel where Lady Benton was anxiously waiting.

H e found her by the window, gazing out at the settling fog, and she turned at once to say, "There you are. I was beginning to hope there was news."

"Nothing so far," he said. "I found the florist. Apparently, Mrs. Lowell had ordered flowers as usual, but she hadn't come in to collect them. I took them on to the churchyard."

"That was kind of you. But now I'm rather frightened. Nothing short of serious illness would have kept her from going there early yesterday morning." She shook her head. "I've been trying to think where she might have gone. Or where else we might look. If she'd been called away, she'd have left me a message, so that I could find someone else to mind the café."

"Inspector Hamilton is starting a search. Let me drive you home, and then I'll go out as well."

"Thank you." She collected her gloves and handbag, then went with him out to the motorcar.

"This is turning into a heavy fog," she said as he got in after turning the crank. "I do hope Mrs. Hailey let the staff go early. There won't be any visitors today."

"Which reminds me. Are any of the other women close to Mrs. Lowell? Someone she might confide in?"

"I don't believe there's anyone in particular. We go on very well together, all of us. Surprisingly, since there's such an age difference. Mrs. Stevens is the eldest, at sixty."

He was threading his way out of Walmer, but once out on the main road, he found the going much harder. The fog came and went, drifting across the land and muffling sound. Rutledge was suddenly reminded of the waves of gas floating across the battlefield, oddly beautiful sometimes, and always lethal.

Behind him, he could feel Hamish stirring as well.

In spite of himself he coughed as it seemed to drift into the motorcar.

Lady Benton said, "Should we turn back?"

"We'll just go very slowly," he promised, and concentrated on the nearly invisible road ahead. The fog lamps of the big motorcar gave him no real assistance, forcing him to stay in the center of the road for safety.

She sat beside him, tense, her hands clasped tightly together, but she had nothing more to say until they were nearing the Abbey. "I can't bear to think about Patricia, not knowing where she is, or why. I shan't sleep tonight." As the gates loomed out of the fog, seeming to have no top, she stopped Rutledge from turning in.

"If Mrs. Hailey let everyone go home—as I'm sure she must have done—the bar is across the main door. But I have keys to the door near the stables. If you wouldn't mind—"

"Of course."

He crept along, searching for the opening that would be the stable lane. And then he saw it, almost a difference in shadow and light rather than a space in which to turn.

"When we had one of these, the flights either went elsewhere if they were up, or stayed on the ground, if they hadn't left. A little respite in the midst of war. Ah, just there, I think?"

He turned down the lane, and found the gate. Lady Benton said, "Shall I get down, and open it for you?"

"No, stay here."

He opened it, driving through into the stable yard before walking back to close it again. His footsteps seemed muffled in the stillness. The fog stirred briefly, as if to welcome them, then came down thicker than before.

As Rutledge came around to the other side of the motorcar, she was collecting her handbag and gloves, preparing to get down, thanking him again for his help.

"I'll walk with you to the door," he said.

"No, of course not, there's no need. I can find my way in the dark."

"I'll see you safely inside," he told her firmly.

She gave him a wry smile, as if still reluctant to let him accompany her.

They started forward, had gone perhaps ten paces, when she said, "Ah. I only have one glove. I must have dropped it as I got down." Rutledge turned, but she stopped him. "I lost it, I'm perfectly capable of retrieving it."

And so he waited while she walked back to the motorcar. He could hear her opening the passenger's door, but he couldn't see her, only a moving darkness in the shrouding mist.

And then she screamed.

Racing back to her, he said quickly, "What is it?"

Her bare hand covering her mouth, she pointed a shaking finger.

He set her behind him and started toward whatever it was that had frightened her, although he could see nothing. But she caught his arm.

"No, you mustn't—"

And in the same moment, Hamish shouted, "*There*!"

The mist swirled once more, and he could just see the gate, still closed. There was something beyond it, he couldn't tell what it was. Ignoring her pleas to stay where he was, he ran to the gate—and then stopped short as the mist moved again.

Across the lane by the fence there stood a dark shape, monstrous in size, facing them but saying nothing. Like something out of a nightmare.

It hadn't been there when he'd opened and closed the gate . . .

"Dear God," Lady Benton asked softly, "What is it?"

"I don't know," he said over his shoulder. "Get back into the motorcar and lock the door. I'm going to find out."

"*No*," she exclaimed. "Let's leave. While we can."

"The gate is closed."

"Break it down," she urged him. "I don't care—you aren't armed—we have a better chance in the motorcar."

Ignoring her, he stared at the figure. Whatever it was, it hadn't moved. He was a tall man, but it was taller. And broader, with what appeared to be massive shoulders. Was that a cloak? And he couldn't tell what it was wearing on its head. A helmet of some sort?

And then it moved slightly, as if bracing to face Rutledge.

It was alive, then. Not a straw man to frighten her.

He didn't bother to open the gate, he vaulted it instead, and walked out into the lane, prepared for anything.

The unpredictable mist kept shifting, making it difficult to judge what was in front of him. He was almost all the way across the lane before he could see the figure clearly—

Rutledge felt a sudden, unexpected urge to laugh rising in his chest.

A tall black horse, wearing a blanket, stared calmly back at him. And yet in the fog, the shape had been almost human. The odd headgear was nothing more than its ears pricked forward. As if it had come to look for human company when it heard their voices.

Behind him, Lady Benton called anxiously, "Inspector?"

"It's all right. Just a horse."

But she wasn't convinced until he opened the gate and took her across the lane to see for herself.

"It—it's one of ours—yet it appeared—appeared grotesquely human," she said. "And I can't think why it should be in this field. I must have a word with Henry. He's in charge of the tenant farms." She reached up to stroke the horse's nose, as if making sure it was real. And as she did, Rutledge saw that her hand was still trembling.

The horse blew, reaching down for more. But she pushed it away, telling it to go home, and it turned and ambled away, like an obedient dog.

They went back across the lane, and once more started toward the house door, along the line of hedges.

As she handed him her keys again, to unlock the door, Lady Benton said, "Would you care to come in? I don't know what Mrs. Hailey has left for dinner, but there's always more than enough for two. And I can manage to put a kettle on." It was an attempt at lightness, but he could hear the undercurrent of lingering shock.

"That might be a wise idea," he agreed. "To be sure all is well."

They locked the door behind them and made their way down to the kitchen, Rutledge carrying the lamp that was waiting on a side table in readiness.

Shadows danced in the great rooms as they passed through, briefly catching a line of gold frame or a tall silver candlestick, casting shadows across the bust of King Charles or a pair of marble nymphs dancing together. In the dining room the salt cellar shaped like a galleon in full sail seemed to move in the silver water beneath its hull. In the flickering light, the Madonna took on a malevolent appearance, sad eyes peering over the veil at them.

Rutledge found himself thinking that Lady Benton was a brave woman to walk through this house after dark. But then it was familiar to her, not as foreign as it was to him.

In another hall, they went down steps into the kitchen quarters, the lamplight catching on the row of brass bells on one wall, before she lit two more lights to brighten the large room with its gleaming cooker and an array of pots and pans hanging above the worktables.

"We can take a tray to the sitting room," she suggested as she reached for the kettle, and then stirred the cooker into life. "Or eat here. I sometimes do, if I'm too tired to bring my dishes back down."

"This will do nicely."

He helped her set out the plates of food that had been left for her, as she made a pot of tea and found a tray of tarts in the pantry, along with a pitcher of milk.

As she worked, Rutledge said, "What do you know about The Salt Cellar? It's a pub down by the harbor."

"It serves rather rough custom. At least that's what the men from the airfield told me. They didn't care to go there. As far as I know, it's never been more than a nuisance. Mostly occasional drunkenness, that's all I've heard. Why?"

"I was driving past it and noticed the rather unusual sign. Very clever. I haven't gone inside."

"Yes, there was a smith in Walmer who did wonderful things. He made the rack for the bells, there by the stairs. He's gone now, sadly. As for the pub, the owner is rather an odd sort, or so I've heard. Bill Johnson is his name." She smiled. "His mother was one of the leaders of the Temperance movement, which was probably his reason for buying the pub in the first place. She lived and breathed sobriety, responsibility, and self-respect—firm middle-class Victorian values—and no doubt it was tiresome to hear it night and day at home. Margaret—Mrs. Hailey—avoided Mrs. Johnson if she could. Demon gin and demon beer were all she talked about. The other pub by the harbor, The Viking, is less savory, and there's been talk about closing it for the public good. But in its day, when the salt ships came in, it was quite popular."

The tea had steeped and the sandwiches were ready. He dropped the subject of The Salt Cellar and asked instead about the other women who worked at the Hall.

"They're good for me. They give me the energy to keep going. It's a daunting responsibility to keep up this house. I'd probably be wiser to sell it or hand it over to the Trust. But it feels like such a betrayal. It's been in the family so very long." She shrugged lightly. "Women have had to take on such responsibility because of the war. Mrs. Hailey would never have considered being a housekeeper, but she enjoys coming here every day. Mrs. Peterson had never dusted and polished furniture in her life, but she finds taking care of the rooms such a pleasure I never have to show her what needs attention. On the other hand, Mrs. Broughton discovered she's a remarkable needlewoman, and she can work wonders with frayed bits of chairs and drapes and tapestries. They are widows, their children grown and flown, as Mrs. Napier likes to say, and they found time heavy on their hands."

She stared down at her plate of food, her concern for Patricia Lowell, returning as she talked about her staff. "These are not women who cause anyone any trouble. I can't imagine what's become of Patricia. Why anyone would wish to harm her."

"We'll find her. Try to rest tonight, and leave it to Hamilton to conduct a thorough search. He knows his patch."

"I wish that was a comforting thought," she told him. "I feel so responsible—I'm afraid that whoever is behind this has something to do with what happened to me. It can't be purely coincidental."

"You aren't responsible for what happened last Friday night."

Sighing, she replied, "Then why can't I believe that?"

The meal finished, she went with him back to the door leading to the stables, and as he stepped out into lingering fog, she said, "So silly of me to be unsettled by a poor horse, looking to see who might be wandering around the stables."

"We were both taken in by it," he reminded her.

"Good night, Inspector. Will you be coming by tomorrow?"

"Very likely. Good night."

He waited until she had locked the door behind him, then walked on to the stables.

The horse had gone. His gaze swept what he could see of the pasture, but he couldn't say with any certainty whether the horse was still there somewhere or had been taken away.

Putting on his Wellingtons, he climbed over the fence and began to make his way through the shrouding fog. Hamish, grumbling, went with him.

He found the horse finally, but in another field. It was grazing and raised his head to stare at Rutledge before going back to feeding.

When Rutledge reached the fence again, he took out his torch to scan the long grass where the horse had been standing. Even with its light he couldn't see anything that might have drawn the animal to that particular spot. No apples, no corn scattered about.

He went back to the stable yard and pulled the motorcar out into the lane before closing and locking the gate behind him. Instead of driving out to the main road, he turned off his headlamps and went instead down to the shadows cast by the hedges that separated the house grounds from the once-wild meadow.

He had told Hamilton that he could vouch for the Abbey, having been searching the rooms himself for other reasons. But he hadn't searched the airfield since Mrs. Lowell had disappeared. Not that there was any chance that anyone had been there since his last visit. Still, it had to be done. Even on a night like this.

It was dark. Cloud cover and the fog had put paid to any sunset or starlight.

Taking out his torch and shielding it with his gloved hand, he walked toward the airfield. The mist was soft and damp against his face.

And Hamish was there, just behind his shoulder as he'd so often been in life. Rutledge did his best to ignore the voice, concentrating instead on where he put his feet.

When he reached the first of the foundations, he had to be careful not to go sprawling over the rough remains, hardly visible even in the torch's shielded light. Then he began a search of the handful of small buildings that had been left standing.

He had to rely on memory to guide him as he moved from one to the other of them. They were as empty as they'd been the first time he'd explored the airfield.

Hamish was saying. "It's a lang way fra' her house. Rough going on a bicycle."

"Are you sure she's here?" he asked before he could stop himself.

"It's as weil to be certain. Ye ken, she didna' seem to be a woman to do foolish things."

It was true. He'd had the same impression of Mrs. Lowell, in that brief encounter in the croft. A quiet, pleasant, sensible woman . . .

By this time there was only one building left. He started toward it— and the batteries in his torch began to go, dimming the light. Twice he stumbled over something underfoot.

This shed was taller than the others, looming out of the mist as a dark shape. He found the door, reached for the handle to pull it open— and it nearly came off its rusted hinges.

Rutledge caught it in time, shoving it to one side, then picked up his torch to shine what was left of the beam into the shed's black interior.

As he did so, the torch went dark.

Rutledge struck it with the heel of his hand, and it flicked on briefly, then died completely.

But not before he had seen what was hanging from the bare rafters above his head.

8

Setting the torch down on the rotting floorboards, Rutledge reached for the lighter he'd been given by one of his men as they had waited for the dawn to break. It had been made from a rifle cartridge shell casing. He'd carried it ever since.

For a wonder it caught the first time he tried, and he held it up.

He'd seen Patricia Lowell only in the café, but he recognized the distorted face even in the patchy light.

And he swore.

Rutledge made his way back to where he'd left his motorcar, and without turning on the headlamps, he barely made it back down the lane to the main road. Creeping along, he took his time reaching Walmer, but there was no one in the police station when he got there.

He roused the doctor, who was already asleep. As Wister pulled on his coat and reached for his bag, he said to Rutledge, standing in the hall waiting for him, "Are you sure she's dead?"

"I am," he told the doctor tersely, and they went together to wake up Hamilton. "I didn't care to leave her there, but there was no one to send or stay."

"This fog is so dense, we couldn't search the Lowell property," the Inspector said, when he'd dressed and come down again, looking a little more awake than he had been five minutes before. "Did I hear you say you'd found the Lowell woman's body?"

"In a shed on the airfield. I couldn't cut her down—it was pitch-dark after my torch died, and I had no ladder."

"And no idea why she might have killed herself? And at the airfield, of all places!" Hamilton asked, climbing into the rear seat of the motorcar.

"No." Rutledge dared not turn and look at Hamilton, in Hamish's seat.

"Damn."

They fell silent as Rutledge made his way back to the Abbey, and took the lane a second time that evening. He looked for the horse as he passed the gates to the stable yard, but it hadn't returned to the fence.

Hamilton fell twice on their way to the shed, impartially cursing the mist and the rubble under his feet as Rutledge, the Inspector's borrowed torch in his hand, led the way.

Before leaving, he'd set the broken door almost in the opening, to keep the scene fairly protected, and now moved it once more, allowing Dr. Wister to step past him and look up as Rutledge swept the light up to the discolored face.

The doctor swore, as Rutledge had done.

"There was no need for this . . ."

They found the overturned stool beneath the dangling feet, and set it upright for Rutledge to stand on to cut her down.

Hamilton and Wister laid the body on the rough flooring, and then, kneeling beside her, Wister said, "You were right, of course. Dead." He finished his examination and rocked back on his heels. "I'll have a better idea when there's enough light to see clearly. But I'd say she's been dead for at least a day, possibly longer. Rigor has passed." He got slowly to his feet. "What the hell possessed this poor woman, to die this way, and in this place? She's a widow—was she still grieving for her husband, do you think?"

It had been the anniversary of his death—two days ago . . .

Mrs. Lowell was wearing a light coat against the chill, and Hamilton went through the pockets as Rutledge watched. He found gloves in one, and in the other a handkerchief, the key to her house, and a crumpled bit of paper.

Rutledge was still holding the torch, and he brought it closer as Hamilton smoothed out the wrinkled sheet.

I can't go on without him

Hamilton read the words aloud in a low voice, as if not to disturb the dead woman lying there beside his knees. "Is that her writing?" he asked, holding up the paper for the other two men to see more clearly.

"You'll have to ask Lady Benton," Wister said.

"Not tonight," Rutledge added. "Let's get her out of here."

Dr. Wister had brought a blanket with him, and they carefully laid the body in the center of it.

Hamilton was saying as they did, "We'll have to come back in daylight. Although we've most likely trampled any clues there might have been. Footprints, the like."

"I looked before I stepped inside. The floor appeared to be clean. No prints at all."

"Where did the stool come from?" Hamilton asked.

Rutledge was searching his memory. "I've seen it before. In the shed out by the field. Where maintenance was done. They'd have needed it to reach the aircraft cowling."

"Sounds about right," Wister said. "I've been on several airfields." He paused. "I also knew the doctor who served here for a year. We met in France toward the end of the war. He had to convey a crash victim to hospital in Chelmsford."

"Captain Nelson?" Rutledge asked.

"No, no. Pilot. Broke both legs, poor man, when the motor shut down too far out. He barely managed to keep control as far as the field. Then she dropped like a stone, ended up on her nose. This was well after the Captain's death, of course." He rubbed his chin, his fingers scraping over the night's growth of beard. "In the ambulance, that young man—the pilot—told my colleague that he'd seen the ghost of the Captain standing in his path as he took off. It had unnerved him, but he managed to get into the air and do what he had to do. And later, the doctor of course mentioned it to me. That wasn't the only pilot— another said much the same thing before he died. Burn victim, that one."

Wister had said nothing about a conversation with one of the air- field doctors when Rutledge had first spoken to him. Only that such sightings had been said to have happened. But here, in the shadows of the shed, the torch on the dead woman, he seemed compelled to give them his account.

There was a brief silence.

Rutledge said, "Is that why you asked me to be careful how I ques- tioned Lady Benton?"

"I don't believe in ghosts," Wister replied. "I'm a doctor. Dead is dead. But the mind can play tricks, Rutledge. It can sometimes con- vince itself that it has seen what isn't there. The danger is, whatever caused the mind to believe in the fabrication can be difficult to assess. And the wrong handling can do irreparable damage."

Rutledge felt cold, careful to keep the light away from his own face. It was too near the truth. And Hamish was hammering in the back of his mind, drowning out what Hamilton was saying in response.

The two men lifted the blanket by its corners, and turned to leave the shed, carrying their burden between them. Rutledge led the way, keeping the torch pointed to the ground, to ease their passage.

At one point, he glanced up at the distant house, but it was lost in the mist. He couldn't tell if Lady Benton had been able to rest or if she were roaming the rooms, looking for peace. He hoped she found it, because tomorrow he'd have to tell her about Mrs. Lowell.

It was a long walk back to the motorcar. And then there was the problem of what to do with the body.

Rutledge said, "Take the motorcar. I'll stay here, and one of you can come back for me." He would just as soon be alone for a while, and it was going to be some time before he got back to the hotel. "Leave me the torch. I'll see if there's anything in that shed that we can use."

Working together, they put Mrs. Lowell's body into the rear seat, and Rutledge turned the crank as the doctor and Inspector Hamilton got in, handing him the torch before he shut his door. "A nasty business," he told Rutledge. "Anything you can find, anything that could tell us why this happened."

And then they were gone, the sound of the motor lasting longer than the visibility of the rear light.

The silence wrapped around him again as the mist closed in. Rutledge stood there for a time, thinking, but came to no conclusions. Lady Benton had worried that Mrs. Lowell was ill, but she had said nothing about her being in distress. And it seemed odd that if Mrs. Lowell had been in such despair over the anniversary of her husband's death, that she hadn't taken flowers to the churchyard before killing herself. A last gesture of love—a last moment by the memorial stone, before choosing to join him in death.

And he had looked in the other sheds before he'd found her body. Where was her bicycle? It wasn't at the airfield, and it wasn't at the Old Rectory. Why hadn't she left it outside the shed before putting the rope in place, and using the stool? Or if she hadn't taken it to reach the airfield, why wasn't it in its proper place?

He turned the shielded torch on the hedge, where he had sometimes left his own motorcar well out of sight. Sweeping the branches, probing the depths for some twenty yards or more. If there was a bicycle here, it had been shoved too far in to be readily seen. He went closer. Using his gloved hand to push heavier branches aside.

It wasn't there.

He couldn't picture her walking alone in the dark from the Old Rectory to the airfield, carrying the heavy rope she intended to use. Again, according to Lady Benton, Mrs. Lowell had been uncomfortable when Fred Newbold stared at her as she passed The Monk's Choice. She wasn't likely to walk past when the pub was noisy, busy with custom, people coming and going.

The more he considered the matter, the more he found it difficult to see Patricia Lowell as a suicide. There was nothing to point to it.

On the other hand, there was nothing to point to murder, either. She seemed to be as unlikely a victim of murder as she was a suicide.

And yet—and yet—she was dead.

Hamish said into the stillness, "Was she mistaken in the dark for Lady Benton?"

Rutledge couldn't see that, either. And yet it made more sense than any other answer he could think of.

Was the airfield haunted? Not in the sense of ghosts wandering the runway to warn pilots of their impending deaths. More likely because of something that had once happened here—and wasn't finished even now. Even with the war over, and the aircraft taken away. And he didn't know why. Or how it was related to what had happened to Lady Benton. Who was searching? Who had unfinished business here?

And what had it to do with Patricia Lowell?

Flicking on the torch again, he started back to the airfield.

Even with better light, there was nothing in the tall shed that he could see. A broken door, a damaged rope hanging from the rafters, the overturned stool, which he'd righted and stood on to cut down the dead woman.

How had Mrs. Lowell managed her own death so well? He wouldn't have expected it of the woman he'd met in the undercroft. Capable, yes, trustworthy, as Lady Benton had described her. But wandering the airfield in the dark, carrying a stool to the shed, putting the rope over the only beam—how had she known these things were there? If she was afraid of passing The Monk's Choice when it was busy, how had she found the courage to come to the airfield and search it for what she needed in order to die?

Surely she would have felt safer using a shed on her own property. Or one of the trees beyond the house, if the shed had not worked.

What had brought her here?

And where was her bicycle? Useless here on the field with the foundations and weeds—but it would have carried her safely past the pub, and down the lane. Yet it hadn't.

Her killer had been particularly careful. If this *was* murder . . .

Why not, if the intent was to let the world believe she was a suicide, have her hang in her own home? It was what a woman would choose to do, rather than end her life among the cobwebs in the rafters, the smell of oil and damp, a place where her late husband had never served. Even cutting her wrists over his grave might appeal to her, so that her blood ran down into the emptiness under the stone. Either was a more likely death for Patricia Lowell.

But it might well come to be the last straw for Lady Benton, who had not been frightened away by the pantomime in her private garden.

There was going to be a long wait before his motorcar came back . . .

He made up his mind, and picked his way as quickly as he dared over the rough ground back to the hedge, and there he set out at a jog down the farm lane toward the road.

He'd often walked on holidays when he was at Oxford. For the exercise and because he'd liked exploring, finding his way over unfamiliar ground. Sometimes alone, sometimes with a friend. He was accustomed to it.

Rutledge's intention was to search Mrs. Lowell's house again, this time not so much trying to discover where she might have gone—or what had happened to her—but to find out what there was in her life that would explain her death.

He'd been walking on the road for what he estimated must be a mile and a half, when Hamish said softly "Hist!"

Rutledge stopped short, flicked off the torch, and as the sound of his footsteps faded, he heard voices. Not close by, he couldn't distinguish words. And the mist effectively disguised where they were coming from.

He reckoned he must be close to The Monk's Choice, but he couldn't see the pub. Not even the glow of lamplight from its windows. He might, he thought, be a quarter of a mile short. But voices didn't travel that far, even in mist. Still, there were not that many buildings along this stretch of road, much of it farmland belonging to the Abbey.

He waited. Listening.

What had seemed to be a low conversation grew louder, taut with anger now. As if they were walking this way as they talked.

Rutledge wasn't sure of the time. One o'clock? Possibly two? Who were they—and why were they on foot along the road? But then they might ask the same of him . . .

Two men. He could distinguish that much. And they didn't sound inebriated. Just very angry.

He tried to move a little closer, but a stone rolled under his foot—and silence fell. He could hear his own breathing, he tried not to hear Hamish's.

Someone was moving away quickly, trying not to make any noise, and then another set of footsteps set off in a different direction, masking each other's sounds.

And a few seconds later, he had the night to himself again.

When he was certain he was alone, Rutledge walked on, toward what he thought was where the voices had been standing. Moving slowly, prepared for anything, he could feel the road becoming grass beneath his feet.

"Ware—"

The sense of something in his path came too late. Without warning, his right foot caught in what felt like tangled wire. He struggled to keep his balance, but his left foot slipped in the wet grass as it tried to take his weight, and he went down hard, his ribs striking something and sending a searing pain through his side.

His last thought as he lost consciousness was that Hamilton, returning soon with his motorcar, would have no idea where he was.

Then the pain and the blackness took over.

When he regained his senses, he could feel cold grass under his face. In place of the mist, no more than shreds now, a wind had risen, breaking it up. It was still dark, and cloudy, because he couldn't see any stars.

He couldn't remember at first why he was lying on the ground, but when he tried to sit up, his ribs sent a surge of pain through his body, and as he lay back, something hard brushed against his head.

Still dazed, he felt around him with his hands, and finally his fingers touched the torch he'd dropped as he went down. Fumbling with it, he found the switch and the light blinded him for a few seconds.

Then he saw what he had fallen over.

A bicycle.

Not a man's bicycle, a woman's . . .

Mrs. Lowell's? There was a basket on the handlebars, small, neat, and tied with a blue ribbon.

Surely someone at the Abbey would recognize it, if it was.

But what the hell was it doing out here, in the middle of nowhere? He flashed the light this way and that, looking for the pub or some other building. There was nothing except farmland.

He tried to get to his feet, but finally had to turn so that his weight went on his arms, without using his chest muscles. It was still difficult enough that he grunted from the pain. He had to squat to retrieve the torch, then managed to right the bicycle.

He was standing there, wondering if he could manage riding it when something caught his eye. There was a small orange glow in the distance.

Even as he watched, it vanished.

A window, a lamp near it. Judging from the height of that orange glow, the room was on the first floor. A bedroom?

He began to walk in the direction he'd seen the light, keeping it in his mind's eye as he moved, using the torch to light his way so that he wouldn't fall again. When he was close enough to recognize the building just ahead, he stopped.

It was the pub. The Monk's Choice. Dark now, no light showing, although he walked around it at a distance, to be sure.

Somewhere a dog began barking.

Ignoring it, he spent several minutes within sight of the pub, waiting to see if anyone came out the door. Whether the lamp meant someone was finished for the night or about to leave the room—and the building.

When there was no sign of anyone moving in or out of the pub, he finally turned and went back the way he'd come.

He was used to measuring distances. He knew to a few yards where he'd fallen over the bicycle.

But when he got there, it was gone.

Casting his light about, he searched for half an hour. It was nowhere to be seen.

Rutledge remembered the dog barking.

Someone had come back for the bicycle and taken it away.

Swearing, he finally gave up his search and started back. Back to the lane and the hedge, where he was to meet Hamilton. There was no time now to reach the Lowell house and return.

Tomorrow.

He was beginning to find it difficult to breathe, and had to slow his pace. He didn't think his ribs were broken, there hadn't been that sense of shock and nausea that came with broken bones. Still, his right side hurt like the very devil. And he thought he must have hit his head as he went down. A lump above his left ear was growing larger with every step, but his mind seemed clear enough.

He was wary when he saw distant headlamps, growing larger by the minute. Moving slowly, as if the driver was searching for something.

Hamish said, "Was yon bicycle real?"

But Rutledge shut away the voice, watching the oncoming vehicle. While he still had time to get out of the high-beam glare.

Then he recognized the familiar shape of his own motorcar, and stayed where he was.

Hamilton slowed as he recognized the figure his headlamps had picked out of the darkness at the edge of the road.

"What the hell—" he said, tired and short-tempered. "Rutledge, I've searched the damned airfield for you—I was going back to gather a search party—is that blood on your forehead?"

Rutledge put his hand up, and found a cut, wet with blood but not bleeding profusely. He remembered now, hitting it on the rim of the bicycle's tire as he tried to sit up.

"Never mind that. Did you take Mrs. Lowell's body to the surgery? Is there anything you could see there that might help us?"

"Yes, of course—and no, we didn't. Nothing obvious. Wister will know more tomorrow. But it doesn't appear she was interfered with. Clothing intact. Get in, man, or it will be dawn before we see our beds. Do you want to drive?"

"No." It was difficult climbing into the motorcar. He had to set his teeth against the pain.

"What's wrong?"

"I tripped over a bicycle, of all things. Lying along the road near where I'd heard two men arguing. I think it was Patricia Lowell's."

"Then let's take it back with us. You should never have left it."

Rutledge was in no mood for it. He said tersely, "It's gone now. But I can describe it."

Hamilton was cross. "Damn it, you should never have let it out of your sight. Who was arguing? Why is it gone?"

"Just drive. There's nothing more we can do tonight."

Grumbling, Hamilton reversed, and started back toward Walmer.

They drove in silence after that, until they were in sight of the first house in the village. Then Hamilton said, "We'll go back at first light. In case you misjudged where you saw it."

"Go if you like. It isn't there."

Hamilton left the motorcar in the hotel yard, started to walk away, then turned back.

His words echoed Hamish's but he spoke quietly, so as not to wake up anyone in the rooms above.

"There's that cut on your head. Are you sure there was a bicycle? Or was it on your mind when you fell?"

Rutledge turned. He hadn't bruised his ribs on grass. But he said, "I'll know when I've described it to Lady Benton and her staff."

He went in the hotel's door and closed it behind him, then walked down the passage to the stairs. They seemed insurmountable, suddenly.

I n the morning, Rutledge looked at his chest in the mirror as he was shaving.

A slanting red and blue line marked his ribs on one side. The knot above his ear had come down, although combing his hair just there reminded him quickly where it had been. But the cut on his forehead had stopped bleeding. It was small enough, he thought, not to attract attention, now.

He managed to dress, and at nine o'clock he was at the door of Wister's surgery.

The man looked as tired as he felt.

"Come back at two. I have patients until noon."

He drove instead to where he had stumbled over the bicycle. The pain in his ribs was not as sharp now, but it had not gone away.

Rutledge couldn't be sure of the exact spot, but it didn't matter— there was no bicycle to be seen in any direction. He found scuffed, bruised grass some forty yards from the pub, but even that might have been caused by any number of things.

Driving on to The Monk's Choice, he knocked at the door. It was several minutes before Newbold came to answer the knock. He looked as if he'd had too much to drink, eyes bloodshot, his clothes rumpled.

"We're closed."

"I haven't come to drink. Where were you last night?"

"You're asking too many questions for a man who came here before asking for a room," he said harshly. "Rumor says you're police. The Yard."

"And you can talk to me now or talk to me at the police station in Walmer. Your choice." Rutledge's voice was cold. Newbold tried to bluster.

"Here. Where the hell do you think I might be?"

"A woman was killed near here last night. Did you see or hear anything suspicious that might help us pinpoint where it happened, or how?"

Newbold blinked. "What woman? I don't know anything about anyone being killed. I closed early. Toothache. Drank myself to sleep finally, took more than I bargained for to do the job."

"There was a witness who said he heard men's voices, arguing in the fog. Not too far from here."

"Yes, well, I daresay it was someone angry about the pub being closed. There was banging on the door, calls for me to open. And I wasn't having it," he added sourly.

Hamish was saying, "Aye, he was drunk, ye can smell it on his clothes and his breath. But it was no' his tooth that was troubling him."

Nor was his jaw swollen.

"If the toothache was that severe, why aren't you on your way to see a dentist this morning?"

"All the way to Chelmsford? And who's to pay for it, if I get there? Whisky is a damned sight cheaper."

He made to shut the door, but Rutledge stopped him.

"If I'd heard shouting outside my window at two in the morning, I'd have taken a look. Did you? And see more than you bargained for?"

Something shifted in Newbold's gaze. But it looked more like fear than guilt. Yet not fear of Rutledge . . .

Newbold moved uneasily. "All right. I heard shouting in the night. But I didn't go down or look out. Trouble on the road late at night? I mind my own business, and I don't have to look whoever it is in the eye when they step through the door the next evening. Like it or not, that's the truth."

Rutledge considered him. He didn't think Newbold had killed Patricia Lowell, the man hadn't been in the war, and watching a woman slowly die would have taken more than simple lust or anger or even revenge. But it was clear he must know something. About the bicycle? But why that and not her death?

He left ten minutes later, unable to break the man's stubborn refusal to admit to anything but hearing voices. Newbold clung to that account with a fierceness that had more in common with a drowning man clinging to anything that would keep him afloat rather than hiding a murder.

Whatever the man knew—or suspected—it would keep for the moment. It was more important to speak to Lady Benton before someone else brought her the news.

I t was quiet on this Friday morning. The gates were closed, and he had to go round to the stable entrance.

There was a knocker, and he used it.

After a time Lady Benton came to the door. She was wearing men's trousers, her son's very likely, a heavy jumper, and a kerchief round her head.

"No tours this morning?"

"None is booked. I'm just as happy about that." She gestured to her apparel and smiled a little. "I'm so sorry. The lady of the manor has been working in one of the rooms." The smile faded. "The truth is, if I don't stay busy, I'll go mad with worry. Do come in. Do you have any news for me? About—?"

She had been covering her embarrassment about last night, running on without really looking at him, but now she stopped in midsentence, something in his silence warning her. Her gaze swept his face, then faltered.

"No. Oh, no." Her hand over her mouth, she turned away but not before he saw the tears filling her eyes.

"It's best to talk in your sitting room. Not here," he said gently, and guided her with a hand on her arm to the door.

It was as tidy as ever, although breakfast dishes were still on a tray, and there was a work basket by the side of one of the chairs.

She sat down, clearly bracing herself. "Was it a motorcar? I'd worried about her bicycling home. It isn't a busy road, but what traffic there is sometimes flies . . ." Her voice trailed off, and she regarded him helplessly, waiting.

Rutledge took the chair across from her. "It wasn't a motorcar. We found her in one of the sheds on the airfield. It appeared to be a suicide—"

She shook her head vehemently. "No, not Patricia. She'd weathered the grief for her husband. She was herself again, cheerful and hopeful," she told him firmly. "I refuse to believe she would do such a thing. She had a strong faith, she simply *wouldn't*."

He said nothing about the bicycle. This wasn't the time. And she hadn't asked how Mrs. Lowell had died. He didn't want to tell her, unless she wanted to know. But he added, "If it wasn't suicide, the only alternative would be murder . . ." Testing her.

She found a handkerchief and wiped at the tears. "I don't—that's hardly a *comfort*." Steadying her voice with an effort, forcing herself once more to face and deal with the unthinkable, she said, "Who would harm Patricia? She's—she had a little money, but she wasn't rich by any stretch. There's nothing to be gained by her death."

"There's the house. The property."

"The Old Rectory? At her death, it was to go to the school she'd attended. In Surrey, I think. To be dealt with as they saw fit. She had no one else, and there was no money for an endowment. I know this because she asked me to be her executor."

When he said nothing, she went on, her voice husky with grief. "I can't wrap my mind around this! I can't think beyond the news that she's dead." She sat there, staring at the tapestry on the wall. And he watched as she struggled to cope. As the unthinkable struck her suddenly. Turning to him, alarm in her eyes, she said, "You don't believe—surely this has no connection with Friday last and what happened here."

"I don't know," he told her truthfully. "We're still looking into her death."

Her voice was thick with the tears she was fighting to hold back. "Where is she now?"

"Dr. Wister's surgery."

"Yes. Of course. I should have thought—but when did you find her? This morning?"

He hesitated, knowing how it would strike her. "Last evening. After I left you."

She colored slightly. "After I was frightened into hysterics by a horse. I was going to send down to the Home Farm today to see why there was one in that pasture. It's for winter grazing, the grass is all used up." Clearing her throat with a cough, she added, "How did you come to find her?"

Rutledge told her, keeping the worst to himself. She listened, then nodded. "I'm glad you thought to look there. I can't bear to think of her, all alone, waiting to be found." She straightened her shoulders. "Dear God . . ." as she fought for control. Finally, rising, she said, "I-I think I should like a cup of tea. Will you come down to the kitchen with me?"

He picked up her breakfast tray, and carried it down for her. While she was dealing with the kettle and the teapot, she said, sadly, "She was such a kind soul."

"You told me once that she felt uneasy, passing the pub. Do you think there was anything to that? Or just a general unease?"

"The owner is not a particularly nice man. She said he *leered*. But as I've told you, he never said a word to her or approached her. Much as I dislike him, I don't believe he'd harm her."

But he'd been awake very late last night. Rutledge had watched his lamp put out.

"I've been thinking about getting a dog. I haven't had one since Eric's died just before he enlisted. But what am I to do with it when we have visitors? I can't simply lock him in my bedroom all day."

"You can build a run near the stables for days when there are tours. You'll want one to protect you. Not a lapdog."

"My staff will spoil it terribly, whatever breed I choose," she replied wryly. Then, reverting to the death of Mrs. Lowell, Lady Benton sighed and added, "I shall have to notify Patricia's solicitor. And stop in at the Old Rectory for her copy of her will." Biting her lip, she looked at him. "Would you go with me? We can take my motorcar, then I'll drop you at the stables before I run in to Walmer. I won't keep you long."

She offered him a cup of tea while she changed but he chose instead to walk through the rooms, thinking.

When Lady Benton came down again, dressed for going out, she found Rutledge in the sitting room. She had put a little powder on her face, to hide the ravages of grief, but her eyes were still red. He said, "You told me once that you had a rather troublesome visitor. In what way, troublesome?"

"He didn't appear to be the sort of man who toured historic houses. And he asked questions that seemed out of the ordinary. How many people lived here now, how many rooms were in actual use, how many staircases there were. And he was always slow to keep up. When one of my staff—Mrs. Sutton, I think it was—asked him not to linger after the tour had moved on, he told her he'd paid for his visit and intended to make the most of it. It made the other guests uneasy, and Mrs. Hailey, who was in the next room and overheard the exchange, came to find me. I offered to return his money, but he told me he had no intention of leaving before the end of the tour. Rather aggressively, actually. And so I asked one of the gardeners to help him leave. You could hear the man cursing all the way to the outer door. It was very embarrassing."

"He never came back?"

"No. Not to my knowledge."

She collected her gloves and handbag, and started toward the door.

Going ahead to open it for her, he said, "Do you recall when this was?"

"It was after the airfield was dismantled. June? July? 1919."

"Could you describe this man, do you think?"

"Absolutely." She locked the outer door and he followed her to the stable yard. She was saying, "He was fairly tall—not as tall as you—with dark hair, cold gray eyes, and a scar down one cheek. The left one. A strong man, physically, but Bert, the gardener, was more than his match. The odd thing was, Patricia was just coming up from the crypt, and she thought the man who was waiting for our visitor in the drive seemed familiar. But she only saw him for the briefest moment."

"Did you ask her to describe him? For future reference, if either man returned?"

"I never thought to ask. To tell you the truth, I had a feeling both men had been sent by that man, Wilbur. I told you, I think, that he's been persistent."

"Why would he try to disrupt a tour?" And yet the man was just the sort who might think of forcing her to sell, one way or another. With ghosts in the private garden . . . ?

"If word got around, and the tours fell off, I might be forced to sell the meadow."

"Did Bert, the gardener, see the other man?"

"He must have done."

"Where is Bert now? I'd like to ask him."

"I've no idea, I'm afraid. I had to let the gardening staff go last year. and I don't know where he might be now. So far we've managed, the staff and I, but it's beginning to show. I'll have to find new people soon."

He had just turned the crank and was getting into his motorcar beside her when she began to work with her keys. Taking one off the heavy ring, she handed it to him.

"You ought to have this," she said. "It was Eric's—to the door we just came through. In case."

He took it, added it to his own keys, and then started through the gate, which he'd opened earlier. He saw her scan the field for the horse, but it was empty, as usual.

"I must speak to Henry at the Home Farm. About the horse."

"Do you think Henry had anything to do with it?"

"Oh, no. He's sixty and hardly the sort to play practical jokes. Or put a mare in the wrong field."

At the Old Rectory, he walked through the house while Lady Benton went up to Mrs. Lowell's room to collect the will.

He could swear that no one else had been in the house since he and Lady Benton had searched it the day before. It felt oddly empty now, as if the personality of the owner had faded away with her death. Returning to the parlor, he went to look at the photographs on the round table by the window. They were mostly of Mrs. Lowell with her husband or her parents. None of them appeared to be more recent than 1914.

Hamish was saying, "There was nothing, ye ken, he wanted in the house."

"Or he found it without disturbing anything."

And then Lady Benton was coming down the stairs. He went out into the hall to meet her, and he could see that she'd been crying, but she held up a sheaf of folded papers.

"I so disliked going into her desk to find the will. She was such a private person."

"Still, she knew you'd come for it, if the need arose," he reminded her.

"Yes. There's that."

As they left the house Rutledge took advantage of the moment to ask, "Where did she keep her bicycle?"

"There's a little shed out back. As I mentioned to Inspector Hamilton, I would have noticed if the doors were standing open. But they weren't, they were closed."

"What sort of bicycle did Mrs. Lowell ride?"

"She bought it at the start of the war, I think. I don't know the name of the firm. She had one of the men at the airfield help her attach a basket to the handlebars."

"Who was it? Gerald Dunn?"

"No, one of the other mechanics. I don't think Private Dunn arrived. The men kept coming in for nearly a month, before the squadrons were at full strength. Some were here before the buildings were even completed. That autumn was rather chaotic, if you remember."

He did. England had been scrambling to keep the Germans from cutting off the French coast roads, the Expeditionary Force fighting to hold on as Belgium collapsed.

"What sort of basket?"

"A rather nice wicker one. And it had a blue ribbon woven into the side at the top. Her workmanship."

Then he hadn't imagined it after all. The bicycle had been there . . .

9

Rutledge waited in the stable yard until Lady Benton drove her motorcar out of the shed, then closed the gate after both of them passed through. She waved a hand in thanks, and started up the lane.

He followed.

In Walmer, he saw her motorcar again, outside a house with a solicitor's plate beside the door.

Driving on, he went to look for the young woman who worked at The Salt Cellar. But he didn't see her on the street or coming and going from the shops.

"Later," Hamish told him. "When she walks down to the pub."

Impatient to speak again to Wister, he went back to the hotel to leave the motorcar and then had a simple lunch. At five minutes before two, he was standing again outside the door to the doctor's surgery.

He was drying his hands when he opened the door to Rutledge.

"There isn't much to tell you," he said, leading the way to a back room. There, Patricia Lowell lay under a sheet. "A blow on the head while she was still alive. And she was alive as well when she was hanged. Possibly unconscious, but alive. Cause of death, strangulation.

She was hauled up after the noose was put around her neck, she didn't kick that stool out from under her feet. There was no fall, to end it quickly."

Rutledge said, "A cruel way for her to die. But this eliminates the possibility of suicide."

"Yes. It does. A clumsy attempt at covering up a crime." He crossed to the table and lifted a portion of the sheet. "The reason I believe she was unconscious is that I see no defensive wounds. That would be more consistent with suicide, of course. But then there was this."

He dropped the sheet in place and crossed to a table where her clothes lay spread out.

"That's the belt to the dress she was wearing. And look here, on the prong that closes it."

Rutledge leaned forward. "It appears to be several strands of thread."

"Yes. Picture this—she's dazed or unconscious. He can't leave her where she is—or he can't take her just now to the shed, because it was still light enough for him to be seen with her. And so he puts her over his shoulder and carries her somewhere until it's dark. And that belt buckle pulls a few threads from his coat."

"It appears to be khaki. A uniform, then?"

"More likely an Army greatcoat. The thickness of the wool."

Half the ex-soldiers wandering the countryside, looking for work, wore greatcoats from the war. They were warm.

"If she was taken somewhere, surely she would have regained consciousness before being taken to the airfield."

"Yes, I'm coming to that. Her killer must have given her something to drink. Water, tea, I haven't looked yet. And put something in it to knock her out."

"Whisky?"

"Yes, that's more likely to cover the taste. Laudanum, at a guess. Although one doesn't wander the countryside as a rule with a vial of opiates in his pocket. Ready to give to a victim."

"Unless," Rutledge said slowly, "he's still bothered by an old war wound to have something at hand to keep him going."

"I agree. The khaki thread, the laudanum for a war wound. An ex-soldier?"

"Or someone still serving." Rutledge shook his head. "Or just now demobbed. I need a list of men associated with the airfield."

Wister ran a hand through his hair. "I'm not comfortable asking this. But do you think this is the first time he's killed?"

Rutledge said, giving it some thought, "He was calm enough to carry out Patricia Lowell's hanging. That would have needed a strong nerve." He was already considering what he knew of that stretch of road, any buildings that a killer would have had access to. The pub? Farm outbuildings, sheds . . .

"Death is a part of life. But I hate to cut open the young. It's somehow wrong."

Rutledge looked across at him. "Yet you chose medicine."

"I did. It was the war that cooled my joy in it." He walked back to the table and stared at the sheet covering the body of Mrs. Lowell. "Such a pity."

"It is. Thank you. Do you mind if I take her belt with me, along with that strand of thread?"

"No, not at all." Wister hesitated. "Not to be a rumor monger, but should I have a look at you? I've heard you had a fall last night."

Rutledge knew he should agree to be examined. But he said, "I'm all right. I'll see a doctor in London if need be."

"The cut on your forehead is all right. But let's leave this poor lady in peace, and step into the next room. If you're driving to London, you'll be glad of a bit of tape."

As it happened, Dr. Wister was right. Sitting for several hours behind the wheel of the motorcar, his ribs began to protest long before he reached London.

There were a number of ways to achieve what he wanted to do. The quickest way was to call on Haldane. And Rutledge was reluctant to leave Lady Benton for too long, just after Mrs. Lowell's death.

He was even more reluctant to speak to Haldane.

The man lived on a quiet street in Chelsea, the door guarded by his manservant. Rutledge's first impression on meeting the manservant—he was hardly a butler or a valet—was that he had once been Haldane's batman and had chosen to remain with him once the war was over.

Haldane himself claimed to have been in the Foot Police, but it was more likely that he had been a high-ranking member of Intelligence. His contacts were too wide and too well placed to be those of a simple military policeman.

Rutledge had met him quite by accident in the course of an inquiry into a murder that had its roots outside England, where he himself couldn't travel. He'd asked Haldane for information, and in a roundabout way it had been supplied. But Rutledge had been very, very careful not to draw on that source unless there was no other way of learning how the war and murder might have come together. And he could never be sure of Haldane's help. Sometimes he was told blandly that Haldane was not at home.

There was another reason for him to be chary of asking anything of the man. Rutledge had always felt that any service Haldane rendered was a personal debt rather than assistance to the Yard, and the price of that service would inevitably be collected at some point in the future. It had never been addressed in words, but there was something in the man that Rutledge, a soldier himself, recognized: a sense of duty that bordered on the ruthless.

When he left his motorcar and went up the short walk to the door, it was opened almost as soon as he'd let the knocker fall against its plate.

"Good morning, sir."

"I've come to call on Haldane." Rutledge had never known any other name, Christian or surname, by which to address him. And wondered sometimes if even that was fictitious.

"If you will step in, sir, I'll see if he's receiving visitors."

To Rutledge's ears that had always struck him as regal rather than social.

He nodded and moved into the foyer.

After several minutes, the man returned. "He will see you now, sir."

And Rutledge was admitted to the large study where Haldane was often found working. He was setting some papers aside as Rutledge entered, careful to turn them facedown so that their contents couldn't be read across the desk.

He greeted Rutledge as quietly as he always did, and pointed to the chair in front of the desk, his face unreadable. Hamish had commented once that he would not choose to play cards with Haldane. Rutledge had agreed.

"How can I help you?"

"There's a small airfield just north of Walmer, on the Essex coast."

"Yes, I seem to remember that its purpose was to watch for Zeppelins, guard the coast, and escort troop and supply ships crossing the Channel. That changed with the war. Some fine pilots in that squadron."

"I need a list of personnel posted there. From late 1916 to the end of the war."

"That's a rather impressive request. Why do you need it?"

"A man was killed in a car crash during the war, and another was listed as a deserter. The officer in charge of the airfield took his own life at war's end. Now a woman has been killed, her body left in one of the remaining sheds on the site. By themselves they can be explained away. Together, they raise questions."

"And you believe that these are somehow connected with the men who were posted to the airfield?"

"I don't know," Rutledge replied truthfully. "So far I haven't found any direct connection with Walmer itself. That leaves the airfield."

"Or the house that stands nearby."

Rutledge hid his surprise. Haldane knew about the Abbey. Why?

"It can't be discounted."

"Let me see what I can do. With no promise of results, you understand."

"Absolutely."

"Come back tomorrow at ten."

It was a dismissal, and Rutledge left.

As he was walking back toward the motorcar, Hamish said, "He doesna' tell you what's going on in his heid. It would be helpful if he did."

Rutledge smiled grimly. Haldane had actually told him more than was intended.

He debated going to the Yard, but chose to drive on to his flat instead. There would be questions about his return to London when he was expected to be conducting an inquiry in Essex.

As he turned the crank and got into the motorcar, he tried to imagine explaining Haldane to Markham.

For that matter, he himself was never really certain why Haldane was willing to provide information to a mere Inspector at the Yard. Unless he had very good reasons of his own for doing it. If nothing else, it might allow him to clarify something where he didn't wish his own hand to be seen.

In this case, did Haldane's cooperation have to do with Major Dinsmore's death?

There were several letters waiting for Rutledge on the silver tray where his daily put his post, and he read through them, then spent two hours working on his notes. The more he looked at them, the less he felt he understood about what was happening in Walmer. Or to be more precise, the Abbey. Where could he find the key that would unlock the secrets surrounding it?

Hamish said, "Yon Lady Benton is the center of it. Ye're tae close to see it."

If that were true, then she was in danger. But she was connected with the Chief Constable, if only through her dead son. She couldn't be killed without raising half the county to find the person who had done it.

Or so he told himself. Still, he hadn't counted on being away overnight, and he hadn't warned her to be careful while he was in London.

In his mind's eye he kept seeing the still body of Patricia Lowell under the sheet in Dr. Wister's surgery. He had a niggling feeling that his arrival might have triggered her death, that there might have been something she knew—but didn't know the importance of it. And she had had to die before she became aware of it. But what could someone like Mrs. Lowell know? A quiet widow who worked at the Abbey, seldom went into Walmer, and spent most of her free time alone? She was uneasy, passing The Monk's Choice—if she had been interfered with, it would have been the first place he, Rutledge, would have looked. But he couldn't quite see Newbold as a killer. Besides, there appeared to be no motive. So far.

Restless, he paced the floor, was tempted to go out to dine, and then remembered that he wasn't supposed to be in London. And Hamish, reflecting his unease, was there, waiting for him in the dark.

It was a long night.

It was hard enough to endure in an hotel somewhere in England. Harder still when he knew that in the trunk beneath his bed was respite in the form of his service revolver.

In the morning, he rose early in spite of lying awake for hours, staring at the ceiling, reliving the war in his head.

And he was on Haldane's doorstep at ten sharp.

The manservant opened the door at his knock and said, "He asks you to forgive him for not meeting you as promised." He produced a blank white card and a pen. "If you will leave your direction, he will contact you as soon as possible."

There was nothing to do but leave the name of the hotel in Walmer. As he wrote that down, he had the feeling that Haldane could find him in the mountains of Peru, if need be.

The man thanked him and shut the door.

Rutledge was irritated. There had been no need to stop over in London last night. He went back to his flat and put clean clothes in a smaller valise and took it out to the motorcar, put new batteries in his torch, and closed the boot. Then he went back inside to leave a note for the daily, who would be coming in the afternoon.

He was just capping his pen and putting it in the pocket of his coat when there was a knock at his door. It was so light a tap that he almost didn't hear it. Thinking that Haldane might have sent a message, hoping to catch him while he was still in London, Rutledge strode back through the flat and opened the door.

Kate Gordon was standing there, her face pale, her mouth set in a resolute line. And then he noticed the valise at her feet.

His surprise showed before he could stop himself, and she said, "I know, I'm so sorry, Ian, but I stopped at Frances's house first, and she wasn't in. Could you do me a very great favor? I hesitate to ask, but I can't think of anyone else to turn to."

"Kate, yes, of course, anything," he said, and stepped aside. "Come in. We can't talk in the open doorway."

She stood there, uncertain. "Your neighbors will be shocked."

He smiled. "Let them be."

But there was no answering smile. He knew then that whatever had happened, Kate was in desperate need. He couldn't imagine what it was that had brought her here. He could only be grateful that she had trusted him enough to come to him.

She stepped into his flat, leaving her valise by the door.

"Please, sit down, Kate. Would you like a cup of tea?" He tried for a light note. "I learned how to fend for myself in the trenches."

She shook her head, adding wryly, "I probably need a whisky more than I need tea. It's what my father always turns to in times of stress."

He sat down across from her. "What is it, Kate, what's happened?" he asked gently.

She took a deep breath. "Would you mind terribly taking me to an hotel, posing as my brother, and finding a room for me? It would shock my grandmother no end if I appeared there alone. And I've never done it before. There was never any need."

"Of course I will, but first you must tell me what's wrong."

She looked away, blinking back angry tears. "My father and I quar-reled again, you see. It was rather awful this time. And at the end of it, he told me to leave the house. I quickly put what I needed in my valise and left. He expected me to change my mind as soon as the door shut behind me—he expected me to beg. Ian, I couldn't. I have money of my own, I thought I might go to an hotel until he calms down. My mother took his part—she likes Thomas, and she thinks I should be grateful that he wants to marry me. And so I may have to wait until *both* of them come around."

This time Rutledge was able to control his face. "Does Thomas know how you feel about him?" He had no idea who this man was.

"I hope not—he's a thoroughly nice man, Ian, and I shouldn't wish to hurt him. But I don't *care* for him—well, not enough to marry him." She bit her lip. "That sounds very ungrateful, but I'm old enough to know my own mind, I'm not just out, and carried away by my first proposal. Only Thomas hasn't proposed—yet. He did ask my father for his blessing. And my father gave it. Without asking me how I felt."

Thomas was a lackluster suitor, in Rutledge's opinion.

Keeping that to himself, he said, "Do you have friends you could turn to?"

"I can't ask them. They would find themselves in trouble with their own families. I went to Frances, because she isn't Army, and if she and her husband took me to an hotel, my father couldn't make their lives unpleasant."

"She's in Cornwall, visiting friends," he told Kate, his mind work-ing swiftly as he tried to sort out what he must do. "But I don't feel an hotel is the answer. For one thing, you'd be forced to take your meals there, and someone might see you and tell your parents." He wondered what Melinda would think if he arrived on her doorstep with Kate. "I have a friend in Kent. You might recall her from the engagement party at Jean's home. Melinda Crawford?"

She frowned. "Oh—yes, I remember Jean telling me that you'd pro-posed to her in Mrs. Crawford's lovely gardens. And my father was especially pleased to be introduced to her at the engagement party. She's something of a legend in Army circles."

He laughed. "She wouldn't like being called a legend. But she will keep you safe, and she's infinitely respectable. Not even your father would dare to lay siege to you there."

She smiled this time. "That's all very well, but she's Army, Ian. She might not wish to cross my father. Besides, she doesn't know me, and I shouldn't care to impose."

"Melinda is friends with half the General Staff. Your father might not wish to cross *her*."

The smile faded. "Did I do the right thing, Ian? I've upset my family, heaven only knows what Thomas will think of me. I've wandered about London valise in hand, trying to make the best of it. But this isn't 1910 when whatever Papa says is law. I'm of age, I can choose my own future."

She wanted reassurance.

"I don't know how I would feel if I had a daughter and she quarreled with me. But Frances was free to marry where she pleased, and no one—least of all me—would have expected her to do anything else. Still, I'd have spoken up if I'd believed that her choice was going to bring her unhappiness. I had a duty there." He didn't add that Frances had nearly made the wrong choice, and had come to him for advice. That was his sister's confidence, not to be shared even with Kate.

"Thank you," she said simply. "Thomas would be good to me. Kind. I don't think he would mind that I didn't love him. But I would care. And I would never be able to tell him what I felt. It would hurt him terribly to *know*. I've thought it through, you see. This was no mad or rash decision, when my father told me to go."

"Catch your breath, then we'll leave for Kent straightaway. And Kate—if you changed your mind—if you decided you wished to go home—you can depend on Melinda to arrange everything. She wouldn't try to persuade you either way."

"But the Yard–"

"Never mind the Yard. I'm in Essex at the moment. Kent is on my way."

———

Rutledge would never forget Melinda's expression when he arrived on her doorstep with an anxious Kate Gordon standing just behind him.

She had heartily disliked Jean. That made no difference, as he knew it wouldn't. Melinda took in the scene, smiled warmly, and said, "How lovely, Ian, you've brought me company. I've had no one to talk to for a fortnight."

And she swept Kate into the house, leaving him to follow, while Shanta came out to scoop up Kate's valise. She raised her eyebrows, asking if his own valise was still in the motorcar boot, but he shook his head slightly, and she disappeared with Kate's.

Rutledge stayed until he was sure Kate was comfortable. And by the time he left, Kate was already ensconced in Melinda's favorite sitting room, and no longer anxious. There was color in her face again, and less strain in her voice. The problem hadn't gone away, but she was calm enough to cope.

Melinda walked to the door with him, and before he could apologize for arriving with no warning, she said quietly, "You did the right thing, Ian. I'll see to her."

And lifted her cheek for him to kiss.

As he reversed and went down the long drive, Hamish said, "Ye ken, ye've made an enemy of yon lass's father."

"What else could I have done? Persuaded her to return to her house? Perhaps I should have done. It was probably my duty as a policeman. But Kate was in distress."

She had come to him as a friend—and yet he had had to be almost avuncular in comforting her. Thank God he'd thought about Melinda. It would, he believed, allow both Kate and her family to come to terms with her refusal to marry Thomas Whoeverhewas. And she had been spared the unpleasantness of spending days if not weeks in an hotel, a young woman on her own.

He would have to resist the temptation of telephoning Melinda on any excuse to find out how Kate was faring.

Coming out on the main road, Rutledge tried to concentrate on traveling back to Essex. His thoughts stubbornly refused to leave Kent behind.

Hamilton had left a curt note at the hotel desk. The clerk handed it to Rutledge as he came through Reception and started toward the staircase.

Unfolding it, Rutledge saw the black dash of words across the page. *Where the hell are you?*

Crumpling the note in his fingers, he thanked the clerk and went up to his room to leave his valise.

That done, he went to find the Inspector.

He wasn't in his office, and the desk sergeant shook his head when Rutledge asked for him.

"He was called out to Abbey. Early this morning. He hasn't come back."

"What's happened?" Rutledge snapped.

"I dunno, sir. He was summoned."

Rutledge thanked the Sergeant and left. Cursing himself for being away overnight.

He drove too fast, his mind churning. *He should have warned her . . .*

When he arrived at the Abbey gates, they were standing wide. Not a good sign . . .

He pulled in, saw the Hamilton bicycle resting against the steps, and went to knock at the heavy door. As he waited for someone to come, he realized, looking around, that there were no visitors this Friday afternoon.

There had been none yesterday . . .

He turned as the door swung open. Inspector Hamilton stood there.

"You just missed Wister," he said tersely. "You'd better come in."

"Why was Wister called to the Hall?"

"It's Lady Benton." Hamilton waited until Rutledge had stepped into the Hall. "Mrs. Hailey is with her."

"What has happened?" At least, he thought in a corner of his mind, she wasn't dead . . .

"You'd better ask her yourself. She won't tell me anything."

With Hamilton at his heels, Rutledge set out through the public rooms to the stairs at the far end, expecting to find Lady Benton in her sitting room. But she wasn't there. Without a word, he went to the staircase just beyond, took them two at a time, and was hurrying down the passage to the bedroom she used.

Mrs. Hailey came to the door.

"She's asleep. Don't wake her," she said in a whisper. With a last glance over her shoulder, she stepped into the passage, closing the bedroom door behind her.

"Damn it, what happened?" Rutledge demanded for the second time.

"I told you," she said, vehemently, "that she wasn't safe alone here in this house. Just look at it! Room after room, no lamps lit for fear of fire, and she walked through them as if she can see in the dark. All hours of the day or night. It was trouble waiting to happen—"

He cut her short. "Is she all right?"

"No thanks to you," Mrs. Hailey said, still incensed.

Rutledge made to move past her, intending to open the bedroom door and walk in, but Mrs. Hailey caught his arm.

"No, let her sleep."

He looked from the housekeeper to Inspector Hamilton. "I'll go in there and shake her awake if someone doesn't tell me what happened to her."

He meant it. It was clear in his voice and in his face. Even in the dimly lit passage.

"We were expecting a tour, this morning. It had been booked for weeks. She was up early, seeing to it that all was well. And since Mrs. Lowell's death—"

"Come to the point," he snapped.

"She was going down into the crypt." Hamilton stepped in. "The stairs there twist and turn. She fell. It was Mrs. Hailey who found her there, when she came in at eight. She wouldn't leave Lady Benton until one of the other ladies arrived. A Mrs. Jenkins. Mrs. Hailey sent her straight to the surgery. Wister was dressing a farmer's wound, and he came at once."

"How badly is she hurt?"

"She hit her head, bruised a shoulder, twisted her knee. She was still unconscious when Wister got here. He wanted to take her to his surgery, but Mrs. Hailey here didn't want her moved. Wister's nurse sent word that he had gone out to the Abbey, and I immediately followed. Together we got her to her bed, once Wister was sure she could be moved. I stopped at the hotel on my way, to let you know as well, but the clerk told me you hadn't been in for dinner or for breakfast."

His tone was accusing.

"I was in London," Rutledge answered curtly.

He turned to Mrs. Hailey. "What did she tell you?"

"She was confused at first, telling me to go—I couldn't follow what she was saying, her words were slurred. Only half conscious, really."

Rutledge didn't believe her. Glancing at Hamilton, he said, "Let her sleep, then. Bring me a chair, and I'll sit here in the passage until she's awake."

They had been speaking quietly, some ten or twelve feet from the bedroom door.

When it opened behind them, they turned as one, caught off guard.

Lady Benton was standing on the threshold. With the glare of the afternoon sun behind her, it was difficult to see her clearly.

Her hair down, her clothes—usually so perfect, as befitted her station—were rumpled, and there was a dark splotch on her skirt, where her knee had bled.

Rutledge was swiftly revising his opinion about what Mrs. Hailey had told them.

As she opened the door a little wider, he could also see the cut on her forehead, a scrape on her chin. Or rather the dried blood that marked them.

Into the uncomfortable silence, she said wearily. "Go away, all of you. Yes, you as well, Margaret. And leave me in peace for a bit."

With that she closed her door firmly—and they could hear the distinctive *click* of the lock that shut them out.

Mrs. Hailey looked from Hamilton to Rutledge, and said, "Now look what you've done." And without waiting for an answer, she marched away down the passage.

Hamilton watched her go, then said to Rutledge, "Can you give me a lift back into Walmer? I don't relish pedaling all the way back."

It was the last thing Rutledge wished to do, but he said, "Yes, of course."

They walked in silence back to the stairs and the door leading to the stables.

"The main door is still bolted, I think. And my motorcar is just there by the stables. We'll fetch the bicycle as we leave."

Hamilton stepped outside, and as Rutledge shut the door behind them, he said, "What do you make of this fall? An accident?"

"We can't be sure until we speak to her."

Hamilton turned the crank and then closed the stable yard gate behind them.

"What do you make of all this? Ghosts on the lawn, Mrs. Lowell killed. And for all we know, Lady Benton attacked in her own house."

"I thought it was a fall?"

"Early days," Hamilton said darkly as they went up the lane.

"That's assuming someone managed to get in and lie in wait."

"It's possible. I had a look around. Anyone could force those old locks."

"*Had* anyone broken in?"

"No. Not that I could see. But Wister told me Lady Benton might have been seriously injured. She went down those steps with some force. He was surprised nothing was broken."

Rutledge turned to look at him. "Truly?"

"He said if she hadn't somehow had the instinct to twist at the last minute, she might have snapped her neck." Hamilton shook his head. "There's something about that house. All those rooms, a labyrinth of them. With no life in them unless a tour walks through. Like something dead, left to rot. You could lose half a regiment in there, and not find them for days."

"I've been through nearly every room in that house. There's nothing that I can find to account for anything that's happened. And yet it's clear the house is at the center of what's going on. Or the airfield. I haven't decided which, to tell the truth." They were on the main road now.

"God knows there's enough in that house to make a poor man rich. And you wouldn't have to be greedy about it. I don't know much about the paintings, but even I can see the silver everywhere. Tea services—those platters—that bloody great ship on the dining room table. Just the inkwells and the serving spoons would be enough to set up most people for life."

Rutledge shook his head. "It would be hard to sell many of the treasures. They've been cataloged for death duties twice over. Still, if you know someone who could melt it down, you could sell the silver itself."

"Did you see that cabinet in the library? An entire fox hunt—riders, dogs, trees, even a grinning fox—all in silver. My wife would faint if I brought that home one Wednesday after market day." Then, more serious, he added, "If most objects would be hard to sell, because they are famous, just what is someone after in that house?"

"I don't know. Nor do I know what the airfield has to do with anything."

They stopped for the Inspector's bicycle, and Hamilton said morosely, after it had been lashed to the boot, "My grandfather always claimed there was Viking treasure to be found somewhere here. There was a famous battle, you know. Long before the Normans came. The Anglo-Saxons against the Vikings. Fairly bloody, but the Vikings won. My grandfather said that while they were fighting, an Anglo-Saxon thane found their treasure ship, took everything out of it, and hid it. Then he was killed in the battle, and the secret went with him. But none of that appears in any history of Walmer. Yet the story survived all these centuries."

There were stories of buried treasure all over the country. If the monks hadn't buried it before being attacked, the invader had buried his plunder before he did battle. King John was even said to have lost the English treasury when he crossed The Wash in Norfolk.

"If that was what they were after, someone would have been digging up the meadow every night after dark. Or the Abbey gardens. No, if something is buried there, it has nothing to do with Vikings. But it's worth killing for. And that's what worries me."

Even as he said the words, Rutledge had a sudden image of Mrs. Dunn's worn face, as she asked him to find out what had become of her son . . .

Had Patricia Lowell somehow learned where he was? Alive or dead . . . And was killed before she could tell anyone?

IO

As soon as he'd seen Hamilton safely home, and the bicycle unloaded, Rutledge turned around and drove back to the Abbey. He left his motorcar down by the hedge where it wouldn't be seen and walked back to the house.

He let himself in with the key Lady Benton had given him, and after standing in the stairwell, listening, he quietly made his way through the rooms to the great hall. The stained glass in the window above the main door made a pretty pattern against the floor as he went to the stairs leading down to the undercroft.

He had brought his torch with him, and now he scanned the steps carefully.

There was no evidence that someone had laid a wire across, hardly visible in the dimness of the stairwell, to trip up Lady Benton or anyone else who started down.

Only partly satisfied, he turned the light against the far wall, finding the place where Lady Benton had struck her forehead as she lost her balance. There was still a faint smear of blood on the rough stone surface.

The account he'd been given matched what he'd found here, and he flicked off his torch, preparing to leave.

As he started back up the steps, he nearly ran straight into Lady Benton.

"I'm sorry—"

His words clashed with hers. "I thought you might be here—"

She had pinned up her hair, but she still wore the clothes he'd seen earlier.

"I thought there might be signs that someone had left a wire across the steps."

Lady Benton shook her head. "I was pushed, Inspector. I distinctly felt a hand against my back. And before I could do anything to prevent it, I went headlong."

Rutledge said, "Forgive me. But are you sure?"

"It was warm. Human. Not my imagination. And whoever it was, meant for me to fall and be seriously hurt. If the stairs hadn't curved, I'd have gone all the way to the bottom. The floor down there is flagstone."

She turned to walk back through the hall, and he followed her. "That means that someone is in this house. I've just been round to all the doors, and they're locked. Just as they were last night. How, then, did he get in? And—is he still here?"

"I don't know. I came back to find out."

"Do you have any idea just how many places one can hide in this house? I do. Eric loved to play hide-and-seek with his friends from school. We'd have them for a weekend. And as long as they didn't break anything in the state rooms, they had the run of the house."

They were walking to her sitting room, and when they reached it, she went to the decanter on a table by the hearth and poured two whiskies, one for herself and the other for him.

"Don't tell me you can't drink it because you're on duty," she said brusquely. "I prefer not to drink alone. It's a dangerous habit to fall into."

"You were unconscious. Do you think whisky is a good idea?"

"We'll soon find out. The tea Margaret brought me didn't help me. Or harm me."

She sat down in her favorite chair. "Will you spend the night in the house, Inspector? For the first time, I am not comfortable in my own home."

"I think it might be a very good idea."

"Thank you."

He said after taking a sip of his whisky, "Do you trust Margaret?"

She stared at him. "What do you mean, trust her?"

"She's in your confidence. She knows your schedule. She knows your way of doing things. She's often, so you told me earlier, the last person to leave."

"Of course I trust her. But I'm no fool, either. I inspect the doors every night. I read the ledger of guests, the money we've taken in, I keep a watchful eye on my house and my accounts." She sighed. "I have to depend on someone. I believe Margaret deserves the trust I have in her."

Rutledge took that with a grain of salt, but said nothing.

When she had finished her whisky, she rose and set her empty glass on the tray. "We might as well start with the ground floor."

He finished his glass as well, handed it to her. "The monks in abbeys that were in danger from invaders often had a way of escaping if they were trapped in the church. Is there anything like that here?"

"No. Nor is there a priest hole. The Bentons were thoroughly Protestant, which is why they were in King Henry's favor."

"You're certain of that?"

"When his father died, my husband went through archives. If he'd found any such thing, he'd have told me. And Eric."

Then someone with access to this house was involved, he thought to himself.

Aloud he said, "You gave me a key to one door. Who else have you given keys to?"

"You make it sound like an accusation. Only Margaret has a key, and that's to the kitchen door."

"Could someone have copied hers when she was occupied elsewhere? One of the staff, for instance. Or even a visitor."

For the first time, she looked away. "I gave one to Roger. Captain Nelson. So that he could use the library whenever he liked."

"To which door?"

"The terrace doors. They're closest to the library. He wouldn't disturb me, if he couldn't sleep and wanted a book. Eric liked to read late at night too . . ." Her voice trailed off, and as she faced Rutledge again, her eyes were sad.

"What happened to his keys, after the crash?"

"I—I never thought about that," she said in surprise. "When the Major boxed up Roger's things, he returned the two books Roger had borrowed. It didn't occur to me to ask for my key as well."

And the "ghost" had crossed to the terrace doors, after he'd appeared to kill someone. Lady Benton had been frightened because in one part of her mind she remembered that he'd had a key when the Captain was alive.

Who had that key now?

"I must speak to Wister. He'll know where Nelson's belongings were sent." But the Captain had been buried in Walmer. Did that mean there had been no one to claim his personal effects?

Rutledge said, thinking aloud, "Why was the Captain buried in Walmer?"

"It was his sister's choice. It was during the war, travel was difficult."

As he prepared to leave, he said, "You ought to rest. Lock your bedroom door. I will always let you know if I come back to the house."

"You didn't this time."

"You asked us to leave you in peace. I wanted to see where you'd fallen."

"To be sure it wasn't a figment of my imagination, like the ghosts in the garden?" she asked ruefully.

He smiled. "I think your ghosts were real, and so was the hand at your back."

"I'm glad to know that. I was beginning to fear—" She stopped. "Thank you."

———

Wister was at home, finishing a late dinner, when Rutledge came to his door.

"Is there no peace?" But he invited Rutledge into his surgery, and said, "It was a nasty fall, but I don't believe there was serious damage done. Although it could have been."

"I agree." He took the chair Wister pointed to. "I've come to ask what became of Captain Nelson's personal effects. He's buried here, he wasn't sent home."

"I've told you, I wasn't here at the time. But according to his file, he had no family in England. That's why he was buried here. Afterward, Major Dinsmore and Dr. Gregson apparently decided to give most of his things—clothing, and the like—to the church for use where they might be needed. The more personal belongings were sealed in a box, in the event someone came forward to claim them, later on." He gestured toward the ceiling. "I expect they have long since been relegated to the attic. Want to find out?"

"Absolutely."

And so they climbed the stairs to the attic floor and began to search.

"I haven't been up here," Wister was saying as they looked into another box. "I arrived with two valises and my medical kit, but Gregson was a widower, and I simply took over his house, his medical books, and his surgery until such time as I could choose furnishings of my own. So far, there's never seemed to be a good reason to do that. I expect if I ever marry, my wife will be more than glad to sort that out."

Rutledge laughed and passed another box Wister's way. So far they had found Christmas ornaments, trunks of clothing belonging to Gregson and his wife, and odds and ends that had been relegated to the attic over the years of their own marriage.

And then Wister said, "Look here. This could be it."

Rutledge came across to see what he'd found. It was a small black metal box, the key still in the lock. He turned it and lifted the lid.

Inside was an assortment of small things. A man's belongings and military effects. Cuff links, a wristwatch, a compass, a Webley revolver, his uniform insignia, including a medal, a photograph of a woman who appeared to be Nelson's mother, a wallet with several pound notes and coins still in it, a fountain pen of good quality, a dozen other odds and ends, pathetic reminders of a hero's life—and a ring of keys.

"Ah," Rutledge said. "Do you mind if I borrow these?"

"The airfield is gone. I doubt they'll fit anything now. But go ahead."

Rutledge thanked him, and they dusted their hands and knees as they started for the stairs. "What became of the wrecked motorcar?"

Wister shook his head. "Damned if I know. I expect it was sold for scrap. Apparently, it was beyond redemption."

At the hotel, Rutledge took out the ring of keys and began to sort through them. He couldn't be sure what all of them might have opened. And in the end, he scooped them up, returned them to the ring, and was starting to leave the room when he noticed something on the coverlet where he'd been sitting.

A tiny bit of yellow something. Wax? From the cheap candles they'd used in the trenches and elsewhere?

He rolled it in his fingers, but it fell apart, pieces too tiny to tell him just what it was. Yet he was nearly certain that it hadn't been on the bed when he sat down. Nearly certain that he'd have noticed it . . .

The only way to test the keys, he told himself, was to take them to the Abbey.

He was nearly out of petrol, but it was still Sunday, and he could only hope that he had enough to last until Monday.

When he reached the Abbey stable yard, he drove on to the hedge. Getting out of the motorcar, he noticed a man crossing the field where the horse had been.

Rutledge climbed the fencing and started toward him. As if the man sensed someone else in his vicinity, he turned, then stopped short.

"Thought you was her ladyship," he said gruffly as Rutledge hailed him. "Who are you?"

"A friend," he said, when he was closer.

The man was dressed in work clothes. Medium height, gray hair, still streaked with the sandy color it had once been, a beard that needed shaving, and blue eyes, one of them clouded by cataracts. Still, his shoulders were straight and strong for his age, and he'd walked like a man used to long distances on foot.

"You must be Henry," Rutledge said, remembering that Lady Benton had used his name.

"Mr. Warren to you," the man retorted, having looked Rutledge over. "Never saw you before."

"No, I've only been here a few days. In fact, I was here when Lady Benton saw the mare in this field. She said it was winter pasture, and she needed to speak with you about that."

"Well, if she'd come herself, I'd have been happy to tell her."

"I'm afraid she had a fall, and hasn't felt well enough to pay you a visit."

"Why didn't you say so, to start. The mare is in foal. I've kept her close to the house, because her last foaling was difficult, and I wished to keep an eye on her. Some fool left the gate open, and she must have wandered in. No harm done, you must tell her ladyship."

"Who works for you at the farm?"

"My daughter and her son. And a lad from the next village over. He's all right. Better than my grandson was, come to that."

"Could it have been someone else, playing a prank?"

"I do hope not!" he retorted. "She's a valuable mare."

Rutledge thanked him, and went back to the lane, crossing over into the stable yard. He was careful as he made his way around the house to stay as close to the walls as the various plantings and borders allowed. He avoided leaving a footprint in the soft earth, keeping to the grass.

At each door he passed, he tried the keys on Captain Nelson's ring, but none of them fit until he reached the terrace doors. There, as he began to insert a key into the lock, the door moved under his hand. He stood there for a moment, then pulled it wider. No one spoke—the room appeared to be empty.

He stepped inside.

This was a garden room, high ceilinged, with wicker furnishings and wrought iron tables. The wallpaper was a pale green, with painted trees full of painted birds and flowers. A welcoming room, bright in the late afternoon sunlight. There were lamps on the tables, and if the pale green drapes were open, there was a lovely view out across the private garden. A low shelf by one of the chairs held several books. He went to them and found that they were about famous English gardens, with sketches and drawings of each.

He returned them to the shelf and went to the tall double doors at the back of the room. On this side, the paneling was painted, with a tall great white egret facing each other on each one. The knobs were elegantly made wrought iron feathers.

When he opened them, he found himself in a passage, and decided not to explore farther. But the door facing him across it was ajar, and he looked in.

The large room was filled with glass-fronted cases full of leather-bound books. There were comfortable chairs and a desk in the center of the room, lamps on several tables, and a sliding ladder on railings that ran down each side, to allow access to the upper shelves. These, he thought, held the older, more fragile books. A map table stood against the far wall.

This then was why Captain Nelson had had a key to this door. As Lady Benton had said, he could use the library without disturbing her.

Then he went back the way he'd come, stepped out on the terrace, and while the doors were still ajar, tried the keys here as well. But there was no fit. He left the double doors as he'd found them, and had just stepped down from the terrace when the sound of voices carried to him from the garden room. Mrs. Hailey, he thought, speaking to one of the staff. He moved away quickly.

He finished testing the keys at the remaining doors, but whatever they were intended to open, the keys matched nothing here. It was more likely that they belonged to the long-vanished buildings of the airfield. Then where was the key Nelson had used?

Rutledge left the Abbey.

As he came to the junction where the lane met the road, he headed back toward The Monk's Choice. He was still unsatisfied with Newbold's answers.

He left the motorcar on the road and walked across the yard to the door. Intending to give no warning that he was coming. He'd raised his hand to knock when he heard voices.

At first they were indistinct, as if the speakers were in the kitchen. And then they began to move closer to the door. Rutledge could hear a man's voice, gruff, angry—cornered. Curious to know who might be there with Newbold, he reached for the latch.

And a woman's voice—lighter, demanding—stopped him.

He stayed there, listening, trying to pick out words. Leaning closer, he heard the woman say, "Mrs. Lowell was a *friend*!"

And the door opened in his face.

Rutledge and Lady Benton stared, speechless, at each other. And over her shoulder Newbold stood there in the dimness of the room, grinning.

She collected herself with an effort. "I don't care to walk back to the Abbey. Do you mind taking me there?"

He'd believed that she was resting. God knew where she thought he was, although he'd been under her windows not a quarter of an hour ago, opening the terrace doors.

Rutledge said tersely, "Wait in the motorcar." And stepped aside so that she could walk past him.

Without a word, her head high, shoulders squared, she did as he'd asked. But he watched her until she got in and took her seat. Then he turned back to the pub's owner. The grin had gone, and there was uncertainty in the man's face now.

Rutledge said, "Two nights ago, there were two men nearby with a bicycle belonging to a murder victim. Your light was on at the time. Tell me what you know about them."

There was something in his voice—the officer on the battlefield— that reflected his anger, and Newbold backed up against the bar as Rutledge stepped into the room.

"I wasn't awake. Whoever says I was is lying."

"I watched the light go out."

Newbold said, "I don't know anything about that."

"Then I'll take you to London, to answer there. Turn around."

Rutledge didn't have his cuffs with him—they were in the motorcar standing across the road. But the man believed him.

"All right. Yes. I was awake. I told you before, I had a toothache. I don't know anything about men and bicycles."

"They were not fifty yards from this building. And they were quarrelling. And you were one of them." He couldn't be certain about that, but it was worth testing the waters. "When the other man walked away, you went inside, shut your door, and turned off your bedroom light. I want to know what became of that bicycle? It's evidence in a police inquiry. If you don't produce it, you'll be held as an accessory to murder."

Newbold nervously wiped his upper lip. "I never *had* that damned bicycle you want, only my own. I never touched this dead woman she was going on about. I don't know who those men were. There's been talk. I've heard it when there have been people here, drinking."

"What sort of talk?"

The man shrugged. "That something is going on at the Abbey. People walking about in the night. Coming and going at all hours. Lights moving around the airfield. It's unsettling. This is a quiet road, the men who come here to drink don't want any trouble. I keep my mouth shut, my eyes closed."

"Could you identify those two men quarrelling, if we take them into custody? I'll know the voices again if I hear them. It won't be long before I have the speakers." Again, he was testing the man before him. But the question only served to make Newbold more anxious.

He said, "Here, I don't need to do any such thing! I don't want to find myself in trouble with my custom. I shouldn't have told you what I did."

"Then they *were* here—"

"You're putting words in my mouth! I never heard anything that night. I'd drunk too much whisky, I was never out in the road, I was cursing my bloody *tooth*."

Once more he refused to budge. But Rutledge was convinced that he knew something.

Hamish said, "Ye ken, he more afraid of someone else than he is of Scotland Yard."

Rutledge thought that was very likely true.

But he said to Newbold, "If you don't send me word when you see them again, you'll be in more trouble with me than you will with two murderers."

There was a sneer on the man's face now. "Oh, aye? And how many people have you killed?"

With an effort of will, Rutledge kept himself from showing his shock. He said, something in his voice now that wiped the sneer from Newbold's face. "I was in the war. I know how it feels. And the first time is the easiest. Be careful that they don't turn on you."

And he turned, walked out, and left the door standing wide.

By the time he reached the motorcar, he'd got himself under control. But Hamish was hammering at him, and his voice, when he spoke to Lady Benton as he got beside her, had an edge to it.

"I believed you were having a rest."

"I couldn't sleep. And since you hadn't spoken to that man, to ask if he'd seen Patricia on the day she went missing, to see how far she might have got—or even if she had been taken at her own door—I asked him myself. Do you have any idea what it's like, waiting for news?"

"And you expected him to tell you the truth?"

"Did he tell *you* the truth?" she demanded.

"If he's a part of what happened, he wasn't fool enough to keep either the bicycle or Mrs. Lowell at The Monk's Choice. For the simple reason that he *might* have seen her that day."

"I did learn one thing," she said, angry with him. "I learned that she had pedaled past the pub ten minutes after she'd left the house on her bicycle. That's about right."

"The distance between the Abbey and the pub is shorter than the distance between the pub and Mrs. Lowell's house. When they took her, whoever they were, they'd have waited until then. It's more open there. The Home Farm is between the Abbey and the pub. There are several pairs of eyes there." Exasperated, he said, "Look, if I wished to abduct Mrs. Lowell, I'd allow her to see the house ahead of her. She'd feel safe then, past the dreaded pub, within reach of sanctuary. It was broad daylight, after all, they couldn't just rush up behind her and throw sacking over her head. Even in the open."

She looked at him. "That's cruel."

"People who kill usually are cruel."

Silence fell.

As they turned in at the stable yard, he said, "They were very likely waiting in or near that little shed, where Mrs. Lowell usually keeps her bicycle. Then they took it with them to throw doubt on her where-abouts. After she was killed, they had to rid themselves of it. Or who-ever had been hiding it, wanted to have it gone before it was found in his possession. And while they were about it, I stumbled into the thing in the fog."

She shivered. "I can't bear to think about it. About how frightened she was. But *why* did they kill her?"

He'd asked that question before, and had no better answer now. And so he said, "It would have been quite easy to abduct you today, walking along that road alone, and no one to know where you had gone, or when. It wasn't very safe."

"I can't imagine anyone wishing to abduct *me*."

"I'm sure Mrs. Lowell had no idea anyone would take her—or kill her."

He came around to open her door. "What is missing, that someone needs to find?"

"What?"

"It must have been either something Mrs. Lowell saw that cost her life, or something she knew. Would someone who had been here during the war have trusted her to keep something for them, while they were away fighting? Something someone else now wants?"

"Surely not! She wasn't that close to any of the squadron. Friendly, yes, but not close enough to encourage confiding in her."

"Did her husband send her anything—a souvenir—something in a letter that might have caused trouble if it were known?"

"If he had, she would have asked me what to do about it. She wasn't a secretive person, Inspector."

He took a deep breath. "There's a piece of this puzzle that's missing. Does this really have anything to do with the war? Or is that only because the airfield is out there, confusing the matter. I wish I knew."

She stared at him. "I have no earthly idea what you're asking me."

"It isn't important." It was. But he still didn't know why, and she was already unsettled enough by what had happened.

"Then why are you still here?" she asked. "If my ghosts and Patricia's dying aren't important? No—I can find my way to the house. Thank you." And she strode on toward the door, leaving him standing there.

Rather than ask Lady Benton, Rutledge drove all the way back to Walmer, interrupted Inspector Hamilton's day once more, to ask, "I need to find Margaret Hailey. Any idea where she lives?"

"Mrs. Hailey? Here in Walmer." He gave Rutledge the direction.

It was an older house, set back from the street, with a small garden in front. It was a prosperous part of town, not wealthy so much as quite comfortable. As he drew up in front of number 14, West Road, he wondered why Mrs. Hailey needed to work at the Abbey.

Hamish said, "She's the kind of woman who doesna' want to sit still."

And Rutledge thought that might very well be true. When he knocked at the door, she answered it wearing an apron.

"Oh," she said, staring at him. "I thought you were the neighbor's boy. His mother isn't well, I was making soup for the family. Come in. Has Lady Benton sent for me?"

"I'm here as a policeman," he said, smiling to make his words less official.

"Indeed." She led him into the parlor. It was what he'd rather expected, tidy to the point of stiffness, although it was an attractive room, bright and pleasant with the sunlight coming in the windows. They were polished to such a perfection that the glazing might not even be there, it was so clear.

"Is it about Lady Benton? Or Mrs. Lowell? She's been very distressed over Patricia's death. And the fact that it was on her own property—or will be as soon as the meadow is returned to her. She feels somehow responsible. I think that's why she fell, too much on her mind to pay attention."

"You don't believe she was pushed?"

Mrs. Hailey sighed. "I don't know what to think—except that the house was locked. We aren't careless about that, Inspector. I close up and Lady Benton herself makes the rounds again, after me."

"A window, then?"

"I don't see how someone could manage to climb through a window. Those in the rooms open to visitors are double locked. Mr. Eric saw to that." She looked away. "Such a tragedy, losing him. I grew quite fond of him myself."

"Is there anything missing from the house?"

"I've worked in that house since 1911. I know every inch of it by heart. If someone took something, I'd spot it at once. Not to speak of Lady Benton."

He considered that for a moment, then asked, "Is there something that ought to be there—but isn't? Or isn't, any longer?"

"Death duties were punishing, I can tell you that. But so far she's not had to sell anything to keep the house up. I'd know if she had."

He couldn't think of another way to reach the answer he needed. He was about to thank her and take his leave, when she said, "Sadly, there *was* something Mr. Eric was sending to her from France. But it never came, and she's always wondered what it might have been. He couldn't say much in his letters—the censors kept a sharp eye out for anything that mattered. But they had a code of sorts, Lady Benton and her son. They'd worked it out before he left, and so he could ask about his favorite rose, and she'd know he was going to be in the rear that week. Out of danger. It kept her going, that code."

"Had he sent her packages before this?"

"Just the usual. A small vase made from a shell casing. Lovely little piece. One of his men did the engraving. And when he was sent to Paris to recover from a leg wound, he found a book about the Duc du Berry's *Book of the Hours* in a French shop. I saw that myself, exquisite engravings."

None of these were worth stealing, in a household of treasures.

Rutledge thanked her, then left.

He was reviewing what he knew—it seemed to be precious little— when he suddenly saw the connection he'd been unable to find for days.

What if it wasn't the house that mattered, not directly? It was the airfield. And Lady Benton was involved only because she would soon own the meadow again?

But what would a man like Wilbur, the profiteer, want with a meadow that had once been an airfield? It had made no sense. The concept of a museum cum a children's park in the middle of nowhere, no sea bathing, nothing that would draw hordes of Londoners eager to spend a weekend at the seaside, wouldn't appeal to a man like Wilbur. He was more likely to cut down the wood at the far side of the meadow and build cottages by the sea.

Or if he did revive the airfield as a museum, that might cover small-scale smuggling. What better way to move small packages—even stolen goods—than in an aircraft, under the pilot's seat or in the small compartment near the tail. A good many art treasures had been looted during the war, while there were men who had grown rich making shoddy goods for the war effort, and now wanted grand houses in which to display their wealth.

It was the mechanics who kept the aircraft flying. A stop at another field in France for some trumped-up emergency, a package added, then removed when the aircraft came in. Very likely only one of two pilots were involved. But war's end had put a stop to the game.

Hamish said, "It doesna' explain yon lass's death now."

And that was the sticking point . . .

But it did account for the disappearance of the mechanic Gerald Dunn, accused of desertion, but more than likely he'd been killed when he stumbled over something. Had he spoken to Captain Nelson, who began to ask questions?

But for the life of him, Rutledge couldn't fit Patricia Lowell into the picture. If she had died while the smuggling had been going on, it would have been different. Why was she a threat?

Still, he could understand now why Haldane hadn't kept his morning appointment with him. Haldane must have known another part of the puzzle, but had said nothing for reasons of his own.

And that was both maddening and intriguing.

It was nearly eight o'clock by the time he returned to the hotel. He left his motorcar in the back, but that door was locked and so he walked around to the main door.

As he turned the corner, he saw Liz, the young woman from The Salt Cellar, speaking to someone—one of the staff, he thought—on the street just in front of the hotel. She nodded to the other woman and turned away.

But not before he'd glimpsed a cut lip and a red mark on one cheek. He realized that she'd been slapped.

As the other woman went back inside the hotel, Rutledge hurried on and caught up with Liz.

"Hallo," he said. "What seems to be the trouble?"

She turned her face slightly to keep him from seeing the mark. "I—I was just asking if there was a position open at the hotel."

"And is there?"

"No." Her voice caught on the word.

"What has happened?" he asked, and took her arm lightly, guiding her into the churchyard.

"No, I must go—"

"Who struck you? Was it Johnson?"

She stared at him in surprise, as if she hadn't expected him to know the name of the pub's owner. Swallowing hard, she said, "No—oh, no.

He yells at me. It was one of the other girls. I—I nearly dropped my tray on a man, and she was angry, because he leaves her a nice tip. But he was about to stand up, and it was truly an *accident*." She looked up at him, pleading for him to believe her.

"I'm sure it was. Is the hotel not hiring?"

"I-I have no experience. All I've ever done is wait in the pub. And—and it doesn't have the best reputation, and I know Mr. Johnson wouldn't give me a reference. He's that way. He'd shout at me for wanting to better myself. And I do. I don't want to work there any longer." There was determination in her face.

"I understand," he said, nodding. "Shall I have a word with Johnson?"

"Oh—no—please! He'll let me go, and who will take me then?"

"If it happens again, you must come and tell me. I'm at the hotel. The desk clerk will give me a message if I'm not in when you come."

"There's nothing you can do. It will only make matters worse."

"Let me be the judge of that."

"Why would you bother?" Liz asked, suddenly wary. "I don't even know you."

"I'm a policeman," he told her. "I deal with men like Johnson all the time. And expect no favors."

"Then you must take Ivy into custody," she said, suddenly angry. "She thinks because Mr. Johnson fancies her that she can treat me like a scullery maid!"

Rutledge suppressed a smile, for she had clenched her fists and was truly cross with Ivy. Then, as the spurt of anger faded, she said contritely, "You mustn't do anything. It will only cause more trouble for me. Promise?"

"I promise, if you will tell me if there is more trouble."

"But you'll go away soon, won't you? And then what?" She turned and walked off down the street.

Rutledge watched her go, then went back to the hotel and walked into Reception.

The clerk came out of the dining room and called to him. "Mr. Rutledge, sir? Sir? There's a message for you. Hand delivered sir!"

Rutledge heard the man's last words, and turned to come down again.

"What was hand delivered?"

The man went to the desk, opened a drawer, and took out a large envelope.

There was nothing on the outside, as Rutledge took it from him. And when he opened it, he found a ticket for the Dover ferry to Calais, and a map.

Nothing else.

No explanation, nothing to indicate who had sent it or why.

"Did you see the person who delivered it?"

"I was at the desk when he came in. He looked like someone's valet, sir. Not much to say for himself, except that this was for you, and urgent. And he—er—made it worthwhile for me to see that it was delivered promptly, sir. But you weren't in, sir."

He thanked the man and went upstairs.

Haldane. It had to be. But why a ticket to France?

Or was it a wild goose chase, to get him out of Walmer?

When he looked at the ferry ticket, it was for an early morning crossing. Tomorrow.

That meant an even earlier start, if he was to drive there in time to make the damned ferry . . .

He packed what he needed, ordered his dinner, and went back to the Abbey. It was late, when he stepped into the sitting room. Lady Benton had left pillows and blankets to hand. He slept in the chair.

There would be a telephone in Dover. He could call Haldane from there and ask what the devil was in France. Unless it was the other end of a wartime smuggling affair . . .

II

It was just dawn when Rutledge walked out of the Abbey and went around to his motorcar. Even the gulls were quiet at this hour, and he had the roads to himself, except for the van delivering milk. There was a petrol station just opening as he passed, and he made the necessary stop.

He had to push the motorcar hard to reach Dover before the ferry was scheduled to leave. What's more, the crossing at Gravesend was delayed, putting him on an even tighter schedule.

And it was imperative to have the time to find a telephone.

He was successful in that at least, and put through a call to Haldane. The man answered almost at once.

"Rutledge. Are you in Dover?"

"I am. Why should I take the ferry to France?"

"You rather owe me, I think. There's a small matter to attend to there."

"I'm in the middle of an inquiry—"

"Nevertheless, you will be on that ferry. It's important to both of us."

"Where am I going? And why?"

"Did you read the map?"

"Yes. Somewhere close by the Ypres road, apparently."

"Exactly. A motorcar will be waiting for you in Calais. You can't miss it. The port master will know. Drive to the village circled on the map, and don't use your name or title. Find the house of one Michel Vermuelen."

"Who is Vermuelen?"

"You'll see soon enough. Don't miss the ferry."

And the receiver was put up, the connection broken.

Rutledge debated whether or not to go to France. For one thing, it brought back too many memories, grief that hadn't healed. For another he was not a man who liked being used.

He'd always suspected that one day, Haldane would call in his debt.

He left the motorcar in the ferry office compound, told the Customs Officers why it was there—official business, even though he had no idea what that business was. He had no jurisdiction in France. Besides, it would require a great deal of bureaucratic formalities to arrange for him to do more than travel there as a private citizen.

Rutledge was the last passenger to come aboard the ferry. He'd made certain of that, still uneasy. And as the ferry pulled out into the road and started the crossing, he felt a stronger surge of uneasiness about what he might be leaving behind in Essex.

The motorcar was waiting, a Citroën, the first one produced, almost at war's end, in 1919. He looked it over, decided he could cope, and got in.

It was not a comfortable motorcar compared to his own, but it seemed to drive reasonably well, and he left the harbor, climbed to the town at the top of the hill, forcing himself not to remember marching his men up the winding approach to Calais, where they were given their orders for proceeding to the Front.

It was here too that he and Meredith Channing had begun their journey to Belgium. That was another memory he didn't wish to relive. The traffic coming out of Calais and finding the road north toward Ypres managed to keep Hamish at bay, and then he could see how the wounds of war had healed—or not.

And then he was on the long flat stretch of road he knew too well.

Heavy fighting in 1914 and onward had left scars. Shattered trees, buildings in ruin or patched together sufficiently to be habitable. The road itself had had to be regraded, to make it passable.

He found the little village of Langville on a side road closer to the sea, but in spite of himself, he found he couldn't take the turning.

Instead he travelled on to the Belgian town of Bruges and bought flowers at a tiny shop on the street. It didn't take him long to find what he was after, the pretty little church that he and Meredith Channing had visited, with the perfect little Madonna with Saint John. As he approached the church, the priest, just stepping through the great door, nodded to him, pausing to see if the stranger might be calling for him. Satisfied he was not, he disappeared inside.

There were a number of fresh graves, but after a time, Rutledge found what he'd been looking for.

There was a joint stone, and he winced as he saw that her husband was buried beside her. He told himself that the man lying there with Meredith Channing was not to blame for what had happened to her. And yet what had happened was unforgiveable.

Channing had been ill, damaged by the war to the point he hadn't known his own name when he had been found wandering in the middle of nowhere, a released prisoner with no idea who he was or where he'd come from. Even whether he was French or German or Belgian. His torn uniform could have been stolen from the living or the dead.

The nuns had taken him in, they had worked diligently to learn which army he might have belonged to, and in the end, they had found out his name, and through the Red Cross or some such, they had found Meredith.

She had been searching for her husband since he'd gone missing,

presumed dead. Her own sense of duty had never let her stop searching, even when all hope had gone. And yet Channing's survival had
shocked her as much as it had shocked Rutledge. But when the letter
had come from the nuns, inquiring if this shell of a man could be her
husband, she had asked Rutledge to take her to Bruges to find out if the
man with the broken mind was Channing.

Rutledge had begun to fall in love with her. But he took her to
Belgium—and tragically she had recognized Channing. Rutledge had
had to leave her there, at her bidding. Even though he had known that
she didn't love the shambling, half-mad figure who had stared blankly
at her without any idea who she was. That she had stayed out of duty,
not love.

Had stayed and nursed the man who would eventually kill her in
one of his violent fits.

He hadn't known Meredith was dead until the nuns had written
again—and she was already in her grave by then.

Rutledge knelt there in the churchyard for a time. Remembering
her, remembering what he'd felt for her. What he'd believed she'd felt
for him.

And then he laid the flowers by her half of the joint stone.

I came back . . .

It was all he could find to say, as he got to his feet.

As he was leaving, the priest came out of the church.

"I saw you there. Is it a loved one you visited?"

"Yes . . ."

"Do you need comfort, my son?" the priest asked in concern.

"Thank you, Father, but no."

"So many come here, and to the graves of the war dead." He shook
his head. "It was not the peace we'd hoped for."

"No."

With a nod, the priest went back inside.

He didn't remember finding his way back to the motorcar.

———

It was late when Rutledge came back to the turning to the little village near the coast. Later than Haldane might have liked, but then Haldane wasn't here, he thought grimly.

There was a man walking along the road, on his way to a row of houses, hardly more than cottages, that heralded the village of Langville, Rutledge pulled over and asked for the home of Michel Vermuelen, but the man shook his head.

"Why do you wish this man?" he asked in French with a heavy accent that made the question difficult to follow.

"I knew him in the war."

The man studied him in the reflected light of the headlamps. "Then you also know he is dead."

"I think not. Or someone would have told me."

"Who are you?"

"My name is Broadhurst." He'd put a man in Dartmoor by that name. It would do.

"And who is Monsieur Broadhurst?"

That was trickier. Rutledge said, "We—did some business once."

"What sort of business, then?"

"Profitable."

If Vermuelen had been a soldier, he would have had little contact with the English forces. But then again, if he were an older man, he might have helped the Expeditionary Force with information or as a translator . . .

To himself Rutledge swore at Haldane for not giving him more information.

But that response seemed to be the right one.

"He is in the house two from the church."

Rutledge nodded and drove on.

Villages this near Ypres had seen heavy fighting. Patched roofs, broken walls and chimneys were proof of that. Gaps where houses had been, piles of bricks and wood where others had been shelled, and a church without a tower. He mentally cataloged these as he passed by a few shops, one with boarded windows, and reached the church itself.

There were no houses next to the church on this side, except for the priest's house. On the far side the one nearest the church was dark. Its neighbor had a lamp lit, a bright rectangle in the gathering darkness.

Pulling up in front of the small, two-story house, he stopped the motorcar and got out.

The yard was more rubble than grass, but the door appeared to be solid enough as Rutledge knocked.

After a time, a nun answered it, her headdress wide and curved like sails. Her face was lined and sad. But she said calmly in French, "Oui?" Behind her there was only darkness, as if the household was asleep.

"I'm looking for Michel Vermuelen. I'm told he lives in this house."

"He does. But he is very ill, and does not have the strength to speak to visitors."

"I've come from England to see him. I knew him once, in the war."

The nun frowned. "In his present state, I do not think he wishes to remember the war."

"Nevertheless," Rutledge told her, "he would not wish to die with certain matters on his conscience."

At that she moved aside, returning her hands to the sleeves of her habit, and led the way down a dark, unlit passage to a room near the end.

When she opened the door, the smell of sickness struck him.

Vermuelen must be very ill—and important enough, to have a nun for a nurse . . .

Rutledge stepped into the room. It appeared to have been a sitting room converted to a sickroom. He didn't recognize the man in the bed, but as he approached, he wondered if even those who had known him would know him now.

In the light of a lamp shaded by a shawl, his body, once strapping, was wasted and thin, now, though he must have been tall, for his legs were long under the coverlet.

He appeared to be asleep, eyes closed, his mouth slightly open in the thin face.

Rutledge said to the nun in a whisper, "What is his illness?"

"Gangrene. It is not contagious."

"How did he come by his wound?" Rutledge had seen gangrene in the trenches. It was ugly and not an easy way to die, bit by bit.

"A knife. The other injuries healed. The leg did not."

Approaching the bed, Rutledge said quietly, "Michel? Are you awake?"

The man's eyes blinked several times, then opened. They were wells of pain.

"I have come from England to see you."

"Who are you?"

"My name is Broadhurst."

"I don't know you."

Taking a chance, Rutledge said, "Haldane sent me."

To his surprise, the name brought recognition. The eyes focused sharply.

"Tell him I am dying."

Rutledge had a feeling that the man in the bed was accustomed to being careful. That it was ingrained in him, even as he lay desperately ill.

"He sent me to you. He must know that."

"What is your business with Haldane?"

What to answer? Rutledge finally replied, "I have come from Essex. About a murder."

"I knew him in the war. We did good work, then."

He wondered if Vermuelen was even aware of what he'd said. The man's eyes had closed again.

Then he spoke. "What the Germans did in Belgium was not human."

"I was not there. I was on the Somme. But there were refugees. We heard enough." He paused, then added, "What can you tell me about Walmer and the Abbey there?"

The names didn't seem to mean anything to the man on the bed. There was no sign that he recognized either of them.

"The airfield?"

Silence again. The weary, pain-ridden eyes stayed closed. Behind Rutledge, the nun said, "He must rest."

Rutledge turned to her. "There doesn't appear to be much time," he said softly, so that her patient couldn't hear him. "I must talk to him before the end comes. Then he will rest."

"You must leave him now."

There was no point in arguing. "Is there another part of the house where I can wait until he wakes again?"

"Most of the house is closed. But there is his workroom."

"That will do."

She led him down the passage to another door and opened it. "There is a lamp on the table. Matches by the hearth."

"Where will you be?"

"In the kitchen. Just there." She nodded toward a door across from the sickroom and then went away.

Rutledge took out his lighter, and found the lamp on the table without barking his shins. He lit the wick, turned it up, but the chimney was grimy with smoke, as if it hadn't been cleaned in some time. As the light strengthened, he turned to look around the room.

It *was* a workroom of sorts. The table was covered with maps, layered one on top of the other. The top one showed the countryside around Ypres. There were two chairs, and shelves against the wall holding books. The hearth was cold, and there was no fire lit, nor was it laid.

He sat down in one of the two chairs, just as Hamish spoke.

"I dona' like this."

Nor do I, he answered silently, glad of his heavy coat. The house was cold.

"If yon man worked for Haldane, why did you need to come here? He could ha' sent that man of his."

"I don't know. Yet."

He tried to make himself more comfortable, but there were no cushions in the chairs, and the furnishings, as the wick caught well and the light improved, were battered and chipped. Some of the books in the shelves were either missing—long gaps between them—or their spines were torn. Who the hell was Vermuelen?

The closer it got to dawn, the colder the house seemed to grow. Rutledge stood up and began to pace, but that was no help. Finally resigning himself to no sleep, he turned to the worktable.

He'd seen the map of the surrounds of Ypres, lying on top. And as he lifted it to see what lay beneath it, he realized that these were military maps of the French and Belgian coastline. How had Vermuelen come by them?

And on the bottom were military maps of the Essex coastline, with all its estuaries and waterways, marshes and lone strands.

Rutledge, frowning, pulled those out, just as the wick began to smoke. He had to stop and trim it by the glow of his lighter, but in the end he could at least see what he was looking at.

Turning to the bookcase, he randomly pulled out books and looked at them. In a few of them, words and page numbers were underlined, but without rhyme or reason. The others had no such markings.

A cipher?

Intrigued now, he began to search the room, quietly and thoroughly. Vermuelen, it appeared, was Flemish by birth, the non-French-speaking half of Belgium, but had been brought up in Brussels when his father worked for the postal service there. Several letters from his sister were in the bottom drawer of his desk, some of them full of family news.

Rutledge found a torch in another drawer, and decided to explore. Leaving his boots in the workroom and walking the cold floor in stocking feet, he let himself out into the passage. But the other rooms of the house were ordinary, with no secrets that he could discover. It was clearly the home of a working-class family, the heavy dark wood of furnishings handed down in generation after generation, a crucifix over the beds in the four small bedrooms, and a shrine to the Virgin in a corner of the parlor.

Disappointed, he returned to the workroom. Remembering something one of his friends—an Intelligence officer—had told him during the war, he started to search all over again.

And against the back of the smoke-darkened painting of an elderly bearded man over the hearth, clearly someone's ancestor, given the style of clothing he was wearing, was a thick envelope. It had been taped in place.

Rutledge took it to the table and opened it.

There were a dozen sheets of tissue-thin paper, the sort that could be used to attach to the legs of pigeons. The British had used pigeons to send messages to the Front and to people behind the lines in occupied Belgium who hated the Germans and were willing to risk their lives to provide whatever information they could on reinforcements moving through their tiny country. But the sheets were clean, unused.

What had all this to do with Essex? Or with Haldane, for that matter?

It was full light outside now, a cloudy dawn, almost as gray as the view from the workroom window.

Rutledge had put his boots back on, and now he cleaned his hands as best he could on one sheet of the tissue paper before walking to the kitchen and knocking on the door.

The nun, awake and dressed, opened it and invited him in. There was a cot up against a dresser, clearly where she slept, but of more interest to him was the pigeon cage outside the window, in the back garden.

She had made coffee, and offered him a cup. It was black but hot, and he was grateful for it, nodding his thanks as he sat down at the narrow table in the center of the room.

"I have borrowed bread and a little chicken from the priest. It is for his breakfast and mine. There is no other food."

"I understand," he told her. Then, he asked, "Tell me about Michel Vermuelen?"

"I was sent by my convent to nurse him through this illness."

"When was he hurt? How long has it been?"

"A fortnight ago. On the road to Calais. He came home, only the leg wound had become septic. There is nothing to be done. A slow poisoning of the blood."

"He was in the war?"

"I think not. He is lame. But he was a patriot all the same."

That explained why her convent had sent her here. But the man had done something in the war . . .

On an impulse, he said, "I have looked at the maps and books in the workroom. He served in his own fashion. But there is nothing to take back to England with me. I should like to speak to him again."

"It is not necessary. I think this is what you came for." She turned, opened a small cabinet against the wall. It was where spices and flour and salt were kept. In the sack of flour was an envelope.

"Take it and go." She opened a drawer in the dresser, found a cloth, and cleaned off the flour dust before handing it to him.

It was tightly sealed.

"Leave him now to die quietly." But when Rutledge didn't go, she sighed. "He did not trust the post," she went on, and turned away to begin preparing a broth for Vermuelen, adding a raw egg to it.

Rutledge looked away. "Thank you. I'd still like to speak to him."

"We shall see, yes? As God wills."

Finishing his coffee, he thanked her again, and took the envelope back to the workroom.

It was indeed tightly sealed. But Haldane had sent him here without a word to help him find what the man wanted from Vermuelen. And Rutledge told himself that he'd be damned if he wasn't going to open the wretched envelope and find out what it contained. He needed to return to Essex—but if Vermuelen was dying, this could be his only chance to ask questions.

Inside the envelope, there were pages of that tissue-thin paper, and this time, they were covered in writing. Someone—Vermuelen?—had kept a running account in the tiniest handwriting he could manage. In the dim light of the lamp, Rutledge was hard-pressed to read it. Fortunately it was in English, not Flemish or French.

At first he had no idea what the report was about, and then he began to understand. It was dated, clear, concise, logical. Rutledge wondered if the writer—or Vermuelen himself—had been a policeman in Belgium before the war, for there was a recognizable policeman's viewpoint about it.

It began with troop movements in Belgium, which regiments the Germans were bringing into that country and staging to march into France. There followed a description of the heroism of the Belgians as they fought back, giving the Allies nine days to get their own armies into the conflict. There was a gap, and then the report began again at the French-Belgian border days later, again noting German troop movements and strategy. As if he had changed his location.

This continued—with gaps, apparently as Vermuelen moved his area of operations to another location. This time he was watching the French coastline and reporting on the submarines and other German naval movements. Once he rescued a British airman, leading him back to his own lines.

Rutledge was beginning to realize that this was a record, not a report, a duplicate of all the information he had managed to get into British hands during the course of the war. In the event that any messages were lost, the information in those messages would not be.

Rutledge began to scan. It wasn't the war, three years in the past, that Haldane was interested in.

His eyes aching from the tiny print and his stomach growling from missed meals, he forced his mind to keep at it, looking for anything that might be useful. Searching the parlor again, he found a half empty bottle of whisky, and took that back to the workroom. As time passed, he was beginning to think that there was nothing of interest here. Nothing to do with Essex and murder.

He drank from the bottle, unwilling to ask the nun for a glass, and then went on with his search. By the time he'd read the last page, he knew this couldn't be what he had come all the way from Essex to find. He would see that it reached Haldane, but there had to be another reason for this journey.

Folding the pages and returning them to the envelope, he put it safely in his pocket, capped the bottle of whisky, and returned it to the parlor. Then he went in search of the nun.

She was in the sickroom.

"How is he?" Rutledge asked quietly.

"He fights to live, but it's only a matter of time."

"Is he awake?"

"He hasn't spoken for some hours."

Rutledge moved closer to the bed. He could hear the man's rough breathing, but he didn't think he was actually asleep.

Drawing a chair up to the bedside, he said, "Vermuelen? Haldane sent me. I found your reports, what you'd done in the war. But there must be something else. I understand your need to be circumspect."

There was no response from the man in the bed.

"If I had come here to find out what you knew, or to kill you and the Sister, I would have burned down the house with both of you in it, and been done with it. Instead, I have waited for the truth."

Rutledge sat patiently, then was about to try again when Vermuelen spoke.

His accent was heavier, his voice weak as he fought for air. "Notes."

"I have the war notes."

"Not war. More."

"You will have to tell me. I don't know where to look."

The man lifted a hand trembling with weakness. "Not finished." He pointed to a table by the window. It held medicines, a bowl of what appeared to be broth, several glasses, and a spoon. Nothing else.

"Where?"

"Under. In case—someone came—to kill—"

Rutledge stood up and went to the table. It was old, very heavy wood, intended to last down the generations. As it must have done. But there was nothing to be seen. He turned to speak to the nun, but she had quietly left the room.

Dropping down on one knee, Rutledge ran his hands up under the table's top, where the wood was unfinished. At first his fingers found nothing, and then just as he was about to give up, he felt something.

Not an envelope this time. A roll of papers, taped to the inner front edge.

He pulled them out carefully, then rose and returned to his chair.

"These?"

The man on the bed made an effort, opening his eyes. "Not finished," he said again with a brief nod. "Ask. Ask him."

"I shall. And I'll see that these and the other papers reach London. Is there anything else I can do for you? Is there any message for Haldane?"

But what followed was almost unintelligible, sometimes a rambling murmur, and then the occasional single word. Rutledge found it nearly impossible to follow what Vermuelen was trying to tell him. From the effort the man was making, it was clear that it mattered in some way.

Were these instructions for Haldane? Information for Rutledge, that there hadn't been time to add to the pages? Vermuelen himself had said that they weren't finished. Or was his mind wandering as the poisoning in his blood spread? Several times, Rutledge thought he could make out what sounded like *lake,* and then more clearly, *must look,* followed by *lake* once more, and possibly *body* or was it *bloody?*

Twice Rutledge had to ask him to repeat something that made no sense at all, but it seemed that Vermuelen was struggling to pass on something that was on his mind and paid no attention.

A pause, finally, before he managed to speak as if to Rutledge directly. "Sister. She will stay."

Rutledge couldn't be sure whether the man was speaking of the nun or a relative. And then there was something more, hardly above a whisper. He leaned closer to Vermuelen, but couldn't make it out.

And then he said, struggling to form the words, but still clearly enough for Rutledge to understand him, "Tell—tell him that it was a privilege to—to—"

His voice faded into silence. For an instant, Rutledge thought the man had died, but he was asleep, the deep sleep of medication. The nun had been giving him his next draft of laudanum or morphine, Rutledge wasn't sure which.

He sat there for several minutes longer, then rose and went to the kitchen.

The nun was sitting at the table, her head in her hands. She looked up.

"He's asleep."

She nodded. "Better that way."

"Are you his nurse? Or his sister?"

"Both," she replied, her voice weary. "I will not leave until it is finished."

"Shall I stay?" he asked.

But she shook her head. "It will happen in God's good time. I am patient."

"Who was he?"

"He hated the Germans for what they did to our country. He was lame, he couldn't be a soldier. He found a different way. It took great courage. He was taken prisoner three times, and three times, he escaped. But not without cost each time. It is a wonder he has lived this long."

"You must be proud of him."

"It isn't pride," she said harshly. "It was duty."

And then she added in her usual tone of voice, "I am sad there was no food to offer you. If you have found what you need, please go. He will be with God soon."

He thanked her and left. But he stopped by the workroom and took up the map of the Essex coast, rolling it carefully.

And then he got into the borrowed motorcar and drove back to Calais.

He had much of the ferry to himself on this crossing and sat where he could read Vermuelen's additional notes without someone looking over his shoulder. He had purchased some food in Calais, a little cheese and bread, and was glad of the hot tea on board.

The notes were as cryptic as the report had been. It was clear that after the war had ended with the Armistice, there was still work to be done.

Vermuelen had only a brief respite to return to his family in Belgium, and then he was in Paris, where he was set to look for deserters as a cover. But what did he need a cover for?

He was also, it seemed, searching for a killer . . .

Rutledge sat back, staring out at the sea and just ahead, the towering white cliffs just above Dover Castle.

So this was why Haldane had sent *him* to call on a dying man.

Hamish, quiet in the back of his mind as he had struggled to read the finely written lines on the thin sheets of paper, said, "Ye ken. It's no' verra' much."

That was true. But Vermuelen's notes and Haldane's insistence that he go to Langville had convinced him that he wasn't hunting a ghost. If Haldane was right, he was after a cold-blooded killer. Who had come back to Essex, where he was killing again.

But who the hell was he *now*?

12

It wasn't until the ferry had docked and he'd retrieved his own mo-torcar that Rutledge could put in a telephone call to Haldane. And then he thought better of it, because there would be other ears on the line.

He went to find a shop that sold postal cards. There was one of the castle on its hill overlooking the Channel, dark against a stormy sky. He paid for it, wrote a short message, added a stamp the woman in the shop had offered him, and then dropped the card in the nearest post box.

It read simply, *Sadly, our uncle is dying. I am back, I was given the cuff links he wished you to have. More when I see you. R.*

If Haldane wished to play at cryptic messages, he, Rutledge, could do the same.

As he took the road to Gravesend, he was tempted to drive a little farther, to call on Melinda. And Kate.

But he'd been away too long as it was, and there was a murderer to find.

He went over what he'd learned in Vermuelen's report, trying to compare it with what he already knew.

Early in the war, a man named Miles Franklin had killed three people in Dorset, had been caught and taken into custody, and somehow had managed to escape on his way to trial. He had disappeared.

Shortly after that, a man's nude body was found in a ditch ten miles away. It was soon identified as Timothy Robinson, a soldier home on compassionate leave. The Army was informed.

It was wartime, 1915, and spy fever was at its height. But no one tried to infiltrate an Army post or use Robinson's identity to approach a factory or other vulnerable target. It was as if Robinson's name and history had died with him.

The Foot Police and other interested departments began to suspect that while wearing Robinson's uniform, Franklin had approached and killed someone else, with more time to dispose of the body than he'd had in Robinson's case. Six months later, a decaying corpse was found under a railway bridge in Derbyshire, confirming that theory. It was never identified. But in the pocket of the ill-fitting uniform he was wearing someone had written the name Timothy Robinson. Many soldiers had done just that, in the event they were killed in action and unrecognizable.

Who the dead man was, no one ever discovered.

By early 1916, it was decided that Franklin, whatever name he used now, had probably enlisted somewhere, and used the Army to transport him out of the country and to safety. There had been no German-related incidents, ruling out the earlier questions about a German spy. And as far as anyone knew, there were no further killings. Once he was in France, Franklin could travel to Switzerland or take ship from Portugal to Canada or anywhere else he might choose.

That was where the search for Franklin had stopped.

The war had ended and the British Army came home. Franklin had become a dusty file on someone's desk.

And then some two months ago, Vermuelen, who had already been looking for him, had come across Franklin—or someone, an Englishman, who fit the vague description and used a knife in his killings—in Picardy. To the police questioning Franklin about a murder, he was simply an ex-soldier who had known the victim. The false name he'd given was cleared as having no record, and he was released.

Michel Vermuelen had arrived in Picardy too late to look at the suspect, but managed to follow someone who might have been him as far as Ypres, where the man was looking for transport to Calais. Certain now that the man must indeed be Franklin, Vermuelen had approached him and told him that he himself was going there and would like company on the road. Vermuelen had wired Haldane before the two men set out, alerting him to the fact that Franklin might be returning to England. Franklin was using the name Tom Barnes, but had no passport in that name, claiming that the Picardy police had kept it. Somewhere outside Calais, either Franklin had grown suspicious or was already covering his movements, and he tried to knife Vermuelen. They fought, and Vermuelen was stabbed several times. He managed to make it back to Langville, but by then he had lost track of Franklin.

The ports were watched for one Tom Barnes. But the man never arrived. It was likely that he hadn't left France at all. That he had used Vermuelen. The trail had then gone cold.

And Vermuelen's leg, refusing to heal, had continued to drain. In the end it had turned septic before he could go after Franklin.

Small wonder Vermuelen had feared that Franklin might track *him* instead.

Had Franklin crossed to England after all? Using another name?

And why would he come to *Walmer*? A small town where strangers would be noticed?

Unless he had been there once before . . .

Why had Haldane, listening to Rutledge's request for the names of all the men posted to the airfield, connected that with Franklin? Did he have a reason to think that Franklin had served there during the war? Or was it simply the way Haldane's mind worked, when Rutledge had said he needed those names in connection with an inquiry?

But there had been that wisp of wool that Dr. Wister had found on Patricia Lowell's clothes, and the possibility that it had come from a military greatcoat . . .

A down-on-his-luck ex-soldier looking for work? Or a murderer looking for a place to go to ground?

The ferry across to Dover pulled in to the port, and it was time to leave it.

Hamish said, "Aye, it fits together. But is it true?"

"Hamilton will know if someone has come to Walmer recently, or is looking for work. That's where I'll begin."

But when he walked into Hamilton's office, he was greeted with an angry, "Where the hell have you been?"

"Chasing a possible lead."

"Yes, well, it might have saved a good deal of aggravation if you'd told me how to find you."

That hadn't been possible. Hamilton couldn't have reached him in Langville, if the police station itself had burned to the ground.

"It wouldn't have helped if I had. You have no telephones here. What's happened?" He kept his voice level with an effort. Hamilton had resented having the Yard thrust into an inquiry he'd dismissed. And now he resented not being kept informed.

Hamilton took a deep breath. "For one thing, someone burned down the hut where Mrs. Lowell was killed. There was wind, we were concerned about the house."

"Had you searched it carefully?"

"Of course I had. There was nothing to be found."

"I'll have a look."

"Too late. You'll find nothing but ashes. By the time Lady Benton got here and the fire brigade went out, there was nothing left. She's talking about having a telephone installed. But who would she call? Chelmsford?" he answered sourly.

"Lady Benton is all right?"

"You know how she is. Unflappable. I got an earful from Mrs. Hailey."

"I'm going out there now."

"I'm serious, Rutledge, if you leave again, I'll see the Chief Constable is told."

"Which reminds me," Rutledge said, "are there any new people who have come to Walmer recently?"

"New people? As in a family—a man—a woman?"

"It doesn't matter. Anyone."

"No. It's not a village that's famous or popular. We make salt and Thames barges, hardly a draw for workers. Besides, that sort of work often runs in the family. I can't think of the last newcomer."

"What about someone who had served here during the war?"

Hamilton shook his head. "A few men and several grieving families have come from time to time. I don't know that any of them stayed longer than a day or two."

Rutledge thanked him and left.

He drove directly to the airfield, and walked down to where the blackened ruins of the hut lay, tiny wisps of smoke still stirring in the sunlight as the wind blew.

Why burn it down? he asked himself as he dropped down on his haunches and gazed at the ashes. The hut had served its purpose, it had been the perfect place to leave the body of Patricia Lowell. And standing there, well within sight of the house, where anyone looking out the Abbey windows in this direction would see it instantly, it was a constant and powerful reminder of what had been done there. From that perspective, it was far more haunting than these black embers.

Why burn it?

The words kept repeating themselves, a litany in his mind.

And then the answer came, like a flash of light.

There was something here the killer didn't want to be found. Or was afraid that it might be found?

Something he'd left behind? Or lost, and suddenly realized it was missing and where it must be . . .

But Hamilton had searched the hut. Apparently Mrs. Lowell's killer had as well. And neither of them had had any luck.

Not something of Patricia Lowell's. Something that belonged to the killer?

Rutledge got to his feet, and set out in a jog for the stables. There he found what he wanted, an iron rake, and he carried it back to where the ashes lay.

He carefully began to smooth out the embers, spreading them this way and that. Hamish, busy in his mind, told him it was useless.

"Ye ken, it burned in the fire. That's why it was set."

But he kept telling himself that the hut had had to be set on fire because it would cover something that wouldn't burn, something that would be concealed by the very ashes he was so carefully inspecting.

And then something clinked against the iron tongs of the rake that wasn't an ember, and he brought it toward his feet where he could pick it up.

As he did, he saw that it was part of the iron door hinges.

He kept at it, found the other set, then the latch itself.

Hamish urged him to give up, but he worked on, coughing sometimes when the last of the smoke moved with the little breeze.

And finally he was rewarded. Something rolled out of the ashes nearly to the toe of his boot.

He reached down and picked it up.

At first it appeared to be a twisted piece of metal, but when he'd taken out his handkerchief and rubbed away where the fire had touched it, he could see that it was a ring. A man's, judging from the size of it. The question was, how long had it lain under the rough planking of the flooring of the hut? Slipping unnoticed through the cracks. Who had lost it? A killer—or the men who had once worked here.

He dropped it into his pocket and continued to rake. There a charred bit of paper, a halfpenny, and what might have been a coat button. The last thing he managed to find was a key. He turned that over in his fingers. It was very like the one he'd been given by Lady Benton.

Hamish said, "It's more likely one o' the officers."

That was possible too. Giving up, he raked the remnants of the hut back where they'd come from, then picked up the rake to carry it back to the stables.

Hamish said something in warning, and he looked up.

Someone was standing on the terrace overlooking the lawns, a hand shielding her face as she watched what he was doing. He couldn't tell if it was Lady Benton or one of her staff.

Rutledge returned the rake to the stables and was about to go back to where he'd left his motorcar when he heard his name called. Turning, he saw Lady Benton coming toward him.

He greeted her, but she didn't smile. "Where were you when we had the fire?"

"I had business in London."

"I thought your inquiry was here?"

"It is, of course. But there was information I needed about the airfield."

"What sort of information?"

"The names of the officers and men who lived down there at the airfield."

"What on earth for? And as to that, I have all of their names. In a book that they signed. You had only to ask." At his look of surprise, she said, "I bought the book, thinking that when Eric came home he might like to look through it—possibly might even know some of the men. And I kept it up, out of habit when Eric didn't come back."

"I'd like very much to see it."

She led the way back to the door, and into the small sitting room. "The Major was kind enough to let me know when there was someone new, and I'd invite him to tea." Shrugging slightly she added, "It made me feel safer, in a way. A hundred or so strangers on one's doorstep is not usual."

As she went to a cupboard and took out the leather-bound book, she added, "Why were you looking through the ashes? It was rather macabre. I couldn't sleep at all last night, thinking that if we hadn't found Patricia, she might have burned with it. That would have been horrible. Unthinkable." She shivered a little. "I can't forget that she died on my land. Well, once my land, and soon perhaps mine again. It makes me feel that I could—should have done something to save her."

"There was nothing you could do. You didn't know she was there."

"But I knew she had gone missing, you see. I keep feeling responsible. That perhaps her death is related to the Abbey. To the—the men I saw in the private garden."

"We don't know yet."

"Still . . ."

She handed him the book, and he opened it.

There were several signatures on each page, as if the men had come in twos or threes, sometimes. He found Nelson's name, and that of Gerald Dunn, as well as the Major's, as he'd expected. Looking up from the page where the Captain had signed, he asked, "Are these names all the men who served here?"

"Yes, as far as I know."

"Did any of them make you feel—uncomfortable?"

"Several did," she admitted. "Some of the ranks had so little in common with Lady Benton. As you'd expect. I tried to put them at ease, but it was clear, coming here to tea was comparable to an invitation to a hanging."

He smiled. He'd read the names on every page, and none of them leapt out at him as a possible suspect.

She was saying, "Some of them were quite charming. I expect others wrote to their wives or their mothers, telling them all about tea here. They had probably never been in a house like this one. One or two undoubtedly believed this was far too much for one person to own. Very Bolshevik in their thinking." She smiled. "One of the men was local, and he'd probably heard stories about the Abbey all his life. He asked to see the Madonna."

"What did he think of her?" he asked, curious. This was very likely Gerald Dunn.

"He asked who had carved her. It was one piece of oak, and that fascinated him."

Frowning, she added, "I was quite shocked to learn later that he'd deserted. He didn't seem to be the sort."

"In what way?"

"He had nice manners. He was quiet, until he spoke of his younger brother, and then he was quite animated. He clearly liked the child, and enjoyed spending his leaves with his family." As he closed the book, she took it from him and put it back in the cupboard.

"Why did they burn down the hut?" she asked, turning back to him.

"I don't know. Unless they feared they'd left something there that might betray them." He took out his handkerchief and unfolded it. "I found these things."

She came to stand beside him, looking at the items. "This key. Do you think it's to the house?"

"We'll try it and see."

"And this ring. It's rather odd, don't you think? Not the sort of thing one might find in a jeweler's shop." She set it aside. "And this bit of paper. It looks like part of a ticket of some sort. Too bad there isn't more of it." She carried it to the window where the light was better, but shook her head. "I expect it's nothing in particular."

When he collected the items and put them back in his coat pocket, they took the key and tried it in each of the house doors.

It didn't fit any of them. Turning it over in her fingers, she said, "I feel much better knowing that it doesn't. I only gave out one key, and that was to Captain Nelson. I shouldn't care to think someone else had a copy."

He left soon after that.

But not to return to Walmer just yet.

He stopped in the yard of The Monk's Choice, and went to knock at the door. There was no answer. And so he took out the key again, and tried it.

It didn't fit.

As he went back to the motorcar, he looked up at the windows on the first floor, but there was no one watching him—not that he could see at any rate.

Pulling out of the yard, he looked across at the fenced-in field of the Home Farm, where in the mist he'd seen the mare standing.

He thought it was empty at first, then saw that someone was walking back to the barn. At this distance it was difficult to tell if the man was Henry.

On the off chance that Henry had seen something the night of the fire, he went on, pulling into the lane that ran past the house toward the barn and stables and other outbuildings. But there was no one around, although he called.

From there he went to Patricia Lowell's house, to test the key in her door.

To his surprise, it didn't fit. He'd been almost sure that it would, that it had been her key, since it hadn't worked at the Hall. That it had fallen from her pocket as the noose was put around her neck and she was hauled up into the rafters.

The house had two other doors, but they too were no match for the key.

Hamish said, "It's for a lock that doesna' exist. For a door at the airfield, long since taken doon. It could ha' been there for years."

Rutledge was tempted to agree. But why else was the hut burned?

He went on into the village—little more than a hamlet, except that it had a small church. Twenty houses, he thought, on the main street, a dozen more on each of the smaller lanes that turned off the road.

There was someone in the Rectory garden, weeding between the rows.

Rutledge stopped and got out, walking around the Rectory house to the kitchen garden. This was, he thought, the New Rectory, smaller than the old one, which had been Patricia Lowell's home and that of her family.

The Rector looked up as he heard Rutledge approaching.

"Good day," he said cheerfully, standing up to greet his visitor. "You find me with time on my hands. And as the Devil is said to find work for idle hands, I'm ridding the world of a few weeds. How may I be of service?"

He was an older man, graying and tired for all his lighthearted greeting. Rutledge had seen the man's name on the board by St. Matthew's churchyard. It was MacNeal Farmer. And he could hear the slightest hint of a Scottish accent in the man's voice.

"My name is Rutledge. Scotland Yard. I'm looking into the death of Patricia Lowell. Was she a member of your church?"

"She was indeed," he replied, his expression changing to sadness.

"As were her parents. A sad end for a lovely young woman. If you'd care to step into the kitchen, I'll put the kettle on. I could do with a cup."

And so Rutledge followed him into the house through the kitchen door. The room was spotless, the kettle on the cooker, and the curtains at the open windows stiff with starch.

As if he had noticed Rutledge's glance, Farmer said, "My wife is away doing good works. We have an ill parishioner, and she's sitting with her for an hour." He began to make tea with practiced ease, as if he had done it many times. "But it's Patricia you wish to know about. She had a kind heart. And widowhood was difficult for her. She and her husband were very close, and she took his loss quite hard. I think it was the work at the Hall that saved her. Got her out of that lonely, empty house, gave her something she felt she was contributing, and brought other people into her day, even though they were strangers."

Bringing cups and saucers out of the cupboard, searching in a drawer for spoons, he shook his head. "It must have been the nights that were hardest. Clara stayed with her the first week after the news came about George. I feared for her, to be honest. But the young are resilient. And it helped, I think, that he had been away for two years by that time. She was used to his being gone."

"Did she have any close friends?"

"There was Betty Hicks, but she died in the influenza epidemic. It took a toll here. I'm priest in two churches. The Rector in the next village died in the war. And the Church hasn't seen fit to replace him, so far. He was killed on the Somme, ministering to the ill and dying. So many of them died, you know. He wrote to tell me how it was, how many couldn't be saved." He drew a breath. "I can't begin to think what it must have been like out there."

But Rutledge had been there, had seen it for himself. He could feel the rising tide of memories, and fought them off. And so he made no answer, and Farmer took that as disinterest.

"Forgive me, it was Patricia you came to ask about, not the war."

Bringing the teapot to the table, then fetching the little jug of milk from the pantry, he added, "What else would you like to know?"

"Anything out of the ordinary, anything that was different—unusual—in the last week before her death?"

"I didn't see her at all that last week. Well, at services on Sunday, of course. She was in the congregation, I don't recall anything untoward about her then, no anxiety or sadness, nothing that would have led me to feel a concern for her." He passed a cup to Rutledge, adding, "Sometimes the shepherd must go to his flock when someone is in trouble. Too many eyes, you see. Or they haven't the courage to call. I try to make it easy for them to speak to me."

"Nothing in the village that might have affected her. A death—a newcomer—an illness—anything?"

Farmer shook his head. "I'm sorry." And then, brightening a little, he went on. "Oh—it escaped my mind. It must have been a fortnight ago, she came to the Rectory to speak to me. I was visiting the sick, my wife was here, and when Clara asked her if she would like to come in and wait for me, she said she had come about the flowers in her husband's memory. She always honors him with flowers in the church. And that it could wait."

"Did she seem unsettled when she spoke to your wife?"

"Clara didn't notice it if she was."

"And you didn't follow up—the shepherd going to his flock?" Rutledge tried to keep the sarcasm out of his voice.

"Actually, I did, but she wasn't at home. Since she didn't call again, I assumed she had talked to someone on the flower committee this month."

What in hell's name had she intended to speak to this man about? Rutledge asked himself, drinking his tea. Or had Mrs. Lowell's visit been about the flowers after all, and it was after that when something had happened?

He'd always had in the back of his mind that she must have seen something—someone—on the way from the Abbey to her house. But how to find someone to ask?

Farmer was saying, "And then there's Mrs. Trask, poor soul, who sees shadows under her bed. I don't think she sleeps well. At any rate, she sent her son for me, to tell me that she had seen a stranger lurking about the churchyard in the middle of the night. But when I investigated, there was no one at all. There's a table tomb, old Mrs. Thompkins'. She had a fear of being put in the ground. But it offers a little shelter, and we've had soldiers out of work who sleep rough in its shelter—"

He broke off when Rutledge, who had been occupied with his own thoughts, barely listening to the Rector, suddenly realized what the man was saying.

"When was this?" he asked abruptly.

Taken aback, Farmer said, "Let me see . . . A few weeks ago, I think. I try to help them if I can find them—they are often hungry and have no hope of work."

"I should like to speak to Mrs. Trask."

"But there was no one in the churchyard—"

"When did you look?"

"The next morning—before breakfast—when her son came pounding at my door."

That was well before the Friday when Lady Benton had seen the ghosts in her private garden . . .

He finished his tea. "Will you come with me?" Mrs. Trask might very well speak more freely to her priest than to a stranger.

In the event, once started, Mrs. Trask was anything but shy with a Scotland Yard Inspector in her tiny parlor.

The cottage backed up to the churchyard on the lane that curved around the church and rejoined the main road several more houses along what was called Churchyard Lane.

She was not as old as Rutledge had expected. Seventy perhaps, but her blue eyes were alert, and she was very happy to talk to anyone who came to call. The question was, how good was her vision? She wore gold-rimmed glasses, and in the middle of the night, waking from sleep, she might not have had them to hand.

"Tell me about what you saw in the churchyard several weeks ago?" he asked after the introductions, an offer of tea, a monologue about her son having lived in London for a time and having considered joining the Met.

"But of course he doesn't have the patience of a policeman. He's more suited to railway work. That was, until the war took his leg. And now he's the postmaster with a tiny box of a room in the General Store."

"Does he live with you?"

"His house is next but one to mine. And much as I care for my grandchildren, I do sometimes wish he lived in the next village."

Rutledge forced himself to keep a straight face. "Can you show me the window from which you can see the churchyard?" he asked.

She glanced at the Rector. "It's my bedroom . . . Well, I'm not used to visitors asking to see it."

"I should like to see the view you had when you noticed someone in the churchyard." He turned to the Rector. "This is a police matter, I'm sure that makes a difference. Mr. Farmer can wait for us."

Only partly mollified, she said, "Still . . ."

"Mrs. Trask, you might well have witnessed a felon lurking there," he told her, "and you would not wish someone to come to harm because I didn't have sufficient information to find and stop him before that happened."

Mrs. Trask was nobody's fool. She stared at him in horror. "You aren't saying, are you, that he killed poor Mrs. Lowell?"

He swore to himself. "Early days, Mrs. Trask, but you must keep that to yourself. I am serious, I don't want you to mention this to anyone and find yourself in danger as a consequence."

"Of course I shan't," she snapped. "I can see that for myself. Come on, then, up the stairs with you."

There were only two bedrooms at the top of the stairs, and instead of running side by side, with the staircase in between, they were back to back, one facing the street and the other facing the back garden, with the stairwell and a cupboard in between.

The room was as tidy as the parlor, with a bed, a small armoire, two chairs, and a washstand as its only furnishings. Drapes had been opened, allowing the morning light from a pair of windows to fill the room with brightness.

Mrs. Trask neatly stepped ahead of him to stand between him and the chamber pot discreetly set to one side of the washstand, and pointed to the windows.

"The moon was up, I could see clearly. The church clock had only just struck three, and there was someone moving about old Mrs. Thompkins' tomb. He stayed there, he didn't leave, and I went down to be sure my doors were locked, even though the churchyard wall stands between us. He was still there when I came back up the stairs. I watched for half an hour or so, but he didn't move. I thought perhaps he was sleeping rough. And there was a little chill that night. Not that the dead could warm him."

"Are you certain it was a man?" Rutledge asked her. She was right, he could see the table tomb from here. "Not a dog?"

She was affronted. "I may be seventy, but I'm not blind," she told him sharply. "Even without my glasses. I can still tell two from four, and he had two legs. And before you ask, he had on trousers, not skirts."

Hamish said, his voice seeming loud in the small room, "She's a verra' sound witness."

And he was right, Rutledge thought. The woman's gray hair covered a very clear mind.

"He was not there in the morning?"

"I usually rise with the sun, and he was not there."

"You hadn't seen him there before that night?"

"I draw the curtains most nights. But the moon was bright, and after I turned down the lamp, I decided to open them."

Oddly enough, very like Lady Benton, she enjoyed the moonlit nights.

"Still," she was saying, "I did look the next night, and there was no sign of him."

"Did you report this to the police?"

"The nearest police are in Walmer. How was I to report to them? I sent my son to speak to Rector."

She had done her duty.

He stood for a moment, looking out at the back of the churchyard, the table tomb clearly visible from here, the only one of its kind that he could see. And then he turned to leave. "Thank you very much, Mrs. Trask. I will look into it."

Satisfied, she escorted him down the stairs, offered them tea again, but Rutledge told her that he must pay a visit to the churchyard.

On the way back to the Rectory, Farmer asked, "Do you truly believe there's anything to this business?"

"Probably not, but I should take a look. Still, I would advise you not to mention my interest in it. Or even that anyone had noticed anything in the churchyard. It's best."

"Yes, yes, I understand."

They walked in silence back to the Rectory, and Rutledge left Farmer at the house door, not wanting anyone else tramping about on the ground before he'd had a good look.

But whoever had been there, he'd left nothing behind, not a bottle, the paper from a packet of sweets—nothing.

There was the imprint of a boot some three feet from the table tomb, in the soft ground near an older, sunken grave.

Rutledge squatted there to take a closer look.

A military boot, meant for long marches, perfect for walking any distance, if they fit well enough that no blisters formed. The tread was well worn, especially on the inner side of the heel, as if the wearer had some problem with his leg. Other than that, the sole was ordinary.

Hamish said, "Ye canna' know who walked here."

It was true, but he had something to be going on with.

The road perforce passed the Old Rectory, and Rutledge pulled in. There was little hope of find a matching shoe print here, but he owed it to Patricia Lowell to try.

It took him two hours of scouring the ground around the house and then around the outbuildings.

And there, by the shed where Mrs. Lowell had kept her bicycle, was a faint heel print just inside the door. Someone—it looked like a woman's boot—had stepped on the print, obliterating much of it. But not that distinctive wearing down on the inner side of the heel.

Hamish said, "It's a vagrant looking for something to steal."

But was it?

And where else could he search?

He got back into his motorcar and drove on to the pub, The Monk's Choice.

Rutledge really didn't care if anyone saw him or not.

But there were too many prints for him to pick out the one he was after. He widened his circle, getting farther and farther from the door.

And there it was, left in a bit of mud where the grass grew close to the pub yard.

Whoever it belonged to, the owner of the boot had been here.

Hamish warned him again. "Ye canna' be sure."

13

Hamish quarreled with him all the way back to the Abbey, where Rutledge left his motorcar by the hedge.

Try as he would, the airfield was too vast a site to search. And even though he looked closely at the ruins of the burned-out hut, too many shoes had passed through here at the time of the fire to pick out any distinctive boot.

When he went to the stable yard and looked, he found a partial heel that was very like the one he had found in the churchyard.

Hamish was right, it proved nothing.

Rutledge left the stable yard and drove back toward Walmer, without speaking to Lady Benton. There was nothing he could tell her that wouldn't worry her more.

As he came around the hotel to the main entrance, he found Mrs. Dunn just leaving.

"I thought you'd left, with no news for me about my boy."

"I haven't left. And sadly I have no news to give you," he told her.

She nodded. "I'd hoped you weren't like the others. Inspector Hamilton, and the Major." Turning, she walked away.

Rutledge said, "I promise you, I haven't forgotten your son."

But she kept going, as if this was only one more false promise.

He watched her until she turned down one of the side streets, out of his line of sight.

Instead of going inside the hotel, as he'd planned, Rutledge went back to his motorcar and drove back the way he'd come. At the hedge where he'd left the motorcar before, he got out. And this time instead of walking through what was left of the airfield, he put on his Wellingtons and set out to cross the meadow to the line of trees that marked its boundary. Moving through them, he came out finally on a marshy finger of land where the sea had come up so many times that it had soured the soil. The footing was treacherous, and he was glad of his Wellingtons. The marsh was unable to drain because of a barrier of sand that had been left by retreating tides. They brought in the sea, but couldn't retrieve it as they pulled out again. Seagrasses had grown in patches here and there, and beyond them was the strand and the ripple of water. On the far side of it was the Continent, France and Belgium. And here was a perfect place to land the troops of an invading army. But that hadn't happened, although it had been a fear throughout the war.

He walked down to the water's edge, discovered a few razor shells, and the tracks of seabirds, then found a piece of wood that looked from the flecks of paint still caught in the grain as if it had come from a ship that had been sunk by one side or the other, in the war.

Turning, Rutledge walked the edge of the marsh for some distance, but he could see nowhere that would provide more than the shallowest of graves, for storm tides could easily uncover it. If Gerald Dunn had been killed somewhere on the airfield—at the farthest end of the runway, for one, where could his body have been taken?

Hamish said, "It's no' likely he was killed here. Ye ken, a live man is easier to move than a dead one."

Then he'd been lured somewhere else.

If that is what happened, he *was* dead, and not hiding out in the tenements of Manchester or Birmingham. It would take an army of men to find him there, or the Foot Police . . .

Did Haldane know what had become of Gerald Dunn? Rutledge rather thought not. Men like Haldane left the Dunns of this world to subordinates . . .

He had walked far enough to find himself at the edge of another of the countless Essex inlets, where a scruffy dinghy was pulled up into the reeds, out of reach of the tides. In the distance on the far side of the water, he could see two men dragging a hose pipe to one of the tide-fed rectangles where salt accumulated through the evaporation of seawater. Rutledge watched them at their work. It was labor intensive, but they went about it with accustomed ease.

The hose pipe inserted where they wanted it, one of the men walked back to the sheds where the collected salt-laden water was pumped into vats and skimmed as the mineral rose to the surface. The other man began to look at several more rectangles, bending now and again to test them. Finally satisfied, he too disappeared in the direction of his fellow worker.

Reminding himself to buy a packet of Walmer Salt for Melinda, Rutledge turned and walked back through the marshland and the trees to the meadow.

From there, at the edge of the trees, he could see the house rising on its knoll, the westering sun silhouetted it, and from here it could be the Abbey that it once was, with the refectory and the dorter, the workrooms and the chapel.

He was still thinking about that when he reached the hedge and walked past the broken place where the Captain had died. He looked up at the house again. This close to, the sun's spring brightness was blocked, and he could see the terrace and steps that led to the broad spread of the lawns. The windows were dark, empty, as if no one lived there now—except for one at the very top of the house, the old attics where the servants had once lived in the sixteenth century. A light moved past the glass, brighter than the surrounding darkness, and Rutledge set out at a run.

It took him a good ten minutes to reach the door to which he possessed a key, and, breathing hard, he made himself take his time inserting it into the lock. The door opened, and he went up the stairs, leaving it standing wide behind him, his mind busy remembering how he had found his way when he was searching the rooms.

He reached the floor where the last of the servants here had lived, and searched for the stairs to the next level. It was partway down a long narrow passage, and it opened under his hand. The stairs here were dusty, and he saw the prints as he climbed, coming out into a passage with a single window at the end facing the stables. He stopped, making an effort to calm his breathing as he listened.

The light was fading as it moved farther west, and as he stood there, he could feel the emptiness. Still, he went down the side that overlooked the meadow, opening each door and closing it after peering in. The tiny windows gave very little light, but the rooms were so small it didn't matter. There was no place to hide in any of them. Any furniture that had once been here had been taken away years ago.

Rutledge came to the room he was nearly sure he'd seen from the airfield, flung open the door. There were more footprints in the dust, a different boot from the print he'd seen in the courtyard, but he thought close to the same size. They had disturbed the dust more there by the window, he noticed, but no one was here now.

Unsatisfied, he continued his search, and finally came to the end of the passage and the tiny window overlooking the stable yard. He peered out, but there all he could see were the stables below, beyond them the tennis courts, and in the distance, the rooftop of the Home Farm's barn.

When he'd looked into every room on the other side of the passage, Hamish said derisively, "Ye've seen your ain ghost."

But ghosts didn't carry lamps or torches. And one or the other was needed in these attics, where the only illumination came from those tiny windows.

He walked back to the stairs, and went down them, bent on searching that floor as well, but as he stepped out into the dim passage, someone leapt out of the shadows and swung something in his direction.

Even though he ducked, he wasn't in time, and whatever it was brushed by his head with enough force to send him to his knees.

Hamish was shouting, "On your feet!"

Shaking his head to clear it, he was in time to see someone just start-ing down the next flight of stairs. He could hear the clatter of boots on the treads.

Rutledge stumbled to his feet, and followed. These were the back stairs, now, leading down in darkness to the kitchen passage. He was moving fast and he could still hear whoever it was he was following, a flight ahead of him.

The passage door to the back garden swung open in a momentary shaft of light, bright after the darkness. Rutledge saw a figure dressed in black dart out and turn left, toward the stables.

He had only one more flight to go when the passage door into the kitchen was flung open, and a woman stepped out.

"What in God's name are you playing at?" she snapped.

He nearly cannoned into Lady Benton.

"Out of the way," he ordered, but she refused to move, and he had to physically set her aside as she protested vehemently, one hand clutch-ing his arm. But he got clear and went through the door, turning left through a bed of young beets, trampling them underfoot as his quarry had done before him. But when he reached the stable yard, there was no sign of the man he'd been after.

Rutledge went into the stables and the carriage house next to it, flushed his quarry from behind a handsome landau, and chased him into the yard.

He had vanished again. Swearing, Rutledge searched everywhere he could think of, but the man was nowhere to be seen. He had just come out of the small shed where gardening tools were kept when he stopped abruptly.

Lady Benton was bearing down on him, her face flushed with anger.

"Go back inside. There's an intruder—" he began.

"Where? Not in the house, surely!"

"The old attics. Go inside, I tell you. Find the other women and make sure they are all safe."

"What was he doing up there? And how did he find a way inside?"

"Wait here," Rutledge said, still breathing hard. And ignoring her protests, he turned and ran toward the lane. But it was empty in both directions as well. Had the intruder hidden in the hedge? He started after him again but whirled as he heard running feet. But whoever it was had reached the road, and was out of sight.

It was useless to follow him, there were endless places to hide in the fields across from the Abbey's wall.

When he turned back to Lady Benton, she was waiting impatiently. "You must tell me what is happening."

And this time he caught the anxiety beneath the anger.

"I was coming up from the airfield. I saw a light in the old attics. I let myself in and went to see who might be up there. It isn't a likely place for your staff to go."

"Oh, dear—Margaret had just gone to the servants' floor to look for a pail she remembered seeing there—"

"I might have caught him, if you hadn't stepped out of the kitchen just at the wrong time." He was still angry with her, while her own anger had changed to worry.

"I heard someone racketing down the stairs when I went to fetch more milk for the undercroft. We have visitors. I thought one of them had dropped out of the tour and was wandering about on his own. I didn't recognize you at first, and when I did, I thought perhaps that's who you saw."

"It's late for a tour," he told her.

"They asked for the evening. A half dozen couples. It seems they were staying in Chelmsford, and someone who had toured the house before suggested it. They wrote to ask for this evening. They wanted to see it by candlelight, as it must have been ages ago. A good deal of work for us. But they offered a great deal of money, and so I agreed. They're having a special tea in the undercroft."

"Then let's go there now, and see if there are still six couples." He started toward the door to the house.

"I won't have you disturbing them," she said, hurrying after him.

"Lady Benton, I'd rather disturb your guests than know someone got into your house." He kept walking, long strides.

She had no choice but to try to keep pace.

Rutledge opened the door into the house and held it for her, then followed her into the sitting room and beyond. Mrs. Hailey had a long-handled candle snuffer and was putting out the candles in the third room they came to. Beyond, on the way to the chapel, evening shadows were thick. But Lady Benton led the way with the assurance of long practice.

In the dimness, lit only by the windows high above, the Madonna was almost ghostly in her gray robes.

He could hear voices and laughter coming from the undercroft, and as he descended the stairs, Lady Benton was speaking to him. But he ignored her.

There were four tables set with white cloths, china and silver, and tall candelabra gave a flickering softness to the low-ceilinged room that the usual lamps lacked.

He did a quick count. Six couples, twelve people. They were all there. At the long serving table, the middle-aged woman attending it looked up and smiled when she saw Lady Benton.

But Rutledge turned, and with a hand on her back, gave Lady Benton no choice but to retreat back up the stairs.

"I thought—" she began, but Rutledge shook his head.

"There were twelve people at the tables. None of them appeared to have been racing back to take his seat. And Mrs. Hailey would have seen him."

Exasperated, she said, "Well, what am I to do, pray? Are you certain he's gone? Or did he slip back into the kitchen passage, where we left the door standing wide?"

Rutledge said, "Do you want me to search?"

"No—no. But I expect you ought to stay until the guests leave. Just to be certain all of them do." She sighed. "I must admit, this is getting on my nerves. And I'm not usually timid or easily frightened."

"I don't believe you saw a ghost. What you saw was real enough. I'm nearly certain that the second man was an accomplice, who got up and walked away."

"But who is doing this, and why?"

They were in the hall, speaking softly because their voices echoed. "We need to be a bit more private," he suggested, but she shook her head.

"They're due to leave in another twenty minutes."

He began to say something when Mrs. Hailey came out of the state rooms and reported, "All the candles are out. I went back through, to make certain of that. They did enjoy going through, I can tell you. I heard some of the comments, and so did Elizabeth and Sara. I told them to go into the kitchen and put the kettle on."

"Yes, that was well done. Ah—I think I hear movement."

She turned, waiting, and a few minutes later, the first of the guests began to appear at the top of the steps, smiling and talking, clearly pleased with their evening.

Lady Benton turned toward the main door. Mrs. Hailey was already pushing it open.

"You'd better stay. The butler?" she said to Rutledge, and then to Mrs. Hailey, "Will you begin to see to the locks?"

"Yes, of course."

And then the guests were saying good night to Lady Benton, profusely thanking her for a marvelous evening, commenting on the beauty of the rooms by candlelight, and slowly making their way out the door.

As the rest of the party came up the stairs and began to leave, Rutledge examined them more closely. The men were mostly in their fifties, he thought, two of them probably ex-officers, their backs ramrod straight. Even so, none of them as agile as the man he'd been chasing.

From the stairs, the woman who had been serving signaled Lady Benton that they were all accounted for, and then she went back down to clear away.

Several of the women glanced sideways at Rutledge as he stood behind and to the right of Lady Benton, as if wondering who he might be. He kept an appropriately formal expression pinned to his face, all the while wishing they would hurry out the door.

And then they were gone, in a flurry of goodbyes and final words of thanks. He stepped forward and swung the heavy door shut as soon as they had reached the drive and the motorcars waiting for them.

Setting the locks and putting the bar in place, he said, "We need to talk."

"Not until everyone has gone. If you'll help Cynthia clear away the trays from downstairs? We can leave the rest until morning. We don't have a tour scheduled for tomorrow."

As she left for the kitchen, he did as he was asked, carrying up the heavy trays of food and the used dishes. Cynthia, grateful for the help, was chatting about the guests. "Sir Anthony knew the late Lord Benton," she was saying. "They had gone to school together, and he was remembering coming here for a weekend as a boy. I think that's why he asked to bring his houseguests over."

He listened with half an ear, trying to finish here and move on to the kitchen.

When they got there, the tea was ready, and the staff helped themselves to the remaining sandwiches and little cakes.

Excusing himself, he went out the back passage and quietly tested all the doors. Mrs. Hailey had been thorough, and they were locked. By the time he came back to the kitchen, the staff was beginning to leave. Lady Benton or Mrs. Hailey let them out the stable yard door, and then Mrs. Hailey herself left, in a hurry to reach Walmer before dark.

Lady Benton came back to the wreckage that was the kitchen, and shook her head. "I couldn't ask them to stay any longer. Do you mind if I wash these dishes and the silver? They are our third best, but I don't care to leave food on them."

Mrs. Hailey had cleared them and put them into soak. Rutledge was given a cloth and asked to dry as Lady Benton washed. She looked up once, smiling. "I've had any number of distinguished guests in this house, but never has Scotland Yard dried my dishes. What is it you want to tell me?"

"I don't know what is happening, at least not yet. But it's possible that a man who was known to have committed three murders and very likely two more, might have been a member of the squadron posted here."

She stopped what she was doing. "How could that be? I met most of the young men who served here. Some of them were rough around the edges, but I can't think of one of them who might have done such things. And how, pray, did he come to be in the Royal Air Force? Did they not look into the backgrounds of the men they trained?"

"He was very likely using another name. And we were desperate for men, out there. Even if his credentials were stolen, when someone examined them, they would appear to be in order. There would be no reason to question their authenticity. As long as the photograph, if there was one, appeared to match the face, the credentials were accepted. God knows, their likenesses were poor enough at the best of times."

"No, I don't believe anyone I met was a murderer."

"Did you meet all of them?"

"Yes. Not right away, but eventually. Well, they had access to the grounds here, I had to be careful myself." She finished the plate she was washing and passed it to him. "Do you have a name? Any name?"

"Franklin. Miles Franklin."

She said the name over to herself silently. "I can tell you he didn't use that name. But there were at least three men with the initials *M F*."

"He wouldn't have had a choice in his new name. It would have had to match the orders he was carrying. Otherwise, he would arouse suspicion. The trouble is, we have no idea who those orders were actually written for. And the man who took them over was very careful to show that he was capable of carrying them out. No one had any reason to doubt him."

"But all the men *left*. Why would he come back?"

"As far as I know, he went to France shortly after war's end—as soon as he was demobbed—before the airfield was taken down. He's probably been there ever since. Now he's come back to England, and we think he might have come here."

"Why?"

"That's the difficulty. We've no idea. Possibly because he can't continue to use the false name he had assumed in France. Or even more likely, because he wants to change it, and there is something that prevents it. And he's focused on this house."

"But I couldn't have known him, could I? I'm fairly certain Eric didn't."

Rutledge took a deep breath as he dried the last cup and set it aside.

It was a leap. Still, he asked, "Could Captain Nelson have discovered the truth, and that was why he had to die?"

"How could the Captain have known the truth? Besides, he'd have warned me."

"He might have believed you would be safer, if you didn't know. Until he had alerted the authorities and steps could be taken."

She hung up the cloth she'd been using to wash up, and took the tea towel from him to hang that up as well.

"Why would this man have killed Patricia?"

"Perhaps because she saw him and recognized him. And he didn't know just how much the Captain had told everyone in the house."

"That's rather awful to think about."

"Yes."

"Why was he in this house? If he believes I might also recognize him?"

After a moment he said, "Could he be searching for something? Not money, not something to take away and sell. For something that he believes would incriminate him."

"Now you've frightened me."

"I'm sorry. It's what I believe. And you need to know."

There had been something on her mind. He'd sensed it since Margaret Hailey had left them alone in the kitchen. But he had waited. In her own good time, he thought.

Now, after a pause, she said, looking out the window at the shadows in the garden. "He pushed me on the stairs to the undercroft. Didn't he? Why didn't he kill me then, and be done with it?"

"I don't know," he told her truthfully. "Perhaps because you are friends with the Chief Constable. Or perhaps because he misjudged his push, and you survived after all."

Hamish, speaking up in the lamp-lit kitchen, the pots and pans overhead catching the light now and then, the glasses and cups and saucers lined up like soldiers on the deal table, said, "Because he doesna' know if he will find what he's after. The house will be shut, and he canna' come and go sae freely."

Rutledge found himself agreeing, but he didn't share it with Lady Benton.

She was saying, "Do you think he's in the house now? That he came back while we were in the great hall?"

"There's no way of knowing. But I think not. We're aware now that he has been inside at least once." But to himself he added, *He'll wait and catch us unprepared.*

Hamish said something, reminding him.

Rutledge said, "There's a favor I'd like to ask."

"Yes. Of course."

But it clearly wasn't what she was expecting as he answered her. "There's a young woman—her name is Liz—who waits table in The Salt Cellar. She's treated rather roughly by the barmaids and some of the patrons. She applied for work, of any kind, at the hotel, but was turned away. Too many people associate her with the pub. I'd like to see her out of that situation."

"How did you come to know this young woman?" She was frowning.

"I had looked for Nelson's grave. And she came along. It appears she knew him, and he'd been kind to her."

There was a flicker of something in Lady Benton's eyes. "I don't see how? Was she telling the truth?"

"Yes. He came to The Salt Cellar a number of times, apparently, not wishing to meet anyone from the airfield. I gather it was off-limits to the ranks. He walked her home, when she had to stay late."

He could read her face, now. She was jealous of the time Liz had spent talking to Nelson. The Captain had been given special privileges at the Hall. He didn't consort with prostitutes, and then call on her the next morning . . .

"He felt sorry for her. And did what he could, inside the bounds of propriety. There is no way out of what will eventually become a very different life for Liz. In the end, she'll have to survive, and do whatever she's told."

"What would you like me to do?"

"The hotel is better than The Salt Cellar. Or somewhere she will be treated decently. She has very little training."

"The women who worked there had a—a reputation, and the medical officer warned the men about possible syphilis. All right. I'll put in a good word for her at the hotel. Or rather ask Margaret if she would. It might seem less like patronage, if Margaret handles the details."

"Thank you."

But her heart wasn't in it. He could see that, in her choice of letting Margaret deal with Liz. Still, she would keep her word, he thought.

She took a deep breath, then said, "It's late. If you don't mind, I'll see you out now." And with a wry smile, she went on, "Perhaps I should find a dog."

"Lock yourself in your bedroom. Is there anything you might like in the night? A Thermos of tea, more sandwiches? We can collect them now."

"No," she said calmly. "I refuse to be a prisoner in my own house. But my husband has always kept a revolver in the estate room. I shall carry that with me if I must come downstairs in the night."

"Do you know how to use it?" he asked, alarmed.

"Yes, Eric taught me how before he went to France. He teased me, begging me not to shoot him by mistake, when he had his next leave. But he never came home . . ."

Her voice caught, and she turned to lead the way out of the kitchen.

Rutledge, following her, remembered the word on the scroll across the closed gates. *A place of weeping.*

For the woman walking ahead of him, the lamp held steady in her hand, it had been just that.

After Lady Benton had locked the door behind him, Rutledge went around the house and tested each door himself. Then he retrieved his motorcar.

By the time he'd reached the junction where the lane stopped at the main road, he turned toward The Monk's Choice rather than toward Walmer.

Tonight it had what must for the pub be a goodly crowd.

Newbold was busy behind the bar, and the level of noise indicated that most of those present were enjoying themselves. They wore the usual clothing of men who worked on farms or in the salt beds. Boots with their corduroy trousers stuffed into the top, a heavy shirt and—for the benefit of the pub—a jacket over it. The ages ranged from twenty to sixty, Rutledge decided.

The noisy laughter and chatter began to fade as more and more men became aware of the differently dressed stranger joining them. They stared, reserving judgment.

Newbold's face flushed with anger, but he said, almost civilly, "What can I get for you?"

Rutledge ordered the first half of a local brew he'd seen on a poster along the road.

Newbold served him. Rutledge, paying for it, said, "Any strangers here of late? Other than me?"

"Not here." His voice was as cold as his expression.

"The airmen sometimes stopped in, I think."

"Most didn't."

"Get to know any of them well? Anyone in particular?"

"If you're asking if the Captain came in, the answer is no."

"What about Gerry Dunn?"

The man behind the bar shifted his weight. "I had nothing to do with the Dunn lad. He was never welcomed here."

"Why not?"

"His mother lived near my mother for a time. After my father died. She was temperance as well."

Rutledge set down his glass. "I understand you have rooms upstairs. I'm thinking of moving closer to the Abbey. Shorter drive. I'd like to see what you have available."

The man was polishing the counter with a damp cloth, rubbing at a spot that only he could see.

"I've taken over the best one myself. The shed out back leaks," he said after a moment.

"It doesn't matter. I'm seldom in my room."

One of the patrons nearest the bar looked up and said, "Show it to him. The sooner done, the sooner gone."

Cornered, Newbold said, "There's no one to take over the bar."

"I'll be happy to have a look on my own." Rutledge started toward the stairs, and Newbold hesitated, began to follow him, then thought better of it.

Rutledge took the steps two at a time and found himself in a narrow, dark hall with three doors facing him. He opened the one to his left, saw that it was occupied, clothes hung over the bedposts and flung across chairs, the windows grimy and the cheap coverlet on the bed stained and worn in places. The odors of sweat and stale beer filled the air.

He shut that door, discovered that the one in the middle was a shallow closet with shelves that were once intended for extra towels and bed linens but now held extra stock for the bar.

Moving on to the third door, he found a smaller room, stuffy with disuse, an underlying odor here of cigarette smoke. Otherwise, the bed against the inside wall was made, there was dust on the small washstand between the windows, the pitcher and bowl completely dry.

He turned to go, then noticed that the coverlet was long, the side he could see nearly touching the floor.

Rutledge dropped to one knee and lifted it. There was dust under the bed as well, and he was about to rise when he realized that there was something pushed far to the back wall, close to the front leg on that side.

It looked very much like a battered valise. He was about to reach for it when Newbold called from the stairs, "What are you about, up there? Doesn't take this long to look at a spare room."

He rose and walked to the stairs. "Admiring the view," he said, coming down. "I'll take the smaller room."

"It's already spoken for. Norm, here, he's had words with his wife, and wants to take it until she's calmed down."

Norm stood behind him, grinning. "A regular scold, my Dora is."
That brought a laugh from the rest of the men watching the exchange.

Rutledge had the feeling that Dora was not, and the others knew it.
"Very well." He'd paid for his half, and started toward the door.

A large man sitting by the bar rose. "You'll have a game of darts,
then, before you go."

The laughter had faded, there was now an odd tension in the room,
waiting for his answer.

Hamish said, "'Ware . . ."

Rutledge sighed. He had no desire to fight his way out of the pub.
"Why not?" he said, walking across the room, his gaze on the man
who'd challenged him. "Loser buys the next round, agreed?"

"Agreed."

The man joined him in front of the dartboard, as Rutledge picked
up the darts. He fumbled with them, dropped one, and quickly retrieved it, seemingly embarrassed. There was a low rumble of laughter
behind him.

Handing them to the large man, he said, "Why don't you throw
first?"

It was unexpected, but the man nodded, threw the darts with practiced ease, then turned and grinned.

"Better that," he said.

Rutledge stood there for several seconds, as if uncertain. When he
looked around the room, he could see that every man was leaning forward, eager to watch how his first throw might go.

Then he turned, lifted his arm, and threw the first dart. It hit the
wall instead of the pitted elm board. There was a roar of laughter behind him.

The large man walked over and picked it up, bringing it back to
Rutledge. "Point is, you want to hit the board."

Rutledge took the three darts, set his foot, and this time threw them
in quick succession.

They hit the outer rings, doubling the large man's score.

There was silence in the room for an instant. Then shouts of laughter at the large man's expense. His face turned a dark red, more anger than embarrassment for being taken as a fool. Then, thinking better of whatever was on his mind, he had the grace to laugh with the others.

He clapped Rutledge on the shoulder and said, "What'll you have, then?"

Rutledge accepted the other half, and when he was finished, he said a good night and left without hindrance.

As he stepped out into the cool evening air, he smiled grimly.

There was more to an Oxford education than Greek and the Classics, he thought, bending to turn the crank. The man was dead who had taught him how to play—his chest ripped open by machine-gun fire at second Ypres.

14

It was too late to go in search of Hamilton when he reached Walmer, and so he went to the hotel, asked for a tray to be brought up to his room, and went up the stairs.

A packet of papers lay on the coverlet of his bed. He could just make out the outline, against the paler cloth. He lit the lamp first, set his hat and coat on the chair, and went to pick it up. Curious.

It was heavily sealed, impossible to tamper with without tearing the packet open.

He took out his penknife and slit the top, drawing out the contents.

The thickest pages were the names of all the men who had served at the Abbey airfield. He scanned them, and they appeared to be as complete as the album of signatures that Lady Benton had shown him.

There was also a cutting from a newspaper, and a note attached.

Hardly worth including, but there you are.

It was a grainy view of several men coming down the passage inside a courthouse, on their way to a particular room.

He could pick out the barrister in his wig and robe, and a turnkey, whose faces were reasonably clear. Between them was a man in street clothes, his hands cuffed before him. Franklin, surely? He was looking down, trying not to face the camera. All that Rutledge could judge was his general height, perhaps five foot ten, and dark hair. Hardly enough to make a swift arrest in Walmer, Haldane was right there.

Rutledge read the attached article.

This photograph was apparently taken just before Franklin had broken free of the two men with him, and made a dash through the front doors of the courthouse to freedom.

He had been charged with the murder of his wife, her mother, and a sister-in-law. He had steadfastly refused to give the police any explanation for the crime, claiming he was innocent. They had taken him into custody only because he was the primary suspect, but the inquiry had also revealed that his sister-in-law had told a friend that he was tiring of her sister and their mother, who had been living with the couple. The article concluded by reporting that Franklin had no family living in the county, and the newspaper had failed to discover if he had any living relative at all.

The question then would be, who had provided him with protection in those first several seconds of his escape? In the immediate chaos after he broke free, the fact that he was dressed in a dark suit for his appearance in the dock would have made it difficult to spot him in busy streets on market day. By the time the authorities had collected themselves and started after him, chance favored him, and not the police or the prison guards.

Had someone spirited him away? Then who? Or had it truly been a simple matter of chance, and he was out of sight before anyone had reacted?

Rutledge set that aside, and picked up the cutting under it.

This was from a different newspaper about the finding of a soldier's body, left in a ditch just off the road, his clothing and all his possessions removed.

There was a notation in ink just under that.

Before Rutledge could read it, there was a knock at the door. His supper had been brought up.

He collected his tray, poured a cup of tea from the pot, and ate most of his meal.

So far, while the material that presumably Haldane had had delivered to his hotel room was interesting enough, there was very little that was useful in tracking down Miles Franklin or anyone else who might have killed Mrs. Lowell and was, in a very real sense, haunting Lady Benton. Hardly worth, in fact, paying for the service with that journey to France. At least, he had found Meredith Channing's grave. And that had eased some of the pain he'd felt at her shocking death. He owed her that final tribute, an acknowledgment of what might have been . . .

He got up and went to stand by the window. There were no diners in the garden tonight. No candles lit to mark each table. Only darkness, where on other nights there had been voices and laughter. Fitting, he thought, because there had been so much darkness in his relationship with Meredith—his shell shock, her missing husband, standing between them like shadows—

Hamish said, "There—by yon gate."

And Rutledge saw what he was talking about.

Taking his time, he turned from the window and stretched. Then, out of sight of the watcher below, he took the papers he'd been examining and shoved them under the bed. Keeping low, he went to the door, stepped out, and shut the door. And began to run.

He leapt down the steps, turned, and went out the main door, nearly colliding with a young couple just starting to walk in.

He reached the corner and stopped, catching his breath before easing around the side of the hotel, among the plantings there.

At the corner where he could see the rear gate into the garden with its tables, he paused.

The figure was just leaving, walking briskly toward the yard not far from where his motorcar stood. There were no more than a handful—four or five—other vehicles there, as most people who came to dine usually walked to the hotel.

Keeping the railing that set off the garden from the lane between him and the figure, Rutledge followed at a distance.

He saw the other man stop by the boot of the Rolls, then move toward the bonnet, fumbling to lift it.

Rutledge moved fast then, coming up before the man could react. And because his own reflexes were swifter, he had caught the man's left arm, swung him around and pinned him to the side of the motorcar.

"What the hell did you think you were about?" he demanded savagely, not bothering to hide the fury he was feeling. Yanking the man forward, he twisted his arm behind his back and marched him to the hotel, ignoring his prisoner's struggles and protests. He was taller, he had a longer reach, and there was nothing the other man could do to get free.

In front of the hotel, where the light from the windows was good enough to take a look at what he'd caught, Rutledge turned his captive so that he could see his face.

It was the man called Norm with the scold of a wife. From The Monk's Choice . . .

His disappointment only increased Rutledge's anger. "What were you doing with my motorcar? If you lie, I'll have you in for malicious mischief and vandalism."

Norm wasn't laughing now. Grimacing at the pain in his arm, he said, "Newbold—it was Newbold's idea. To damage your motorcar—for what you did in the pub tonight. Making us all look like—like fools. Let me go, damn you!"

"What were you doing to it?"

"Pull some of the wires—I don't know—"

Another couple walked past, staring, but kept going without a word.

"If I catch you—or anyone else—near my motorcar again, I'll have Newbold's license, and bring the lot of you in for plotting to obstruct the police in the course of carrying out their duties."

"You can't do that! I was only going to—"

"Can't I? I'm Scotland Yard, remember? Not your local Inspector. Now go home and apologize to your wife for calling her a scold in a public house."

He gave the arm a last twist, then released the man.

Norm turned and glared at him, but Rutledge said quietly, "Don't even think it. Next time it will be your neck, I promise you."

Something in that quiet voice reached the other man. "We intended no harm—"

"Tell Newbold to go to hell."

And he walked into the hotel, leaving Norm standing there, one hand clasped at his aching elbow. But he quickly left.

Satisfied, Rutledge let him go. Newbold was irascible, a man who had carried his father's rancor into the next generation. But he hadn't come to do his own mischief, he'd sent someone else. The question was, had it been done privately, or was it with the knowledge of all the patrons there?

Hamish said, "He's no' a murderer. But he could run with one."

And that was a good point.

He went back upstairs, ignoring the stares of the desk clerk and a few people sitting in the lounge.

In his room, he finished the tea before it could go cold, then retrieved the papers under his bed. He found the article again, about the dead man in the ditch who had finally been identified as a young soldier by the name of Robinson. Just as Vermuelen had written. Rutledge sat down in his chair and scanned it until he came to the comment in ink.

One of those missing possessions the police did not list. It was something that the dead man had found as a child, playing in the strand along the Cornish coast. A roughly made silver ring, twisted rather like a snake. According to the family.

Rutledge stared at it, read it a second time, then took out the handkerchief with the bits he'd found in the ashes of the hut fire.

And there it was. The sea must have worn off some of the details, but when Rutledge held it under the lamp, turning the ring in his fingers, he could see now the remaining pattern of a snake's body.

To be sure, he went to the washstand and cleaned the ring with soap and water.

After drying it, he went back to the lamp again. And if he'd had to answer under oath what the design was, he could truthfully reply that the ring looked very much like a snake swallowing its tail.

It was an ancient symbol, the Ouroboros. Found in ancient myths and in alchemy. A snake or even a dragon biting its own tail. Eternity.

A man's ring. He slipped it on his own finger, and it was tight. A slightly smaller hand, then. But it had fit Robinson's killer too, and he had kept it. Only to lose it somehow as he tried to hang a dead woman. And he was desperate enough to burn down the hut to be sure that no one else found it and could connect him with a murder.

Hamish said, "If no' with the lad's murder, it might connect him with yon airfield."

And it might, if someone remembered it. Was that someone Patricia Lowell?

Hamish added, "But there isna' a lake."

Lake . . .

Rutledge set down the cutting and went to the armoire and his valise. In it were the papers that he'd brought back from France.

He returned the pages concerning the war to the valise, and took the later pages to the desk.

He was halfway through them when he remembered. Vermuelen had spoken of the lake in that last rambling monologue at the end.

His English, sometimes muddled with French, and his heavy Flemish accent, added to the weak voice of a dying man, had made it difficult to find a thread.

Hamish said, "He said *lake* twice."

That was true.

Rutledge closed his eyes, his head back as he tried to recapture that last conversation.

There had been the reference to the nun, the man's sister—his final message, barely finished, for Haldane, but before that, what had he said about a lake?

Must look . . . And *bloody*—no, possibly *body*.

Haldane must have told Vermuelen to look for what had been taken from the body—not a lake, nor even a snake. A snake *ring*. And he, Rutledge, must look for it as well.

The one piece of information that hadn't been made public. That Franklin had kept and was possibly still wearing it, because he hadn't known the importance of the ring to the soldier he'd killed for his identification.

And Vermuelen must have seen that ring, still on the killer's hand, before he asked Franklin to travel with him to Calais.

He was trying to tell Rutledge that it was a means to find and identify a killer.

Rutledge sat back in his chair. Franklin had lost the ring in the hut.

While he, Rutledge, had found it in the ashes, without knowing its significance.

He got up and began to pace the room.

Franklin might have lost it, but before that, someone would surely remember it. A woman noticed such things as rings and clothing and the like.

Lady Benton hadn't known what it was, as he'd spread out the items left from the fire. Perhaps she hadn't had that much to do with the man wearing that ring.

But Patricia Lowell might have recognized it. The question was, in what connection? Why had it meant something to her? And even if she had connected it to someone who had been serving at the airfield during the war, that surely wasn't motive enough for murder.

And that was why the bicycle had had to disappear . . . somewhere on the road she had encountered the man wearing it. Trouble with a tire, the chain—and she must have seen it and remembered. Why didn't matter—the fact was, she had. And therefore remembered the man.

He put away everything he had been reading, locked all of it in his valise, and then locked the door to his room, after setting his tray from the kitchen outside the door.

Leaving the hotel, he went to Mrs. Hailey's house.

It was late, but she was still up. As he stood at the door, he could see a light in the kitchen.

He knocked. And after a time she lifted the lace curtain in the top half of her door and looked out, a frown between her eyes. But it smoothed out as she recognized him.

Unlocking the door, she opened it and said, "Is something wrong at the Abbey?"

"No, sorry, there was something I needed to ask you, and I didn't want to wait until morning."

"Come in then." She stepped to one side, and gestured to the parlor. "Could I offer you a cup of tea?" she went on, crossing the room to light the lamp on the table.

"Thank you, no." Then, as she sat down across from him, he said, "Was Patricia Lowell working at the Hall during the war?"

"Yes, of course. Well, not for the first few months. But one of the other women knew her and suggested that Lady Benton ask her. She told us that Patricia was anxious about her husband, and it would be a kindness to put her to work. She had been rolling bandages, that sort of thing, which only made her think about wounds and death and the war. The Hall on the other hand offered a very different day. Needless to say, she was very grateful to Lady Benton, and was fast one of our most dependable members of staff."

"When the airfield was put in, was she involved in Lady Benton's efforts to make the men's lives better?"

"Not at first. She was the youngest member of staff, and she was married. She didn't find it as easy to mix as I did, or Lady Benton. She did try to help some of the shyer ones, which was typical of her."

Ah.

He said, "Anyone particular?"

Mrs. Hailey frowned, and in her usual blunt way, she asked, "Inspector. Where do you intend on going with this sort of question?"

"I'm sorry. I'm not suggesting that there was any impropriety. I'm interested in the men of the squadron." He improvised. "I'd like to know how they got on together, with the household, with the people here in Walmer."

"I thought you'd come to find out who was killed in Lady Benton's private garden."

"One of those men pretended to be Captain Nelson. I want to know why."

"There was a young mechanic with a stutter, and she found that he could speak normally when he wasn't anxious or pressed. Or teased. And so she would chat with him from time to time."

Not Franklin then. There had been no mention of a stutter in any of the articles.

"Anyone else?"

"There was a man who always spent his free time alone, a knife in his hands, and a piece of wood. I never saw what it was he was carving. He wasn't rowdy with his mates, never took part in any games or pranks. She tried to bring him into any planned activities, but he always refused. I told her he was unlikely to change his ways."

Franklin had used a knife on his victims in France.

Including Vermuelen.

"What was his name?"

She smiled. "If you mentioned it, now, I'd know it straightaway."

"Was anyone else close to him?"

"I don't know that anyone was. He kept himself to himself. Someone did say—I think it was young Dunn, the local lad—that he was a fine mechanic. Or was it Captain Nelson? He'd know, wouldn't he? And, yes, it was Patricia who told me he'd been apprenticed to a blacksmith when he was only twelve. She thought it explained his aloofness." Taking a deep breath, as if to remind him of the time, she added, "If I remember anything else, I'll leave a message at the house for you."

He thanked her, apologized again for the late hour, and left.

She had been the right person to ask, he thought, walking back to the hotel. The one person who kept an eye on everything at the Abbey including Lady Benton.

Hamish said, "She would ha' been a guid minister's wife."

It was true, she would have recognized every parishioner by sight and known their family history, their needs. And made certain in her own quiet way that her husband was aware of everything that might affect his flock.

Rutledge had known women like that, and felt a healthy respect for their abilities.

But she hadn't come close enough to the man carving wood to notice his ring . . .

Patricia Lowell had.

In his room, he took out the sheets that gave the names and dates of each man in the squadron. From date of birth, date of enlistment, rank and promotions, to what had been said of him in every post where he'd served. Everything a man's commanding officer might need to know about those under him.

Except what they had done to make a living in private life.

Even crossing out officers and those who actually flew the aircraft—assuming another man's life meant assuming his skills or lack thereof—there was nothing in the lists to help there. But what if Franklin had also been a good mechanic, and chose the man he was going to kill for his identity *because* he could play the part? For some reason Robinson hadn't been what Franklin needed.

Rutledge went back to the cutting about the body in the ditch.

Hamish, seeming to lean over his shoulder as Rutledge worked, said, "There's dependents."

Rutledge swore.

Each man's dependents would be listed, those who received a share of his pay and if he died, his pension. Someone who could, if questioned by the Army, report that they hadn't heard from their son or brother in weeks or even months . . . Who might even contact the Army to ask why their loved one had failed to write. The soldier would be summoned by his commanding officer and reminded that it was his duty to see that his family heard from him. If nothing else, for the sake of Home Front morale. Rutledge himself had done just that on occasion.

He went back over page after page of squadron names, searching for anyone who had no dependents.

And there were six men who had no dependents listed—and therefore no parents or wife or children eagerly awaiting letters.

He sat back and looked at the notes he'd taken.

Howe, Jonathan. Mechanic
Betterman, Joseph, Clerk
Cooper, Allen, Mechanic
Reed, Albert, Mechanic

It was after two in the morning, far too late to call on Lady Benton. Or even Inspector Hamilton.

On impulse he went back to the article about Miles Franklin, reading everything that had been written about the man, committing it to memory.

There was damned little. He had come to the small town of Lambert Magna as the schoolmaster, married the daughter of Mrs. Lambert, a widow, and three years later had killed both of them in their sleep, along with his wife's sister, who was visiting. No motive was discovered. Except for the sister's remark that Franklin was tiring of his wife and a demanding mother-in-law.

Hamish said, "He's killed before."

Rutledge said, "Very likely. And the wife's sister may have feared that something was going to happen. Not precisely murder, but perhaps that the husband might walk away one evening and never come back. It may explain why she told someone. Why he waited until her visit to act."

He collected all the papers he had been reading and locked them in his valise before calling it a night.

And found it hard to sleep. Not because of the nightmares that always hovered so close in the dark, but because he felt for the first time that he understood what Miles Franklin was.

A s soon as the first rays of dawn brightened his window, he got up, dressed, and went down to his motorcar. On the drive ahead, he used his time to arrange his thoughts.

Rutledge walked into the hotel in Colchester where he'd used the telephone earlier, and despite the early hour, he put through a call to Haldane.

"We need to meet," he said as soon as the man had come to the telephone. "There's something we must discuss. About that matter of business in France, and about what I've learned here."

"Come to London."

"There isn't time. We must meet halfway. It's urgent."

"Very well. There's a small inn outside Little Upton. Do you know the village?"

"I don't. I'll find it."

The line went dead.

Rutledge went to the front desk and asked if the clerk knew Little Upton.

"Yes, sir. It's just across into Hertfordshire. Only a village. No hotel there to recommend—"

"I need to find it. Not to stay the night."

The clerk provided him with a rough map, and Rutledge thanked him. The hotel's dining room was just opening, and he stopped for a cup of tea. And then he went back to the small, uncomfortable telephone closet. Against his own better judgment.

H e had given Kate space in which to work out her problems with her father. Trusting in Melinda to see that all was well. Much as he would have liked to take the matter in hand, for Kate's sake, he knew that would only cause more trouble for her. Mrs. Gordon had made it plain that a policeman had no room in her daughter's future.

Shanta answered the phone. He quickly recognized the guarded tone of voice.

Was there trouble?

He kept his own voice light as he greeted her, and was rewarded with a relieved, more cheerful, "Good morning. Madame will be glad you have called."

And there was silence at the other end until Melinda herself said, "Good morning, Ian. It's quite early."

He made himself laugh. "And so it is." He paused, then said more seriously, "I've been caught up in the latest inquiry. I also felt that it was best not to add my presence to Kate's troubles."

"That was wise. I've come to like her immensely, Ian. I'm glad you brought her to me. We went to Rochester at the weekend, to visit the haunts of Mr. Dickens. It was a very nice outing."

Hardly the information he was after.

"Have matters improved with her family?"

"I think not."

"Let me know if there's anything you need. Anything I can do."

"It's best if you don't. Do you mind?"

Something was wrong, he could hear it in Melinda's choice of wording.

Formal, almost cold. As if he himself were somehow at fault.

He couldn't stop himself from saying, "Is it something I have done? Was I wrong to interfere?"

For the first time there was that familiar warmth in her voice. "My dear Ian, of course not. I'm so glad you called. I've wanted to ask about Essex. Is it going well? Have you found any answers?"

"I think I'm about to."

"I should like to know the outcome, when you are free to talk about it."

"I'll call again when I'm back in London."

"Yes, please, I'd like that very much."

And she rang off.

The only message that he'd been sure of in their conversation, was that Melinda had taken to Kate. She had disliked Jean, Kate's cousin, had felt that he shouldn't propose to her. And he hadn't listened, he'd been so besotted with Jean and her effervescence, her charm, that he hadn't seen beneath them to the selfishness they concealed. He'd known she liked having her own way, but he hadn't realized that it was more than just her upbringing as an only daughter. It was her true nature.

The operator's voice broke into his thoughts.

"Do you wish to place another call?"

He hadn't realized that he was still holding the receiver in his hand.

"No, thank you." He put it up.

And now he had to face Haldane.

15

Little Upton lived up to its name, *Little*. As Rutledge passed through it, he found that it was the perfect place for a quiet meeting. Neither he nor Haldane would be likely to encounter anyone they knew.

The inn was two miles outside the parish, a small coaching station in the past and now a country inn catering to the nearby villages. The board by the road showed a coach and four above the elegant script spelling out THE COACHMAN. Haldane had somehow managed to command a private room—or perhaps, Hamish suggested wryly, had used this place so often that he had an arrangement with the owners.

Rutledge was shown there by a pleasant woman in her fifties who asked if there was anything he might like while he waited.

"We are still serving breakfast. Or perhaps an early lunch?"

He settled on breakfast, and had just seen the dishes taken away when the door opened again and Haldane stepped in.

"I've been told," he said without a greeting, "that our mutual friend has died."

"I'm not surprised. He was very ill when I saw him."

"Yes. I received your postal card."

Rutledge bit back a smile. Touché, he thought. Two could play at being enigmatic.

Haldane set a case on the table, and sat down across from where Rutledge had been seated.

"What did you find there?"

Rutledge had brought the envelopes he'd taken from the Vermuelen house with him in a smaller valise he'd purchased in Chelmsford as he passed a shop.

"Three envelopes. One concerning the war, which I've read because I expected it to concern me. It doesn't. The second was merely clean sheets of paper, possibly a smoke screen. And a third, which details the movements of the man we appear to be hunting in tandem."

Haldane nodded, took the first two envelopes, and put them away.

Rutledge had the sudden thought that the empty pages—for all he knew—were covered in secret ink. They did, he noted, still leave a sprinkle of flour on the table as Haldane picked them up. He said nothing. Haldane noted it with a raised eyebrow, but didn't question it.

"And that was all?"

"From what he told me—and the papers indicated—our friend was ahead of me by perhaps a few weeks. Time enough to have planned the ghost scene. But there was no proof that he was in the village. Someone was, that was apparent, but was it our friend? I've only just had confirmation that it was." He reached in his pocket and brought out the snake ring.

Haldane reached for it and studied it carefully.

"Yes. This must be the ring. I had the dead man's family sketch it for me. The sketch was quite good because they had seen it over the years. The father had worn it until his son was of an age that he could be given it. Where did you find this? Start at the beginning."

And Rutledge began with the ghost in the garden.

When he'd finished, Haldane nodded.

"We had no idea where he'd gone. The man whose identity he took after killing him in Derbyshire has been a blank. No one came forward to report him missing or to tell us where he had been expected to arrive.

Of course they couldn't—he appeared to have been accounted for, all through the war. He could have been in France—Egypt—or even killed in action, for all we knew, because we had no *name*."

His emphasis on the last word was a trenchant indication of the frustration Haldane and the authorities must have felt with a corpse wearing a murderer's stolen clothing, but nothing to indicate who he was or where he'd come from, much less where he was going. No way to trace the man's killer, much less the victim. Franklin had chosen his victim very carefully.

After a moment Haldane added, almost to himself, "He stayed on our watch list as a question mark, because he might have been up to no good. A spy. A saboteur. Why else kill a soldier and take his place? If a killer wanted to escape having to serve, he'd have chosen a civilian."

"Did he kill in France, do you know?"

"Vermuelen was attempting to backtrack him when the wound turned septic. And so we have no answer to that. But from what I was able to understand, there was something in Picardy." He didn't elaborate.

"I have a feeling he'd killed before. Before the victims in Dorset."

Haldane regarded him sharply. "We had kept that out of the papers. Only five of us knew that."

"Who were the victims?"

"They lived in Hereford. A young woman and her father. Mrs. Lambert's daughter had gone to school with her. She must have thought she recognized Franklin. The deaths are still unsolved, because without Franklin we have no way of learning the truth. After he was tried in the Dorset case, he was to be taken to Hereford. But he used a different name, and the photograph that was sent to Hereford raised some doubt. I expect he'd changed his appearance."

"I should have been told this in the beginning."

"Neither the Chief Constable nor Markham had any idea this was related to Essex. But anything that had to do with a military installation had been flagged during the war, and so it came across someone's desk when the Yard was sent to Walmer. It would have been no use to you, if the ghost had been no more than a prank. But when you queried the airfield, we paid attention."

"Still—"

"It was more helpful to us for you to make the connection on your own. Rather than jump to conclusions."

Rutledge said nothing.

Haldane added, "I must say, it was well done, all the same. And that's why you were sent to France."

But Rutledge was not mollified by praise. He found himself thinking that Haldane and he had a very difficult relationship at best. And trust was not necessarily a part of that relationship.

"What happens now?" he asked.

"I think it best if you finish what you've begun. You know the people, you know the ground. And most importantly, you've kept what you've learned to yourself. He still believes he's safe, there has been no talk about an arrest coming soon. A new face might make him decide to cut his losses and disappear."

"And what if I don't find him?"

Haldane shrugged. "That would be unfortunate. Given the number of people he's killed."

"What does he want in the Abbey?"

"I don't know. It's possible that Mrs. Lowell had unwittingly left something in the house that could lead to him. From his days there with the squadron."

"Why there? Why not in her own home?"

"Whatever it is, he must know by now that it isn't in her house. I daresay he looked long before she was killed, and then turned his attention to the Abbey."

It made sense, in a way. But Patricia Lowell hadn't struck Rutledge as a keeper of secrets. The little that Rutledge had seen of her had given him the impression of an open, rather naive person. Easily taken advantage of? She had tried to help the lonely and the outsiders.

He said only, "That's possible."

Preparing to leave, Haldane asked, "Is there anything you need?"

"Markham will be demanding a report on progress. And the Chief Constable here in Essex is related to Lady Benton. He'll be asking as well. What do I tell him?"

Haldane gave the question some thought. "If need be, tell both of them that you believe that this began as a blackmail plot to force Lady Benton to sell her estate. Give them no details."

Rutledge wondered if Haldane knew something about the man Wilbur, who had pressed to buy the meadow once the land was returned to Lady Benton.

"Is there anything you're holding back about Franklin? Like the ring?"

Haldane regarded Rutledge. "There is one other thing. Be very careful. He's quick with a knife."

R utledge left before Haldane.
      He was not so far from Melinda's house. As the crow flew. Across the Thames into Kent. An hour, possibly . . .

It might as well be across the sea.

Turning away, he drove out of the inn's yard and turned back the way he'd come.

"Ye heard the man. Best to keep your mind on what's to be done. The sooner ye finish wi' Franklin, the sooner ye'll be free."

It was some miles before he could force himself to think about Walmer again.

W here do you disappear to?" Inspector Hamilton asked him crossly when he walked into the police station sometime later. "I came by the hotel just after breakfast, and they told me you hadn't come down. I pounded on the door, and there was no answer. When I went out back to look for your motorcar, it wasn't there."

"Sorry. I went for a drive to clear my head."

"What sort of drive? You'd be in the Irish Sea by this time."

"Just—driving. I'm here. What's happened?"

"There's a body."

"Whose? Where?" he demanded.

"Ah, you're interested now, are you? Head all clear and ready for bones?"

Bones . . .

Long dead.

"Tell me."

"The salt works. You know how they collect the salt?"

"Yes. They work in the marshes along the coast. As the tide recedes, it leaves salt behind in the shallow pools created for the purpose. When a pool has enough salt to be salvaged, they pump it into large sinks, where the salt finally comes to the surface."

"Yes. That's right. Only this time, when they set the pump in a pool it ran slow. When someone got around to taking a look at the pump, there was a bone stopping the end. They're out there now, trying to find the rest. Dr. Wister says there are bound to be more."

"Take me there. Now."

"Got anything for wading?"

"In the boot of the motorcar."

Hamilton nodded.

They left straightaway.

Where the salt pools were, the ground was boggy but not sour. They trudged through the marsh, toward a group of men working at the far end. Rutledge saw Wister there, but didn't recognize the others.

This pool was at the very edge of the marsh. Hamilton was saying, "It's not very productive—the tides don't always come up this far, and the land there is starting to dry as well. There was a high tide last week, and someone thought to take a look last night. The verdict was, it was finally ready."

Rutledge could see the salt rind on the stalks of plants growing next to some of the pools, which were more or less a catchment for seawater left behind as the tide went out.

The men digging in the pool looked up as Rutledge and Hamilton approached. Wister turned and nodded. At his feet were several more bones. They were not clean.

"What have you got?" Rutledge asked.

"Not much so far. That looks like a tibia. And those are part of a hand. Over here, there are several toes. Whoever it is was dismembered and buried here. This isn't an animal's leavings. No signs of gnawing. My guess is a male, judging by the length of the leg. He's been here some time. But the salt has preserved some of him. Rather nasty."

Although they worked for several more hours, they didn't find much more.

Rutledge asked one of the men, "How long has this section been used as a salt pool?"

"Before the war," he replied. "It was expanded then, but dried too quickly to be much use."

"And so it has been sitting here untouched for some years. Eight? Ten?"

"Closer to ten," the man answered.

"We're going to need that area adjacent to the pool dug up as well," Rutledge said. "And we need more men."

Hamilton went off to find them, and Rutledge watched the work here until Wister said, "It's useless. Let's start to expand it to your right."

The work went on, laborious and careful. More bones began to come to light.

As more men appeared and helped, the work went faster. And then a woman cried out.

Rutledge turned to see Mrs. Dunn coming toward them.

He hurried forward, with Wister in his wake. Catching her by the shoulders, he stopped her, although she struggled against his hold, crying out for him to let her go.

"You mustn't," he said gently. "We've only begun, we don't know what we've found."

"I have a right to see. It's my Gerry, isn't it? *Tell me*—I've waited all these years—I have a *right*—!"

Dr. Wister said, "Mrs. Dunn—Mary—you need to go home and wait. Mr. Rutledge is right, it could be anything, a Viking burial—"

"No. It's my boy, and I want to be there." She was crying now. "I said, it didn't matter, alive or dead, as long as I *knew*. But all along I wanted him back, alive. I'd have hidden him from the Army—I'd have done anything—"

Another woman came running. "I couldn't stop her," she called. "Let me take her home."

Mary Dunn, her shoulders slumped, let her neighbor take her by the arm and lead her away, certain now and brokenhearted. "None of you know what it was like, waiting. Else you'd understand," she said over her shoulder. "He's still my *boy* . . ."

Wister watched her go. "Poor woman."

Rutledge said, "This is the worst part of murder."

Wister turned. "Here—I never said it was murder—"

"You told us the body had been dismembered. What the hell did you think it was?"

Wister answered quietly, "I know. I just didn't want—" He stopped. "I wish to God it *is* a Viking grave!" He left Rutledge standing there and walked heavily back to where the men were digging.

By teatime, the rest of the body had emerged, scattered about ten square feet of marsh and the adjacent higher ground.

"How did anyone not see him?" Hamilton was demanding.

"It was at the start of the war," one of the younger workmen answered. "They had rolls of wire here, and it was off-limits because of the inlet yonder. There were even stories that it was mined. No one ever tried to test that. It was '14, and invasion fever. Mum slept with an axe under her bed, for fear the Germans would break through the coast road and come in the night."

"His killer must have thought that when the ravens and gulls had finished with the body, it would wash out to sea. Then he came back and discovered it hadn't."

"But who is it?" someone asked as Wister began to place the bones on a length of canvas someone had brought out.

"I thought Gerald was a deserter," another man put in. "That's what the Army called him."

"I heard he went away in the night," someone else commented. "And the Army had no choice but to call it desertion."

"It's not desertion if he's been murdered," the first man retorted. "Army jumped to the wrong conclusion."

"Best not to let her see him brought out," Hamilton told them. "It will have to be a closed casket."

"Reminds me," an older man said, "of the war. Caskets went into the ground empty, until someone said how foolish that was, until the body came home. But most never did. My son's one of them, still lying in France." They stood in a half circle, caps off, as Wister and three other men lifted the corner of the canvas and began to walk back to the harbor and then up the long hill to the surgery. Women were standing in their doorways, watching the somber party pass by. One or two were weeping.

When they arrived at the surgery and the bones were deposited in a back room, everyone walked out except for Rutledge, Hamilton, and Wister.

It took the doctor the better part of an hour to assemble the bones on the long table covered with a sheet. When it was done, he straightened and turned to the two policemen who had silently watched him work.

"All right. I'd guess he was twenty? Not more than twenty-one. And he hadn't been in the ground very long. A few years. Five? Give or take. They're still finding bones in France and Belgium, did you know? The grave teams. Terrible work. But necessary." He went to a sink against the far wall, washed his hands with water from a pitcher and then dried them carefully, as if washing off the smell of death.

He turned and walked back to the table. "I can't tell you with any certainty that this is Gerald Dunn. Nor can I tell you it isn't. The age fits, from what I was told. The time of death, mid-1917, seems likely. The ribs were smashed, as you can see. But if you look here"—he pointed—"I would guess that's a knife wound. You can see where the blade scraped that bone. Very different to the heavy hammer blows that broke up the bones later on. There's nothing to suggest blunt force or a shooting. A few pieces are still missing—some of the smaller bones of the hands and feet. The head. But we were remarkably lucky to find as much as we did. Poor Mrs. Dunn. She'll have to be told something."

In the event, they found her waiting stoically, her younger son beside her, on the street in front of the doctor's surgery.

She took one look at the faces of the three men who came out to speak to her, and didn't wait to hear what they had to say.

She turned, taking the younger boy by the hand, and walked on.

"I'll send word to the undertaker in Chelmsford," Wister said quietly. "She can't see him like this. Tomorrow we'll have to dig again. Where in God's name did the head go?"

And he went back inside, firmly shutting the door.

Hamilton said, as they walked back to the station, "Who killed him, then? If he was stabbed."

Rutledge took a deep breath. "We'll have to find that out, won't we?"

Hamilton turned to look at the man walking beside him. "Nothing happens when you're here, does it? And you've been damned mysterious about those times away."

"They were necessary," he said tersely, cutting of any further questioning.

But Hamish was hammering in the back of his head. "Yon killer knows when you're no' in the village. He's watching. And waiting."

Hamish was right, Rutledge thought. His motorcar was distinctive enough, and it was either at the hotel or at the Hall. Easy enough to keep track of its whereabouts. But not even the killer could have known the bones would appear—that it had been decided to work on a flat that hadn't been productive, hoping to bring it back to usefulness by digging it deeper where Time and lack of attention had seen it grow more shallow.

Hamilton was still asking questions when they reached the hotel, but walked on rather than follow Rutledge inside. For which he was grateful.

———

After his supper, Rutledge went to call on Mary Dunn, to be sure all was well.

The neighbor who came to the door said, "She's not seeing anyone. She's just sitting there in the dark in Gerry's room. I tried to bring her a cup of tea, but she asked me to go away. She'd kept telling Major Dinsmore that her son wasn't a deserter. He wouldn't listen. That's what's gnawing at her the most, that everyone called him a deserter, when he wasn't. And him dead and not able to defend himself from the stories."

"Tell her I called. We can't make a positive identification, but the doctor feels the age is right, and the time of death."

The neighbor's mouth drew up in a tight line. "That's only offering her hope. And there is none," she said finally. "She knows. A mother knows. Let her bury her boy."

And she closed the door gently but firmly.

Rutledge turned away, angry still with Franklin, who discarded people who were in his way, like Patricia Lowell and now Gerry Dunn.

Almost over his head, the church clock struck the hour. Half past eleven. There was nothing more he could do tonight, but tomorrow—tomorrow would be different.

He was on his way to the police station when he encountered Liz coming down the street.

She stopped him. "Is it true they've found Gerald Dunn?" she asked.

"It's possible that the body could be his."

Liz sighed. "He was older, he never teased me, when we were in school. Sometimes he'd take up for me when they were particularly nasty. Everyone told me he was a coward, he'd deserted. I didn't want to believe it. He'd stood up to the bullies."

"It's very late, you shouldn't be out on the street like this."

She smiled. "I've been to see Mrs. Hailey. She's teaching me how to serve properly. There's a place coming open at the hotel, it's only in the kitchen, but she told me that if I showed promise, I'd be taken on in the dining room."

"I'm pleased to hear it," he told her.

"Yes, she stopped me on the street, and asked me if I was free to leave the pub whenever I wished. I told her I had no other way to keep myself, but I hated The Salt Cellar." The smile widened. "I can't believe anyone would do such a thing for me, but I'm not to tell, not until I'm ready to give my notice."

"Yes, that's very wise." His mind still on Franklin, he added, "I hear the pub has rooms to let?"

"You don't want to go there. There are cockroaches." She shivered. "I see them on the walls of the kitchen."

"I'm not going there. But I'm curious about someone who might have stayed there at one time. Several weeks ago, perhaps."

"There hasn't been anyone staying, not for months. People who come to Walmer stay in the hotel if they have any sense at all. And I told you before, the rooms have other uses."

He thanked her, and watched her on her way, then went on to the police station. Hamilton had just come in from his own dinner, and was finishing his report on the body. He looked up, and Rutledge saw the dark smudges of worry under his eyes.

He said, "The Chief Constable wants to speak to me. Two murders and no one taken up for them. You're to come as well. He's worried about Lady Benton."

"Put him off if you can. It's too soon."

Hamilton shook his head. "I don't know if I can. I'll be here long after you've gone. I'm the one who has to think about the future." He rubbed his eyes, and said, "What is it you want at this hour?"

"You've told me that there have been no strangers in Walmer recently. Since all this began. Are you sure of that?"

"Of course I am," Hamilton snapped. "If there were, I'd already be questioning them. I don't know anyone in this village who might want to kill Mrs. Lowell. Damn it, most of us pitied her, losing her husband so young. As for Gerald Dunn, the Army was thorough in their search for him. I wonder if Wister is sure about that knife wound. I'd be more willing to believe he killed himself. But then who dismembered the body?"

"I'd like four or five men for a search party. It shouldn't take long."

"At this hour? What in hell's name for?"

Rutledge ignored the sarcasm.

"In the morning. I want to begin with the pubs, the hotel, the lodging houses. Anywhere that a man might sleep for a night—perhaps two. A stranger who came to look for work. A traveler who might even have been here before, in the past. I need to find him."

"You're wasting your time. I live here, I know who comes and goes."

But when Rutledge arrived at the station just after seven the next morning, Hamilton had collected a handful of men and was already giving them their instructions. Ten minutes later, Rutledge and Hamilton stopped at the Swan Hotel themselves, to look through the register at the desk.

The flustered clerk kept demanding a name. "It's easier to look for a name. You must have one, surely?"

Rutledge handed him a slip of paper. On it were the four names he'd come to think might be his quarry: Jonathan Howe, Joseph Betterman, Allen Cooper, and Albert Reed.

They had never stayed at the Swan.

Outside, as they moved on, Hamilton asked, "Where did you get those names?"

"The Yard," Rutledge told him, and refused to answer any more questions. "I'd like to question Johnson at The Salt Cellar myself. Your men know the few lodging houses, and where people take in occasional guests."

Hamilton was still grumbling as they made their way down to the harbor. Walking into the door of The Salt Cellar, he called, "Anyone here?"

It was too early for custom.

Chairs had been piled on tables, and the floor was wet in places where it had been mopped. The interior was clean, with dark paneling and the handsome old bar. The brass shone even in the dimness of the room. A far cry from The Viking, its neighbor along the harbor road.

The owner, Bill Johnson, came through from the kitchen. Drying his hands on a towel, he laughed when they asked to see the register for the rooms he had available.

"Why should I need a register? More often than not, it's the man too drunk to make it to his own bed who sleeps there. I've known three to a bed, on busy nights."

"We'd like a quick look," Hamilton told him, and started toward the stairs.

Johnson said, "Go ahead."

Hamish said, "There's naebody here."

Rutledge waited until Hamilton had disappeared above, his footsteps moving about overhead.

"Know any of these people? We're looking for them," Rutledge said casually, putting the list of names on the bar, where Johnson was standing.

He scanned the names, looked up at Rutledge, and said, "Haven't had the pleasure of meeting them." He turned and came around from behind the bar.

Oddly enough, Rutledge thought, Johnson's reaction had been one of relief.

Why?

Because the name he'd been braced to see on that list wasn't there?

Was there someone else, one of the long list of other names, that he, Rutledge, had missed?

Johnson was saying, "What have they done, those four?"

Hamilton was already on the stairs.

Rutledge said quietly, before he came into view, "Smuggling."

"Oh, aye? I thought that had died out in my granny's time."

"Apparently not."

Hamilton said as he came down the last few steps, "Nothing."

They thanked Johnson and left. There was the other pub, and Rutledge kept his own council, moving on to The Viking. But the only room above was a storeroom, and not for guests.

Hamilton shook his head as they stepped out into the morning's bright sunlight. "I told you this was a waste of time. And we've run out of options, unless my men come up with something."

"One more to go. The Monk's Choice."

Where there was a suitcase shoved under the bed . . .

Hamilton grumbled all the way out there, much to the discomfort of the Constable sitting in the rear seat. They had collected him at the station as they drove up the long sloping hill back into town.

Hamish's usual place . . .

As they got out in the pub yard, Rutledge said, "Have you been looking under beds? In armoires?"

"Of course I have," Hamilton snapped. "Behind the drapes and under the table as well."

Newbold was unhappy to see them, staring balefully at Rutledge as soon as he and Hamilton stepped through the door.

"What, again?"

"A routine police matter," he said. "You're the last pub on our list."

Hamilton showed him the names while Rutledge and the Constable went up the stairs.

They looked into the bedroom where Newbold slept, opened the door of the cupboard, and went into the empty room. Rutledge opened the armoire while the Constable got down on his knees and lifted the coverlet, shining his torch under the bed.

"I don't think he's cleaned under here for a month," he said, getting to his feet and sneezing loudly.

"What did you find?"

The Constable shook his head. "Nothing." And at the look on Rutledge's face, he added, "See for yourself?"

Rutledge got down on one knee, shone the torch under the bed with one hand while he held up the coverlet with the other.

The Constable had been right. The floor beneath the bed was empty. But in the back corner, where the suitcase had been, there was a rectangle of wooden flooring that was relatively free of dust.

Where the suitcase had recently been removed.

Rutledge went back to Newbold's room and looked again to be sure. But the valise he'd seen was not there.

Someone had already retrieved it.

H amilton had much to say about coming up with nothing, taking the time of the police, and accomplishing aggravating a good many people all morning.

Rutledge let him grumble, all the while wondering if Franklin was about to do a runner. If that was why the suitcase had gone.

The two pub owners, Johnson and Newbold. Was there a connection between the two men? Or was he searching for straws where there were none.

He broke into Hamilton's monologue as they reached the outskirts of Walmer. "Are Newbold and Johnson related?"

Hamilton stopped. "What? No. They aren't. Constable?"

"No, sir. I'd have heard."

Rutledge put them down at the police station, turned the motorcar around, and went to the little village where he had spoken to the Rector, Mr. Farmer. But the man had no other information to give him, saying finally, "I am haunted by the fact that I wasn't at home the day Mrs. Lowell came to see me. There's no reason to think that whatever was on her mind had anything to do with her death. Still, I would sleep better if I could believe that."

"Is there anyone she might have confided in? Something that she might have felt was too trivial to worry Lady Benton about? Anything at all that might help me find an answer to her murder?"

They were sitting in the Rectory kitchen, and Farmer got up to pace. "I've been over and over every conversation we've had in the past two months or more. I've questioned my poor wife until she's as unsettled as I am."

Rutledge recalled something Farmer had told him earlier. "You said you had gone to Mrs. Lowell's house, after she had come here to look for you."

"Yes—yes I did. But she hadn't come home from the Abbey. The hours there aren't regular, I'm sure, depending on whether or not they have an afternoon tour."

"And there was nothing at the house that seemed irregular?"

"If there had been, I'd have told you on your last visit. I was there for no more than five minutes, I'm sure. I knocked at the door, there was no answer. The handyman came around the corner of the house and told me she hadn't returned from the Abbey, I thanked him and left. That was all."

"What handyman?"

"I didn't ask his name. He said Mrs. Lowell had hired him to clear out the bicycle shed. Rats had taken up residence in a back corner, and he had dealt with them. He was waiting for her to come home to pay him for the day's work."

Rutledge swore to himself. "What did he look like, this handyman?"

"Thirties, I expect. Polite. Brown corduroys and a flannel shirt. I thought perhaps he'd come from the Abbey. He didn't appear to be itinerant, or living rough. It wouldn't have taken more than a few hours to rid her of the rats. It was the sort of thing Lady Benton would do for her."

But Lady Benton had told him that she had had to let Bert and the gardening staff go in the autumn . . .

"Was it usual for Mrs. Lowell to take on someone to help her at the Old Rectory?"

"Bert, the gardener at the Abbey, often did a bit of work for Mrs. Lowell on his days off, and I have recommended someone to Mrs. Lowell when she needed help. A plumber in February, when there was trouble with the drains, and another time she needed someone to chop wood for the house fires. I myself went over back in December to help her put up a small Christmas tree, then returned in the New Year to take it down. In March my wife helped take down the curtains in the kitchen and wash them, then put them back up . . ."

Rutledge wasn't listening. Farmer didn't know that Bert and his helpers had been let go.

He thanked the Rector and left.

On his way back to Walmer, he made two stops.

The first was at the Old Rectory, where he spent ten minutes looking for any sign of rats in the shed where Mrs. Lowell had kept her bicycle. But he found no sign of them, and there was no indication someone had been there to destroy a nest.

He went on to the Abbey. Lady Benton was busy but Margaret told him what he wanted to know.

"Bert left in early November, and the two under gardeners left about two weeks before him, because they'd found work at one of the estates in Suffolk. There hasn't been anyone else."

"Had Mrs. Lowell told you about the rat problem in her shed?"

"Rats?" She made a face. "Were you there at the house? Is that how you found them? She would have hated that. Nasty things, rats. We keep a sharp eye out for them here."

He thanked her and left.

If the man the Rector had seen at the Old Rectory was Franklin, if the suitcase left at The Monk's Choice was his, where was he now? And had he been the man the elderly woman had seen sleeping by the table tomb in the Rector's churchyard?

That would mean he'd reached England, had had to sleep rough the first night, then was given a room at The Monk's Choice.

But when Rutledge stopped there to demand an answer, Newbold swore that there had been no strangers there. And he denied all knowledge of the suitcase under the bed.

Oddly enough he appeared to be telling the truth.

Frustrated, Rutledge set out for Chelmsford. He'd have preferred London, to speak to Haldane face-to-face, but if he was being watched, he dared not stay away another night.

Someone was using the hotel's telephone when he got there, and Rutledge paced for a good ten minutes before it was free.

He put through the call to Haldane's house, was asked to wait—another five minutes—and by the time Haldane's voice came over the receiver, he was in no mood to be kept in the dark.

He said, "There's something missing in the information I've been given about Franklin. I need to know if there is any link he or his family might have had to East Anglia—or Essex in particular? Why, if he was here during the war, did he come back here? Why not Northumberland or Cornwall?"

"We can't seem to find any more information about him. It's possible that Franklin isn't his real name. Still, there is no evidence to support that either. He seems to have come out of nowhere."

"He was a schoolmaster in Dorset. There would have to be some credentials. Some proof that he was trained for that profession."

"When we looked into them, they proved to have been forged. The headmaster told the police that Franklin gave every impression of having been well educated. But where is still a mystery. We can't trace him beyond that first set of murders, the ones before Dorset. Which leads me to think he's had to change his name several times. The barrister who took on his case in Dorset told us Franklin claimed he had no family living."

"And you've been to Somerset House?"

"We have. The only Franklin who might have been our man died as a child."

"Then he found the name in a churchyard."

There was brief silence on the other end of the line. Then Haldane said, "A very good guess, Rutledge. The child died in a small village near Lancaster in 1876. But there was no trace of Miles Franklin there. One of the other schoolmasters in Dorset did mention to the police that he thought Franklin had a brother, but they were estranged. The question arose because Franklin never got any mail addressed through the school. The schoolmaster asked if he had any family, and that was why the mention of a brother came up. Another lie? Or the truth? So far we've been unable to trace so much as a cousin. But then the man is an accomplished liar."

There was a reply swirling in the back of his mind now, but he wasn't ready to put it to the test. He thanked Haldane and hung up.

Then stood there thinking. . . .

He'd asked over and over again if there had been any strangers in the village, and the answer had consistently been no.

Because there *were* no strangers. But there was someone's relative, accounted for and accepted, for the simple reason someone could vouch for him. It was the only explanation for the man's ability to come and go without attracting attention.

Hamish said, his voice loud against the bustle in the lobby just around the corner from the telephone closet, "Newbold."

That made sense. It explained why, having to leave France so abruptly, Franklin had come back to Walmer. It was where the valise had been shoved to the far corner underneath the bed in the other room upstairs in The Monk's Choice. And Newbold could lie with a straight face about strangers staying there.

He must have enjoyed deceiving the police . . .

And Newbold could easily have been the "victim" in that charade in Lady Benton's garden.

The question that still needed to be answered was, given that Franklin had found temporary sanctuary in Essex, why had he brought attention to himself by playing at being a ghost, and then killing Patricia Lowell? Franklin had always appeared to kill for his own benefit. What was the benefit in Walmer?

16

Rutledge went directly to the Abbey as soon as he reached the turn for Walmer.

The gates were open, and two motorcars were waiting in front of the great doors.

There were guests today.

He walked in, went through the state rooms toward the sitting room, and encountered a party of five being taken round by Lady Benton herself.

He nodded to the surprised guests, and went on through to the sitting room.

Almost an hour later, Lady Benton came to find him.

"I heard that the body of Gerald Dunn has been found. How awful! I'm afraid my first thought was gratitude that he wasn't on my property. I don't think I could have borne it."

She sat down in her usual chair, and almost in the same moment, the door opened again and Mrs. Hailey brought in a tray of tea and biscuits. She nodded to Rutledge and said to Lady Benton, "They've gone. And very happy with their tour."

"Thank you, Margaret. That's marvelous."

When Mrs. Hailey had left, Lady Benton busied herself with the tea things, and when she had given Rutledge his cup, she sat down and sipped hers gratefully.

"I don't find the same joy in the tours as I once did. I'm almost afraid I'll find a body in one of the rooms, much to the horror of my guests."

He said, "I've come to ask you about four names. I'd like to know if you recognize any of them."

"Names? Of the airmen, you mean?"

"Yes." He took the list from his pocket and read them one at a time, waiting for her to respond. "Jonathan Howe. He was a mechanic."

"Howe . . . Oh, yes, he was too large to fly, perhaps taller than you, and several times he came in to help us shift a heavy piece of furniture."

"Joseph Betterman. A clerk."

"Yes, he was a bookkeeper before the war. Tall, thin. He helped Margaret set up a much better accounting system. We still use it."

"Allen Cooper. Another mechanic?"

"I didn't know him well, but Roger—Captain Nelson told us he was thorough and dependable. As was Gerry Dunn, for that matter. He often assigned them to his aircraft, because they were so good at hearing the slightest change in the pitch of the engine."

"Albert Reed. Another mechanic."

"I don't—or was he one of Patricia's pets?" She bit her lip, then said, "We should never have called them that. She had a soft heart, always trying to make other people happy. If someone was generally by himself, when he came up from the airfield, she would try hard to find something to interest him. Croquet. Tennis. That sort of thing. But some of the men just seemed to prefer their own company, and they'd find a quiet corner to write letters to their families."

"Mrs. Hailey told me he liked to sit and carve."

"Was that Reed? Actually, I don't know that I ever saw him carve anything. He would watch the other men, a stick of wood in his hand, the knife too. As if they were just there as—as props, so that he could appear to be busy and people would leave him alone."

"Was he a good mechanic?"

She frowned. "Yes, I expect he must have been. Someone mentioned that before the war, he had worked designing motorcars. At least I think it was Reed? Perhaps it was one of the other men. Still, all of the mechanics would have to be experienced, wouldn't they, to keep all those aircraft ready to fly?"

"Did you ever hear of any disciplinary problems with any of these names?"

"I never thought to ask about that sort of thing. I tried to keep a distance from airfield matters. The men came here to relax. Sometimes to mourn a pilot who had been killed. It wasn't my place to judge them. I left that to Major Dinsmore."

"Would you recognize Reed if you saw him again?"

"Good heavens. Well, if he came into the sitting room in uniform, I just might. Those I often talked with, I'd probably have no trouble recognizing. But there were so many who came and went, and I didn't get to know many of them very well. Patricia of course-"

She broke off. "No. You don't think—you aren't saying that—that she recognized him, and he—he killed her? But in God's name *why*?"

He weighed how much to tell her. How much was safe, how much was very likely dangerous.

"That's speculation at the moment. Do you know if he had any family members living close by? Like Gerald Dunn, for example, whose mother lives in Walmer."

"Relatives? I have no idea. Many of the men talked about their parents or their wives and sweethearts. Especially in the beginning, when they were so homesick. Major Dinsmore frowned on having family members visit, it was a distraction. After all, family members weren't allowed to visit airfields in France. Why?"

He was about to ask if she had ever seen Reed with Newbold, then changed his mind. "Did many of the squadron go to The Monk's Choice in the evening? I've been told it was popular during the war."

"It probably was, since it was so close to the airfield. Men could walk there. The Captain did say once that he had tried to put it off-limits, because the men who went there usually drank too much. But Major Dinsmore overruled that. The men went into Walmer when they could get leave. Especially the pilots."

"Do you know why he overruled the Captain?"

"I was only told that he had."

"Was Reed one of the heavy drinkers?"

"Again, I wouldn't know. Where are you going with these questions?"

"I'm trying to narrow my list of names."

But she wasn't to be put off. "I think you already have." She carefully set her cup on the table by her chair, then said, "Was he—was this man Reed the one Captain Nelson appeared to kill that night in my garden?"

"We haven't got that far in our inquiry."

She rounded on him. "Stop it. You're leading me down the primrose path! 'Speculation.' 'Haven't got that far.' That's not like you, Inspector. What are you keeping from me?"

He took a deep breath. "The less you know, the less the risk to you."

"That's rather chivalrous. And just as impractical. What do you know? You must tell me the truth."

"Very likely there was an imposter among the men at the airfield. He had stolen the identity of a dead man, and used the war to avoid being found and charged. He's a murderer. I don't why he's back in Essex. There's a strong possibility that he came back here either because of the airfield or because of this house. Or even for the grounds. It's even possible that he put on that little drama in your garden to frighten you away for a few days. Did the Captain—Major Dinsmore—anyone from the squadron ask you to keep something for them? And never collected it again?"

"No. Absolutely not. That isn't to say that something wasn't left here. If it was, none of us knew about it."

She swallowed hard, taking it in. But she said only, "Thank you. I feel safer, knowing what it is that I'm facing."

"You must come back with me to the hotel. Where it will be more difficult to find you."

"And leave this house unprotected? My husband's inheritance, and my son's? Thank you for your concern, but the answer is no."

"You're carrying your sense of duty too far. If this man killed Mrs. Lowell, he will have no compunction about killing you. For all we know, his was the hand that pushed you down the crypt stairs."

"He can find me at the hotel. There are other people about, I won't see him coming for me. Here, I know who ought to be here and who shouldn't be. I'm safer."

"You can't watch every window, all the doors. You can't guard every room."

"Then I'll borrow a dog. Mrs. Bradley owns one, a great hulk of a beast. Not too bright, but he has a ferocious bark. And you should see his teeth. He'll hear what I can't."

"Is she still here?"

"I expect she is—there were dishes to be dealt with, and some rather nice lemon poppy seed cakes. You just had one." They had finished their tea. She rose, and as he stood to follow her, she shook her head. "No, I don't want to frighten the staff. Or worry them. I'll go and ask for Bruce. She will be happy to lend him for a night or two, if I tell her that we have a rodent problem."

She left him there, and as soon as the door was closed, Hamish said, "Ye canna protect her forever. He'll only wait for his chance."

"I'll leave the motorcar in the carriage house. Out of sight. He's taken the valise. It's very likely that he knows he has to move on. Either he'll cut his losses and go, or if he's desperate enough, he'll strike soon."

"You've no' got a weapon."

"There's a gun room. I'll borrow one, then lock the door."

"Ye're a fool."

And he fell silent.

The door opened and Lady Benton came in. "She's delighted to lend Bruce to me. She's gone to fetch him now."

"I'll put my motorcar out of sight. You'll be safe enough with the others still here."

The main gates were still open. He got into his motorcar, drove around to the stables, and opened the wide doors of the carriage house. The Rolls fit neatly into a space behind a handsome landau with the family arms on the side paneling.

He took his time going back to the house, first searching the stables, then making a circuit of the grounds, testing the seldom-used doors. Making certain all was well, even though it was too early yet for anything to happen. The staff was still clearing away.

Hamish said, "There isna' a reason why he'll come tonight."

"He can't put it off much longer. But whatever it is he wants, he's already taken a risk coming back here for it. That tells me he's convinced it's worth it. Someone—most likely Captain Nelson—could have led him to believe there was damning evidence in his possession. For that matter, we don't know how the Captain or anyone else got on to Franklin in the first place. Franklin has been very clever from the start. He's left no trail to follow. Unless the Captain had some reason to think Reed wasn't the man he was pretending to be, I can't imagine how he uncovered any evidence at all."

"It might no' be evidence. He kept yon ring. It could be anither thing that belonged to the real Albert Reed."

Rutledge shook his head. Then realized he'd been talking aloud to Hamish for a good five minutes. Breaking off, he went back toward the stables.

Using his key, Rutledge let himself in to the house and locked the door behind him. As he opened the sitting room door, something large and dark came at him fast.

"Bruce!" Lady Benton commanded him. "Down."

But the shaggy gray animal was trying to lick Rutledge's face. He caught the big paws resting easily on his shoulders, and set him down.

"I told you, he's not too bright. He took you for a villain as soon as he heard you at the outer door. Long before I knew you were there, I heard him growl. But I don't think he's going to be much protection." She handed him a handkerchief to wipe his face.

"He got here quickly enough."

"Yes, he lives just up the road, toward Walmer. Mrs. Hailey is locking up, then I'll make my rounds. Will you stay, at least until I can learn to manage Bruce? We don't have another tour scheduled for today. She tells me there is a sufficient amount of sandwiches left for our supper."

But he had already made up his mind to stay.

When the usual routine of closing up the house had been carried out, Rutledge went round with Lady Benton to be certain the locks were in place and all the lamps had been turned out, while Bruce whined behind the door of the sitting room.

They spent the next hour going back over the past.

Rutledge hadn't told her that he believed Franklin had killed Captain Nelson because he had somehow stumbled on the truth. That was the only explanation for the death of Gerry Dunn after the Captain's crash. A mechanic himself, Dunn might well have discovered whatever had been done to the motorcar to cause it to crash. His mother had said he was mad about all things mechanical.

And so when they had brought a fresh pot of tea back to the sitting room, Rutledge said, "Did the men from the airfield come inside?"

"I've told you. I spoke to all of them, but in various places. On the lawns, in the kitchen, the old butler's quarters. The Captain had the run of the library, but that was because I trusted him to be careful, discreet, and to lock up when he left."

"Could the Captain have put something in the house for safekeeping? Something he wished to keep private? Flying as often as he did, he left his quarters unguarded. Anyone might go in. And he was killed in the crash before he could recover it."

"What could he possibly have wished to leave here? And why didn't he tell me it was here?"

"I don't know. Something about the squadron, perhaps?" Rutledge wasn't ready to tell her that it might have to do with a murderer.

"That's not like Roger—Captain Nelson. If there was a problem at the airfield, he'd have gone straight to Major Dinsmore. And he only came into the house to borrow books."

"Then we should go to the library."

Once in the handsome room with its row on row of books, shelves climbing nearly to the high ceiling, with several lamps lit to enable them to search, it appeared to be a daunting task. They had brought Bruce with them, and as he curled up on the hearth rug, content, Rutledge asked, "What in particular did the Captain like to read?"

"The Classics. Books on navigation, history—memoirs. I never asked. I saw him with a Cicero once, and again with an account of the Great Mutiny in India. We had a fine collection of books with lovely plates of Greek statues. I pointed those out to him, myself."

Rutledge considered shelves running around the room. "Did others know his tastes in reading?"

"I have no idea."

Then Hamish spoke, and Rutledge turned away, to hide his expression.

"He wouldna' leave anything in a book he had read."

And that made a certain sense. Rutledge began to scan the shelves. He found a book on flowers of the world, and took it down to search. Lady Benton, watching him, said, "I see what you're thinking. That he would choose something less likely to appeal to him."

It was almost as if she too had heard Hamish's comment.

She picked out a book on the development of firearms, another on the Moghul Empire, and two on ancient architecture. Rutledge meanwhile looked through a multivolume set of County Records.

He moved the ladder and climbed to look on the higher shelves.

Bruce lay snoring on the Turkish carpet in front of the hearth.

Lady Benton sat down, resting her head against the back of her chair. Looking at her hands, she said, "These shelves need a good dusting."

A few minutes later she was back at work.

It was growing late. Rutledge looked at the tall coach clock on the mantel, and decided they could devote only half an hour more to what was becoming an impossible task. It would, he thought, take several people days to do a thorough search.

He had just found a three-volume set on fishing in Scotland when Lady Benton said in a surprised tone of voice, "Inspector? I think— you ought to have a look."

He climbed down the ladder and crossed the room to where she was standing.

Rutledge couldn't have said afterward exactly what he was expecting to find. Anything, from a newspaper cutting to a letter from the real Albert Reed's solicitor trying to find him, even a military file.

Instead Lady Benton was holding a photograph.

It was of a wedding party. The bride and groom, smiling. A brides-maid beside her, and another man standing next to the groom. It was an excellent photograph, quite sharp, quite clear.

"What is it? Do you recognize these people?" he asked.

"No. Well, yes. That's to say—I'm not sure—perhaps the groom?" Her voice was doubtful. "Who are they? Ought I to know them?"

"Possibly. Someone did, or the photograph wouldn't be here. Tell me who you think he might be?" Rutledge tried to keep his voice level—interested, but not alarmed.

Her answer was not what he was expecting.

"I'm not sure. He's so much younger here." She shook her head. "He's—well, I believe he's working at the Home Farm. Henry took him on for the planting season. I'd told him to look around for a man. He's getting too old to do everything. Even with that new tractor." She shook her head. "I've only seen him once, at a little distance . . . always work-ing." Looking up at Rutledge, she said, "But why is his photograph—I expect it must be his wedding photograph—in one of our books?"

Rutledge had seen the new farm laborer as well, but standing well back, head down, when he'd asked Henry about the horse in the wrong pasture.

"What is his name?"

"Blackwood? Blackburn? Yes, I believe it's Blackburn. Henry sees to his wages, you see. I try not to interfere—Eric left Henry in charge of the Home Farm when he went to France. He's been very good too, and I leave him to it. We go over the books every quarter."

"Have you ever seen this man before? At the airfield?"

"I—I don't think so." She rubbed her chin, trying to remember. "Certainly not one of the pilots. Possibly one of the mechanics? Margaret might be able to tell us."

Patricia Lowell might have answered that, if she'd lived.

He said, "Mrs. Lowell might have remembered him."

"Oh—yes! Of course! One of her pets. Um . . . Perry? The one with the stutter? No, I think it must be Reed." She stared at him. "Are you telling me that Blackwood is also Sergeant *Reed*?"

"I think it's very likely."

"But Patricia never said anything!— It was—she had a flat going home on the Saturday after what happened in the garden—Blackburn was waiting by the road for someone to take him somewhere, and he—he came to her rescue and fixed the flat for her. She told me on Sunday how grateful she was."

"Did she recognize him? Realize that he was Reed?"

"She'd have said something if she had. Surely?" Lady Benton shook her head. "I'm sure she didn't. Or perhaps it didn't occur to her that he was Reed. At least possibly not then—but later—" Her fingers went to her lips, pressing them as the next thought came. Rutledge read it clearly in her eyes.

"If she asked questions, if the police investigated, they might well discover he was a wanted murderer. And he hadn't finished what he came here to do. He wasn't going to take a risk that she knew Reed was using the name Blackburn now." He waited the space of a moment, then asked, "Did Henry have much to do with the men at the airfield?"

"Hardly at all. You can't imagine what it was like, with everyone enlisting, no one to plant or harvest—making do at every turn. I worried about him—he was working day and night, he kept us fed, and the animals as well. And he was much older. He had nothing in common with the men who were here. They were all so—so very young."

He took the photograph from her and turned it over.

Someone had written on the back.

Brides are so lovely, aren't they? Overshadows yours truly.
Much love, Penny

"Who is Penny? Do you know?"

"Ah, she was Roger's sister. She married a young American and they went back to his home there. She was Roger's only family, and he took her leaving hard."

And that explained why he'd been buried here. Why no one had come to Essex to take him home.

But was this bride the wife that Franklin killed three years later? Or someone else? *Another victim?*

If it was, then this was the only known photograph of Miles Franklin, other than that unclear one in the newspaper cutting.

No wonder the Captain had hidden it. Rutledge looked at the title of the book that Lady Benton was still holding. *Myths and Monsters: A History of Strange Beings.*

A fitting title, he thought.

Lady Benton was saying, "There's a second volume. Perhaps we should look in there. Would you bring it down?"

Rutledge found it and handed it to her.

She thumbed through the pages, and stopped toward the end. "There are cuttings here. I don't recognize them. Roger must have put them in as well." She passed them to Rutledge.

He took them, expecting them to be copies of what he already had in his possession about the murders in Dorset. But they were not.

Here was the first murder—earlier than the one where Franklin had escaped from a courthouse and disappeared. At the least, the first one that anyone had found, searching what they could of Franklin's life.

MURDER MOST FOUL was the headline. And beneath that was the story.

Last night the bodies of Mary Elizabeth Morton Franklin and her father, Jerome Andrew Morton, were discovered by a cousin who had come to the house to return a cooking pan she had borrowed for a Maundy Thursday dinner at St. Joseph's. According to Constable Merriman, Inspector Williams was brought in to take charge of the inquiry into their deaths and is seeking Mrs. Franklin's husband, whose present whereabouts are unknown. There has been a search for his body, but it has not yet been found. Mrs. Franklin and her father died of multiple stab wounds, and it is feared that Mr. Franklin may have suffered a similar fate. Neighbors interviewed by the police can offer no explanation for the deaths. "They appeared to be such a nice family" according to one, while another told us, "They were lovely people. This makes no sense to any of us."

The second cutting reported that Mr. Franklin had not been found, alive or dead, and the police were still searching for him. A third reported that the police now believed that Franklin was a person of interest in the deaths of his wife and father-in-law. He had disappeared, and it had been learned that he had made numerous large withdrawals from accounts at the nearest bank before his disappearance, and that items were also missing from the home. He was being actively sought by Scotland Yard.

The date on the cutting was 1911.

A note had been added at the bottom of the third cutting.

Roger, darling, you remember Mary, don't you? We were in school together, and I was in her wedding party some years ago. I never cared for him, I could easily believe he has killed her. But the police haven't a clue.

And the note was signed with a *P*. Penny . . .

Appalled, Lady Benton looked away. She had been reading over Rutledge's arm as he scanned the cuttings.

"Why did he kill them? Why not a divorce—or simply leave? Disappear? I can't understand it."

"I don't know that anyone can. Perhaps Franklin believed that a divorce would take too long and be too difficult. That it was safer just to be rid of them, if he could get away with it. Needless to say, he was never caught. There's a very good chance he's killed others. Not just Morton and his daughter." He said nothing about the other cuttings in his possession. This wasn't the time. Instead he added, "Men like Franklin find it easy to kill, if someone is in their way. They feel no shame and no remorse. It's merely self-protection."

She was frowning, working it out in her own mind, putting the pieces together.

"Is—is *Reed* this man Franklin—and dear God, the man at the Home Farm as well?" She found her handkerchief, and wiped away tears. "I don't want to believe it. I don't want to think of Patricia dying at his hands." She set aside the book lying in her lap, as if it were contaminated by what had been hidden among its pages. "Roger knew, he *knew* what Reed—Franklin—was, didn't he?" Reaching out, she caught Rutledge's arm, her fingers gripping it hard. "Inspector—it was an *accident*, wasn't it? Roger's crash? Please tell me it was!"

"I can't. I think the Captain must have done or said something to alert Franklin. Or perhaps he even confronted him. Who can say for certain? He may have intended to talk to the Colonel—the police—someone in authority, and he had to be stopped. Without drawing attention to his death. Everyone seemed to know the Captain drove fast. Fiddle with the steering or the brakes, and let nature take its course. I don't think Franklin expected it to happen in front of witnesses, who could vouch for what they *thought* they were seeing. He was fortunate there. If the crash had occurred somewhere on the road from Walmer, late at night, there might have been a formal inquiry. It's very likely that Gerald Dunn discovered what had been done to the motorcar. That sealed his death as well."

"But how could he be certain the Captain would be killed? Not simply injured and able to tell the police what went wrong? Even who might have done something to the motorcar?"

"I daresay he was hoping it would be fatal. Desperate as he was, Franklin could hardly kill Nelson himself and toss the body into the sea. It might be believed that Dunn deserted. But not Nelson. Not the air ace. There would have been an uproar, and London would have sent people down here to help in the search." People like Haldane, but he didn't say that aloud.

"If this is true," she asked, her voice husky, "why on earth did that man come back to Walmer? Why not leave well enough alone—leave these hidden forever?"

"For one thing, it's possible that he didn't know for certain just what the Captain had hidden. If this is indeed the only known photograph of Franklin, he'd want to destroy it. If it wasn't in the Captain's quarters, if it wasn't in the records in Dinsmore's office, it had to be here. And you might eventually come across it. Again, the simplest solution would be to kill you. But like the Captain's death, yours would have to seem natural. Like a fall down the crypt stairs. It's very likely Franklin was already planning a new life and name elsewhere, and he wanted to be certain there was nothing in the past that might follow him. He's always carefully removed anyone who could prove who he was. For another, it's likely that the real Franklin and Newbold, at The Monk's Choice, are brothers. He'd feel safe here."

"No, that can't be true. We've known the Newbold family going back generations. He *has* no brother. Anyone can tell you that."

"Are you sure?" he asked sharply. "Newbold's father wasn't married twice?"

"Of course I am sure. Ask Inspector Hamilton—or look in the church records at St. George's. I don't think he ever set foot outside Walmer."

He was collecting the cuttings, and she handed him the photograph, and he took a last look at it, committing the face to memory.

Lady Benton leaned forward to see it one last time.

"Who is the bride? Is this the woman he killed? Is this Mary Elizabeth?"

"I expect it must be. Nelson's sister sent it to him, and the clippings. She identified her on one of them."

Lady Benton shivered. "Put that back where we found it. It's safer there, and I don't want to have to look at it again. And then we'll go to the police—to Inspector Hamilton."

"I think it's best to wait until morning. I don't want to leave the house unguarded."

"You aren't armed. There's the gun room. My husband has a shotgun, and a set of dueling pistols that came down in the family—"

He was already closing the pair of books *Myths and Monsters*, crossing the room to put them back on the shelf. "That's not a bad thought."

She stopped halfway to the door. "Henry. At the Home Farm. Dear God, what are we to do about him? He's got a murderer sleeping in the tack room in the barn!"

"It's best to do or say nothing. He's safe because he has no idea what's happening. Leave it that way until we can take Blackburn, or whatever his name is, into custody."

He had just turned from putting the books where they had come from, his hand already reaching for one of the lamps, to put it out, when Bruce lifted his head from the Turkish carpet and growled deep in his throat, a low, rumbling warning.

Lady Benton turned slowly, staring at the dog, then looking at Rutledge, her face suddenly pale.

Bruce lumbered to his feet, his massive head turned toward the terrace doors in the garden room on the other side of the passage.

"Keep him quiet," Rutledge ordered her in a whisper and put out the other lamp, plunging them into darkness. She had already gone to the dog, taking him by his collar, he could hear her speaking softly to him. Rutledge joined her, and together they stepped into the passage.

He closed the door to the library as softly as he could.

She reached out, fumbling for his arm.

"This way. The gun room is this way," she whispered softly.

Bruce was pulling against her grip, still growling deep in his throat, and Rutledge reached for his collar. "Good boy. This way."

And she walked down the pitch-black passage as if it were noon and the doors were opened to all the rooms, letting in the light.

He brought the dog with them as she guided him. Opening doors and shutting them with ease. He had shifted his hand to her shoulder, so that both of her hands were free.

And he had a sudden vivid memory of the war, and gassed men, their eyes bound against the pain and the light, stumbling along in a grim line, each man's hand on the shoulder of the soldier in front of him, trusting in someone ahead to lead all of them to safety and medical care.

He shuddered, remembering, saying to Hamish next to him, "Poor devils."

He hadn't realized he'd spoken aloud.

He felt her turn slightly. "What?"

Hoping his voice didn't betray him, he said, "Speaking to the dog."

He felt her nod, then move on.

Rutledge had always had a good sense of direction, and he'd searched nearly every room in the house, but the twists and turns of passages in pitch-darkness worried him. He needed to know where he was, which direction the danger was coming from.

He was about to ask how much farther they must go, when in the distance both of them heard the muffled sound of breaking glass.

Bruce jerked against the grip of Rutledge's hand on his collar, growling again as he tried to turn back the way they'd come.

There was no more pretense. Franklin was no longer playing at ghosts and hiding his real motives. This time he would kill anyone in his way.

Lady Benton hesitated at the sound, then opened a door. "Wait here."

He could hear her striking a match and lighting a lamp. But she kept the wick low.

And he stepped into the gun room. It was hardly that, closer to an estate office, although in a case were the shotgun and a hunting rifle. On a stand were the dueling pistols in a velvet-lined case. Two revolvers had been in a third case. One was missing.

"That one is in my room."

He opened the case and took out the remaining revolver as she handed him a box of cartridges. As he loaded it, he put the rest of the box into his pocket. "Take this. And then we need to hide the long guns."

"Oh, yes, of course." She had been digging in a drawer, found what she wanted there—a torch—and then unlocked the long case and took out the shotgun and rifle, handling them gently. "There's a blanket or two in that small chest. For sleeping rough."

Rutledge found them and took them out. When they had wrapped the weapons, he asked, "Where should we take them?"

"I know just the place." She turned out the lamp, closed the door behind him, and led the way down a set of back stairs. The torch swung back and forth as they walked, and then steadied as he saw large sinks just ahead of him, racks for stretching curtains, and ironing boards. "When my husband was a little boy, there were full-time washerwomen, and this room was filled with steam from heating water, and smelled of lavender soap. He said." She pointed to the larger sink, and he set the longer guns inside, then reached into one of the baskets on the floor for several sheets, piling them on top of the weapons.

"Where do we go from here?" she asked softly.

"As far as possible from where these guns are hidden. And where he's not likely to look."

"I thought you'd want to catch him. Once he was inside."

"I do, but I want you somewhere safe, meanwhile."

"No," she said firmly. "In the dark, we could just as easily shoot each other."

"His weapon of choice appears to be a knife. He could be standing and waiting in the dark, and stab you before you knew he was there."

"No," she repeated. "I won't let him destroy the library. I'll shoot him myself first."

"Then stay out of the way. I want to take him alive, and see him tried."

"I'll bear that in mind," she replied, but she had turned away, and he couldn't be sure just how far he could trust her to follow his lead.

With the shielded torch, Rutledge could make his way back to the library fairly quickly. Bruce had been locked in the gun room, for his own safety.

They moved quietly down the last passage by the library door, and paused to listen. But there was only silence.

With Lady Benton behind him, Rutledge reached for the knob and slowly began to open the door.

The room was pitch-black. Rutledge flashed the torch beam left and then right, but no one was there. Either searching the shelves, as they had done, or simply waiting for Lady Benton to come down to investigate the sounds of breaking glass.

He waited a full minute, then crossed the room, opened the far door. No one was in the far passage. But the door to the garden room was standing wide. Beyond, in the flash of his torch, he could see pieces of a large vase scattered across the floor, smashed to bring someone running.

Behind him he heard Lady Benton draw in a breath, as she saw the wanton damage. "Where is he?"

"I don't know. The outer door is open. Leave while you can. And send word to Hamilton."

"There's only one torch. I'm safer here."

Rutledge said, "We wait in the library. He's hunting you, at a guess. And so we stay where he least expects to find us."

"I'm worried about Henry and his family. Do you think he's already harmed them? We ought to do something. I just can't think what."

"If he's harmed them, it's already too late."

They moved back to the library, and shut both doors behind them.

Rutledge switched off the torch. "I'll take the revolver now. If you are sure I'm down, find the weapon and use it."

"Let me go to my room—the other revolver is there—"

"There's no time. The safest place for you is up on that ladder. Unless he has a light, he won't see you there. But I will know precisely where you are."

Reluctantly she crossed to the ladder, and he switched on the torch for a few seconds, until he was certain she had climbed safely. And then he sat down to wait.

Waiting. The hardest part, he thought.

And without warning, he could feel the nightmare rising, could feel himself in the trenches, his feet in the dank water where rats ran and parts of the dead hadn't been found, a cold wind blowing, and dawn ten minutes away. He was at the bottom of the ladder, his eyes on his watch, the whistle ready in the other hand. Some of the men were praying, he could hear them, while one man swore softly, a constant stream of coarseness. Two men had rosary beads—

By an effort of sheer will, he forced himself back to the present, making a sound in spite of himself as he fought for control.

"Are you all right? Inspector? Mr. Rutledge?"

The whisper out of the darkness reached him.

He cleared his throat. "Smothering a cough."

Hamish said, "Listen—"

Someone was coming down the passage, he thought, the sound just at the limit of his hearing. Not trying to conceal the footsteps . . .

There was no time to warn Lady Benton. He got to his feet just as the door opened, flung wide enough to hit the wall behind it with a soft thud.

The intruder was making certain no one was standing behind it.

The sound was met with silence.

Rutledge held his breath, for he was closest to the door.

And then a torch went on as whoever it was walked into the room.

Rutledge couldn't see more than a shape behind the sudden flare of light, but it pinned him.

There was no choice but to attack. He came at the man fast and hard, and the intruder dropped the torch to meet the sudden onslaught. From the floor it cast its light upward on their faces as they fought, shadows and brightness, distorting their features.

Rutledge had served in the trenches, he'd fought hand to hand, and survived. Franklin had killed without mercy, but his victims had been unsuspecting, vulnerable. Still, he was fighting for his freedom now.

There was a flash, something bright, caught for an instant in the torch's beam—

A knife—

It was in the intruder's free hand, and he was using all his strength to bring it up.

Rutledge reached out and caught the man's wrist, bringing it down hard, with such force that the other man cried out, dropping the blade.

They went down, hitting the floor hard, and Franklin grunted, freeing his hand and reaching up for Rutledge's eyes. Rutledge hit him, and the hand fell back.

They were rolling across the floor, and Rutledge had him now, about to pin him, when Franklin's boot, drawn back for a kick, struck the ladder where Lady Benton was watching.

The ladder began to move fast, rolling on the groove designed to make every shelf accessible. It hit the far wall with a thud, and from the semidarkness in that corner came a cry of alarm. And then the sounds of a struggle as she fought to regain her footing.

For a split second Rutledge looked up, and in that one instant, Franklin broke free. He bolted, flinging the ladder back across the room as he passed.

Lady Benton was clinging to it by one hand, her other hand flailing, as it tried for a grip. Rutledge got to his feet, leapt forward, and managed to reach the ladder. But as it abruptly stopped, she lost her grip completely, and came down in a flurry of skirts. He caught her, set her on her feet, and was gone, after Franklin.

He heard her cry out, "Shoot him—don't let him get away—"

Rutledge's boots crunched in broken glass as he raced through the garden room and out into the night.

There was no sign of Franklin.

But there was only one way out of the private garden, and that was the arch in the hedge, and the gate there.

It was standing wide, and he set out in pursuit.

17

Rutledge came through the gate and onto the lawn at a dead run. His eyes were adjusting to the darkness, and he saw Franklin racing across the lawns, with no shelter until he reached the place in the hedge where the airmen had had access to the Abbey grounds.

Hamish was saying, "Yon's a clear shot—"

And it was. He could bring down Miles Franklin—the revolver was still there in his belt and loaded.

But the weapon was unfamiliar, and if he stopped now, took aim—and missed—he wouldn't have a second shot.

And then even that chance was gone as Franklin disappeared down the slope that led to the airfield.

Rutledge ran on, went through the gap after him, and nearly lost his footing as a root caught at the toe of his boot.

But the airfield offered very little cover to the fleeing man, and he knew it. He turned and ran close by the hedge, deep shadow enveloping him.

Rutledge followed him, was gaining by the time Franklin reached the far end of the hedge and turned into the lane.

Rutledge heard a horse whinny, and as he rounded the far side as well, he saw Franklin climbing the fence where Lady Benton had seen the ghostly horse.

And it was there, saddled and waiting.

This time Rutledge didn't hesitate. He skidded to a halt, had the revolver in his hand, and was already aiming as he fought to steady his breathing.

Franklin was silhouetted against the night sky for an instant as he reached the top rail of the fence and was about to swing himself over. Without hesitation, Rutledge fired.

He saw Franklin throw up an arm, then bend as if twisting sideways, and knew he'd been hit. But the unfamiliar revolver had pulled slightly to the left, and as Franklin began to fall from the fence, he caught himself, for an instant, hung there before he half-fell, half-leapt to the ground. He got to the horse only feet away, swung himself up into the saddle, even as Rutledge fired again. But the horse was already on the move, Franklin leaning forward in the saddle so that it was impossible in the darkness to tell animal from man.

The horse set out at a gallop, straight for the fence where the lane met the road, and was put to it. It cleared the rails handily as Rutledge watched. Even in the dark, he could see the fast-moving blur turn toward Walmer.

He was already turning, heading for the carriage house, shoving the heavy door wide, racing toward his motorcar standing behind the landau. He turned the crank, the motor caught, and he was in the driver's seat, pulling out, narrowly missing the landau, almost clipping the gate as the heavy motorcar roared through it.

He reached the main road, sure that even at her full gallop, the mare couldn't have gone farther than the closed gates to the Abbey. And the motorcar was faster, its headlamps cutting through the night.

Rutledge glimpsed her ahead of him, passing now where the old Abbey gatehouse had stood, and then she was lost, a heavy stand of trees by the road masking her flight as it blocked what little light there was.

By the time he too had reached the ruined gatehouse there was no sign of her on the road. It was as if she had vanished among the trees or was lost in the fields that stretched on the far side of the old gates.

He lost precious minutes, making certain the main gates of the estate were still locked, that they hadn't been tampered with. In the great headlamps of the motorcar, the brass scroll with *Lachrymosa* etched in it seemed to glow like molten gold.

Satisfied that Franklin couldn't have doubled back, he started toward Walmer again.

I should have shot him when I had that first chance, he told himself grimly. It's on me if I lose him now.

To his left as he drove, scanning both sides of the road, movement caught his eye.

There was a stretch of fallow ground, running down to a line of trees in the far distance. And a horse was coursing diagonally across the field toward an inlet, and beyond, the lights of Walmer.

He couldn't tell, as he drove, whether there was a man on the horse's back or not.

What's more, there was no way to follow across the fields. No access at all from the road. He had to drive the legs of the triangle, but he had no idea where the mare was heading.

Swearing, he sped up, perilously taking a sharp curve, as Hamish warned him to take care.

The outskirts of Walmer were ahead, but he had lost the horse behind the brambles and scrub trees that bordered the fields already well behind him, and then he was among the cottages and small houses that led into the High, and was forced to slow.

There were options—the harbor for one, where Franklin could steal a boat and disappear. There were The Salt Cellar and The Viking, where at this hour he might think he could take refuge. What would he choose to do? Were there motorcars in the yard behind the Swan Hotel? Had he already found one and had a head start toward Chelmsford? What would he choose?

Hamish said, "I'd choose yon motorcar."

There was the brother, Rutledge suddenly remembered. And according to Lady Benton, it couldn't be Newbold.

Whoever he was, would he help?

Rutledge drove down to the harbor, but there was no horse wandering about, and The Salt Cellar, like The Viking, was dark.

With the motor still running, he got down and knocked at the door of The Salt Cellar. But no one came to answer it. He had no idea where Johnson lived, just that it was not in the rooms above the pub. And then he saw what he had nearly missed in the shadowy doorway. Someone had tried to force the lock. The heavy door had held.

Nor did anyone come to see what the fuss was about when he knocked at the door of The Viking.

He got back into the motorcar, reversed, and went to find Hamilton.

Hamilton answered the door on the third knock. "Damn it, Fred, I—"

He broke off as he saw Rutledge in the shadows of his doorway. "What the hell do you want?"

"I need you—as many men as you can collect as fast as possible. I've tracked Mrs. Lowell's killer as far as Walmer. He was on horseback—a mare he'd taken from the Home Farm. He broke into the Abbey tonight."

"Lady Benton all right?"

"Yes." He kept thinking about the broken door into the garden room. There was no way to lock it now. Still, there was the dog . . . He said, "If we don't find him now, we'll never catch him."

"All right, let me get my clothes on. Constable Brown is on Church Street. I'll collect the other two."

"Where does Johnson live? The owner of The Salt Cellar? Someone—possibly the killer—tried to force the lock. He may have found another way inside. I'm going to find out."

"At the foot of the hill. It's a semidetached, his daughter lives on the other side. Look for the house with a little barrow in the front garden. She plants things there."

As Rutledge turned to go, Hamilton added, "We'll sweep from this end, you begin at the harbor."

He drove to Church Street, roused the Constable, wasting precious time answering his questions. He said, "The harbor. Start there. I'll be with you shortly."

It was not difficult to find Johnson's house. He didn't need to look for the barrow. There was a dim light just showing at the back of the house, and it went out as Rutledge knocked on the door.

No answer. He knocked again. "Johnson? Scotland Yard. I know you're—"

The door opened, and Johnson said, "For God's sake, keep your voice down." He caught the sleeve of Rutledge's coat and pulled him inside. "This way. I daren't light a lamp."

Rutledge followed him to the kitchen. Johnson lit a small lamp, then covered it with a towel before setting it on the floor.

The table was covered with bloody cloths. And to one side of the room stood a young woman, presumably the man's daughter, who lived in the other side of the house. Her face was pale, her hands trembling.

"He was here," Johnson was saying. "Bleeding. I didn't know—I let him in. And he told me that if I didn't help him, he'd kill Sally, there." He gestured toward her. "I believed him—"

"What did he want?"

"First, someone to bandage his shoulder. It was bleeding heavily. I did what I could, but I'm no doctor, I didn't know what to do. He ordered me to take the bullet out, but when I looked, it had gone through." He shook his head. "He didn't believe me, he said it was bleeding because the bullet was still in the wound."

"What else did he want?"

"I've a small boat. I keep it in the river, not the estuary. He wanted me to take him there and row him upriver."

"And you didn't?"

"She's in Brooks's boatyard. Planks need recalking. He told me to go and get her, but she's not seaworthy, she'll take on water faster than I could bail. He was angry, I've never seen him so angry."

"Where did he go from here?"

"I don't know. I was glad to be shut of him. I locked the door and turned out the lights."

"Just now? I saw the light go out just now."

"Sally come over to ask what the yelling was about. I'd just come finished locking the doors. I didn't want her to see the bloody towels, but she lit the lamp before I could stop her." He sighed. "I tried to keep her out of it. For a bit there, I thought he was going to take her with him. To be sure I didn't tell anyone he'd been here. I've never seen him like that," he said again.

"All this time—when we were searching—you must have known what your brother was." Rutledge was angry now.

"But I didn't know," he retorted. "He came to my door four or five weeks back, telling me he was down on his luck, asking me to find him work. I didn't even recognize him at first."

That fit the timing that Rutledge knew. Franklin had left France after trying to kill Vermuelen, and then made his way to Essex somehow. Without attracting attention.

"And he's not my brother," Johnson was saying, aggrieved. "He's my half-brother. Ma took me back to Essex when my father died. Miles was left in Wiltshire with his grandmother—his mother's mother. When she died—the first wife—my father married again, and I was born. I hadn't seen Miles since he was *ten*."

"He was here—at the airfield—through the entire bloody war!" Rutledge snapped.

The surprise on Johnson's face was genuine. "He couldn't have been—you're wrong. I'd have *known*."

That was very likely true—Franklin hadn't used his own name. There was no reason why a grown man in uniform, by the name of Reed, would have meant anything to Johnson. But how did Franklin know where *Johnson* lived?

He was still talking. "I tell you, he knocked at my door, told me he'd just come back from Australia, and said he wanted to find work so that he could move on to Staffordshire, where he had friends. He said he'd had to leave the village where he'd been living, that the woman's husband had turned up and brought his brothers with him. I didn't know whether it was true or not, any of it, but I told him they were looking for work at the Home Farm. He said he'd go there and ask. I was glad to be rid of him, I was afraid he'd want to work at the pub. When he pounded on my door tonight, I tried to persuade him to go to Dr. Wister. He told me then he'd killed a dozen people, and I'd be next if I didn't help him. Sally too." He wiped his face with his hand, still shaken. "He was always strange. I never liked him."

"And yet when he came to you, asking your help, you found him work at the Home Farm. How did he find you, if you'd lost touch with *him*?"

"His grandmother must have known where my mother was going. Or they corresponded. How the hell do I know? I was only six when my mother took me and left."

Rutledge, watching his face, couldn't be sure whether Johnson was lying for his daughter's sake, because she'd known nothing about this half-brother until now, or if Johnson was telling the truth. And it didn't matter.

"Stay here, keep the doors locked, the lights off. And pray we find him before he has nowhere else to run."

Rutledge tracked down the Constable by the harbor, searching among the boats anchored there. "Any luck?" he called as he approached.

"None, sir. And no one answers in the shops and either of the pubs. I don't know where else to look."

"House to house, then. Test the locks on all the shop doors as well. The outbuildings. He's armed, he's killed before. Don't take any chances."

Another Constable came running down the hill, sent to join them.

Rutledge was growing restless. There was no sign of Franklin, but more urgently, no sign of the horse. Had he turned back after luring the hunt to Walmer? Had Johnson bandaged his wound, and afterward Franklin had set off toward the Abbey?

He turned to the newly arrived Constable, told him where, so far, he and Brown had searched, and told him he would be back shortly.

As he retrieved his motorcar and drove up the hill toward the High, Rutledge felt a compelling need to hurry. But Hamilton stopped him at the other end of the village, flagging him down. "I thought you were searching the harbor."

"The man was there—but I can't find the mare. He may have doubled back when he discovered we were searching. And Lady Benton is alone in the house. With a broken door."

"Then go on. The Chief Constable will blame *me* if she comes to grief."

The road was empty—he made good time, but when he reached the gates to the stable yard, he left his motorcar outside, vaulting the gate, and then made his way around the house to the private garden.

The doors were still broken but someone had pushed a bench across in front of it.

Lady Benton, he thought. Waiting somewhere now with her late husband's revolver? He wouldn't have put it past her to go upstairs for it the minute his back was turned. He stopped at the bench, called to her, added his name and then called again.

He was about to call a third time when he heard a low bark, and Bruce came dashing down the passage and through the door into the garden room, leaping over the bench in his eagerness to greet someone he knew. His momentum carried him through the doors and out onto the terrace, launching himself to hit Rutledge full in the chest. He had all he could do to stay on his feet as the dog tried to lick his face.

Lady Benton appeared in the doorway to the room, the revolver in her hand. "He likes you. Where is Reed or Franklin or whatever that man's real name is? Did you kill him? I thought I heard a gunshot."

"Clipped his shoulder. He got as far as Walmer, but I haven't found the mare. I thought he might have decided to double back."

"Oh dear—I hope he hasn't harmed her. I've sat in the library, on guard."

He saw that she had wrapped something around her left wrist. "There was no time to see if you were all right."

"I think I've strained it a little," she said, lifting her arm. "I came down on it rather hard."

"I've got the motorcar by the stable gates. Come back with me. Until we know where he is."

"There's the dog. He was terribly unhappy being locked away from all the excitement."

"We'll take him with us."

"I won't leave the house like this. I can't."

"He uses a knife, Lady Benton. It won't be pleasant if he finds you in his way. I don't have the time to persuade you. I shouldn't have left Walmer, as it is. I might not be able to get back to the Abbey tonight."

Something in his voice reached her. "You're saying I'm a distraction. All right, let me collect a few things—"

"Later. You must come as you are. There's literally no time now."

She went into the library, found the lead for Bruce, and snapped it on his collar. "It seems we're taking a ride, whether we care to or not," she said to him, and Rutledge moved the bench far enough for the woman and the dog to leave.

He had to unlock the gate, expecting to have to persuade Bruce into the motorcar, but the dog made short work of it, jumping in, settling into the rear seat, tongue lolling. Taking up most of it, crowding Hamish into a corner. As Lady Benton took her seat, Rutledge turned the crank and got in beside her.

He drove fast, reached the outskirts of Walmer, and only slowed when he saw one of Hamilton's Constables just coming out of a house. "Any news?"

"Not yet, sir. We haven't heard from the men down by the harbor."

"Tell Hamilton where I am."

The Constable tried to see who was in the motorcar with him, and leapt back when Bruce stood up and thrust his head out the window, over Rutledge's shoulder.

Rutledge drove on to the hotel. "I'll give you my key. Stay there until I come for you. You'll know it's safe then."

"I'd rather go to Margaret. If she knows what's happening, she'll be worried for me. And I can get a cup of tea. I need it rather badly."

She smiled wryly. "In the war, I felt safe, with the squadron at my doorstep."

He wasn't pleased, but he drove on, pulling up in front of Mrs. Hailey's door.

"I just remembered. We can't take Bruce inside," Lady Benton warned him. "Margaret has a cat. But we must keep him safe. He's only borrowed."

He waited by the motorcar, watching as she went up the short walk and tapped at the door.

Mrs. Hailey didn't respond for a minute or two, and Lady Benton turned toward Rutledge, where he stood impatiently by the motorcar. There was a rueful expression on her face, and just then Mrs. Hailey opened the door. He could see that she was wearing a robe or her nightdress.

"I'm not well—" the housekeeper began apologetically, just as Bruce began to bark frantically from the rear seat of the motorcar, his head and shoulders pushing against the rear door.

And in the same instant, Mrs. Hailey was roughly shoved out of sight. Before Rutledge was halfway up the walk, a hand reached out, caught Lady Benton's bad wrist, and pulled hard, dragging her into the house. He heard her cry out with the pain.

She was already across the threshold and the door slammed shut before Rutledge, shouting her name, could reach her. Bruce was out of the motorcar, jumping down and bounding toward the door, then throwing himself against it. When it didn't open he began to leap frantically up and down, barking madly, in his efforts to reach Lady Benton.

Rutledge caught the dog's lead and physically heaved him away from the door and across the front garden.

But his mind wasn't on Bruce.

It was on the revolver Lady Benton was carrying with her.

If Miles Franklin found it, he could hold off any effort to break into the house.

18

Rutledge ducked as the glazing in the window next to the door shattered, and a shot went just wide of his head. He heard someone scream as he moved clear as swiftly as he could, yanking the dog with him across the side of the house, in an effort to get both of them out of range.

Another shot was fired, this time closer, as he reached the corner of the house and threw himself around it. The dog whimpered, and at first Rutledge thought he'd been hit, but Bruce's foot was tangled in the lead.

Relieved, he caught the lead and managed to tie it to a fruit tree well out of range.

He heard men calling to his left, and the sound of running feet. Hamilton yelled something, and Rutledge realized he was shouting questions.

"Who's firing? Damn it, Rutledge, where are you?"

Rutledge called, "I'm all right. But he's got Lady Benton and Mrs. Hailey. And he's armed."

Hamilton was giving orders as Rutledge, bending low, was running toward the rear of the house. But the kitchen door was locked, and as he hit it with his shoulder to break it down, he realized that it was blocked from the inside.

The curtains had been drawn on all the windows, there was no way to look inside or even to hope for a good shot.

He made his way around the next house as lights came on, people calling to each other. Reaching the street, he stopped just as Hamilton came running down the street.

"I've been around to the kitchen door. It's blocked. There's no way in."

"He'll kill those women if we try," Hamilton told him. "And if he harms Lady Benton, I'll be demoted to Constable in the Outer Hebrides. What the hell happened? And where did that hairy monster come from?"

"She borrowed it from a neighbor." They could hear Bruce barking again. "I wanted to take her to the hotel, where she would be reasonably safe, but she insisted that she would rather stay with Mrs. Hailey. And he was already there."

"Clever bastard. We've seen nothing of the damned horse. I was just going to look in on Dr. Wister, in the event the wounded man had gone there, when I heard the shots. Who the hell *is* he? Johnson was trying to tell me something about a half-brother."

"He's many men. It's a long story, but he's wanted for a number of murders under different names."

"How did you find out about him? Why did Lady Benton come into the village? Did she know him?"

"Not now, there isn't time. It will be light soon. Clear out the houses on either side and across the street as soon as possible. Do you have anyone who can use a rifle?"

"No. And it's rather chancy, trying to hit him in that house, shooting blind."

"I was intending to draw him out."

"Constable Brown was in the war. But he's no sniper. He has a German rifle, a souvenir."

"Does he have any ammunition for it?"

"No idea. I'll find out. But I tell you, it's madness to use it."

"We might not have any choice." He started to walk away.

"Wait, where are you going?"

"To move my motorcar. It's in the way."

"He'll shoot you."

"No, I don't think he will. He's got four shots left, and he'll be as glad as I am to see it out of the line of fire."

He walked down the street openly. Hamish was thundering in his head, and he ignored the warnings. Franklin had been a mechanic, not a foot soldier. He would very likely worry about what Rutledge was up to. Trying to think what the logic behind such a move might be. Whether a trick was involved. The only difficulty was, this would put him on edge. And that would be dangerous for Mrs. Hailey and Lady Benton.

Tensing as he came within range, he walked on, reached the motor-car, and as it shielded him, he took a deep breath. Then stepped out into the open to turn the crank.

With any luck, he told himself, Franklin would be debating whether it was worth killing Rutledge and finding himself with only three shots left.

The motor caught, he folded the crank back into its place, and walked back to the still open door.

Without looking at the house, he got in, closed the door, and re-leased the brake.

Out of the corner of his eye, he saw a shadow at the broken window, and held his breath, driving away without hurry, ignoring the mur-derer and his two women shields.

It worked. He got the motorcar well out of range, and as he walked back, he saw moving shadows as Hamilton got the closest families to safety. The two Constables from the harbor were running up the hill to help him.

He was still watching when someone spoke behind him, making him jump.

"I came to this village because nothing ever happens here. No gun-shot wounds, no broken bodies." It was Dr. Wister. "Do you always bring chaos wherever you go?"

Rutledge, turning slightly, said, "Sometimes."

"He has hostages, doesn't he? How do you expect to get them out of there safely?"

"I don't know yet. He's wounded. The shoulder. But it's bleeding rather badly. Or was, when someone cleaned and bandaged the wound."

"Now that's the first bit of good news I've heard. But much can happen before he bleeds to death. Shall I offer my services as a doctor, and see what I can do to hasten the situation?"

Rutledge considered him. "What about your oath? To do no harm?"

Wister smiled. "There are a good many things I can do that won't harm him but might render him incapable of fighting back."

"Then be ready. It might come to that."

Wister looked up at the sky. "It will be dawn soon enough. Have you had any sleep?"

"No. But I'll be all right."

"I'll make you a cup of tea with a little whisky in it. That should help."

"Thanks."

Wister left, but Rutledge stayed where he was. For one thing, he had a better view of Mrs. Hailey's house from here. And the villagers knew and trusted Hamilton and his men. If they told someone to leave, there would be less argument. He wasn't absolutely certain it was necessary, but it was a precaution that was wise to take. If Franklin decided to make a break for it, there was less chance of someone being in the way.

Suddenly there was shouting from Mrs. Hailey's house.

Rutledge moved closer.

Franklin must have been standing beside the shattered window, because his voice carried clearly.

"There are two women in here with me. I'll kill them if I have to. But I know how to use a knife, and if you don't listen, I'll send you a few bits to get your attention."

Hamilton shouted, "It will go harder for you, if you harm them."

Rutledge heard Franklin laugh. "Will it now?"

He let the two men bargain. If Franklin was convinced that Hamilton had the authority to give him what he wanted, then he, Rutledge, was free to do what had to be done.

There was silence for several minutes. Behind him, someone called, "Mr. Rutledge? Sir?"

Turning, he saw that Constable Brown had somehow circled around, gone to his house on Church Street, and brought him something wrapped in a sheet.

It was the German rifle.

"It was loaded when I found it. But nobody said anything. Even when I brought it back to England in my trunk. I was thinking that I might take my youngest brother out one day, and let him fire it. He's only thirteen. Too young still." He was starting to unwrap it.

Rutledge said quickly, "Get it out of sight, man. He's at the window, talking to Hamilton."

Brown backed away, the rifle behind him now. "It's here. If you need it."

It was a last resort.

Rutledge turned back as the shouted conversation resumed between Franklin and Inspector Hamilton.

The problem was, while Franklin held the better hand with the two women he'd taken prisoner, what could he bargain for?

Hamish said, "A chance to disappear."

That meant leaving the coast of Essex and traveling inland, walking until he felt safe enough to buy a ticket for the train or an omnibus. The other option was to be given a small boat that could carry him across the Channel, back to France or Belgium.

An idea began to form in Rutledge's mind.

Farther up the street, Hamilton was at loggerheads with Franklin, his voice sharper as he tried to deal with the man.

The light was growing now.

Rutledge turned and raced down the hill toward the house where Bill Johnson lived.

He didn't bang on the door, as he wanted to do. Instead he called, "Johnson? It's Rutledge. I need your help."

Several minutes passed, then the curtain in the front room twitched. He called again. "Open the door, Johnson. I need to talk to you."

It finally opened. Johnson's worried face appeared in the crack. "Is he dead? I heard gunshots—"

"No. He has two women shut up in a house with him. He's threatening to harm them if he's not allowed to leave. Hamilton's talking with him, but it's hopeless. I'm not sure Franklin knows that."

"Here—I don't want any part of him." He tried to shut the door, but Rutledge had his boot in it.

"If you don't help, people will die. Just as he threatened you and your daughter."

He shook his head vehemently. "No, I tell you." He backed away, turning to walk back down the passage, leaving Rutledge in possession of the door—and nothing else.

But Johnson kept shaking his head, refusing to listen. Or help.

Rutledge said, "Look. I want to help him escape. We'll find him eventually, but I want those two women out of there and safe, before he decides to force Hamilton's hand by sending out a finger—or God knows what."

Johnson covered his ears.

Rutledge shoved the door back against the wall as he stepped into the passage. He went after the man, caught Johnson by the shoulders, turned him, and slammed him against the wall.

"Listen to me, damn you. All you have to do is walk to the harbor, find a boat, and with the backing of Scotland Yard, prepare it to sail. Not tonight—not tomorrow—now."

"I won't go with him—I refuse to be a party to this."

"You found him work—you never reported him to Hamilton, or told the Home Farm that you wouldn't want him working for you. You protected him, and that makes you an accomplice to the murder of Patricia Lowell. And if anything happens to those two women, the Chief Constable will personally see to it that you hang next to Franklin."

"You can't do that! I didn't bring him here. I'm not responsible for him. I don't want to be dragged into this any more than I already have been!"

"You're a fool, Johnson. All I'm asking you to do is to find a boat. One that is seaworthy, and prepare it to sail. You own a boat, you know what needs to be done with this one. I'll shoot you myself, if you don't do as you're told."

"Scotland Yard isn't armed—"

"I am." He pulled the revolver free and held it up for Johnson to see. "I was in the trenches, I know how to use it."

Johnson's shoulders sagged. "All right! I'll do what I can. I'll get the bloody boat. Hubbard will let me have his. It's seaworthy, but you can shoot me if you want to, I won't go with Miles. If Hubbard wants his boat back, Scotland Yard can fetch it for him!"

"Who is Hubbard?"

"He works over in the salt mill."

"Fair enough," Rutledge answered. "And hurry. Before there's more on your conscience."

Johnson caught up a coat from the rack in the hall, and with a bitter glance at Rutledge, he left.

Someone was coming down the hall. Rutledge turned quickly, expecting trouble. But it was Sally, Johnson's daughter. "You shouldn't ought to have done that," she said, glaring at him. "My father is a good man."

"He looks the other way, when he doesn't want trouble. Ask Lady Benton, who watched a ghost try her door."

"Dad said my uncle had been drinking—they meant no harm. It was a *lark*!"

"He never spoke up afterward, when it appeared there was a real murder. He never spoke up when Liz was tormented by the other women at The Salt Cellar. He did nothing to protect her from their taunts."

It was harsh, he could already hear Hamish objecting to what he'd said. But he was angry still. "Mrs. Lowell wouldn't have been killed, if your father had spoken up."

"That man is only his half-brother. Dad isn't his keeper. How was he to know? Besides, why can't Lady Benton look after herself?"

He turned on his heel and left, shutting the door behind him.

Rutledge went as far as the turning to the harbor, to be certain Johnson had kept his word. And he saw him in a distance, speaking to another man.

He hurried back up the road, to the Hailey house, stopping well out of range, and searched the darkness at the window for Franklin. But he wasn't visible. On the far side of the house, well up the street and out of range, Hamilton was arguing with one of his Constables.

Watching the window for a moment, Rutledge called, "Reed? Are you there?"

There was silence. And then he saw Lady Benton at the window. There was enough light now to see the red mark on one side of her face.

"What is it you want, Inspector? Reed refuses to come to the window. He saw the rifle."

"Yes, well, it was German and there are no cartridges for it. A war souvenir." He moved forward a little. Bruce was still under the tree, on his feet now as he heard Lady Benton's voice. "I had a word with Bill Johnson. He's at the harbor, speaking to someone by the name of Hubbard. The man has a seaworthy boat. If Reed will agree, I will offer safe passage to France. Or Belgium, if he prefers. He can use you and Mrs. Hailey as shields as far as the harbor. I give him my word, he can take the boat and leave. From the moment he releases the two of you unharmed, he has safe passage. No one will touch him. If he harms either one of you, I shall withdraw my offer, and he's fair game."

She disappeared from sight, and he hoped she was relaying the message to Reed, if he hadn't heard it for himself.

After several minutes, she returned to the window.

"He says, as soon as he leaves this house, the man with that rifle will use it."

"As proof of my good will, I'll see to that now."

And he walked up the street to where Hamilton was standing, listening.

Hamilton said at once, "Damn it, Rutledge, I never agreed to any such offer."

"I outrank you. Where's the rifle?"

Brown stepped forward. "I'm sorry, sir. My fault he saw it." He held out the covered weapon.

Rutledge removed the sheet. "Thank you. You'll have it back shortly."

He turned, walked back toward the house, ignoring Hamilton's arguments. When he'd approached close enough for Franklin to see what he was holding, he stopped.

"As promised," he called. And bending down, he laid the rifle in the street, in plain view. That done, he walked back to where he'd been standing earlier.

"Will you honor my offer?" he called then.

There was silence from the house. Rutledge was beginning to think that it was no more than a trick on Franklin's part to take the rifle out of play.

And then Lady Benton came back to the window. "I'm to tell you, escaping in the boat, he's got only the clothes he stands in, and no money. A hundred pounds."

Damn the man!

"I will agree to one hundred pounds. Yes, all right. But it will take some time to raise that sum. Will he give me his word that nothing will happen to you or Mrs. Hailey while I am collecting it?"

She turned, listened to something, and then she turned back. "He has agreed. And he wants medical supplies and a bottle of Johnson's best whisky in the boat, waiting."

"He'll get those handed to him when he releases you and Mrs. Hailey. Along with the money."

Another conference.

"Yes. All right."

"In exchange, I want to see both of you at the window. Now. Otherwise, the offer is withdrawn."

Mrs. Hailey joined Lady Benton at the window.

"Have you been hurt?" Rutledge called.

Mrs. Hailey answered for them. "No. Not so far."

"I expect to hear the same when I return at noon." And he walked away without looking back. He could hear Hamilton shouting at him, but ignored it.

H ubbard was a thickset man with straw-colored hair. Rutledge had trouble convincing him that the boat would be returned to him. "If I must travel to France myself to retrieve it," he promised.

Wister supplied the medical bag, and a bottle of his own whisky, bringing them down to the harbor himself.

Rutledge took both and set them in the road some distance from the rifle. And then went to find Hamilton. As the light began to brighten he could see, at some distance to the Hailey house, a gathering crowd of watchers. Waiting for whatever was going to happen. One of the Constables was keeping them from coming nearer.

The Inspector was seething. "I didn't expect Scotland Yard to let a killer walk away."

"It has to be done. He meant what he said about what he'd do to the women. Are you prepared for the repercussions of that?"

"It's my patch, damn it. You should have conferred with me."

"He's a killer, Hamilton. Now, where do we find the money he's asked for?"

In the end, they borrowed it from the hotel.

At eleven o'clock, Rutledge carried a bowl of water to the dog tethered to the tree, then went back to the road.

"We have collected most of the money," he called. "It won't take too much longer to find the rest. You can see for yourself the bandages, salves, and something for the pain. A bottle of whisky. As promised. When you are ready to come out, Constable Brown will take them up and carry them to the boat. Once I have all the money, I'll bring it here, then count it while you watch me. When you're satisfied, I'll add it to the medical bag, while you watch. Do we still have an agreement?"

There was silence from the house.

Without waiting for an answer, he walked away.

It was all set in motion, he thought as he went back to the harbor to be sure the boat was waiting. Then he took Johnson by the arm and marched him up the hill to where the medical sack and bottle of whisky stood.

"Call to him," Rutledge ordered Johnson. "Tell him that I haven't lied to him."

"I can't—"

Rutledge's grip on the man's arm tightened. "You will. Now."

Johnson took a deep breath and then called, "Miles? It's me. Bill. Are you there?"

The curtain twitched but there was no answer.

"He made me do it, Miles. He threatened me. But I spoke to Hubbard, and the boat is there, waiting. He's telling the truth about that."

"Do you swear to it?" Franklin called.

"I saw it for myself. We made sure of it not ten minutes ago."

Rutledge said softly, "Now walk away. Back to your house and lock the door. If you don't, he could ask you to handle the boat for him, and bring it back."

"No—" Johnson began, but Rutledge cut him off.

"Go."

And he turned and hurried away alone.

Rutledge called, "I'm going to bring the money now." And he walked past the cottage, toward the hotel.

The money was waiting. Rutledge counted it himself, then nodded to Hamilton. "Thank you."

"If this goes wrong—" Hamilton said.

"I know. Just—pray."

He took the money back to the cottage, stood there in plain view and counted it carefully. It was in single notes, fives, and tens. Nothing larger. Then, still holding it where Franklin could see it, Rutledge took it across to the medical sack, and carefully opened it and dropped the money inside. Setting it down, he said, "I'm going to find Constable Brown. He'll be unarmed."

And he walked away.

Hamish said, "You're taking a terrible risk."

"I know."

When he was out of sight from the cottage, he turned, and set out at a run. Weaving through empty back gardens, he reached the back of the Hailey cottage, and when no one in the house noticed he was there, he quietly slipped past the windows and stood at the nearest corner.

Constable Brown appeared, lifted the medical sack, and held it gingerly, as if it contained a live mortar round.

Rutledge looked at his watch. Eleven-fifty-nine. Then noon . . . Five minutes after. He found he was holding his breath. Another five minutes passed. Constable Brown was growing restless. But Rutledge had left the sack positioned where Brown couldn't see him by the side of the house.

Lady Benton called from the window. "Constable? We're coming out."

"Yes, my lady."

The door to the house opened slowly. Margaret Hailey stepped out first, Rutledge could hear her speaking quietly to someone behind her. And then another lighter step. Lady Benton.

And finally, Miles Franklin.

Rutledge could just see them now, they took another tentative step forward. Mrs. Hailey. Then Lady Benton, and in the rear, Franklin, with his revolver pointed at their backs.

Bruce saw Lady Benton and began to bark wildly, pulling at his lead.

What happened next took mere seconds.

As Franklin hesitated, then warily stepped across the threshold, leaving the house door wide behind him, the dog broke loose from the tree, the broken lead dragging behind him, and launched himself forward, crossing the space between the tree and the three people in a blur.

Startled, Franklin turned to meet the onslaught, crying out. Lady Benton was pulling Mrs. Hailey down.

And Rutledge, his revolver already in his hand, brought it to bear and fired.

In slow motion Miles Franklin dropped the revolver, went down to his knees, and then pitched forward on his face. Ignoring the figure lying there, the dog was greeting the two women with lavish joy.

In long swift strides, Rutledge was there, picking up the revolver, and dropping to one knee by the man on the ground.

Dr. Wister came running, and Constable Brown stood there with the bag in his hand, staring, his mouth open in shock.

Rutledge stood up and Wister took his place by the fallen man, turning him over, examining the wound. "You clipped his hip. That was a damned good shot," he said, glancing up at Rutledge. "He'll live to hang. Let's get him to the surgery, fast as you can."

Hamilton was running toward the sound of the shot, coming to a sudden halt as he saw the two women standing there beside the huge dog, and Franklin just beginning to stir, already groaning in pain.

The Inspector started forward again, had the presence of mind to take the sack from Constable Brown, and managed to say, "Good God, Rutledge, you took a devil of a chance!"

Wister was calling to Brown to come and help with the wounded man, and with Hamilton's aid, they got him up, and began to carry him toward the surgery. Franklin was swearing now, cursing Rutledge, cursing the pain, cursing the men who had him in their grip.

Lady Benton came up beside Rutledge, saying, "That was brilliant. Will he live?"

"Wister says he will."

"Then I'll see to Margaret. I think she's in shock."

And she turned back.

They reached the surgery with their burden, and Wister held the doors wide until they could get him inside and on an examination table. Rutledge took out his handcuffs, and put them on Franklin while Wister was washing his hands.

The doctor then came forward, saying to Constable Brown, "Help me get his clothes off. I need to look at that shoulder as well."

Hamilton, waiting to wash his own hands, sticky with blood, turned as Rutledge stepped away from the table. He said, "Why didn't you wait until the two women were in the clear? It was a risk, he could have fired at them as he went down. And you didn't tell me what you were planning. I should have been told, ready to cover your back."

"You would have been watching me. As would Constable Brown. And Franklin would have known I was there. Besides, you weren't armed. Don't let him out of your sight until he's been locked in a cell. Keep a Constable there with Wister all the time he's working on Franklin." He handed Hamilton the revolver in his hand. "Use it if you have to."

"Where are you going? Who is this man? You called him Franklin, and Reed as well. How do I charge him?"

"Charge him as Miles Franklin. He's wanted for murder in several counties. He's Bill Johnson's half-brother, as well as a laborer called Blackburn at the Home Farm. During the war he was at the airfield, serving under the name of Reed. I expect he's also Lady Benton's ghost. Now I'm off to be sure Mrs. Hailey and Lady Benton are all right. They've had a bad shock."

He left the room as Franklin swore at him again, and walked on out of the surgery.

Hamilton started to follow, then thought better of it.

Rutledge found the two women in the kitchen of the Hailey house. Lady Benton was trying to breathe some life into the cooker, the kettle waiting to be set on. A small cupboard still blocked the door he'd tried earlier.

Mrs. Hailey was sitting in a chair, saying, "I didn't think we'd survive. I truly didn't. He's the most frightening man—" As Rutledge stepped into the room, she stopped, then said to him, "I believed him when he told us he'd kill us if we offered any trouble."

"Just as well you left it to the police." He gestured to the cupboard. "Shall I shift that for you?"

Mrs. Hailey shook her head vehemently. "Leave it. I'll sleep better. There's already the broken window in my parlor."

"We'll have that mended tomorrow," Lady Benton promised.

But Mrs. Hailey wasn't comforted, and went on to Rutledge, "I thought you meant it—about the boat. But I worried that he'd take one of us with him." She was still wearing her nightgown and robe, her feet thrust into a pair of blue slippers that matched the color of the robe. Her hair was still down her back. He watched as she reached up to push several strands out of her face. Her fingers were trembling. Very different from the brisk woman who helped run the Abbey.

"It's finished," he told her gently. "You don't have anything more to worry about."

Lady Benton glanced at Rutledge, but said nothing. The cooker had come to life, and the kettle was warming. She turned to her friend. "Margaret. Is there any whisky? I think we could all do with a little."

"In the cupboard, I think. In the dining room."

Rutledge went to find it, bringing the decanter back to the kitchen in time to hear Mrs. Hailey say, "When that shot was fired, I thought it was *him*. I thought he'd decided to kill one of us."

"I was afraid he'd shot at the dog." Lady Benton dropped down on one knee beside the dog, on the floor by her feet. Hiding her face against the long hair on Bruce's head, so that Rutledge couldn't see the toll the night had taken of her. "Such a brave boy," she said softly, smoothing the large ears. Rising, she took a deep breath. "What did Dr. Wister say?"

"He hasn't changed his opinion. Franklin will live, if there's no infection. I've got to retrieve the motorcar. He can't walk to the police station. It was bad enough, carrying him to the surgery."

"I have no sympathy," Lady Benton said. "He showed none to Patricia." She bit her lip. "Roger had that photograph. Those papers. Do you—is there any real proof to show that that man killed him? To stop Roger from turning him in? Is there enough evidence to charge for that too? I'd like to see it happen."

"It's very likely he did. And then there's Gerry Dunn, who probably discovered how he'd managed it. Even if we can't prove it beyond a reasonable doubt, Franklin will most assuredly hang. There is a long list of people who died at his hand."

"Then I wish you hadn't missed, when you fired." It was clear she meant it.

"I didn't miss," he told her.

Lady Benton asked to stay a little longer with Mrs. Hailey, and Rutledge went back to the surgery. Hamilton and Brown were still there. Franklin was awake, but lying silent on the table with his eyes closed as Dr. Wister worked with his wounds.

"I gave him something for the pain," he said as Rutledge walked to the table. "If you've come to ask when he can be moved, I'd say this evening."

"Fair enough. There's paperwork to be done." And one task remaining.

Another Constable arrived just then, and Hamilton said, "You'll stay in my place. I must see this money back to where it came from. Rutledge, are you coming with me?"

Rutledge said, "I must still find the mare. And make certain the manager of the Home Farm and his family are safe."

He went out with Hamilton, who said, "At least he'll stand his trial. It's a good thing you weren't a better shot, or he'd be dead."

Rutledge said nothing, and let him go while he walked back to where he had left the motorcar.

He could feel the fatigue setting in as he drove out of Walmer and turned to the road leading to the Abbey. As he passed it, he braced himself for what he might find at the Home Farm.

As he pulled into the yard and got out, Henry appeared from the barn. "Was it you who rode that mare so hard?"

Rutledge let out a sigh of relief.

"No. Is she back home?"

"She was standing in the yard when I woke up this morning. And I can't find Blackburn. I had to milk the cows myself, and there's the milking shed to be washed down, the stable to be mucked out—"

Rutledge stopped him. "I'm afraid Blackburn won't be coming back."

"Won't be— Why the hell not?"

"He's been taken up for the murder of Mrs. Lowell."

For once, Henry was at a loss for words. "Are you mad?" he managed at last. "He didn't even know her. And he wasn't one to go running off to the pub, out all hours of the night. Said he was saving his wages, to marry a lass in Yorkshire. Why would he want to harm poor Mrs. Lowell? I ask you!"

"He did know her. He was at the airfield during the war. He was called Reed, then. Albert Reed."

Henry frowned. "Did you say Reed?"

"Yes. His name is actually Franklin. Miles Franklin. I need to search his quarters. And anywhere else he might have hidden something of hers."

"Wait, now. Mrs. Lowell stopped in to ask if she might speak to a Mr. Reed. My son Josh told her there wasn't anyone here by that name. She was puzzled, then said she must have misunderstood, she thought he might work here. Josh remembered that, when we heard she was dead. He said he was sorry he couldn't have helped her find the man she was looking for."

"Was Blackburn here when your son mentioned Reed?"

"He didn't like taking his meals with us. We made up a tray to carry out to the barn. But he could well have heard her himself, when she asked. Josh said they were working in the shed, where he was repairing a beam."

"When did she come and ask for Reed?"

"I expect it was a Monday morning. It was the Wednesday when we heard the news."

She had remembered Reed . . . Had gone to the Home Farm to ask why Blackburn was using a different name.

And Franklin, living there as Blackburn, had known then she had to die.

"I need to search his room," Rutledge reminded the farmer. But when he found nothing of interest there, except for a handful of French sous, they moved on to the rest of the barn.

An hour later, Rutledge and Henry found the suitcase that had been under the bed in the smaller upstairs room at The Monk's Choice. It was in an old well on the property that they discovered Mrs. Lowell's bicycle.

It took another hour to drag that inch by inch to the top of the well. Rutledge had no difficulty recognizing it, though the front fender was crumpled and the basket broken. The blue ribbon was still there.

On his way back to the Abbey, he stopped in at The Monk's Choice. He didn't bother to knock. He pushed the door open so hard it banged against the wall behind it, and Newbold stepped out of the kitchen, saying, "What the hell—?" He broke off as he saw who had come in.

The expression on his face changed.

In Rutledge's hand was a worn valise, still dusty around the hinges.

"You lied to me," Rutledge said, before Newbold had stepped around the bar.

"Is he dead?" His face was drawn now. "*Tell me he's dead*!"

"He'll live to stand trial for murder."

Newbold seemed to sink into himself. "He'll try to take me with him."

"Why?"

"Because I refused to help him hide that bloody bicycle. You heard me quarrelling with him. It was me on the road that night. And he told me that if I said anything, he would swear to the police that he had seen *me* with the Lowell woman. That I had killed her. But I hadn't. I liked her. I never said two words to her, but I'd watch her pedal past the yard."

"Why didn't you speak to Hamilton? He'd have sorted it out."

"Because of that damned, infernal valise. He left it here early in 1919. Several men did, and came back for them later. All except him.

He told me the police would find it, and there was proof of murder in it. They'd think it was mine. And I'd hang."

Rutledge said, "There was indeed proof of murder in the valise." He swung it to the top of one of the tables and snapped the locks. Lifting the top, he turned it so that Newbold, bracing himself, could see the contents.

Newbold leaned forward, stared, and then turned back to Rutledge. "That's just old uniforms! The bastard lied to me!" Face flushed now, his hands clenched at his side, he said, "I was afraid to open it. It was locked, and I was afraid he might see I'd tampered with it. And all the time it was nothing but unforms he didn't need anymore!" He began to swear, but Rutledge cut him short.

"He wasn't lying. There was proof of murder here."

He lifted out the topmost uniform tunic. Spreading it out, he turned the breast pocket inside out. And there, neatly sewn by a caring mother, were the initial and name *G DUNN*.

"This isn't Reed's valise. It belongs to a dead man who was accused of deserting."

Newbold leaned closer again. "Dunn? I remember him. There was a search, before he was declared a deserter. I heard they might have found his body. Some of the men who come in here work in Walmer." He looked at Rutledge again. "Are you saying that Reed killed him? But in God's name, why?"

Rutledge ran his hand down the side of the valise and lifted out part of the linkage from beneath a motorcar.

"Reed took this out of Captain Nelson's motorcar and substituted a faulty bit. Where it broke finally. He happened to be driving fast, lost control, and was killed. Gerald Dunn was curious, and a fine mechanic, found out what Reed had done. And so he had to die as well. I'm sending it to the motorcar's manufacturer, to see just where it came from. The steering, I should think."

Sitting down heavily at one of the other chairs at that table, Newbold said, "And I'd take the blame if the valise had been found here. They'd think I'd killed them. He was right. My good God . . ."

Without a word about the one other object he had found in the valise, Rutledge folded the tunic again, put the linkage in next to it, then
closed the top and snapped the locks in place. "You'll need to make a
statement for the police. About who left the case here, and when. And
who retrieved it recently. Don't delay. You could be charged as an accomplice."

"No—no, I'll come down. If only to be sure the bastard hangs for
what he's done."

Rutledge studied his face for a moment. "What if I'd found the valise the first time I came here? And asked you to open it, and explain
what it contained. Would you have told me about Reed?"

"Of course I would have done. What do you take me for?"

But Rutledge was nearly certain he would have said nothing about
Reed. He'd been too afraid of the man. He'd lied readily enough about
the quarrel by the road.

"It might have saved Patricia Lowell's life."

He turned, lifted the valise once more and walked out the door of
the pub, leaving Newbold sitting there, at the table.

When he passed the Abbey a few minutes later, the gates were open,
and a van was in the drive by the main door, which was closed. He
stopped. But they had been sent by Lady Benton to repair the damage
to the terrace doors. He made certain that some of the staff were there
to watch the workmen's progress, then he left.

I t was nearly eight o'clock when Miles Franklin was transferred to a
cell in the police station.

They had almost reached it, watched by a silent crowd of people
who were standing outside, when a woman came out of the throng,
and before anyone could stop her, she ran to the stretcher and began to
pummel the man lying there, shouting at him.

Rutledge came to her and pulled her off Franklin. She broke into
tears, then.

"I want to see him hang," Mrs. Dunn begged Rutledge. "Promise me I can come and watch him hang."

He led her away. "I'll do my best," he said.

He went with her back to her door, where her son Eddie, his own eyes red-rimmed from crying, took her in.

"Can you manage?" Rutledge asked. Eddie was only nine.

"Yes, sir. Thank you, sir." And then as his mother walked down the passage toward the kitchen, the boy leaned forward. In a low voice, he added, "I just wish you had killed him, sir. It would have been better."

With that he closed the door.

19

Rutledge went back to the hotel, and sat down at his desk, preparing his report. The Chief Constable had asked for a copy as well. He was finding it difficult to concentrate, when there was a tap at the door.

He called, "Come," and then quickly rose as the door opened, and Lady Benton stood there. "I was told you were still here. Would you mind awfully driving me back to the Abbey? Margaret urged me to stay the night, but I need to be sure they've repaired the terrace doors properly." She looked around with interest. "It's a rather nice room, isn't it?"

He set the pages he was working on in the desk drawer, then collected his coat and hat. "Yes, it's been comfortable."

As they went down to his motorcar through the back garden, the wafting scent of roast ham reached them.

"You have nothing for a meal," he reminded her, and stepped into the kitchen to ask for a box.

It was quickly done, and he went with her out to the motorcar.

"You haven't told me about what happened in my garden," she said as they drove out of Walmer.

"According to what I was told, Franklin appeared to be drunk, and Johnson was trying to humor him before he did something foolish. And so he went along with the charade, sure no one was going to see them anyway. He got the wind up when Franklin began to try the door, testing to see if it was locked, and he left rather hastily while you were pushing something across your door."

"Dear God. I was so sure—so very sure it was Roger."

"Franklin knew him. He could mimic the Captain's stride. I talked to Johnson again today. Franklin had a torch inside his coat, pointed toward his face, lighting it, but casting shadows as well. You saw what you were expected to see. You most certainly wouldn't have expected the figure in the garden to be Reed. He counted on you believing it was the Captain. By the way, I discovered your iron key to the house, the one you gave to the Captain. It was left with other items in a valise belonging to Reed. It will be returned to you after the inquest and trial."

"When I went to the Home Farm, I never saw the man listed as Blackburn in the ledgers. I don't think I would have recognized him if I had—but he kept his distance, all the same." She sighed. "We were all taken in." After a moment she added softly, as if to herself, "I was gullible, wasn't I? Was Franklin aware, do you think, that I was at the window, watching?"

"I don't know." But he rather thought Franklin had done. He'd probably been in that garden several times, seen her lamp go out, and the drapes standing wide open. It would worry her to hear the truth.

"Henry had told me Blackburn was a good worker, no complaints."

"Of course he was. It was close enough to the Abbey he could go across at night whenever he wished."

Lady Benton shivered. "He was frightening, Inspector. I think he would have killed us if it suited him. Either of us. With no remorse."

He said nothing. Even though he knew she was right.

They were in sight of the gates now. They were closed. "Have they replaced the damaged doors, I wonder?" she asked.

"I believe they have. I was here earlier. They'd nearly finished." As they came to the end of the wall and turned down the farm lane, he added, "I shall need that photograph and the cuttings. For my report, and the inquest."

"Yes. Of course." But her thoughts were far away. As he held her door for her, there in the darkness of the stable yard, when he couldn't see her face clearly, she added, "He showed us the knife. We tried not to let him see, but we were so afraid. I couldn't know how that was going to end. I kept thinking that this was the man who had killed Patricia. Who put her there in the hut. And I knew he meant every word he said."

Once more he kept his thought to himself. It was better for her to put it out of her mind now. Or it would haunt her forever.

Into the silence, she said, "He told me I would be first. An ear. A finger. He said he could flense a fish with his knife without touching the flesh. Or joint a chicken with it. Or take off a hand, if he wished to. He wanted us to be afraid so that we wouldn't be any trouble. The worst part was, he talked about it in such a-a sensible voice. As if he were in a shop, demonstrating what the knife could do. As if we had asked to see it and he'd taken it out of the case for us. A-a salesperson, not a killer. And then he put it against my face, and told me that he could shave with it as well. I could feel it, cold, against my skin. Shall I have to testify to that, under oath, in the inquest?"

"No," he told her gently. "Only that you were threatened and believed that he was capable of carrying the threats out."

He could hear her swallow hard, then clear her throat. But her voice was husky as she said simply, "Thank you." And then she walked on toward the door, leaving Rutledge to bring in the boxed dinner.

He didn't stay long. They checked every door, and double-checked the one in the garden room, even though Franklin was wounded and locked in a cell in Walmer. Afterward, together they retrieved the photograph and the cuttings he had asked for.

As she closed the books and he returned them to their proper place on the shelf, she said, "This seems like such a trivial reason to take a man's life—two men, really."

"We'll never be sure just what the Captain told Franklin, but he must have confronted him and given him a chance to clear himself. After all, the Army knew Franklin as Albert Reed, and that had to be explained before the Captain went to the police. Franklin couldn't be sure just how damning the evidence was, he didn't know if they'd found the soldier whose identity he'd taken. I expect he tried to lie his way out of it, wasn't certain Nelson believed him, and realized that he had to kill the man before he took his 'proof,' whatever it might be, to the police. And we don't know what the Captain himself had decided to do. Franklin didn't hesitate. He got rid of the man, but couldn't find his evidence. Still, nothing came of that, no one descended to take him in custody, and Franklin came to believe he was safe. At war's end, he went to France and believed he was finished with Walmer. But he ran afoul of the French police, thought he was being tracked, and had to vanish for a while. It was easier to come back here than it was to try to start elsewhere, and have a suspicious Constable look into the background of whatever name Franklin chose to use there. And there was also what might be hidden here. While he was staying out of sight at the Home Farm, he could easily search the Abbey at night. If he'd had any reason to think that the Captain might have a photograph of him, it would be imperative to find it before you or the police did."

"But Patricia recognized Blackburn as 'Reed,' and he must have thought that once she mentioned the connection to me, I might ask the Chief Constable to find out who he really was. After all, he was working on my property. I could easily have done." She took a deep breath. "I might even have found what Roger had hidden, and never understood it's importance until now. I didn't know Reed that well. I might not have made the connection. But the police would have done."

He could see how drawn her face was, and he asked, "Shall I stay?"

After a moment she shook her head. "I must get used to staying here alone. All over again. Franklin has taken that peace of mind from me. And so I've asked Bruce's owner to find me a dog. But please, not one as large as Bruce."

He smiled, and began to collect the cuttings and photograph. She turned out the lamps, picked up the lamp she had brought with her, and walked with him through the silent house toward the door leading to the stables.

As they passed through the great hall, she stopped by the statue of the Virgin, mysterious and sad as the light from the flickering lamp she was carrying touched it.

Looking up at it, she said, "I understand her, you know. I've lost three men I cared very deeply for. My husband. My son. And a very dear friend. She and I are survivors. The dead have it easier you know. They don't feel. We who are left do."

At the stable walkway door, she asked for his borrowed key. He took it out of his pocket and returned it to her.

And then she said good night, and quietly closed the door.

Rutledge slept for five hours, rose at dawn, and completed his report.

And then he packed his valise and set it ready by the door.

He went to the police station, and Hamilton came out to greet him.

"He's on a suicide watch," he said grimly. "I'm not losing him now. That the report?"

"Your copy. And the Chief Constable's as well. I've kept the one for Scotland Yard."

"You're leaving then?"

"For now. When you've arranged for the inquest, I'll return to give evidence." He paused. "You will have to charge Johnson as an accomplice. He was not complicit in the murders, but he must have seen something in Franklin that troubled him. And he did nothing about it. Even when he was threatened by Franklin and realized how dangerous he was, he didn't come to you. I had to force him to speak to Hubbard about the boat."

"Yes, I've considered his part in all this. He'll have to stand his trial and take his chances with a jury." Changing the subject, he added,

"Mrs. Hailey came by this morning. She wanted to see Franklin behind the cell bars. I took her back. And then she left. The dog was with her. She was taking him home."

"That was my next stop. I'm glad she's recovered enough to send him home."

Hamilton frowned. "As to that, I don't know. There was something in her expression as she looked at Franklin. It made the hairs on my neck stand up."

"It must have been hard for both women. Deal carefully with them at the inquest. There's enough evidence to hang him without distressing them further."

"After that morning? I'll do just that." He took the report as Rutledge held it out to him. "I can't say it was a pleasure working with you. You kept too much to yourself."

Rutledge remembered Vermuelen, struggling to make sure what he knew reached Haldane. "Some of it didn't fall into place until very late You'll find most of the answers in my report." All but what had touched on Haldane. And France.

"Still."

And there was the ring. He'd seen to it that it was mentioned in the report. Now he took it from his pocket and also handed it to Hamilton. "That's evidence. It's explained in the report. But I found it in the ashes of the hut where we found Mrs. Lowell. He burned it down when he realized he'd lost the ring and couldn't find it. It must have fallen through the floorboards as he set about hanging her."

Hamilton took it and looked carefully at it. "Ugly thing."

"It was a treasure to the young boy who discovered it. He was wearing it when he was killed by Franklin. Early in the war. And for some reason Franklin kept it."

"It's as twisted as he is."

They spoke for several minutes more, and then Rutledge left. He called briefly on Dr. Wister, to thank him for his help.

"Not at all," Wister said, seeing Rutledge out. "I'll see you at the inquest then, shall I?"

———

Rutledge returned to the hotel to collect his valise, and left by the garden entrance where the sun was pleasantly warm in the sheltered space. He stood there for a moment, going over everything, making certain that he had tied up the evidence against Franklin to the best of his ability. He had all the statements he needed, there was his own report, and Hamilton's. And there was the photograph, the one thing that tied Franklin to that early murder. It could tie him as well to the deaths in Dorset. The war had changed him—but not so much that the man he was now had lost any resemblance to that Miles Franklin. He hadn't been in the trenches, he'd fought his war in Essex, and had seen France only after it was over.

The one question Rutledge couldn't answer—very likely no one but Franklin could—was whether or not the man had had anything to do with Major Dinsmore's suicide. It would have been like Franklin to be certain that the Major knew nothing about the Captain's evidence by silencing him forever. There was a strong possibility that he had gone to France until he was sure neither he nor the man he'd pretended to be was being hunted.

Hamish said quietly, "It doesna' signify. He can only hang once."

That was true. But Rutledge would have liked to know, for Melinda's sake, if not his own peace of mind. He didn't like the thought of Dinsmore not finding justice too.

Hamish said, "It's best that she doesna' know for certain."

There was some truth in that.

And there was nothing to keep him in Walmer now.

He had already decided to return to London by way of Kent.

He walked out to his motorcar, and reached for the crank.

It was a pleasant drive back to the Thames, and the crossing was no trouble. He remembered little of it. His thoughts were ahead of him, already in Kent.

He managed to find a telephone, dreading to be put off, knowing as well that it was the right thing to do.

He picked up the receiver and spoke to the operator, then waited while she connected him.

Melinda offered him lunch.

Hiding his relief, he took that as acceptance.

And then back in his motorcar, he realized that she would be free to invite him if Kate had already left—had gone back to London and her parents.

He hadn't dared ask. Now he wished he'd found the courage.

Hamish said, when at last they turned off the main road into the long, looping drive, "Dona' dither, ye'll ken soon enough."

Shanta was at the door to greet him, and as she took his hat and coat, she said, "They are in the sitting room. You know your way."

They . . .

He smiled at her. "All is well?"

"See for yourself."

Rutledge walked down the passage, stopped at the sitting room door to take a deep breath, and pin a pleasant smile on his face. Then he opened the door. It was, he thought, rather like walking into Markham's den.

Melinda rose from her favorite chair and came forward, lifting her face for his kiss. And then as she moved away, he saw Kate by the window.

"Hallo," he said, as if he'd met her on Bond Street, shopping for a new hat. "It's good to see you well."

She smiled, a little anxiously. "Hallo, Ian."

He turned to Melinda, to give Kate time, and said, "It didn't end well in Essex. As you've no doubt heard."

"Yes. Sadly. But one learns soon enough that disappointment is a part of living." And then, as if she were the hostess of a dinner party, not a luncheon for friends, she said, "I must see to things in the kitchen. My cook is having a tantrum."

"I don't know why you put up with the man," he said, suddenly reluctant to see her go.

"He's an idiot. But he cooks divinely. He can even manage a decent curry."

And she was gone.

Kate moved away from the window. "I need to explain—" she began, but he stopped her.

"No, not at all."

"But I do," she answered resolutely. "I haven't been able to mend matters with my father. He's sometimes stubborn once he makes up his mind. Melinda has asked me to stay on, but I feel I've taken advantage of her kindness. Will you take me back to London?"

This was why, he thought, he'd been invited to come.

"If that's what you want to do, of course, I'll be happy to drive you. The question is, what will you do? Will you go to an hotel?"

"I was so—so unsettled when I came to you. I needed time—space—to accept what my father had done. I couldn't really think straight, I just knew I had to find a place to stay. And I'm so grateful to you for thinking of Melinda. She's been kindness itself this week. But I know—I know she never cared for Jean. Jean told me herself. And I can't accept her hospitality, now that I've got over the first shock."

He said, "She told me to my face that she believed I was making a grave mistake, marrying your cousin. But I couldn't see it. I know now that she was right. I'd have made Jean as unhappy as she would have made me. Jean knew that too, when I came home."

"Yes. I told her it wasn't very well done to break the engagement so quickly. But she wouldn't listen. And she had met the diplomat. I think she already knew that she wanted most of all to escape from England and everything about the war."

But he winced at that memory—it was still vivid. When Jean had finally been allowed to see him in the clinic where he was still fighting the nightmares and the constant presence of Hamish's voice in his head, she had seen a broken man, and was horrified. He'd stood there and found the strength to ask her to break their engagement for his sake. And the profound relief in her face had hurt him deeply.

He'd not been in love with her for a very long time, now, but that rejection, when he had so desperately needed hope and the courage to believe he could survive, had nearly destroyed him.

Bringing himself back to the present, he said, "I can tell you this about Melinda Crawford. If she hadn't enjoyed your company, she would be perfectly capable of arranging matters for you. She would have found a proper hotel, taken you there herself, and seen to it that you were both safe and completely comfortable. And I wouldn't be standing here now talking with you."

Her eyebrows rose. "You're saying that to make me feel better."

"No. I'm telling you that I have known Melinda far longer than you have done. You would never have guessed that she wanted you gone. But gone you would have been. If she asks you to stay, it's because she likes you. I can't think why."

She smiled a little at that. "I don't know whether to believe you or not."

He said, without an answering smile, "I don't think I've ever lied to you."

Her smile faded. "No. No, you haven't. You've been a very good friend. All right, if you think it's best, I'll stay. A little longer."

"It's for the best. Your father will come round, he'll miss you, worry about you, and then try to find you. Give him time, Kate, and Melinda will gladly give you that time."

She took a deep breath, turning away to hide the tears of relief welling in her eyes. "Thank you, Ian. From the bottom of my heart."

He wanted to go to her then, but he knew he shouldn't. That it was wrong, that it would make her feel that he had brought her here for reasons of his own. He had to stay her friend.

"You'll be sick of curry by the time you go home," he said lightly.

She laughed. "To my surprise I've come to like them, but not as spicy as Melinda does."

As if on cue, the door opened.

"Crisis averted in the kitchen," Melinda said briskly. "I believe we can sit down now, without interruption. When Shanta is shouting in Hindi and he is shouting in French, even the cat disappears."

She led them to the small dining room, where they didn't have to shout down the long table. "Now, then, Ian, must you rush back to London, or can you take the day for yourself?"

He knew what she wanted from him. "I'd much rather stay, but Markham is not a patient man. For the sake of his blood pressure, I expect I ought to appear this afternoon."

"When will they replace him? He's an idiot."

"I understand from Sergeant Gibson that some are already placing bets on that."

When he left an hour later, he was alone in the motorcar. Melinda had seen him to the door, waited for his kiss, and then said softly, so that her voice wouldn't carry to the sitting room, "Well done, Ian. She's fragile still."

He said, "Her mother is no better than her father. How they managed to have a daughter like Kate, I'll never understand."

And he walked on to the motorcar.

There were no ghostly moans when Rutledge walked into the Yard. Gibson greeted him civilly, asked if Essex had come to a satisfactory conclusion.

"Yes. I was pleased."

He left it at that.

Gibson said, "He wants to see you in his office. He's not in a very good mood."

"Thanks for the warning."

But he stopped in his own tiny office to leave his hat and coat. The valise had stayed in the boot of the motorcar.

For a moment he stood looking out the window. It was nearly time to leave for the day. Traffic over Westminster Bridge was already heavier than it was when he'd crossed some minutes ago.

There was nothing for it but to beard the lion in his den.

He picked up his report, walked out into the passage and down to the Chief Superintendent's office. Knocking at the door, he heard "Come in," in a voice that boded no good.

"Rutledge," Markham acknowledged, then continued to sign several papers waiting in front of him. That done, he looked up. "Did you find the ghost?"

He knew Markham well enough to understand this was a well-planned taunt.

"Yes, sir. And the man behind it. It's in my report." He passed it across the desk.

Markham took it but didn't open it. Instead he said abruptly, "Sit down, man, you know looking up gives me trouble with my neck."

Rutledge did as he was told. Something in Markham's expression alerted him, he didn't need Hamish behind his shoulder, hissing a sudden warning.

In the top right-hand drawer of the Chief Superintendent's desk was his own letter of resignation. It had been asked for, and then held over his ahead like the sword of Damocles.

He was never to know when it would come out of the drawer and then be signed by the Chief Superintendent. Irrevocable. Final.

And he watched now as Markham reached into that very drawer and drew out a folder.

Rutledge braced himself for what was to come.

Looking him in the eye, Markham said, "I was against this from the start. I will tell you that before you are puffed up, thinking you are irreplaceable. But I was overruled."

Markham opened the file.

"The Home Office has in its infinite wisdom seen fit to promote you to the position of Chief Inspector. With the salary that comes with said position."

Rutledge sat there, stunned. He fought to find the words he knew he was expected to say, and he couldn't.

"Well. Don't sit there like a lump of stone. Do you accept this position or do you not? It's late in the day, and I should like very much to leave."

There had been several questions racing themselves through his mind. But he set them aside and replied, keeping his voice steady by an effort of will.

"Am I filling a vacancy?" There was one he couldn't bring himself to fill.

"That's not your affair. But you'll hear soon enough. Chief Inspector Matthews has retired. He was a good man, a sound policeman."

"He was." And Rutledge said, facing Markham, knowing he was about to ruin the other man's day, "Yes. I accept this position."

Markham's mouth tightened into a thin line. He handed Rutledge a fountain pen and the papers from the folder.

Using his knee for a desk, Rutledge read through them and signed where directed.

It was done. He handed them back to Markham.

"That's all. You may go."

No congratulations. No best wishes.

Rutledge thanked him and left the office, still stunned.

He walked back into his own office and sat down behind the desk. His back to the window. He heard a door open and shut down the passage, and Markham came walking past his door and on to the stairs.

Hamish said, "Ye should leave now, yoursel'."

He didn't know how or why this had happened. He needed the Yard more than it needed him, he knew that. He had been prepared to serve as an Inspector as long as he could. He had never held any hope of promotion. It was enough to be here.

Who was behind it?

There had to be someone.

And then he knew the answer.

He got up, walked out his door and out of the Yard. It was urgent that he find a telephone.

No one called to him. He realized that no one else knew. Yet.

Better that way . . .

He drove to the hotel where he had used a telephone before, and put through the call.

He tried to order his thoughts as he waited for the connection to go through. They refused to be ordered.

He'd had to ask who he would be replacing. It was one thing to step into a dead man's shoes, and quite another to step into those of someone he'd respected and then destroyed.

It took ten minutes to get through to Kent and Melinda's house.

He had to know, he had to be sure.

Then Shanta was on the line, and he had to wait again for her to find Melinda.

When at last he heard her voice on the other end of the line, pleasant and cheerful, he asked her straight out.

"Did you speak to someone in the Home Office? Is that why I've just been given a promotion at the Yard?"

There was a brief silence. "This is the first I've heard of it, my dear. But I am quite pleased. Did I have anything to do with it happening? No. May I be among the first to offer you my good wishes? Well done!"

He could hear the warmth in her voice. The sincerity. But he had to be sure.

"Please. This matters. I have to know."

"You have always wanted to be your own man, Ian. Even as a boy. I've always respected that. It's why I stood by you when you told your father and David Trevor that you didn't want to be a solicitor in your father's firm or an architect in David's. It was your choice to make, no one else's. You earned this promotion on your own. You're a very good policeman, far better than you realize. It's time others recognize that as well."

He had to believe her. He wanted to believe her. But Melinda Crawford knew half the Government and most of the Army. If anyone could pull strings, it was she.

"Markham was against it. I could see it in his face, hear it in his voice. If he'd had his way, I'd have been passed over. He would never have agreed on his own."

"Well, someone disagreed, and I'm very glad he did." There was a pause. "Do you feel you can make a go of it?"

She knew that he was shell-shocked, although he wasn't sure just how much she knew. Whether Dr. Fleming had confided in her. On the whole, he didn't think Fleming would tell anyone about Hamish.

He took a deep breath. "I'm damned well going to try."

He heard her chuckle, a rich laugh that came clearly down the line.

"Good for you. I'm very glad, Ian. You are very much like your father, you know. And mine as well. I loved and admired both of them. Come and visit when you can. You know my door is always open."

And she put up the receiver at her end, giving him no more chance to doubt himself or her.

He held the receiver for another moment, then put it up before the operator could ask if he wished to make another call.

Hamish said, "Do ye ken she was telling the truth?"

She wasn't one to lie. And yet for the life of him, he could think of no one else who might have put in a word for him at the Home Office. There was no one he knew whose voice carried such weight.

Hamish had the last word.

"Ye'll no' fail. You wouldna' gie yon Chief Superintendent the pleasure of seeing it."

Rutledge remembered something. Markham still kept his letter of resignation in his desk drawer . . .

The man would enjoy nothing so much as finding an excuse to use it. Especially after the Home Office had overruled him.

The news was beginning to seem real, finally.

He found himself wishing he could share it with Kate.

About the author

About the book

Read on

Insights,
Interviews
& More . . .

Meet Charles Todd

Michael Frost Photography

CHARLES TODD is the *New York Times* bestselling author of the Inspector Ian Rutledge mysteries, the Bess Crawford mysteries, and two stand-alone novels. Among the honors accorded to the Ian Rutledge mysteries are the Barry Award and nominations for the Independent Mystery Booksellers Association's Dilys Award, the Edgar and Anthony Awards in the U.S., and the John Creasey Award in the U.K. ॐ

Remembering
Caroline Todd

Caroline Todd

November 13, 1934 – August 28, 2021

To my author, mother, and friend. Caroline epitomized what a kind, giving, and caring person should be. Her legacy lives on not only in her works of fiction, but in the hearts of all who knew her, and in those who continue to discover and read Charles Todd for years to come.

Fame and fortune were never a goal for Caroline. From her earliest childhood she wanted to be a writer. She achieved that lifelong dream with the support of so many readers, friends, and colleagues. It all began because Ruth Cavin (then senior editor at Thomas Dunne Books) believed in Ian Rutledge. *A Test of Wills* was published in 1996.

Caroline had a special place in her heart for reading and sharing that treasure with everyone. Her support of libraries, librarians, and reading was evident in the events she attended. She spoke at libraries around the world.

Caroline loved all living creatures, especially her cats and her children's cats and dogs. She opened her heart, caring for any animal who came to her back door—from opossums to foxes, birds, ▶

Remembering Caroline Todd *(continued)*

and even a lizard—and made sure they were fed. For her, they were all God's children who needed her love.

A child of the Great Depression and World War II, Caroline always gave to charities to help those less fortunate than herself. Providing food and warmth was not only lifesaving, but it also showed people that they were not alone.

A special thank-you to the many friends and readers for their notes of kindness and condolence. Caroline achieved her dream of becoming a writer and touching the hearts of so many readers. I am forever grateful to each and every person who made her dream come true.

Love, Charles ∾

Questions for
Discussion

1. Upon learning that the supposed killer–Captain Nelson–is already long dead, what was your first assumption about what had happened and who the perpetrator could be?

2. Although *A Game of Fear* takes place after the fighting has ended, how did you perceive the significance of World War I in this novel? How do the effects of war appear throughout the story?

3. Rutledge claims that there is a difference between "giving in" and "giving up" when it comes to his internal conflict and survivor's guilt regarding Hamish's death and the nightmares it gives him. What do you think the difference is?

4. What was your first impression of Felicia Benton? Did she strike you as delusional or mentally ill? Did your impressions of her change as you read on?

5. When Rutledge is exploring the airfield for the first time, Hamish tells him, "Here are the ghosts. The buildings that are gone." What does he mean by this? How does this sentiment relate to buildings outside of the airfield? ▶

Questions for Discussion *(continued)*

6. Among the residents of Walmer, who were you immediately suspicious of? Were you right to suspect wrongdoings on their part?

7. What does *A Game of Fear* have to say about the "madness" of women during this time in history? How relevant is this rhetoric today?

8. Were you able to solve the mystery of the murder before Rutledge did? What information provided you with clues?

9. Did you think Captain Nelson's death was premeditated in any way—either by himself or others? Did you consider it an accident?

10. At any point during the novel, did you consider the possibility of something supernatural occurring?

11. Why does Rutledge go out of his way to buy the flowers that Mrs. Lowell usually purchases for her husband's grave, when she appears to be missing?

Inspector Ian Rutledge: A Complete Timeline of Major Events

JUNE 1914—*A FINE SUMMER'S DAY*

On a fine summer's day, the Great War is still only the distant crack of revolver shots at a motorcar in faraway Sarajevo. And Ian Rutledge, already an inspector at Scotland Yard, has decided to propose to the woman he's so deeply in love with—despite hints from friends and family that she may not be the wisest choice. But in another part of England, a man stands in the kitchen of his widowed mother's house, waiting for the undertaker to come for her body, and stares at the clock on the mantel. He doesn't know yet that he will become Rutledge's last case before Britain is drawn into war. In the weeks to come, as summer moves on toward the shadows of August, he will set out to right a wrong, and Rutledge will find himself having to choose between the Yard and his country, between the woman he loves and duty, and between truth and honor.

JUNE 1919—*A TEST OF WILLS*

Ian Rutledge, returning home from the trenches of the Great War, loses his fiancée, Jean, after long months in hospital with what is now called post-traumatic stress disorder and faces a bleak future. Fighting back from the edge of madness, he returns to his ▶

7

Inspector Ian Rutledge: A Complete Timeline of Major Events
(continued)

career at Scotland Yard. But Chief Superintendent Bowles is determined to break him. And so Rutledge finds himself in Warwickshire, where the only witness to the murder of Colonel Harris is a drunken ex-soldier suffering from shell shock. Rutledge is fighting his own battles with the voice of Corporal Hamish MacLeod in his head, survivor's guilt after the bloody 1916 Battle of the Somme. The question is, will he win this test of wills with Hamish—or is the shell-shocked witness a mirror of what he'll become if he fails to keep his madness at bay?

JULY 1919—*WINGS OF FIRE*

Rutledge is sent to Cornwall because the Home Office wants to be reassured that Nicholas Cheney wasn't murdered. But Nicholas committed suicide with his half sister, Olivia. And she's written a body of war poetry under the name of O. A. Manning. Rutledge, who had used her poetry in the trenches to keep his mind functioning, is shocked to discover she never saw France and may well be a cold-blooded killer. And yet even dead, she makes a lasting impression he can't shake.

AUGUST 1919—*SEARCH THE DARK*

An out-of-work ex-soldier, sitting on a train in a Dorset station, suddenly sees his dead wife and two small children standing on the platform. He fights to get off the train, and soon thereafter the woman is found murdered and the children are missing. Rutledge is sent to coordinate a search and finds himself attracted to Aurore, a French war bride who will lie to protect her husband and may have killed because she was jealous of the murder victim's place in her husband's life.

SEPTEMBER 1919—*LEGACY OF THE DEAD*

Just as Rutledge thinks he has come to terms—of a sort—with the voice that haunts him, he's sent to northern England to find the missing daughter of a woman who once slept with a king. Little does he know that his search will take him to Scotland,

and to the woman Hamish would have married if he'd lived. But Fiona is certain to hang for murdering a mother to steal her child, and she doesn't know that Rutledge killed Hamish on the battlefield when she turns to him for help. He couldn't save Hamish—but Rutledge is honor-bound to protect Fiona and the small child named for him.

OCTOBER 1919—*WATCHERS OF TIME*

Still recovering from the nearly fatal wound he received in Scotland, Rutledge is sent to East Anglia to discover who murdered a priest and what the priest's death had to do with a dying man who knew secrets about the family that owns the village. But there's more to the murder than hearing a deathbed confession. And the key might well be a young woman as haunted as Rutledge is, because she survived the sinking of the *Titanic* and carries her own guilt for her failure to save a companion.

NOVEMBER 1919—*A FEARSOME DOUBT*

A case from 1912 comes back to haunt Rutledge. Did he send an innocent man to the gallows? Meanwhile, he's trying to discover who has poisoned three ex-soldiers, all of them amputees in a small village in Kent. Mercy killings or murder? And he sees a face across the Guy Fawkes Day bonfire that is a terrifying reminder of what happened to him at the end of the war . . . something he is ashamed of, even though he can't remember why. What happened in the missing six months of his life?

DECEMBER 1919—*A COLD TREACHERY*

Rutledge is already in the north and the closest man to Westmorland where, at the height of a blizzard, there has been a cold-blooded killing of an entire family, save one child, who is missing in the snow. But as the facts unfold, it's possible that the boy killed his own family. Where is he? Dead in the snow or hiding? And there are secrets in this isolated village of Urskdale that can lead to more deaths. ▶

Inspector Ian Rutledge: A Complete Timeline of Major Events *(continued)*

JANUARY 1920—*A LONG SHADOW*

A party that begins innocently enough ends with Rutledge finding machine gun casings engraved with death's heads— a warning. But he's sent to Northamptonshire to discover why someone shot Constable Ward with an arrow in what the locals call a haunted wood. He discovers there are other deaths unaccounted for, and there's also a woman who knows too much about Rutledge for his own comfort. Then whoever has been stalking him comes north after him, and Rutledge knows if he doesn't find the man, Rutledge will die. Hamish, pushing him hard, is all too aware that Rutledge's death will mean his own.

MARCH 1920—*A FALSE MIRROR*

A man is nearly beaten to death, his wife is taken hostage by his assailant, and Rutledge is sent posthaste to Hampton Regis to find out who wanted Matthew Hamilton dead. The man who may be guilty is someone Rutledge knew in the war, a reminder that some were lucky enough to be saved while Hamish was left to die. But this is a story of love gone wrong, and the next two deaths reek of madness. Are the murders random, or were the women mistaken for the intended victim?

APRIL 1920—*A PALE HORSE*

In the ruins of Yorkshire's Fountains Abbey lies the body of a man wrapped in a cloak, the face covered by a gas mask. Next to him is a book on alchemy, which belongs to the schoolmaster, a conscientious objector in the Great War. Who is this man, and is the investigation into his death being manipulated by a thirst for revenge? Meanwhile, the British War Office is searching for a missing man of their own, someone whose war work was so secret that Rutledge isn't told his real name or what he did. Here is a puzzle requiring all of Rutledge's daring and skill, for there are layers of lies and deception, while a ruthless killer is determined to hold on to freedom at any cost.

MAY 1920—*A MATTER OF JUSTICE*

At the turn of the century, in a war taking place far from England, two soldiers chance upon an opportunity that will change their lives forever. To take advantage of it, they will do the unthinkable and then put the past behind them. Twenty years later, a successful London businessman is found savagely and bizarrely murdered in a medieval tithe barn on his estate in Somerset. Called upon to investigate, Rutledge soon discovers that the victim was universally despised. Even the man's wife—who appears to be his wife in name only—and the town's police inspector are suspect. But who among the many hated enough to kill?

JUNE 1920—*THE RED DOOR*

In a house with a red door lies the body of a woman who has been bludgeoned to death. Rumor has it that two years earlier, she'd painted that door to welcome her husband back from the front. Only he never came home. Meanwhile, in London, a man suffering from a mysterious illness goes missing and then just as suddenly reappears. Rutledge must solve two mysteries before he can bring a ruthless killer to justice: Who was the woman who lived and died behind the red door? Who was the man who never came home from the Great War, for the simple reason that he might never have gone? And what have they to do with a man who cannot break the seal of his own guilt without damning those he loves most?

JULY 1920—*A LONELY DEATH*

Three men have been murdered in a Sussex village, and Scotland Yard has been called in. The victims are soldiers, each surviving the nightmare of World War I only to meet a ghastly end in the quiet English countryside. Each man has been garroted, with a small ID disk left in his mouth, yet no other clue suggests a motive or a killer. Rutledge understands all too well the darkness that resides within men's souls. His presence on the scene cannot deter a vicious and clever killer, ▶

and a fourth dead soldier is discovered shortly after Rutledge's arrival. Now a horror that strikes painfully close to home threatens to engulf the investigator, and he will have to risk his career, his good name, even his shattered life itself, to bring an elusive fiend to justice.

AUGUST 1920—*THE CONFESSION*

A man walks into Scotland Yard and confesses he killed his cousin five years ago during the Great War. When Rutledge presses for details, the man evades his questions, revealing only that he hails from a village east of London. Less than two weeks later, the alleged killer's body is found floating in the Thames, a bullet in the back of his head. Rutledge discovers that the dead man was not who he claimed to be. The only clue is a gold locket, found around the victim's neck, which leads back to Essex and an insular village that will do anything to protect itself from notoriety.

SUMMER 1920—*PROOF OF GUILT*

An unidentified man appears to have been run down by a motorcar, and a clue leads Rutledge to a firm, built by two families, famous for producing and selling the world's best Madeira wine. There he discovers that the current head of the English enterprise is missing. Is he the dead man? And do either his fiancée or his jilted former lover have anything to do with his disappearance? With a growing list of suspects, Rutledge knows that suspicion and circumstantial evidence are nothing without proof of guilt. But his new acting chief superintendent doesn't agree and wants Rutledge to stop digging and settle on the easy answer. Rutledge must tread very carefully, for it seems that someone has decided that he, too, must die so that justice can take its course.

AUGUST 1920—*HUNTING SHADOWS*

A society wedding at Ely Cathedral becomes a crime scene when a guest is shot. After a fruitless search for clues, the local police call in Scotland Yard, but not before there is another shooting in a village close by. This second murder has a witness, but her description of the killer is so horrific it's unbelievable. Inspector Ian Rutledge can find no connection between the two deaths. One victim was an army officer, the other a solicitor standing for Parliament. Is there a link between these murders, or is it only in the mind of a clever killer? As the investigation presses on, Rutledge finds memories of the war beginning to surface. Struggling to contain the darkness that haunts him as he hunts for the missing link, he discovers the case turning in a most unexpected direction. Now he must put his trust in the devil in order to find the elusive and shocking answer.

AUTUMN 1920—*NO SHRED OF EVIDENCE*

On the north coast of Cornwall, an apparent act of mercy is repaid by an arrest for murder. Four young women have been accused of the crime. A shocked father calls in a favor at the Home Office. Scotland Yard is asked to review the case. However, Inspector Ian Rutledge is not the first inspector to reach the village. Following in the shoes of a dead man, he is told the case is all but closed. Even as it takes an unexpected personal turn, Rutledge will require all his skill to deal with the incensed families of the accused, the grieving parents of the victim, and local police eager to see these four women sent to the infamous Bodmin Gaol. Then why hasn't the killing stopped? With no shred of evidence to clear the accused, Rutledge must plunge deep into the darkest secrets of a wild, beautiful, and dangerous place if he is to find a killer who may— or may not—hold the key to their fate.

NOVEMBER 1920—*RACING THE DEVIL*

On the eve of the Battle of the Somme, a group of officers have a last drink and make a promise to one another: if they survive the battle ahead, they will meet a year after the fighting ends and race motorcars from Paris to Nice. In November 1919, the officers all meet as planned, but two vehicles are nearly run off the road, and one man is badly injured. No one knows which driver was ▶

Inspector Ian Rutledge: A Complete Timeline of Major Events
(continued)

at the wheel of the rogue motorcar. Back in England one year later, a driver loses control on a twisting road and is killed in the crash. Is the crash connected in some way to the unfortunate events in the mountains above Nice the year before? Investigating this perplexing case, Scotland Yard inspector Ian Rutledge discovers that the truth is elusive. Determined to remain in the shadows, this faceless killer is willing to strike again to stop Rutledge from finding him. This time, the victim he chooses is a child, and it will take all of Rutledge's skill to stop him before an innocent young life is sacrificed.

DECEMBER 1920—*THE GATE KEEPER*

Hours after his sister's wedding, a restless Ian Rutledge drives aimlessly, haunted by the past, and narrowly misses a motorcar stopped in the middle of a desolate road. Standing beside the vehicle is a woman with blood on her hands and a dead man at her feet. She swears she didn't kill Stephen Wentworth. A stranger stepped out in front of their motorcar, and without warning, fired a single shot before vanishing into the night. But there is no trace of him. Rutledge persuades the Yard to give him the inquiry, since he's on the scene. But is he seeking justice—or fleeing painful memories in London? Wentworth was well liked, yet his bitter family paint a malevolent portrait, calling him a murderer. But who did Wentworth kill? Is his death retribution? Or has his companion lied? When a second suspicious death occurs, the evidence suggests that a dangerous predator is on the loose, and that death is closer than Rutledge knows.

JANUARY 1921—*THE BLACK ASCOT*

After saving an ex-convict's life, Ian Rutledge receives an astonishing tip about a legendary crime from the grateful man. If true, the tip could lead to capturing Alan Barrington— the suspect in an appalling murder during the Black Ascot, the famous 1910 royal horse races that honored the late King Edward VII. Barrington's disappearance before his trial had set off a manhunt that spanned the globe, baffling Scotland

Yard and consuming all of Britain for nearly a decade. But why should Barrington return to England now? Scotland Yard orders Rutledge to quietly investigate. Meticulously retracing the original inquiry, Rutledge begins to know Barrington well, delving into his relationships and uncovering secrets that hadn't surfaced in 1910. As he draws closer to the man, the investigation is suddenly thrown into turmoil when Rutledge's life is changed by his darkest fear—the exposure of his shell shock. The Yard is already demanding his resignation, and Rutledge realizes that the only way to save his career, much less his honor, is to find Barrington. Against all odds, he must bring the Black Ascot killer to justice. But what if the tip was wrong? What if Barrington never returned to England at all . . . ?

FEBRUARY 1921—*A DIVIDED LOYALTY*

A woman has been murdered at the foot of a megalith shaped like a great shrouded figure. Chief Inspector Brian Leslie, one of the Yard's best men, is sent to investigate the site in Avebury. In spite of his efforts, Leslie is not able to identify her, and the killer has simply left no trace. Several weeks later, Ian Rutledge is asked to take a second look at Leslie's inquiry. But Rutledge suspects Chief Superintendent Markham simply wants him to fail. Leslie was right—Avebury refuses to yield its secrets. But Rutledge slowly widens his search, until he discovers an unexplained clue that seems to point toward an impossible solution. If he pursues it and he is wrong, he will draw the wrath of the Yard down on his head. And even if he is right, he can't be certain what he can prove, and that will play right into Markham's game. But what does Rutledge owe this tragic young woman? Where must his loyalty lie?

SPRING 1921 – A FATAL LIE

A peaceful Welsh village is thrown into turmoil when a terrified boy discovers a body in the river. The man appears to have fallen from the canal aqueduct spanning the valley. But there is no identification on the body. The local police turn to Scotland Yard for help. Inspector Ian Rutledge is given few clues to go ▶

on—a faded military tattoo on the victim's arm and an unusual label in his shirt. But eventually they do lead to the victim's identity: Sam Milford, an Englishman. By all accounts, he was a good man and well-respected. Then why was he murdered so far from home? Searching for the truth, Rutledge uncovers a web of deception swirling around a child's tragic fate. But where among all those lies is the motive for murder? To track a killer, Rutledge must retrace Milford's last journey. Yet death seems to stalk the Inspector's every move. This murderer stays in the shadows, and it will take desperate measures to lure evil into the light. ❧

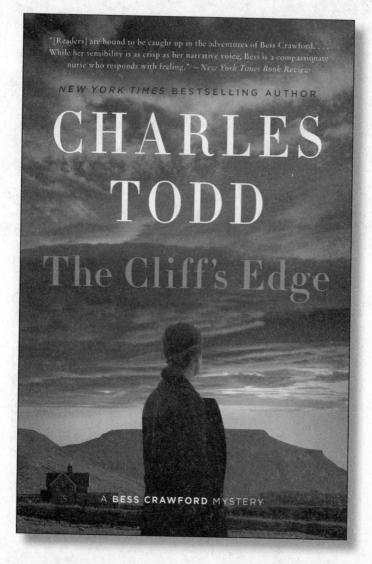

BOOKS BY CHARLES TODD